El Corazon Valiente;

The ballad of Peter Duncan

A Paninaro imprint

www.paninaropublishing.co.uk

info@paninaropublishing.co.uk

www.paninaropublishing.co.uk

Contact - info@paninaropublishing.co.uk

A catalogue record for this book is available from the British Library

ISBN - 13: 978 - 1916088542

Johnny Proctor socials :

Twitter @johnnyroc73

Instagram @johnnyproctor90

Dedicated to Rachel

Writing this dedication in April, 2021, it's been, undeniably, twelve months filled with uncertainty and a life completely foreign to what any of us have ever known previously. While none of us have ever really known what one week was going to be like from the next. *You* have been one of the only real constants through it all x

Chapter 1

El Corazon Valiente Found Guilty on All Indictments; Facing a life behind bars

By Manny Ruiz

April. 25, 2001

The Colombian narco operative, known as 'El Corazon Valiente' was convicted yesterday following a two month narcotics, arms, money laundering, corruption, and terrorist financing trial in New York that - over the course of the eight weeks - revealed the essential parts that he played in his 'Mr Fixit' role within the Ramirez Cartel out of Bogota, Colombia which - over decades - was responsible for shipping tonnes of narcotics and weapons into both America and across the rest of the world. This in addition to directly financing Islamic terrorist organisations until the cartel's demise towards the end of the Nineties.

The guilty verdict handed down to the kingpin, Peter Duncan, ended the freedom and liberty of a man who - over a ten year period - travelled the world procuring and selling in drugs and arms on behalf of the criminal enterprise out of the Colombian capital, whose 'make money by any means' business model saw to it that he could likely be meeting with anyone from Crips from Crenshaw, LA to Hezbollah representatives in Lebanon, from one week to the next. The verdict, effectively ending the career of the British born gangster, notorious amongst anti crime agencies across the world for his almost unshakable ability to evade authorities as his 'value' inside the DEA, CIA and ATF grew.

As Judge Ari H. Berkovic read out the jury's charge sheet in open court - twelve straight guilty verdicts on all counts, documented on the grouped indictments - Duncan sat with a stunned look on his face while appearing to swear under his breath. When the reading of all indictments were complete. Duncan appeared to look in the direction of DEA agents Vinnie Valencia and Tommy Ambrosini - just two out of scores who had taken the stand and given evidence against him - and offer them a thumbs up and a smile before turning to his attorney where the pair engaged in what appeared to be an animated discussion. Duncan was led away from the court soon after and bundled into a waiting car where he was driven back to Fishkill Correctional Facility.

The jury's verdict came a little more than two weeks after the panel had began deliberations at the trial in the Federal District Court in Brooklyn where Department of Justice prosecutors unveiled a treasure trove of evidence against the former cartel member. This including forty seven witnesses which included testimonies from members on both sides of the law with United States government agents (and internationally based personnel flown in specifically to provide evidence for the trial) to cartel informants and former associates of Mr Duncan.

Speaking to reporters outside the courthouse. Vinnie Valencia - now retired Drug Enforcement Administration agent - formerly of the Miami field office, heralded the verdict as a victory for 'good against evil' and that 'the less Peter Duncans that walk the earth, the safer the general public will be for it, and not just inside this great country of ours.'

'If every agency, administration and task force that had Peter Duncan listed on their database as a person of interest were to give you their opinion on today's verdict then we'd be here all freaking day but all I can say is, we gottim. On a personal level. I'd been chasing after him almost as long as I'd been with the Administration so today has provided a sense of closure. Just because he was no longer working for the cartel and was - in fact - in retirement, he may well have forgotten about us but we never forgot about him. This should also serve as a notice towards our friends in Mexico. With today's conviction it showcases that the DEA never forgets. Sinaloa, Juarez, Tijuana and The Gulf Cartel. I invite you to take a look at how big and powerful the Bogota Cartel were. And where are they now? Sleep tight now, senoras.'

Walter Davies, the United States attorney for the Southern District of New York cited the court ruling as a signal to all criminals that 'America will *never* stop fighting the war against drugs.'

'There are people who say that America is fighting a war that they simply cannot win. Today tells a different story. The jury's verdict inside of that court house behind me shows that those people who say that are *wrong*.'

In their post trial press conference at the William Vale hotel. Mr Duncan's legal team from Ron Rosenberg & Partners expressed their disgust at the verdict, but not dismay.

Harry Goldstein, when passing judgment to the assembled press,

'In my twenty plus years as an attorney I have never defended someone facing a case that had so many 'corroborating' witnesses, despite being from different countries, and never having met each other. Due to the high profile nature of my client, he came to America already presumed as guilty through trial by media held *before* we got to court. We weren't just simply fighting a legal case against the influence and power of the DOJ but we were *also* fighting against clear stereotypical oppression.'

While admitting that the mountain of evidence - that the Department of Justice presented - placed beside the multiple witnesses against Mr Duncan would make an appeal almost impossible to find success with, he - without any factual basis - called into question the fast tracked extradition process that had been conducted between Dutch and American authorities and whether it had followed correct procedures and that, moving forward, his team would now be fully focussing on that line of defense.

Duncan's trial - which took place amid extreme intense media exploration and a temporary high level terror alert in the city of Brooklyn which saw bomb sniffing dogs, New York Police Department S.W.A.T snipers and Federal Marshalls fitted with radiation sensors - was the first time that an American court house heard the specifics about the financing, logistical operation, deals, political bribery and alliances struck and the enemies made of the Bogota Cartel in a brutal history that spanned decades and left thousands of bodies lying in its wake.

The Bogota Cartel, ran by brothers Eddy and German Ramirez, had a history of not only importing narcotics of all descriptions into the United States but also worldwide. Their tentacles stretching to all continents. This - coupled with the arms trading that the cartel were also involved in - earning the Colombian brothers billions of dollars in revenue in an enterprise that spanned almost thirty years before the operation was smashed in a cross country joint operation between American and Colombian forces in early 1998.

The trial revealed that - unlike any other South American or Mexican cartel - the Bogota Cartel, while not supplying as much product to the United States as their Medellin or Cali counterparts, were viewed by American authorities as a higher threat to national security due to the unscrupulous way they went about building their empire with no person or organisation that they would not do business with, no matter how toxic the buyer may be, if the Ramirez brothers felt that it would strengthen their business further.

Despite the expansive testimony offered up that told of Maersk shipping containers filled with boxes of money and the murders and deception that made way for those boxes. The trial also divulged the - at times - absurd, comedic and unpredictable nature of Mr Duncan's role within the criminal organization, and the culture of working for the Colombian brothers in general.

Being taken hostage by F.A.R.C rebels - when sent there by the Ramirez brothers as an emissary - in the Colombian jungle after trying to perform a magic trick that involved burning a napkin (to put everyone at ease) and backfiring spectacularly with the freedom fighters taking this as some kind of a trick performed by the devil.

The court left in stitches over the revelation by an ex member of the Russian mafia - now under witness protection in the U.S - that as a mark of trust before doing business, during a meeting in Moscow, that Duncan take a spin in a cosmonaut training centrifuge. This sold to Duncan that everyone entering into business with the Moscow Mafia must undertake, as a form of tradition. This something that the ex Moscow associate admitted to, instead, as 'simply busting the Scotsman's balls' but that the Scotsman had taken it all in good faith, despite spending the rest of the day in an 'Cosmonaut in training' gift shop t shirt due to throwing up over his suit.

How he was blindfolded and rolled up inside a carpet and thrown into the back of a pick-up truck and driven across Afghanistan to meet with Taliban officials in the Afghanistan mountains only to get there and find that Taliban intelligence had discovered a CIA informant near to their training camp and - spooked - fled before Duncan could arrive.

This leading to him being put *back* into the carpet and driven across half of the country before a - by then - prickly Duncan could even *have* the arms for poppies meeting that he'd flown in to negotiate on.

How he had to spend a week stranded in a Colombian jungle after the helicopter he was in developed rotor problems, crashed and how him - and his pilot's - lives were only saved by hunters during a moment of pure chance.

The jaguar that he was responsible for overseeing being presented to an Angolan warlord that escaped on arrival at Luanda Airport and killed five airline workers before being cornered and shot.

The terrorists that he met with who the CIA couldn't have even dreamed of getting as close to. The endless game of cat and mouse between international law enforcement agencies and the man 'technically' from Scotland but who - at times - appeared to belong to the world in general. The millions that he made both *with* the Colombians and then by selling them out when he turned on them as their relationship turned sour. The cars, the houses, the AK-47 with his initials inscribed on it, personally given to him by Mikhail Kalashnikov on his birthday, despite the fact Peter Duncan doesn't know how to shoot a weapon! A champagne VIP lifestyle of excess that came crashing down around him when he was apprehended in an Amsterdam bar last year.

Across the two months. Testimony after testimony played out like a Hollywood movie to an - at times - stunned court. Yesterday, for Peter 'El Corazon Valiente' however, there was no superhero swoop in to save him. No final ten minute plot twist securing a happy ending for the protagonist, when all had appeared lost.

Sometimes stories have a sad ending too, though, and Peter Duncan - to his cost - bore the full brunt of that when his verdict was read out yesterday. Saddest of all, however, is that it took many years worth of death, pain and misery for *others* before the man experienced it, personally, for himself.

Wanted by the Drug Enforcement Agency and ATF through his importing of narcotics and weapons into the country from the years of Eighty Nine through Ninety Six while on a CIA watchlist throughout this same time due to his links to terrorists organisations such as Al Qaeda, Hezbollah and Boko Haram. The worldwide chase to apprehend the narco operative ending last year when arrested by a Dutch anti crime task force in The Netherlands capital.

Mr Duncan now faces life in a U.S state maximum security prison at his sentencing hearing, scheduled for June 4th.

Chapter 2

Peter

A hundred and twenty five years?!

Lets go over those numbers again. One hundred, as in a century, if I can be clear, there. Now add *another* quarter of a century on TOP of that. And, yeah. I'm sure there's probably some old woman in China who is or has lived longer than that but that really is not the point here. One hundred and twenty years is a life - ender. Done, over, finito oh and stick the obligatory fork in it before you leave, will you?

Not that I had desired *any* kind of a sentence, of course, but when you're looking at having your freedom taken from you, the very best that you can hope for is that you get a sentence given to you that only takes one syllable to say. My sentence? Unless I've got my maths (or as they say in this stupid fucking country) 'math' wrong - and trust me on this, I've repeated the numbers there in my cell enough times to know - it takes a full *seven* syllables to spit out. That in itself only serves to reinforce just how completely and emphatically in the shit you really are.

The thing is. You could throw accusations of arrogance, delusions, or simple foolishness in my direction but right up to the very moment the head juror - standing there inside that Brooklyn courthouse - opened his mouth. I thought that I was going to walk.

Despite all evidence that pointed to the contrary. The brutal honesty of my lawyer, - I pay him a king's ransom. If I want to call him a lawyer instead of attorney then that's what I'll call him - the in depth news coverage of my arrest and court case on networks like CNN & Fox News that had already placed me in an underground Colorado supermax prison with my case a mere formality. The slickness of the federal lead prosecutor - Angelo Hernandez, a man that despite the fact that he seemed to have an absolute hard on to see that I would spend the rest of my life behind bars, I kind of liked him - and how much he had done his homework on me. Over the course of the trial it seeming, at times, that he knew more about my life and what I'd done with it than I did myself.

Despite all of that. I still thought I would walk out of there a free man.

I *always* walked away, no matter what. I mean, it was kind of my brand.

Since getting out of prison in the Eighties, that had been my trademark move. It didn't matter which criminal - or at times terrorist - enterprise I would be in dealings with, or whichever international crime fighting agency that was on my tail.

I'd always had the knack for making sure that I was never, ever in the wrong place at the wrong time. Sure, maybe I stretched that theory to the limit at times and, on occasion, had been as close as minutes away from arrest - or worse - but, well, my proof is in my stats.

Amsterdam was, admittedly, a pain in the ass but one that, while I took some time out from the rest of the world in New York State's Fishkill Detention Centre, I was sure was going to be nothing other than a minor blip.

Next thing you know, though. Afternoon plans for a slap up meal and a couple of celebratory glasses of champers in Manhattan, sat in a crisp and fresh new suit are being swapped for a pseudo version of Meat Loaf and mashed potatoes washed down with 7-Up while sitting in that same old orange jump suit watching the panel on CNN sitting gleefully talking about how the DOJ had managed a clean sweep of all twelve indictments on me.

While three of them appeared to be giddy with excitement over the fact that some kind of 'enemy of the state' was now going to be behind bars for the rest of his life (and I don't even know where to begin with that whole enemy of the state stuff) the forth one, Jeb Hawton - the token Republican that they would sometimes throw on for the appearance of balance - was sitting there trying to suck the enjoyment out of them by warning that putting Peter Duncan in prison would not solve a single thing in terms of America's war on drugs and that - while the trial had made clear that he was far from innocent - by giving life to a man who was already retired and living out of harms way in a remote place like Bora Bora. It had been carried out while the Mexican drug lords - the real danger to America - were currently flooding America with larger amounts of drugs than ever before while bodies were piling up south *and* north of the border in record numbers.

You've got to love that Republican spirit, though. *All* that I was tried - successfully - for and their attitude is kind of 'yeah, we *know* he committed a crime but well, that was before so why don't you forget *that* bad stuff and look at this *other* squirrel instead.'

That was a hard, hard night - following the verdict from the jury that afternoon - I must admit. Since being flown into the states from Holland at the tail end of Two Thousand it had been difficult but not impossible to get through. I'd already sampled prison life and that can take you far if you're stupid enough to land yourself back inside again. The time - leading up to the case - had flown a lot quicker than a spell stuck inside a detention centre really should've done but with the magnitude of the trial, and all of the indictments thrown at me, there was barely a day that passed where I didn't have to speak to either my own legal team or an assortment of 'suits' from the Feds.

As a result. I did that time standing on my head and done so with the attitude that I was only there temporarily, not for life.

Technically I was right. I *wasn't* going to be spending the rest of my life inside the Fishkill maximum security detention centre in New York. No, the place that was going to have the luxury of that was going to be the ADX United States penitentiary administrative maximum prison somewhere in the foothills of the Rockies in Florence, Colorado.

That first night - in New York - dealing with the facts that saw a jury find me guilty on all counts. More counts than I could barely even remember *all* I was being charged with. I didn't sleep much. Whatever hope and positivity that I'd held throughout my time in America, that rakish looking head juror stole them from me the moment he opened his mouth and began to speak.

I slept even *less* though that first night in Colorado. If my first night back at Fishkill Detention Centre had been a tough one, as I pondered about the rest of my life behind bars. That first night *inside* the place that I was going to be spending the rest of my days was one hell of a reality check.

In between my guilty verdict, and when I was finally transferred from New York to Colorado, I had learned more and more about the 'ADX' and the more that I learned about it the further scared I became of the prospect of actually going there.

It's stupid, right? Me being scared of going 'anywhere,' with the background that I had. That was one of my main USPs for Eddy and German Ramirez and why they hired me back at the end of the Eighties, *because* I had the ability to go anywhere and fit in. Charm my way in and out of places that other mere mortals wouldn't have had the cojones - or the nous - to carry out themselves.

The ADX scared me, though. It didn't seem right that *I* was being put there. My legal team had advised that due to how high profile my case had been, there was a high probability that I was going to be made an example of, in as many ways as the Department of Justice possibly could.

Placing me in a prison alongside terrorists, mafia dons, serial killers and gangbangers, was but one of them.

At my sentencing hearing, any attempts at appealing the destination - of where I would spend the rest of my years - from my legal team were knocked back without even a consideration from the judge.

While my lawyers argued that I was not a violent man and - in fact - had no criminal charges that suggested as such *or* that anyone who had provided a testimony during the trial had even hinted that I was a dangerous individual.

This angle from my legal team, swatted away effortlessly by the prosecutors on the grounds that with the ADX being a prison of under five hundred prisoners - and through a quick glimpse at who was housed there, and for what reasons - I would be going somewhere that had the *exact* kind of people that I had spent my life doing business with and that the suggestion that their client was somehow going to be a 'fish out of water' was clearly a case of 'reaching' from his legal team.

It hadn't been the 'clientele' waiting for me in Colorado that was my worry. From what I understood, I wasn't exactly going to be bumping into The Unabomber, Ramzi Yousef or Sammy 'The Bull' Gravano in the queue for the canteen in any case. No, it wasn't the fact that I was going to be in the same building as the worst of the worst, as unfair as it all seemed to me. It was the prospect of being locked up for twenty three hours a day and left with virtually no contact with humans that had me so apprehensive. I'd like to think that I was a people person. The ADX didn't exactly seem like it was the most 'social' of places.

I wouldn't have given myself a year inside the place before losing my marbles, never mind a hundred and fucking twenty five of them.

Over the years I'd found myself in some improbable situations over certain parts of the world with the kind of people that you'd really rather didn't know exist, never mind be around, but had always kept my cool, composure never dipping. That night when I arrived - by van under US Marshall guard - into the underground parking complex of the Colorado prison, processed in and given a different - but yet exact same orange coloured - top and bottom to change into and led - shackled - to my cell. Once that door closed behind the guard and I looked around my seven by twelve cell, with window that had been deliberately bricked over (almost as an extra fuck you from the authorities. Yeah look, we built you a window but look some more .. we bricked over it so you can look through the glass, at a brick. Smart bastards, eh?) that was when it truly hit me. The gravity of it all.

Once the tears started, I couldn't stop them. Reality wouldn't *let* them stop flowing. I'd had it all. More than I could've ever dared dream of having when I was a kid. Humans have that tendency to push things too far, though and have been doing so since Icarus thought he could take to the skies. The daft bastard.

I had all the money I could've ever wished for, a beautiful wife, property in some of the most beautiful locations in the world and - my own personal weakness, cars. My Ferraris, Porsches and, my own pride and joy, the Lamborghini Diablo that almost caused an international incident when Prince Albert of Monaco was informed that I - 'a narco' - had been pushed up the waiting list and would be receiving mines before he would. A car that - as it turned out - I only actually ever drove twice. Albert would've been as well having it.

What good was any of that now, though? It was the past. *This* was my present and, more importantly, it was my future. *You'd* have broken down at the very thought of it too, when it ultimately hit you. Like it did on my first night underground in the ADX.

If *ever* there's a time for regrets. It's when that cell door closes on you for the first time. I'd felt those same regrets back in the early Eighties when I'd had my first spell inside but this was different. I was a nobody and had been given a minor sentence. Life was still ahead of me then, I was still young enough. *That* feeling in Colorado, though?

There were no positives to be found and I didn't bother looking for any. It all felt like there had been a certain degree of finality of it all.

It took me the first couple of months - inside there - before I could even begin to lift my head and bring myself out of the malaise that I had sunk into. I hadn't had what constituted as a 'conversation' with anyone in months apart from contact with guards, and it's not like you'd have been able to class any of them as the 'chatty type.'

Despite the front that my legal team had put on at their sham of a hotel press conference in the following hours after my guilty verdict - and how they had plans to challenge the initial extradition between Holland and America - I'd had no contact with any of them. We all knew it was done and that there was no need for our ongoing relationship to continue any further.

When you're sitting in a cell beside the Rocky Mountains in some super secretive maximum security prison. The very *last* thing that you would find yourself needing would be a five hundred dollar an hour billable lawyer.

To my surprise, after around the first month there, letters started to arrive. This, momentarily giving me a temporary lift because of the fact that some people had taken the time to write to me. From the stamped envelopes, all had appeared to have been sent from within the United States - apart from the few that had travelled up from South America - which ruled out any of them being sent to me from anyone that I was close with as, generally as a rule, America had been a country that if I was ever in it I was always in as much of a hurry to get back out of it again. I may not have been Colombian but when it came to the 'Yanquis' I had adopted the same sense of danger when it came to the amount of Americans who were out to get me.

The sight of the letters offered a brief respite in the low mood that everything had left me in. *Brief* in that once I began to actually *read* what was written inside them I found that they weren't exactly of the 'missing you, love you' kind that I'd initially envisaged.

Don't get me wrong. There *were* a couple of supportive letters hidden away inside the majority. The one from Colombian folk singer 'Javi Bermudas' from Bogota who had written to tell me that he had never forgotten the gesture that I had made - back in the early Nineties -

when I had donated ten thousand dollars towards the young offenders rehabilitation centre that he was trying to create and that he had written a 'Narcocorrido' in my honour. *That* would've melted the heart of an Eskimo. Ballads written for narcos were not novel by any means but to have one written for *you* - and sung throughout eternity as a result - was something quite special to have awarded to you. I was more surprised that I had a song *at all,* given the end of how my time was with the boys from Bogota. I was officially a 'rata' yet had folk singers writing ballads in my honour? I guess some people remember the hand that fed them?

In the letter I was informed that he had included a cassette of him performing the song but - for reasons of security reasons - this had not been included with the letter. Not that I'd have had any device to *play* the fucking thing on anyway but the guy meant well, regardless.

I *did* have a small laugh at the attached note from the prison office to advise me that they had removed an item (or items) from the letter and that I would be handed them upon the day that I was released. Ten out of ten for sarcasm and no mistake.

If I was laughing at the thought of receiving a cassette to listen to in a hundred and twenty five years time I certainly wasn't chortling at the majority of the letters that I went through. My god, it was like staring into the gates of hell, and that was just the marriage proposals from women living in trailer parks.

Over the course of that first batch of letters that had arrived - and apart from the ones from thirsty women that were commenting on how attractive they'd found me during the trial and if I'd like to engage in some back and forth with them - I was called a jackass, jerk off, asshole, arsewipe, ass clown, bag of shit, dick smash, fartnocker, douche bag, fucktard, jack wagon, cunt head, shitfucker, sleaze ball, uncle fucker and about another fifty other insults that probably didn't exist outside whatever shitty state the person who'd sent me the letter were from.

The letters, mainly from a mix of people from all over the country. Mums and dads who had lost their kids through drugs. Coppers - both serving and retired - laughing their asses off at me over the fact that I was going to be spending the rest of my life inside the ADX which, it had appeared, they'd expressed their knowledge of how shitty my existence was going to be for the duration. Weirdos and loners who, unnervingly, looked up to me and the life that I'd led and wanted to be friends. The feeling of 'Rock Star' status amongst *those* types left me feeling uneasy every bit as much as the hate mail.

There was that *one* letter, though. From this journalist, the letter itself with the Washington Post logo in the corner. A very formal and respectively written letter by a 'Manny Ruiz' who told me that in his role - as The Post's South America and Mexico correspondent - he had followed my 'career' closely and asked if I would be open to a series of interviews for an article that he was planning, following my conviction. He framed it to me as a way of putting my own story out there, that - no doubt - there were things said during the trial that I would like to take the opportunity to hit back at. It was nothing more than a journalist making an attempt at trying to play mind games with someone.

The irony was not lost on me that - stuck inside a small cell for the best part of a day on my own - *all* I wanted was someone to talk to. Someone, anyone. And when given the opportunity I get handed loners, weirdos, MILFs that maybe 'you' would like to fuck but I sure as hell wouldn't, and scumbag journalists looking to fit you up and twist the knife into you further than it already has been.

It was obviously down to the twenty four hour round the clock news coverage that I'd watched from my cell in New York every day but well, when it came to me and the media - despite the sins that I will hold my hands up to - I'd felt kind of persecuted. I was surprised, more than anything else, that they'd even taken an interest in me. I'd thought that when I'd been stuck on that flight from Schipol to JFK that it would've all been under some kind of radar and that I was going to go from A to B without pause. When I saw all the waiting press - by the DEA people carrier - outside the airport. That's when I knew different.

As a result of seeing *how* the American media had approached my good self. Well, you wouldn't blame me if I was a trifle distrustful of them, in general. Yeah, I agree to the series of interviews with the journalist and what's the actual point of it? He's only going to go away and write whatever it was that he was going to write in the fucking first place, isn't he?

It wasn't Manny Ruiz's fault - all of the negative coverage that I'd received *any time* the subject of me was broached on all the cable networks - but he was the wrong guy in the wrong place as in 'someone' from the media that had given me their address. Was literally fucking *asking* me to reply. So I did.

Dear Manny

*Thank you for your letter that I have received today. I **am** - in fact - in fine health (and thank you for asking) although I do admit to be experiencing some 'freedom and liberty' issues at present. In response to your request that I enter into a series of telephone interviews with you for your newspaper I would just like to express my extreme delight that someone like yourself has awarded me the opportunity to 'set the record straight' and - in turn, through my response to you, a member of the mainstream media - provide me with the welcome opportunity to tell you to go and fuck yourself, sideways.*

Yours faithfully

Peter Duncan

He was dogged, you would have to give him that. What is it they say? *Intrepid reporter?* Because he wrote back straight away. The very next cycle of letters that came into me I saw the 'Washington Post' logo jumping out at me straight away in amongst the collection of sub standard hand written letters that were in the pile.

I'd never expected a reply. The letter - from me - was clearly a 'conversation ender' and something that did not require a response. Someone says one thing > Someone says something back that brings a close to the exchange. It happens all day, every day. For Ruiz to reply *back* to me was - to my intelligence - only ever going to be someone who had taken an exception to my rudeness and wanted to give me a bit back.

Instead, it was quite civil, jovial, even. Whether it had been intended or not it had come across that, despite what I had written in my letter to him, he seemed pleased and upbeat that he'd received a reply back. He should've done considering he was the *only* person that I *had* written back to. He - once again - reiterated that the article that he was planning - and reminded me that with or without my co-operation it *would* be written - was going to offer me the chance to tell 'my' story.

Not specifically just regarding recent times - as had been highlighted during my trial in Brooklyn - but *why and how* someone from Scotland, United Kingdom had come to be working for such a major and notorious outfit such as the Bogota Cartel.

I wasn't sure what he had been looking to achieve with the return letter as he'd never really said anything in it differently to the first one that he'd sent. I *had* toyed with the idea of sending him a much more sarcastic letter in response as - I'd felt that - it would've given me a morsel of a released endorphin, just to abuse a member of the press in some shape or form. This was the day, however, that the new prisoner was brought into the ADX. Something that took me off down a completely different rabbit hole of my own.

'Outside recreation' in the prison was never, ever a guarantee never mind a basic human need and privilege. Even then, when you *did* get to have some outside time you had to do away with any kinds of dignity to secure some fresh air by agreeing to a strip search. Generally you get strip searched going *into* a prison. The ADX - as I'd been told countless times before I'd even transferred there - was no ordinary joint, though.

When Bubba - one of the few African American guards that I'd seen in all my time since arriving - brought my breakfast to the cell in the morning, it was served up with the briefest of info that broke the news that there would be no outside recreation that day. No one had ever said that at the beginning of the day to me so, obviously, it left me wondering why. Had I fucked up somewhere? Was I being intentionally singled out for punishment of sorts. It took me months to even be granted recreational time and then out the blue a guard is making a point of telling me that I won't be getting any that day. Telling me at the very start of it just to ram home that it was going to be an *extra* long day ahead.

'Why's that, then? If I may ask?'

I enquired in the most respectful of ways. Were the guards inside the ADX bastards? Of course they were. It wouldn't exactly be within the realms of fantasy that if you're going to create a super jail, bigger and badder than a standard prison then it would make sense that you were to hire super elite bad bastards to look after the place. Bubba had seemed, I don't know? *Less* bastardish than the others I'd encountered and it was because of this that I felt comfortable about asking for extra details.

'We got some extremist terrorist coming in today. Al Qaeda protege bomb maker, or summit. Place will be on full lockdown until he's arrived and processed.'

As much as I managed to squeeze out of him before he'd gone again.

That briefest of exchanges, however, was enough to offer a reminder of just what kind of a place I was in, that I was going to be neighbours with a Jihadist. The terrorists were a group who - due to work undertaken for the cartel - I was no stranger to. I did business on quite a few times with them on behalf of the brothers, Somalia, Yemen, Afghanistan and Angola. Places I can list straight off the top of my head. *All* trips, I couldn't wait to be back in Colombia from again. Even though we were doing business that was mutually beneficial to both Al Qaeda and the Ramirez Cartel there was never a time where they hid the fact that - as a Westerner - they did not like me, *detested*, even. That evil look never leaving their eyes whenever they looked in my direction.

In the line of business that I was in. Asking questions tended to leave you in the proximity of taking a bullet in the head so for the majority of the time it served you, as well as paid, better to play dumb. Do your job, get paid and then get the f**k out of there.

As a result. All shipments of guns and RPGs that I'd overseen to go to their training camps was done under a no questions asked basis. As long as they paid - and on that score they were as good as their word - then who cared what they got up to with their toys, right?

I'd never heard of them, as an organisation, until the early Nineties and Eddy had sold them to me as a group of freedom fighters who had risen out of the Afghan war and that they had helped send the Red Army back to the Soviet Union with their tails between their legs. Well, if they fought back the Russians, successfully. They must be jolly good fellows, I'd thought to myself when learning about them and how we were going to be equipping one of their training camps in the Tora Bora region of the Afghan mountains as soon as their cheque had cleared, so to speak.

You could never have done my job for the brothers if you were in possession of a conscience. Something that I was prepared to cast aside and did so successfully for a sustained period of years. I believe, however, that it's possible to *reclaim* your consciousness again, if you search for it. As part of your whole reformation, as a human being.

And I *know* that it was all a case of crying after the milk has gone but as the years went by and this unknown group of 'freedom fighters' began to make a name for themselves and force their way onto the world stage with the bombing of the World Trade Centre in New York, US Embassy attack in Nairobi and the bombing of the USS Cole in Yemen, it all left me a little nauseous that I had assisted them years before. I could never have known and even if Eddy and German had (and who knows, maybe they did) they'd have still went ahead and provided the weapons that the terrorists were looking to buy, anyway.

I'd heard whispers that there were already Al Qaeda members there inside the ADX. Ramzi Yousef - responsible for the van bomb left underneath the WTC in New York - was most definitely somewhere else inside the facility. His being one of the names that I'd heard repeated to me when someone was trying to make the point of telling me just what kind of hell I was going to be living in.

It had been held up to me like a mirror as if to say that if Peter Duncan and Ramzi Yousef were being put in the same maximum security prison then, by that reasoning, the two people were one and the same. Which they most certainly fucking well *weren't*.

All thoughts of Al Qaeda and my own direct links with them over the years had been enough to make me soon forget about the letter from Ruiz, or my intentions to send him one back. Actually, only remembering that I *hadn't* when - a few weeks later - I received yet another letter from the journalist.

If the first letter from him had been of the someone trying to sell something to you feel. The third letter was more of the 'offer expires soon' vibe. Specifically engineered to bring their customer out of hibernation to secure the sale.

Dear Peter

I'm sorry that I did not hear back from you with regards to my most recent letter. I hope that everything is well for you and that you are being treated good in Colorado?

I wanted to reach out one final time to remind you that my offer to chat for the article is still open to you, however, due to time restrictions on my end, this window is closing soon and I will be forced to write the piece without your cooperation.

I would appreciate clarification on this within the next seven to ten days.

Best Regards

Manny Ruiz

Clarification? What part of 'go fuck yourself sideways' left the need for clarity anywhere? The letter arriving on what had been one of those extra low days - which would generally fall most days of the week that had a letter 'Y' in them - for me that I didn't even have the motivation to be wound up by the man's unwillingness to take no for an answer.

Instead, scrunching the letter up into a ball of paper and throwing it across the cell. Falling near to the others that I'd already pitched into the corner.

It was the same week that the guards had brought me a TV. Was only a small black and white thing but well, beggars and choosers. I'd been told that I would receive one for my cell but that, first of all, I'd need to prove myself not to be too much of a cunt with the guards. I'm paraphrasing them but that was really about the crux of it.

It felt like Christmas day, the morning the two guards appeared at my cell to install it. One to do the manual work and - I'd assumed - the other to make sure that I didn't kill the one installing the TV. What prisoner in their right state of mind would kill someone that's appearing to try and make their stay inside *infinitely* better than it had been before? Then again, this was the ADX. You think a Ramzi Yousef gives a flying fuck whether he can watch The Simpsons or MTV Cribs?

Once they'd taken care of things and left me to it I was actually pleasantly surprised with what was available on it. Don't get me wrong, it wasn't one of those two hundred and fifty channels kind of affairs but it *did* have a selection of channels that covered all bases. News (which, admittedly, with me no longer being part of the news cycle was easier to watch without the risk of experiencing an aneurism) sports, religion, educational and general entertainment.

I filled my boots that day and went full scale couch potato. Well if you can class lying on a wafer thin mattress sat on top of a concrete bed as 'lampin,' that is. As I'd been conditioned for the previous year. I went straight for the news networks but after around six straight hours of watching Democrats bitching about Republicans and the same back with knobs on I had the moment of clarity that life was already shit, as bad as it could possibly get and that what would be the point of watching people who get *paid* to tell you how shit the world was?

Channel surfing I watched a little piece of college football. University of Michigan 'Wolverines' versus Ohio State 'Buckeyes.' As always with the sport - on the few times I had clapped eyed on it - I didn't have the first clue what was actually going on. I was more taken with the crowd, the commentator saying that there was over a hundred thousand people there. For a college match? Crazy Yanquis.

Reasoning that life was too short to sit and watch a sport I didn't understand, I moved on again. Watching a documentary about Richard Nixon on the Discovery Channel. He was a right shifty bastard, him. He'd have made a brilliant cartel associate, had he not opted for the other life of crime, as a politician. Sometimes with both businesses - and how those inside go about their work - the line is so fine that sometimes you can barely even see it.

After the documentary had finished, I went channel hopping once more to see what I could find. Doing that thing where you flick from channel to channel so quickly you barely give your brain a chance to process what is actually on screen before it's tackling the next visual.

On location news report - Dick Dastardly cartoon - pundits with really loud sports jackets sitting talking about NBA - Aerosmith music video - someone being interviewed on the red carpet at an awards ceremony - episode of Friends - Televangelist trying to persuade you to part with your money.

'Wait up a second.' I thought to myself as I was staring at the preacher on TV urging the viewers to call the number on the screen while my brain was still processing the previous couple of channels that I'd briefly flicked through.

'It couldn't have been him' I told myself as I frantically tried to reverse the steps I'd taken to land me on the channel with the televangelist on it. Pressing the downwards arrow icon on the remote multiple times until it brought me back to the interviewer on the red carpet.

This returning me back to the young and over excitable NBC presenter who was stood there holding her mic in the direction of, my son.

'WHAT IN THE ACTUAL FUCK?'

It had been enough to send me from my horizontal position upwards to the point of sitting on the edge of the bed as I watched on.

'So, Selecao, how excited are you to be nominated for best song written for visual media, tonight?

She asked him while he stood - along with his girlfriend that I'd first come across in Ibiza the year that Eva and I 'visited' Stevie during the summer - in front of a sponsors board. Company logos such as Mastercard, Delta Airlines and Pepsi intermingled with the official crest of the 'Grammy Awards.'

My son, standing there as a nominee at an awards ceremony, as prestigious as The Grammy Awards? Paparazzi cameras flashing in his direction. The famous actors and musicians that were just casually filing past behind him. I should've been sitting there beaming with pride. Cheering him on from my cell shouting

'GO ON, MY SON.'

I wasn't, though. *He* saw to that.

'Well, I can hardly express how delighted I am to be nominated, pinching myself here, really. It couldn't have ever been in my wildest dreams that when I was asked to make a track for an indie filmmaker from Prague would it see that I'd be standing here on the red carpet at The Grammy Awards. It's all a bit fucking ment .. Oh, shit, I mean, emm sorry about that.'

And he had been doing so well up to that point, too.

The girl interviewing him tried to make light out of it and tell him not to worry but you could see it on her face that she knew it wasn't a good look to have someone swearing on a segment, during prime time television, at a major awards.

Standing there in a classic black tux (I assumed) I was struggling to remember a time where I had ever seen him in a suit of sorts. He'd scrubbed up well. Looked good and seemed healthy despite the fact that he'd clearly had a couple of Patsy Clines before arriving at the ceremony. A father knows. *Especially* a father like Steven Duncan's.

I'd have done the same had *I* been the one going to a big awards ceremony with all eyes on me too so there was no judging there on my part when it came to his narcotics use.

'And what a beautiful off the shoulder evening gown you're wearing tonight. Who may I ask is it from?'

The NBC presenter changed tack quickly - and wisely - by directing the next question away from Stevie. Flo replying that the dress was from Giorgio Armani and - when pressed further - that her shoes were by Jimmy Choo. To the delight of the presenter's - as well as visible relief - Flo had managed to articulate her answer in a way - unlike her boyfriend - that would not have had the network switchboard lighting up with complaints.

While the two spoke, Stevie, who seemed to have had his attention captured by someone off screen, had chosen to forget the interview completely and was pointing and smiling at someone before making the international gesture for catching them later for a drink before giving a very enthusiastic thumbs up in the direction of whoever it was he was communicating with.

The presenter seeing this and - trying to take control of this small red carpet interview that clearly wasn't going the way they normally do - immediately tried to bring Stevie back into play and end the interview before she went looking for her next target to grab.

'Now, Selecao. Being nominated for a Grammy is something that people dream of. Your parents must be so proud of you tonight?'

'Yeah, I'd imagine that my mum would be proud that her son is representing on a stage like this. Due to the time difference between here and Scotland I'd imagine that she's probably sleeping but if she's watching right now. I love you mum.'

He replied in that fake accent - he'd spoken with throughout the interview - that was clearly being put on simply so that Americans would be able to 'understand' the boy speak.

'And what about your father, should he be watching from his cell in Colorado?'

You couldn't have blamed her for asking the question. You'd have considered her credentials as a presenter had she *not* taken that subject and ran with it. Grammy Awards or not. Even so, it felt like she'd ambushed him with it.

One second it was all happy shiny award and clothes chat and then BAM she drops in the subject of Stevie's 'narco father' and the possibility that he might be watching from his supermax prison cell in Colorado.

The following few seconds - personally - were an emotional rollercoaster that - by the end of the 'ride' - I was left with a collage of negative thoughts in the kind of way you'd have never thought possible when watching your kid on TV - along with millions of others - on such a big night for him.

When she asked him the question. His face immediately dropped in the way that suggested he wasn't too happy with her for asking. *This* in turn putting a smile on *my* face.

'Who?'

Stevie replied with an arrogant shrug of his shoulders that was more of Cocaine than it was of him.

I could see what he had done and as a result the smile was gone from my face as quickly as it had set. The presenter hadn't, though.

'Your father, Peter Duncan, El Corazon Valiente.' She asked, stupidly.

'I don't have a clue who you're talking about, I'm afraid. Come on, babe.'

He replied with as little emotion possible on his face to the girl fro m NBC before he then turned to Flo and took her hand, squeezed it and led the two of them away and off camera and up the red carpet.

'YOU LITTLE FUCKING UNGRATEFUL BASTARD'

I screamed at the TV, coming scarily close to throwing the remote against the wall (thank god for the voice that screamed at me that if I broke one I sure as hell wouldn't be handed a replacement) and smashing it into pieces through the rage that I'd been filled with.

Seeing him there. On a red carpet, nominated for an award for his music. What seemed to matter most at the time to me was who had *bought* him his DJ turntables back when he was just a kid? Who was it that set him out on the path that had now led to him mixing with some of the biggest names in music? Me, that's who. And he denies me on a night like that?

There was the *other* factor in that I had pretty much been his knight in shining armour back at the start of the decade and it would've been fair to say that were it not for the help of me - admittedly sitting in Colombia at the time - arranging for Davey McKenna in Edinburgh to set up the sting that busted Nora through at that Glasgow trap house.

Putting the psychopath away for a number of years and leaving Stevie to live his life carefree, which he evidently went on to do. Had it not been for me, though. Well who knows? What who *also* knows - and I too - is that you can't play records with two broken arms, or if you're lying in a coffin.

Admittedly there had obviously been some unpleasantness also with the pair of us where not so much mistakes were made but unscrupulous decisions were taken. I know it wasn't a good look to make the decision that a young - and innocent - girl will die before I would be caught but, well. *No one* apart from me during that whole situation understood it from *my* point of view. How I'd had a few years of living 'the Colombian way.' Living on your nerves and your wits at all times to make sure that sicarios do not pop out of the blue and clip you. That when danger presents itself the self preservation of a Bogota barrio kid kicks in and you'll do anything you can to save your skin. The thought of me trading *my* life for Flo's was, frankly, laughable but Stevie - and most certainly Flo - simply wouldn't understand what was so funny about the suggestion.

And if it comes across as cold and uncaring then boo fucking hoo for you. The girl didn't *actually* die. She came close to it but well, the evidence was there to see minutes before on the TV. Standing there talking about her Armani dress and Jimmy Choo shoes.

Whether Stevie would like to admit it - and he certainly wasn't for on NBC - meeting me by accident in Blackburn changed his life, for the better.

And he stands there in front of millions, when he reaches that pinnacle in his career, and denies me? Denies my actual existence?

I felt angry, frustrated, betrayed, cast aside, diminished but worst of all. Forgotten.

And if there's *one thing* that you don't want to be left feeling inside the ADX Florence. It's that you've been forgotten about.

I took my headphones off. Getting up off the bed and taking the few steps required to bend down and collect the scrunched up letter from The Washington Post before reaching for the paper and pen.

Chapter 3

Manny

'Manny, you've still not provided your expenses receipts to me. If you don't get them in by the end of the week then don't bother submitting them at all.'

Beeeeeeeeeep

'Yeah, it's me. I got you the intel on the latest move that the CJNG have made South of the border but it'll cost you. You know that nothing in this life is free, amigo. Call me back when you get this.'

Beeeeeeeeeeep

'Hello, my friend. Me so very sorry for you that Kobe didn't make that last second three pointer but I not so sorry for myself. If you know what I mean? Come and see me, today.'

Beeeeeeeeeeep

'Hey you, you never called me back after our date. Now normally I would just leave it at that and say that it wasn't to be but thought no. I'm gonna ask that piece of FUCKING SHIT just where the hell he gets off on by ….

I switched the machine off at that point. Most days, going through my messages was like trying to navigate your way through a minefield, in a pair of clown shoes. Her whiny, feeling sorry for herself tone was something that I could've done without and not before I'd, at least, had a coffee to start the day.

Gloria. We'd been set up for a date by a mutual friend. Why the fuck friends - who are in a relationship - feel the need to get involved in other people's business. Play cupid and shit? Always trying to pair people up with one another. Taking one person they know who's single and matching them up with someone else that they also know isn't with anyone. Thinking that they are adding two with two and getting four when they're - in fact - no place fucking near.

As was the case with Gloria and myself. Her from Massachusetts Avenue Heights, living in her brownstone townhouse. The pretense of even having to 'work,' something that she did not even feel the need to put on as a front. Mummy and daddy's money seeing to that. And me, in my downtown bedsit that while you could - *technically* - swing a cat inside it. That, however, would all depend on the kind of cat that you were trying to three-sixty, though.

We did our own respective parts, to get our friends off our backs but the actual date was a disaster. Her and I were like trying to put a Sega Genesis cartridge into a Super Nintendo. We just didn't go together. Not that it didn't stop us from having sex at the end of it and *that* could only have been the reason that I was now receiving a tirade on my voicemail, because I hadn't made that phone call that a lot of men say they'll make but seldom do after sex.

Gina from the office moaning at me about getting my expenses in, a source trying to flush me out for a potential paid story and my bookie gleefully calling to let me know that the bet that I had - stupidly - went double or quits on hadn't went my way. All of that I could handle but one hint of Gloria was enough to have me switching the machine off, despite the flashing light which indicated there were further messages to listen to.

I fixed up a much needed coffee and then made a point of checking the Lakers score. The voicemail from Jin had more than suggested to me that I'd lost but - out of morbid curiosity if anything else - I wanted to see for myself what the final score was between them and the Knicks. According to the report on ESPN Sports. The Lakers went down by two points where, in the last second, a three point throw from Kobe Bryant had went agonizingly around the rim before jumping back out again. Leaving *me* 'agonizingly' five hundred dollars in the hole with Jin after trying to claw my way back out of it after that stupid spread bet involving the San Antonio Spurs and the Seventy Sixers.

'Best get those expenses filed, a-fucking-sap' I thought to myself as I opened up a fresh packet of Pop Tarts and shoved a couple into the toaster.

My deal at The Post was that I wasn't required to actually 'attend' when it came to the day to day job. I mean, like, I didn't have a desk and chair for one thing. I only really showed face on an as and when basis. Hence why I had the administrative side of things chasing me for receipts. It was a sweet enough deal. The only real drawback being that if you wanted to get regularly paid, you needed to unearth and write stories on a frequent enough basis to guarantee that.

As such, I was forever on the hunt for a story from the world of the narco, both North *and* South of the border. With my mother and father growing up in the infamous Comuna 13 neighborhood in Medellin. When they had me, they gave birth to a son who would grow up to look *every bit* like someone who, too, grew up in a barrio. With that I was able to capitalize on the looks given to me and - despite being an American - I was left in a position to move more freely in South America and Mexico than a 'gringo' would ever be able to enjoy.

I was able to visit places that 'Brad out of Princeton' working with The Post wouldn't have lasted two minutes in.

And if business was good for the narcos in the South then business was most definitely good for me. And since the Eighties had there ever been a time where profits for Medellin, Cali, Sinaloa or Juarez were *not* plentiful? Obviously, though. You cannot have one thing without the other so while the 'dolla bills' stacked up for the jefe's across the border, along with it would come the pain, suffering and misery of others.

I'd been kept 'busy' over the years since that initial piece that I had written on Pablo Acosta Villarreal from the Juarez Cartel that had been hawked around all of the majors hoping that one of them would take a bite and - fittingly - allowed me to eat that month.

This was during the time of the whole 'Rock & Roll narco' thing that was going on here. The public learning about Escobar and all of the folk stories that went with him. The murders, the terrorism but what held some kind of curious fascination to the American public was the tales of excess. They couldn't get enough of it so I managed to find an opening at the exact right time, professionally.

Once Escobar and - subsequently - Cali fell. Cartel life - in general - found its way back out of the public eye in the main stream media. In reality, however. Things were just starting to heat up. Once the Mexicans took control of things they were going to go on to make Colombia look like a bunch of fucking bambinos. My editor, Will Hessen - at complete odds with rival newspapers - recognised this.

Listened to what I had to tell him and what had gone before. The brutal killings, the corruption and sheer volume of narcotics that had been entering the United States.

That *all* of that - if he could believe it - was going to seem like amateur hour once the Mexicans took it all for themselves. Fucking DEA all high-fiveing each other and holding shit eating grin filled press conferences, slapping each others' backs so hard it was amazing none of their teeth came flying out of their mouths.

I couldn't have blamed the average schmo for looking on and thinking 'shit, we actually did it. We *won* the war on drugs. We got the bad guys.' I, obviously knew better. Knew that, while yeah, we *did* get the bad guys. The only real issue there was that there was even *worse* ones waiting in the wings to take over.

Will, as a boss, had never been anything other than supportive and the most crucial of all, 'got it' when it came to my work and how dangerous it could be at times. Any time I crossed the Mexican border there really was never a cast iron guarantee that I'd be coming back again.

Then again, you choose to take up a job where - in Mexico - someone is killed every week simply for doing it. You can kind of accept that there *is* an element of you bringing things upon yourself.

And yet, back at the offices in Washington it had been suggested that I had a cushy number where - it was believed - I just swaggered around The Americas living my best life … and receiving a cheque for it.

Since becoming Chief Narcotics reporter with the paper, ok, the *only* narco reporter with the paper. I had lost count of the amount of death threats that I had received from all the way down in Sao Paolo to Sinaloa, as well as threats far closer to home inside the States.

Been followed for days on end only for it to mysteriously stop again. Offered bribes from *one* cartel to write lies about *another*. Have been locked up in six different South and central American countries by corrupt police. I even had - and *this*, I have to admit, I found pretty fucking cool - a private and personal one to one phone phone call with one Señor Pablo Emilio Escobar Gaviria.

This coming during the 'end times' for him. On the run from 'Los Pepes' as well as the Search Bloc and DEA coalition.

I'd debunked all of the lovable and cuddly myths about him. Shit like how he'd had to spend a thousand dollars a month on elastic bands to hold his money together. To a 'serious' narco journalist these puff pieces that were full of piss and done nothing but add to his mystique. Meanwhile the horrible bastard is blowing fucking planes out of the sky and murdering politicians and journalists.

I was angry - the day I wrote the piece - and it showed.

'Escobar spends a thousand dollars a month on elastic bands > How the f**k would you or anyone else know how much he spends on elastic bands? You really think that amongst the Cocaine and the terrorism he was keeping track of his receipts from Staples?'

'He has a zoo at Hacienda Napoles' > Yes and the animals treated worse than a dancing bear belonging to a Russian circus.'

'He was so cool that he had international football players all flying in to play games of soccer at his ranch' > Andres Escobar, god rest his soul, admitted to only ever *going* to Hacienda Napoles to play in these exhibition matches through fear and fear only.'

I took on everything in that article.

Myself and the Medellin Cartel were no strangers to each other and it had been a few years before this 'vent' of mines that I had received a bullet in the post with a simple message scribbled on a single sheet of notepaper.

'*A Manny*

Con amor desde Medellin

x'

With love from Medellin. And they even put a little kiss for me at the bottom, how sweet.

That bullet hadn't been enough to stop me writing about them but I'll admit. I wrote that article safe in the knowledge that the walls really *were* closing in on Escobar and that the days of the Medellin cartel - as the world knew it as - were soon going to be over. Knowing that - I think - gave me a larger sense of freedom to write *exactly* what I wanted. And did.

Laying out all of the crimes that Escobar had overseen, murders that he had personally given the green light and been implicated in. Had it been just the sheer volume of Cocaine that he flooded America that he would be judged on then that *alone* would've been enough in itself to put him behind bars for life. It was the terrorism that should've seen him receive a death sentence, which in his own way I suppose, he did.

I called him a menace to society, an evil bastard, a psychopath, in amongst a whole other plethora of things. I also called him 'fat' and *this,* for the soon to be deceased Escobar, was one insult too far.

I genuinely thought that it was a friend, or someone from the paper, pulling my pisser. Trying to put the wind up me, you know? You could tell from his voice, though. You cannot fake that type of rage, plus, if it was someone who was punking me then they just happened to be able to put on a magnificent attempt at his voice. It's not as if I hadn't heard the man speak, where as the average American *hadn't.*

I felt quite privileged, special, even, that despite the delicate position that the man now found himself in. He'd *still* managed to find time to find out the number for the Washington Post. Call there asking to be put through to my office only to find that I didn't have one and - instead - receive my home number where I could be contacted and called it to lambast me over a short phone call where he talked - shouted actually - and I listened.

By the time his tirade had ended - and I was preparing to speak - he was hanging up on me again.

'NO MAS GRRRRRANDE LARGAS'

No more large talk, the last words I heard from him. Made my day to know that I'd riled him so much. Years later when we began to discover what that final year was like for him it brought me even *more* joy to know that he was literally living from day to day, safe house to safe house. Sicarios deserting him in droves.

That during such a claustrophobic time for him. He had still managed to read - or have translated, I suppose - my verbal assault on him and despite the possibility that Search Bloc, the DEA, Delta Force or the lawless Los Pepes lynch mob. Or the high percentage of chance that he was being surveilled from the air by Centra Spike. Regardless of this - in that moment - the *only* thing that mattered to him was that he got hold of me to tell me that if I called him fat again he would kill me.

It was a moment that kept me *in* the industry during the dark times where I felt that things were getting too dangerous, from a personal point of view or when it came to the times where the cheques weren't so regular from The Post. Some stories where you have to dig in, play the long game and trust that once you've collected all pieces of the puzzle, you'll reap the rewards. Like, Acapulco and the disappearance of the soccer team from Los Cabos, who visited for a match against the local team. None of the squad arriving back from the match, or their team bus. As is the case - most of the time - in Mexico. This peculiar story was effortlessly swept under the carpet. The official line - authorities coming up with that they had assumed that the whole team had fled for the American border (together) instead of returning back to Los Cabos - a bambino would not swallow, never mind an adult.

The team had been full of young men, still at university, starting out in the world with life all ahead of them, in their homeland. There was no need for them to be 'fleeing' to America to live life as illegals. When I had picked up on the story of a soccer team disappearing into thin air - this coming up while covering a completely different story - I was left with the loosest of threads that, once I began pulling on it, led to the most sickening of revelations that the entire team, plus coaches, had been shot and killed and buried in a mass grave on the outskirts of Acapulco.

The reason for this? The local cartel had waged several millions on the home side to be the victors and Los Cabos had had the temerity to turn up and win the match. Enraged, the local jefe put out the order that the Los Cabos team was not to leave the stadium.

The driver of the team coach was given a friendly warning that his services were now no longer needed, but his bus was. The Los Cabos playing staff doing half of the work for the Acapulco Cartel by all filing back onto their bus after having their post match showers and changing. Expecting to be making the return journey, instead, they found half a dozen sicarios with semi automatic rifles jumping on board where - with another soldier now behind the wheel - they were taken out to a secluded spot and executed. The bus destroyed - at a cartel owned automobile scrapyard - to wipe out any evidence of the team left behind.

Fearful locals - to a man - repeated the same mantra to anyone who would ask. That they had all seen the Los Cabos players board their bus and their driver pull out of the stadium.

They saw *a* driver drive the players away. That it was under gunpoint was something that had always seemed to skip the minds of those who gave an account of what they had witnessed that day.

Through my digging - over a period of a good year, if not more - it was which led to the exhumation of the bodies in the mass, and shallow, grave that they had been dumped in. Leading to the expulsion of two policemen who were complicit with what took place that afternoon. It dominated the news cycle in Mexico for weeks.

Every now and again something happens in Mexico where even for a country so desensitized to violence, murder and loss. An atrocity is deemed as 'extra.' My reveal was such one of those moments for Mexican society.

And it brought me recognition in my own country too.

'Article by a foreign correspondent' of the year award, in fact.

All I was able to say, at the awards ceremony in Governors Island when collecting my award in front of the great and good in newspaper and magazine in America.

'Thank you for your recognition although I'd much rather that I hadn't been able to write the article. I'd like to dedicate this award to the players and coaches of Club Los Cabos. Taken too soon from this world and in such a unnecessary and needless way. May they all rest in peace.'

That had been years ago now, though. Would barely find an invitation to even *attend,* never mind invited as a potential winner. Ironically, it seemed to come at a time when my work had never been more dangerous. The more unhinged the cartels in Mexico would get the further away I was from any awards of the year.

Of course, that was never the motivation for me, but still. It would've been nice from time to time to receive a little piece of recognition for my work. Some of those political journalists who do fuck all other than put a suit on and stand alongside other suits and let some politician lie to their faces and then - like the fucking stenographers that they are - go back to their laptops and repeat the lies fed. And people worship the ground that some of these journalists fucking walk on?! Like 'their' opinion matters? How the fuck can your opinion matter when all you do is give the opinion of *others*?

To really capture people's attention. Have them looking in my direction - as a respected and known as journalist - it really always came down to two things. Either I uncovered something so fantastical, so random and fascinating about a cartel, or member. Like - for example - the story that I had broken where a certain Tijuana boss had decided he wanted four Maserati's Ghibli's, in green. One for him and other three, one for each of his sons. The only issue with this was that the specific version that he wanted, he would have to pay a deposit and be placed on a waiting list, for one.

To secure *four*, in the same specific color.

Not. A. Chance.

This, however, did not stop the Tijuana boss from finding out who - and where in the world they were - that sat on the list for a green Ghibli and all within the same week. Maserati received correspondence from certain individuals stating that they now wished for their names to be removed from the Ghibli waiting list and, of course, they would be forfeiting their non refundable deposit.

Predictably, upon delivery of the vehicles, the men in Tijuana could not resist flaunting their wealth. That - by now infamous - picture of all four cars lined up in a row with both doors opened and each son - and father - all standing in front of each hood, pulling the same folded arm pose with smiles on their faces. The American public loved that story but that is kind of my point. They weren't interested in the bread and butter and how much of a danger the cartels were to American society. Who cares 'how' they earned the money to *buy* the supercars, right? They just wanted to hear the obscure. And if it wasn't the obscure, they wanted the macabre. Bringing *that* side of things to the public - while what they possibly wanted to read - didn't always make for the most soundest of sleeps on my side.

I sat down with my cup of coffee and magma like temperature, as ever, Pop Tarts - that morning - and finally attempted to go through my mail. The same mail that I'd collected from my post box three days before but hadn't quite managed to get things together enough to sit down and actually open and go through.

Bills (all the way from freshly printed to final demands) - Novelty checks with the news that I may already have won the amount written on it (I may have already won NOTHING, go see fucking Kobe about that) - Flyers for local Asian restaurants (I'm sure the same joints keep putting the same flyers in my post box on a weekly basis) - A copy of the local free newspaper, The Triangle.

(named after the area of the Mount Vernon Triangle that my flat was located and truly a publication that you would even put the New York Post before in terms of if you were stuck for something to read)

Amongst the assortment of shit, however, my eyes were diverted to *that* postal franking stamp. A crest that I'd seen once before, a few months previously when working on a trail that had seemed to go cold. Everything else was dropped instantly as I hurriedly ripped the envelope open to fish out the letter.

Dear Manny

Please forgive the 'tone' of my last letter that I sent to you. You must understand that your original request was received by me when not in the best of places, mentally. Literally and figuratively.

Life in the ADX is challenging at times, to say the least. That does not however excuse how I was with you in my correspondence that I previously put your way and for that, I profusely apologise.

In the event that I am not too late to contribute to your planned article - as mentioned in all of your letters received so far - after careful consideration I would like to now agree to the interview that you have requested.

If this is agreeable to you I would appreciate you recognising this in writing along with further details of how we proceed from this point.

I would, also, like to advise that over the past year plus - since being brought to America - I have developed a deep mistrust of the media and have found myself to be subject of nothing other than a serious case of 'character assassination' since I came onto the media's radar.

Now while I would never wish to threaten anyone - if you've done your homework on me then you will know already that this is not me. And in any case, you would not be receiving this letter had it contained any kind of a threat inside it (the guards - *Hello guards reading this!* - seeing to that) - I would like to take this opportunity to remind you that it was <u>you</u> who came to <u>me</u> seeking the interview and that you told me that this was my chance to put 'my' story across. I will be looking for you to keep your word on that.

Yours Faithfully

Peter Duncan

He had *finally* agreed. And just as I'd given up on him, and most likely the story on him altogether. Already finding myself looking forwards and sideways for an alternative story to run with. Without his input I really was only going to be able to come up with something *slightly* more informed than what had already been made public throughout his trial. Therefore, not much point in writing it in the first place.

I'd tried to play mind games with him by telling him that I was writing the article with or without his cooperation, to no avail.

This changed things, though. Massively.

If my own personal research - and knowledge - of the man was anything *remotely* close to the reality of things.

By the time I was through with Peter 'El Corazon Valiente' Duncan, I'd be taking home a Pulitzer, never mind a fucking 'Article by a foreign correspondent' of the year award.

Chapter 4

El Corazon Valiente - The Ballad of Peter Duncan

The Washington Post goes behind bars in a world exclusive series of taped interviews with infamous narcotics and arms dealer, Peter Duncan, in an expose that offers an insight into the incredible - as well as improbable - journey that took a British citizen all the way from Scotland - via Amsterdam - to Colombia to find work for one of the biggest cartels in the world, only for it all to end in a Colorado Supermax prison. Read how he got there. The inner workings of cartel life, mixing with terrorists and the hunt for him over the globe by multiple international crime agencies. His thoughts on the drugs, guns, money, power and if he now repents his *high* life of crimes and misdeeds.

By Manny Ruiz

July, 2002

Manny - So Peter, let me just start things off with a personal thank you for agreeing to this interview.

Peter - Oh on the contrary, Manfred. It is me that should be thanking YOU. There's been a lot of untruths told about me on TV, radio. internet and in print over recent years - all while I was muzzled and unable to call it out - so it is a most welcomed opportunity to give my side of things.

Manny - Well that's precisely why we're doing this. As I've previously explained to you. While you may not have been known to the average American until the past year, or so, you were someone who I, personally, had known of for a while.

Peter *laughs, self depreciatingly* - To be fair, Manfred. They were halcyon days that I *wish* we were both still a part of. I was a *lot* happier when Chuck from Omaha, Nebraska *didn't* know who Peter Duncan was, I assure you.

Manny - You can speak for yourself there, Peter. I was going through a messy and costly divorce at the time. I'm good with the present! So I guess the question of *all* questions for you is. Just *how* on god's green earth did you wind up working for the fearsome Ramirez brothers, Eddy and German, as part of the notorious Bogota Cartel? Clearly it's not the regular aspirations of a kid in a Scottish high school?

Peter - I know right?! All the other kids saying that they're going to be train drivers, firemen and JCB operators. Meanwhile I'm calculating that if I sell x amount of Cocaine to a bunch of gangbangers from South Central LA and then take THAT profit and add it to the yield taken from negotiating the swap of arms for Opium poppies with the Afghani Taliban it will make me my first million! Obviously, not the case but a funny thought all the same, I'm sure you'll agree?

How did I fall into working with such *colourful* employers, though? Well there's a very good - and you'll find, quite organic - explanation for that. Well, I think to *truly* illustrate how I ended up there - and in return, here, in this f**king hell hole of a facility - and in a way that would give you the most appreciation. I guess I would need to take you back to the very start. And, admittedly, a bizarre start it really all was, although - as you'll go on to find out - to be fair, it only got *more* bizarre from there on in.

Manny - So did you fall into a life of crime at an early age with things escalating from there?

Peter - Life of crime at an early age? I was a BAKER! And a bloody good one at that. Not just a baker but a *Master* Baker. Ok and I admit, that sounds *very* similar to 'masturbator' and when the sign went up above my business premises, announcing that it belonged to 'Peter Duncan - Master Baker' it didn't take long for the town to give my business an unofficial change of name. F**king philistines. They have a master craftsman in culinary arts setting up camp in their town - something that would make the place more of an attraction - and all they can do is take the piss with plays on words.

Regardless of any of that, I made a good go at the business. It was Eighty Three that I opened the place up and by the next again year I'd already had to take on extra staff. People were travelling from outside the town just to buy the cakes that we were putting out. Some days supply couldn't meet the demand. My own design - a D shaped donut filled with custard with a fudge flavoured icing on top - which was called the 'Duncan's Donut' the biggest seller of all. There were some who argued that it wasn't a donut, if it was shaped like the letter D. Maybe they had a point there but customers were a lot less pedantic when it came to getting their hands on one.

For the first time, since opening. I was making a pretty good profit and enough where I was no longer having to pump everything back *into* the business. The day I walked into Laidlaw's - the local Ford dealership -and bought one of the newly released models, The Sierra. It left me with such a proud feeling, you know? That you'd achieved at something in the sense that you could walk into a car dealership and decide to choose one of the cars of the forecourt. I'd never felt like such royalty, in the way that the Ford salesman treated me that day.

The fact that I drove out of the dealership in a shiny new car, paid for through my own hard work, along with the obligatory blood, sweat and tears. Well, it left me with a feeling that I doubt *any* amount of money could've bought.

That feeling, though, working against me, eventually. It was the drive and ambition that crippled me, really. I'd done so well with the bakery in that first year that I really should've just taken a bit time out to breathe. Take a look at things from a distance and be happy with how well things had gone, and in such a quick timescale. That's not me though, unfortunately. With how well things had gone in the first year, this - in my mind - had left me thinking how much further I could grow the business, in the following year.

The logical next step being to open up another bakery, in a separate location. I didn't have the funds to get myself to that point but being the man in a hurry that I was. Rather than bide my time and 'get there' when I got there. I went chasing things, and lost it all in the process.

Manny - How come? Did you go out of business? Bankruptcy?

Peter - Well, yeah. Something like that, I suppose *laughs* Look, it's no one else's fault other than my own, what happened. We're all accountable for our own choices in life but when I found out about the premises that were going for an absolute song, around twenty miles from me, I knew I had to move fast or would lose it. I'd got wind of some other baker who was now well past retirement age and looking for a quick and hassle free sale. Apparently he'd never intended to sell it as had initially planned on handing the business down to his son. Unfortunately his son had been killed in a motorbiking accident earlier on in the year and - understandably knocking the stuffing out of the poor father - this leaving him wanting to sell up. He had others interested and would offer no guarantees to any prospective buyers about reserving the premises. Basically, who ever could put up the money first would secure the place.

I was way off the required amount - but knew that the location equalled an absolute goldmine if I could get the keys to it - with only half the funds needed sitting in my current account. The decision I took next was, unquestionably, *the* defining moment of my life and what - subconsciously - chose the one way street that I ended up going down on.

F**king poker.

Manny - I'm sorry?

Peter - Sorry, just thinking about it - for a moment there - took me back to that night. There was a card school, every Friday night, above the bar of The Athletic. After hours once all the drinkers had gone home for the night. All very hush hush and on a need to know basis with some seriously heavy poker players, heavy people full stop with or without playing cards in their hands. I'd never played a round with them never mind spent a night of gambling above the bar but here's the thing. I was good at cards, *really* good at them. I know - ultimately - it all comes down to what cards are in your hand but if you think that's the extent of how you win a game of cards then you'd be best not picking them up in the first place. I'd been taught by my grandad at an early age - how to play poker - and while most kids would've been playing with their Corgie Cars, Action Man and kicking a football around outside. I'd normally be found sat in front of the fire playing poker for pennies with my housebound grandad.

I didn't just go in there that night with eyes shut - to The Athletic - and gave up all of my hard earned like some sucker. This was not a place for a casual card player. With a two hundred pound buy in price - which may not sound much today but was a fortune back then - it was a table only for the more serious of card players. Which I had thought myself as. To this day I *know* that I was cheated and that - thinking back now - in reality. No matter *what* cards I'd have had in my hand that night ... someone else in the room was going to have better ones.

It was probably the arrogance of myself - to believe - that I could walk into a room like that and walk back *out* again having pocketed various local hard-men's money. *That* was the most sickening of all. How could I have been so stupid? I was so focussed on growing the business and getting hold of the new premises that all logic went straight in the bin, or 'trashcan,' like you'd probably call it.

Not only did I lose the hard capital that I'd built up for the business - and what was meant to be taken and multiplied - but over the course of that torrid night I then went from being in the green to the red.

Over the course of the evening I had gone from the promising position of raising enough funds to see to it that I was going to take the business to the next level. I was - in my mind - already planning my first Edinburgh store after the initial bounce of the second bakery, once that got some steam behind it.

Instead, I was waking the next day to the grim reality that I was going to have a hard time paying the staff at the end of the month, never mind f**king expansions?

Manny - So how did you face up to that? Did you have to let some staff go as a result?

Peter - Sack staff? Oh, Manfred. I'm not sure that I'd have had the heart to do that. Was it their fault that their boss had went and lost his mind and undone over a year's worth of good work, over the series of a few rounds of poker? No, I did what *any* self respecting person would by trying to dig themselves back out of their own hole that they'd dug, by going into business with an enterprising drug dealer. Someone with ambition, not unlike myself. *laughs*

I was sat at the bar on my Jack, in The Goth Tavern having a beer to myself while trying to work out how I could get myself out of things, when Barry Green - one of the locals - slid up the bar to sit beside me.

'Heard you had a bit of a sore one the other night, Pete.'

It wasn't said my way in a sympathetic tone but neither in a cheeky way either. Kind of neutral and in the way where someone -

unhelpfully - draws your attention to something that you're already *well* aware of. Like when someone tells you that you've got a spot on your face when you're already in possession of those facts because you have a mirror and have been able to spy that same thing earlier on and much before they decided to offer input.

All I gave him back was a shrug of the shoulders - how I managed to f**king move them at all when I had the weight of the world resting on them is anyone's guess - as I took another sip of my pint.

'Come over into the corner and and sit and have a chat, I can maybe help you with your current predicament.'

He followed up with which, obviously, showed that he'd actually had an agenda when originally coming over and reminding me of the present state of play.

I followed him over to the corner of the bar - away from the core of regulars that were stood around - and took a seat down beside him where he cautiously 'offered' me a way out of my money troubles. Putting the proposal my way that I allow a contact of his to 'rent out warehouse space' inside the bakery. Putting across to me - in layman's terms - that the amount of money that I was in hock to (and it was handy of him to know just *how much* I was outstanding, without me having told him myself) could be recouped in no time and as far as my *original* plans for expansion? If I rented out the space even further then I'd be cutting the ribbon on my second bakery soon after.

Despite the pair of us only really being casual acquaintances on account of being from the same area, he certainly knew which buttons to press with me.

Half an hour before, I'd been sat there lamenting the fact that I was going to lose my *one* premises and a brief chat with him later and suddenly it was a case of the dream being very much alive once more for a second one.

Obviously, I'd conveniently decided to bypass all thoughts of any potential risk involved. I only thought of the money, nothing else, and the way that he had framed it to me. I was going to make a *lot* of it, and for little effort on my part other than to be there for any delivery coming in and to make sure that the goods were available to go back out when required.

I agreed to do it for two to three months only. Sitting there in the pub doing some back of a fag packet calculations that came up with me being able to square my debts *and* come up with the money to get myself a second premises.

Manny - And how did that arrangement work out. Did it end after the three months?

Peter - *Laughs, for quite some time* What do you think? By Eighty Five I had lost all touch with reality and left with absolutely zero percent sense of discretion. A baker from a small town driving around in Ferraris, Lambos and Porsches. Wearing the best designer clothes from Italy. At times you'd have found more gold on me than you'd have found in the Black Hills of f**king Dakota.

Once a certain Edinburgh underworld businessman - who out of respect shall remain nameless - became involved in the operation, things began to seriously escalate while on a straight trajectory to the moon. Within two years my 'two to three month business plan' had ended with not only my warehouse being used to store kilos of Heroin but the drugs themselves being *hidden* inside various pastries. Masquerading as a Steak Pie when inside was something quite different to a steak and gravy filling. The bakery soon had additional delivery vans that were flying out to various parts of Scotland and northern England with 'deliveries.'

I blame myself for it all going bad. If I'd have just stuck to the Sierra and a pair of Levi's. Hadn't tried to be f**king medallion man. All of that. If I'd just kept things cool then who knows how long it would've went on for. There's *no way* that someone is not going to start asking questions when a small businessman starts driving around in supercars. I just couldn't resist it though. I did it *because* I could and *that* pretty much sums me up.

Manny - And was the 'Edinburgh, Scotland underworld figure' the legendary 'Davey McKenna' one of Scotland's main crime bosses?

Peter - *After a long pause* No comment.

Manny - So what you're saying is that your behavior was what brought attention from the direction of law enforcement?

Peter - Well it definitely didn't help things. You know what though, Manfred.

Manny - You know, you *can* call me Manny, what with it being my name and all.

Peter - No, I'm good with Manfred. Anyway, as I was saying. You know what? That even in your darkest of moments, when you feel like this is it, you're going to sink. Life can throw you a raft. The Edinburgh driver had just driven away half an hour before, when the drug squad came bursting into the warehouse, screaming their heads off, sniffer dogs in tow. Me sitting there - at the time - in my office doing some paperwork, not even getting a chance to stand up before they stormed the office. Half an hour earlier and, f**k me, things would've went in a *way* different direction.

Manny - But you ended up incarcerated, anyway? Right?

Peter - Well, unfortunately, yes.

Manny - How so, if the product had already left.

Peter - Those dogs! One of the kilos that had passed through the warehouse must've been nicked somewhere, leading to some leakage over the bakery floor. You wouldn't have known it was even there because, well, it was a bakery with flour all over the floor. The K-9 unit, though? They picked up on the fact that there wasn't *just* flour scattered over the floor. They - initially - tried to get me on possession with intent to supply, absolutely reaching with their accusation that the flour and heroin mixed together suggested that I had planned to sell it in that form, like any other dealer who would mix their product with another agent.

They really tried to turn the screw on me - in those interviews - and I'm not afraid to admit that - with no prior experience with any police interactions - it was an extremely intimidating and frightening affair. Them telling me that I was going away for over ten years on account of how much heroin they'd found on the floor *but* that they knew that I wasn't the one running the operation and that I was only being used for my bakery and if I helped them with their enquiries they'd be able to start chipping away at the amount of years I would receive until, well, who knew? Maybe there wouldn't be *any* sentence at all.

The thought of prison scared the living shit out of me. Ten years, as well? This, though, countered by the fact that the thought of naming names, especially the one that I *knew* they wanted, from Edinburgh, gave me even more of the fear than a custodial did.

I wasn't from that kind of a world. Ok, yes, I suppose I'd had two fruitful years as *part* of that world but I wasn't *from* it. No one had sat me down and explained the rules of the underworld. The do's and the don't's. There is no tutorial. You're either set out for that kind of life, or you're not. I just knew that there would have been no point in spilling the beans to the drug squad if it meant that I'd be spending the rest of my days looking over my shoulder.

Once I got a lawyer sorted out, - who for my first ever legal representative was a pleasure to witness in action - Crawford Finneson, who came in and wiped the floor with the officers in that interview room, things started to get better.

Once we'd established that I wasn't going to be naming any names and - my lawyer - actually laughing in the faces of the two officers when it came to their claims that I had been mixing heroin and flour to sell to people. We started to get somewhere. Before I was eventually released, my charge had been knocked down to possession but one - that my lawyer grimly predicted - that would see that I would receive a spell in prison over.

Following the bust, I had my food certificate revoked by the council and was left with no choice but to fold the business as a result. The reputation of the bakery was in tatters, anyway. *Everyone* knew about the visit from the drug squad. I guess the bakery - during its existence - made an impact, in many ways.

It began with people referring to it with regards to masturbating and it ended with a saying - adopted by the locals - that went something along the lines of

'You only get high from a Duncan's pie.'

Yeah, it was a dark time and got even darker with an eighteen month sentence handed to me, once the trial eventually came around.

Manny - High from a Duncan's pie! You gots to admit, that's funny?! So tell me about prison, how did you find that, as a first timer?

Peter - Oh yeah, I was completely pissing myself laughing as my business collapsed and I faced a custodial sentence while the locals around me - probably jealous of all of the riches that they'd seen me stupidly flaunt - were gloating. Very droll, indeed, Manfred.

Prison? Well what I *can* tell you is that compared to *this* place H.M.P Barlinnie, Glasgow was like The Four Seasons. And I assure you, 'The Big Hoose' was not what you'd have described as living in the lap of luxury. Character building and educational, that's possibly as complimentary as I can ever get to describing the place. I did make some good friends along the way in there though and - without their help - were it not for them I'm not sure how I'd have managed to serve my time.

The first day I got there and they stuck me in with a murderer. Big Ocho, really good lad, actually. As far as I knew, I'd never met a murderer before but you know what? You wouldn't have known it from speaking to the man. Never seen him lose his temper the whole time I roomed with him.

Manny - Who was it that your cellmate had murdered? Did you ask him?

Peter - Funnily enough, if you can believe this, it was his *dad* that he murdered. Stuck a kitchen knife right into his heart. Christmas Day and everything, too.

Manny - That's horrific. I've discovered a lot of sickening things in my time as a narco journalist but even I have never come across a son murdering his father, and on Christmas Day of all days. Why would he even have thought of doing something like that?

Peter - Well, that was the *exact* same question I asked him although I approached it a wee bit more cautiously. I mean, there's NO excuse for murdering your father. The man that helped give you life but once Ocho had explained things, there was a certain degree of understanding to it.

Manny - *Understanding?*

Peter - 'Pete? The man took some After Eights out of the box and f**king put the empty wrappers back in the box again. I fishes my hand in to take one out. Fancied a couple as we were watching the

Only Fools Christmas special, like. Pulls out the empty wrappers and it all spiralled from there. You know how f**king nippy it is when you stick your hand into the box, feel that paper, pull it out and there not be a piece of f**king chocolate inside it, eh?'

He not so much pleaded with me and more told how it was. Definitely no sign of remorse from the guy in any shape or form. I mean, I'm not saying that I'd knife a parent to death over it but I don't think there's a person in the United Kingdom who doesn't know the pain of when someone has replaced a piece of chocolate with an empty wrapper. It was an overreaction but one that I think a lot of people would be able to understand at some basic level.

Do you have After Eights in America, Manfred?

Manny - Emmmmmm, I'm not sure.

Peter - They're good although, coincidentally enough. Due to where I've lived the past fifteen years *I've* never had a box myself in a while and certainly not had any since I heard Ocho's story involving the - actually - very tasty dark chocolate thin mints. Kind of like your 'Junior Mints' that you've got over here actually, only, if you'd stepped on one.

I did see some sights inside that prison, though. Some horrible nasty goings on that you just happen to be in the wrong place at the wrong time to witness. One occasion a prisoner biting another's nose off and spitting it out into the air before telling the man - who was lying screaming on the ground - 'tell anyone about this and I'll f**king finish you off.'

I'm not really sure how you go about keeping the fact that you're missing a nose on the down low, though? Bit of a dead giveaway when someone's missing a part of them, like that.

Murderer or not, though Big Ocho was a key figure in my 'rehabilitation' as far as life went on the outside. While he - undoubtedly - wasn't going anywhere for a *very* long time and due to the bond that him and I struck up when I was in there, he completely got me set up for when I got out. This coming later in the year in Eighty Seven.

Manny - In what way?

Peter - I'll continue after a break if that's ok with you? I was figuring that I might go for a nice swim then soak it off in the sauna and then probably catch a bite to eat before we continue.

Manny - You have a pool there? In the ADX?

Peter - Oh, of course, Manfred. Olympic sized. I'll catch you soon.

Chapter 5

Peter

I'd been surprised to find that I'd quite enjoyed that first chat with Manny, the journalist from The Post. Before he'd officially pressed the record button on us chatting we'd spoken 'off record' as I'd wanted to know a little bit about him. Figured that if I was going to be speaking to the guy over a period of time then I should at least know *who* it was that I was speaking to.

He looked to be quite an interesting sort and - considering the amount of deaths that occur to those in the game of writing about drug lords - someone, evidently, with cojones of the larger variety. The irony was certainly not lost on me that it was down to men - like myself - doing what we did to put food on the table that - in turn - allowed someone like Manny to eat himself. The food chain, circle of life or whatever you would care to class it as.

Talking about the early Eighties with him was neither painful *or* therapeutic to me. Both - ahead of us chatting - distinct possibilities. I hadn't thought about those days in so long that sitting there on the phone to the journalist and recanting those events. Coming so far before everything *else* that would happen, later in life. It almost felt like I had been describing a movie that I'd watched years back, only, one where I had played the leading role.

Possibly, because of what else followed in life. Being busted by a regional drugs unit and sent to jail for just over a year was kind of like a non event. Insignificant, a footnote barely worth a mention in the scheme of things.

Regardless of the 'subject matter' it actually felt so rewarding, just to be able to speak to someone. It was the closest to what I could've classed as a 'conversation' I'd had since leaving New York. How much just speaking to someone had left me feeling only served to highlight just exactly how much the ADX had stripped me down as a person.

That such a basic level of existence - like conversation with one's fellow man - could leave someone so spirited and uplifted. It was something that was all new to me. Something that - before had been, naturally, looked upon as nothing more than a fundamental human right yet speaking with Manny - and thinking about it that night - had been undoubtedly the best day that I had spent under the care of the Feds at the ADX.

It almost worked counteractively against me as when lights out came I was a galaxy away from sleep. Thinking about those early days, the choices that were made. I lay there wondering if whether I'd have made even just one alternative step if it would have made any kind of a difference or whether I'd have ended up in Florence, Colorado, regardless. You know? The butterfly effect. Had I chosen *not* to store the Heroin in my bakery, would that have led to me ending up marrying a gorgeous model and living in Milan with her? Probably not but you can't help but wonder these things, once you go down the rabbit hole.

Lying there, on that concrete construction excuse for a bed, in complete darkness. And when I mean darkness, when they want to kill the lights inside of there, do they make it dark. With no windows to speak of it could've been the brightest and starriest of skies and you wouldn't know it.

After lights out, save for the occasional prisoner crying, talking in their sleep or generally *unable* to sleep and not feeling too charitable towards those that *were* you were pretty much undisturbed for the night. The guards - whatever they did on night shift - certainly never put in any appearances throughout that period. I'd had enough sleepless nights to confirm that much.

It was because of the darkness surrounding everything that made the small green light on the intercom - fixed to the wall for guards to bark orders at while saving them the trouble of getting up off their fat asses to do it themselves outside the cell door - stand out so much when it lit up.

A small pin prick of glowing green in the middle of all that darkness. Instantly expecting to hear a voice on the other end from a guard, but nothing. The light staying on - however - which told me that someone was *still* holding the button to talk. Technically I couldn't see *any* reason for why one would be needing to speak with me, though.

It went out again and - as strange as it had been - I passed it off as someone possibly pressing it by accident. Like when you call someone from your cell while - in reality - your phone is sitting underneath a butt cheek.

Then, however, the light came back on again. Only this time it was on and off, on and off. Flashing intermittently, almost like if it had sound added it would have come across like morse code.

This time I stood up and walked over towards it. Technically I couldn't see the intercom, just the small green light which continued to flash on and off as I approached. Feeling my way in the darkness I managed to establish where the button was to press into to speak into the intercom.

I held back, though. Unsure of what it was I was going *to* say. The guards call you, not the other way around and - as was explained on moving in day - if you press that buzzer to speak to the guards it better be for a valid reason because the mandatory term in 'Range 13' (the area of the ADX which made *my* area out to be like Butlin's) was two weeks. There was also the worry that I may have landed up with grief from some bored nightshift guard who - knowing I was awake - might cause trouble for me to help pass the time for them.

I stood hovering over the intercom. Finger against the talk button and awaiting the courage of my convictions. All this time the green light flickered away persistently.

Fuck this, I thought to myself, pressing down on the button but - with a mind to the fact that it *was* the middle of the night and I didn't want to bring any heat my way in any shape or form, hesitantly spoke - quiet-ish - into it.

'Hello.'

Nothing came back in return but by speaking into it the green light had now went off completely.

'English, mate?'

The intercom crackled back into life and ended the palpable silence, all be it at a low volume. Much lower than how any commands had been broadcast out of them previously. The weird thing was - and maybe it was the sleep deprivation, I thought to myself - that it had sounded like someone who was English, asking *me* if I was English too.

'No' I replied back but still unsure if I had heard the question correctly which - in turn - was always going to affect my ability to give a clear answer.

'Ah, fucking hell. Fuck's sake. Not English, no? Of course you wouldn't be able to speak fucking English. That would've been too fucking easy wouldn't it?' Yeah he definitely *was* English, now that he was going off on one. Possibly a Cockney and if not, general London region accent, something like that. He sure didn't sound like a guard though, that was one thing that you'd have said. Not there in the Rocky Mountains.

'Hey, I never said I couldn't *speak* English. I said I *wasn't* English.' I said. Well, once he stopped his mini vent that he had went on.

'You speak, English, yeah mate? Ah that is a fucking right touch, that. Where you from then? Maybe it's this intercom but I can't work out the first idea where that accent you've got is from.' He asked, despite the low quality sound that came from the intercom you could still hear the delight in his voice, following the almost near breakdown that he'd just had moments before.

'I'm Scottish.' I whispered back to him.

'Well *that's* good enough for me, mate. Listen, what's your name?'

He asked. It sounded so natural, the way he was speaking to me but - not unusually - I was having a bit of trouble shaking the fact that someone was just having a casual chinwag through the intercom with me.

'Peter,' I replied. Keeping things as simple and short as I could while I tried to figure out just what the hell was going on here.

'Well, I'm pleased to meet you, Pete. I'm Gary, Gary Walters but just call me Gal, mate.'

I half thought that I may have been dreaming because this was *not* happening. I'd never been in contact with a single prisoner since arriving and that had been almost a year by then. Apart from the 'big name' prisoners that were in beside me I wouldn't have known *anything* about anyone else inside there. And here was some Cockney just casually chatting away to me, from the comfort of my cell.

'Listen, Pete. Are you sitting comfortably?' He asked. As if it was some children's story time reading or something.

'Of course I'm fucking not, I'm in a seven by twelve supermax prison cell, of course I'm not sitting fucking comfortable.' I joked with him. Assuming that if he was a prisoner himself then he'd - without question - get the joke.

'Well get yourself comfy, fella because oh does yer uncle Gal have a story to tell you.'

Chapter 6

Manny

As part of our Washington Post world exclusive Peter Duncan article - and to be able to provide the reader a much more rounded and concise look at the life that surrounded him - I also conducted telephone (and in person) interviews with other individuals that were impacted by or played a role in either El Corazon Valiente's rise, demise or were simply neutral throughout but in a position to pass judgement, having known or possessed intelligence on the man.

Below is an excerpt from a telephone interview that I had with Duncan's one and only son, Steven. A young man who - much like his father - has set about making his mark in the world, although, *unlike* his dad. For the right reasons.

Going by the stage name of 'DJ Selecao.' A DJ and breakthrough producer who was a Grammy nominee at last year's awards for his track 'Raise the bar - Spread the bar' which was used in the surprise hit indie film 'Brick City' by Czech Republic director Pavel Novotny. The Scottish electronic music star losing out - on the night - to French duo, Daft Punk. The nomination, however, putting him on the radar within the U.S, sending his stock soaring.

Read on to find out the thoughts of Steven Duncan, on a more personal level. Away from the dark sweaty nightclubs and large sprawling festival fields. Where he tells The Post what it's *really* like having a notorious figure, wanted in all continents, such as Peter Duncan for a father.

El Corazon Valiente - The Ballad of Peter Duncan cont

Manny - Hi, Steven and a very good afternoon to you. It would be true to say that in the past the subject of Peter Duncan has pretty much been off limits when it had come to yourself. Can I ask why you've been willing to break your silence and talk to myself about it?

Stevie - Well, mate. It's obviously something that - over the years - has been a sensitive subject. It's hardly something that you go about broadcasting to people. Stopping them in the street to tell them what your dad does for a living. There is also the - and you *specifically* will know what I mean here - aspect of the 'repercussions' of what might happen to myself or anyone close to me, had I ever acknowledged 'who' he was. I'd also had experiences in the past where him *being* my father had brought danger my way so, understandably, I'd always felt it better to avoid the subject completely, policy wise.

And also. I'm not sure anyone would argue if you were to say that the Washington Post is one of the biggest and - definitely - most famous newspapers in the world. Watergate and that stuff, eh? The amount of people who pick up your publication or read online, all over the world in a day? Impressive stuff, Manny, like. So I thought. If I'm going to break my silence on the whole narco and weapons dealer of a dad stuff, then, I should do it in style.

Now a cynic might suggest that I had only agreed to it because I had a six date mini South American tour (From Medellin all the way down to Montevideo) recently announced and had been persuaded by my manager to take part in the interview as it would be a great way of gaining some free publicity. Shame on those cynics, though, that's what I say. And, please, Manny. Stevie, Zico, Selecao. Call me any of those. 'Steven' is generally what I hear when I've messed up in some way or other. Always gives me negative vibes, like, when someone calls me by my proper name. You know?

Manny - Got it! Now we're obviously here to talk about you and your father's relationship but you mentioned South America? As you know from our chat last week, I've done my research. Hopefully we'll have time to come back to it but South America? Really? Do you *actually* think that's a good idea? *Laughter from Manny*

Stevie - *Also laughing* Aye, that topic *has* come up a few times - from my better half, Flo, mainly - already but well, here we are, eh?

Manny - So, Stevie. Moving things back to your father. How did you feel, the day that he received guilty verdicts on all indictments given to him? The confirmation that he *was* the person that all of the world's crime agencies had claimed him to be?

Stevie - *Laughing again* Aye, like I needed the confirmation from the twelve members of the jury or whatever number there were! I was *there* inside the bar when he was arrested in Amsterdam. By the time that wee detective had finished reading my dad the list of crimes that he was wanted for, the owner of the bar was about putting his shutters down for the night to go home. No really, Manny. You could've grown a beard in the time that it took to read out all his charges to him. I'm not one for believing that where there's smoke there's fire but if someone throws enough shit at you then at least *some* of it is going to stick and - giving the Dutch boy his dues - my dad had had a Chimpanzee house full of it lobbed his way that night. Even just one of the charges that they had for him. Had even just one - alone - stuck then that would've been enough to see him behind bars forever. Some of the more serious stuff, though. Like the terrorists and that? I might think a lot of things about my dad but one thing though that I'd one hundred per cent say is that he most definitely isn't a terrorist. Terrorist, no. Unscrupulous about who fills his pockets and where they're from, aye, without question. He wouldn't even deny that.

You don't want to be seen to be against America either. Definitely not these days. Not after last year, in Manhattan. He's probably lucky that his trial happened months before September the Eleventh otherwise they'd have been carting his unlucky arse off to Guantanamo Bay, instead of Colorado.

Manny - With approx forty Al Qaeda operatives - some currently being force fed due to hunger strike - now detained inside Colorado's ADX, it is almost a *stateside* version of Guantanamo Bay.

Stevie - Well there you go then, eh? One thing for certain though. When he was carted away by the Amsterdam police force - and I even said it to my friend in the bar - that I didn't think I'd ever see my father again, outside of a court or jail setting, like. The guilty verdicts - when they came last year - were nothing other than closure. I mean, my dad is like a fish covered in vaseline. As slippery as they come but had he managed to pull of a series of not guilty verdicts in Brooklyn it would've been more astonishing than f**king OJ Simpson's outcome.

As far as the confirmation that he was the man that all of those - and there were *a lot* of - international crime agencies said? Well I *knew* and had known for a full decade before he was arrested in Holland. Possibly I knew about him before some of them but you have to remember that when I first found out, I was just turned seventeen. Didn't even know what I didn't know about the world. By the next time I saw him - several years later - I was older and wiser. Not so impressionable, you know? *That* was when I got a REAL look at who he was, and what he was capable of. After that mid Nineties meeting in Spain. That was when him and I parted ways as a father and son partnership of any shape or form.

Manny - What changed? From meeting him in Nineteen Ninety and then halfway through the decade?

Stevie - Him - when we were reunited after me not seeing him since the early Eighties he had been working for the cartel in Bogota for around a year. By the next time I saw him - in Ninety Six - he'd had years of living that narco life and I guess it had caught up with him. On the run from the cartel while still trying to hustle his way out of things. He was a mess and, as a result, made even messier decisions.

I'd changed too, though, over those years, and had been able to see him more for who and what he was. I'd been a kid in Ninety and had needed his help and - as a father - he stepped up for me. Put my life back on track like any loving father *would*. By the time we saw each other again, my life *was* on track. The irony of it being him that appeared, trying to do his best to *derail* things was not lost on me. By then, I would have been completely content with a boring father and son dynamic. Instead he went out of his way to bring lies, betrayal and murderous Colombian sicarios my way.

Manny - So yeah, not exactly dull, having him around as a pops? *laughs*

Stevie - Well that really all depends on how you define 'having him around.' If, by that, you mean having him pop into your life - periodically - to completely f**k your shit up, almost tank your career, get you killed by cartel hitmen and leave your girlfriend with PTSD for years to come then, aye? Oh he's a proper good barrel of laughs, Pedro Duncan. You really do need to use the term 'having him around' loosely when it's being used in connection with him. I'm not sure *anyone* could seriously say that they have 'had him around.' He's looked after himself first, every time. That could be the way it *has* to be in that lifestyle though, of course. That's maybe how you keep yourself alive, eh? Anyway, if that's the case then it's never going to be good for family relationships. Not when you hardly ever seen the c**t, anyway.

Manny - So what was it like - when you were at a younger age and before he made the move to South America - having Peter as a father?

Stevie - Pretty much like it was *after* he'd made the move to Bogota. Fits and starts. Listen, Manny. My father was hardly some 'frequent flyer' when it came to spending time with me. If spending time doing stuff together as father and son could be equated into a Focus Point that you used to get inside Regal and Embassy packets of cigarettes. Our collective time spent together wouldn't have been able to be redeemed for a set of steak knifes.

I'm too young to remember living in the house with him - mum and dad divorcing before then but I *do* have some photos to at least prove that there *were* some moments between him and me when I was wee. The photos are ideal for proof to myself because I probably wouldn't have believed anyone had they told me about moments like dad bouncing me up and down on his knee. Big smile for the camera while I looked on, clueless, with drool down the side of my mouth.

Following him and my mother splitting up. Seeing him, after that, was sporadic to say the least. Sometimes you wouldn't see him for two years and then the next you'd see him twice in two months. Even at an early age. I was soon able to see that if reliability was what you are looking for in a person, you should probably look straight past Peter Duncan. Those days where he'd 'said' he was coming. I'd sit there all day waiting, and waiting only for that familiar feeling to start creeping over where you knew that he wasn't going to be coming. *This* - I think - is what has left me able to handle everything in connection with him and the unwanted attention that he has - since his arrest - brought in my direction. The sense of 'detachment' that was already there and that I'd never really known a life of not having when it came to me and him.

Manny - And when did you began to notice the changes with your father, when his career path began to, how should I put it? Diversify?

Stevie - Well you know, Manny? It's really difficult to pinpoint *exactly* where I began to notice any real differences in who my dad was evolving into but - if pressed - I would have to say it was the day that - instead of coming down the street to pick me up in his Ford Sierra - he came slowly - like the f**king pied piper - down the road with all of the kids from around the neighborhood following behind on their Grifters and BMXs as he drove a black Lamborghini Countach.

laughs Getting out of the car to come and get me and revealing that he was in a pair of black leather trousers. Same type that Charlie

Nicholas wore in the papers. I'm thinking to myself here, though, that you won't know who he is.

Just a knob in a pair of leather trousers. Is there anyone who *isn't* one that wears them, though? Goes with the territory, like. Maybe that guy with the top hat in Guns? Slash? Possibly he gets a pass although I *do* remember reading an article in an in flight magazine on a Quantas flight which said that he practically lived in the things and never, ever washed them so. Maybe keep a wide berth if you ever see him out and about, mate.

Aye, I'd have to say. *That* was the day where I thought something was a bit suss. I was too young to appreciate what was behind it. I think the Lambo lasted him six months tops before he cheated death in a crash where he took it into a field, landing on his roof. No worries though, eh? Just get a Porsche 911. The attitude of the man? Yellow, obviously. Just in case the black of the Countach hadn't been eye catching enough for some.

The only reason that I could tell that something had changed, though, was *because* of him showing me, and the rest of the world, that his situation had changed.

The visits were still every bit as unplanned and sporadic as they'd been before. It was just that when he *would* grace me with an appearance it seemed like was always in a different sports car. Doing nothing other than going for a drive so that - I now assume - as many people could stare at us going past as possible. And they would. I'd be bunged twenty pounds (which was an absolute fortune to a kid in those days) at the end of the visit and told to 'keep out of trouble' and that he'd see me soon.

Him telling *me* to keep out of trouble? The man's a comedian.

Manny - And when did you learn - for sure - that your father was involved in drugs?

Stevie - Like mostly everyone else, in the newspaper. 'DRUG SQUAD RAIDS FAMILY BAKER' You know? That kind of deal. You're the one who writes that stuff, not me. F**k knows where they got the 'family' part from but you'd know better than me, there, being in that particular game yourself, Manny, eh? I'd seen him on one of his flying visits maybe a few months before the raid. Ferrari, that time, in case you're wondering. Can't remember which kind I'm afraid. That was in Nineteen Eighty Five and - as it was to turn out - it would be the last time that I would see him until the summer of Ninety. Between the raid and his trial he was a ghost. Not a sign, sound or smoke signal from him. It was through the newspapers that I learned of the raid and it was through them, also, that I found out about his jail sentence.

The family took the decision that I wouldn't go to visit him, inside there. *This* decision, possibly taken due to the fact that he was hardly prolific when it came to visiting his son - on the outside - so why put his son through the experience of visiting his father on the *inside*? Something that I could understand. He never wrote and neither did I. In some ways, when he was in prison it was almost the same as when he was *outside*. I probably missed two to three visits in that space of time so hardly the end of the world. Without question, his spell behind bars impacted him a lot f**king more than it did me.

Manny - What kind of reunion did you both have upon his release from prison, at the end of his time inside? Was it emotional for the two of you seeing each other again?

Stevie - What reunion? There 'was' no reunion. He was released and practically disappeared off the face of the earth. No reaching out to make up for lost time. No contact in any shape or form. While I, obviously, *did* have a 'belated' reunion with him - of sorts - years later. Following his release from prison he just kind of seemed to vanish without a trace. It wasn't until years later before the rumours of him being in South America began to surface but those early years?

Even to this day I don't know what happened to him, or where he went to.

Chapter 7

El Corazon Valiente - The Ballad of Peter Duncan cont

Manny - You left Barlinnie Prison - in Glasgow - towards the end of the year in Nineteen Eighty Seven. How did it feel being a free man again? What was the first thing you did upon your release?

Peter - How did it feel? Manfred? How the hell do you think it felt? Having one's liberty taken away from them. All those small things that you don't even realise that you're taking for granted *until* you realise that they're not there anymore. You don't know what you've got until it's gone? F**k me, isn't that the truth. The biggest loss for me - being inside - was the removal of, quite simply, the ability to do what I wanted *when* I wanted. I'd definitely class myself as a free spirit and well, jail is just about the very *last* place that a free spirit wants to find itself.

As cracking a lad big Ocho was. Would I have chosen to have been locked up for several hours a day with someone who was of the temperament of a person who would stab his father over a chocolate related argument? Or - even when venturing *outside* - the other, equally, mental cases of chancers and nut-jobs that you end up having to mix with. *No one* would choose that, Manfred.

And I'm not slagging any of them off when I say that, even if it possibly comes across that I *am*. I found a lot of them absolute diamonds but did I trust any of them? Hell no. Ocho was the only one who came close to having my full and undivided trust but well, you kind of have to, when you're sharing a cell. Can't trust your cellmate enough for to go to sleep then you'll end up in the nuthouse.

As I've said, though. Ocho is someone that I owe a lot to. I wasn't going back outside with anything remotely even close to a 'future.' Not without his help, anyway. I'll come to that, though.

As for the first thing that I did upon my release? Well despite the fact that I had made no attempt at contacting the outside world when I was on the inside. I had entertained some fantasy that family would be there, waiting for me on the outside when I set foot back into freedom. As far as the boy. While never the best at recognising my own deficiencies I would be the first to admit that I was never going to be in the running for any father of the year contests. Build a soap box racer or Airfix model father and son, we were the furthest thing away from that.

Because of that. I don't know? I just kind of buried my head in the sand over things. I was embarrassed and ashamed of myself that I was inside there and I didn't want Stevie to have anything to do with it. Didn't want him to have any memories of HMP Barlinnie in any shape or form. Told myself that it would've been better off for the lad if he was just to have a couple of 'missing years' from his life, as far as him and I went. Of course, the fact that this proved convenient to myself - and that I didn't have to face up to things - was all just a coincidence, obviously.

Manny - And were there any family waiting on you on release day.

Peter - No, and I deserved it, too. That's not to say that there wasn't *anyone* waiting on that gate opening and me walking through it, though. Initially I didn't think the car was there for me. I mean, you couldn't miss it. This long black stretch limo. I even remember thinking that someone inside Barlinnie was in for one hell of a surprise when they popped their head out later - following their release - to see what their friends or family had organised for them.

I had almost walked the full length of it when the tinted electric window started to make its way down. The noise of it drawing my attention.

'Where the f**k do you think you're going? I hire a stretch for to come and pick you up and you want to take the bus, aye?'

Staring back at me was my Edinburgh connection. Big smile on his face as he held up a champagne bottle. The chauffeur getting out and opening one of the doors for me to get in the back beside him.

I'd had a few years of dealing with the Edinburgh connect - and had heard all the stories that went with him - so I'd had enough experience of him to see that he had come in peace. The smile on his face told me more than any words could have and anyway, who hires a stretch limo to go and pick someone up that they're - ultimately - going to murder? Seems a touch excessive and extravagant, don't you think?

Manny - Well, you *would* think so. However, if the person picking you up that day is who my research leads me to believe that it is then that particular underworld figure *does* have a touch of the spectacular and showman about him so you would never really know.

Peter - I literally have no idea what it is that you mean by that, Manfred.

Manny - Of course you don't Peter, my mistake *laughs* So what did he want with you. He must've thought you as important that he would hire a limo and come and greet you with champagne, to mark your release?

Peter - Well, you know, Manfred? It was the strangest of things because - like I told you earlier - when the raid had happened at the bakery. To serve the time - that I'd surely be handed down come the sentencing - wasn't so much as the logical choice but was the *only* choice. Unbeknown to me, my Edinburgh connect hadn't seen it that way and when I say that, I mean it in a positive way. He *knew* that I had enough knowledge of the whole operation to have talked my way out of things with the Drug Squad, and put the focus primarily on him at the same time. That I'd chosen *not* to had registered with him. Doing my time and keeping my mouth shut the whole time had meant more to him than I could have ever imagined. If anything, you'd have thought that he'd have *expected* it. Demanded, even.

Manny - So he made the gesture of thanks by welcoming you back to the outside in style with a chauffeur driven limo.

Peter - Well, he done a bit more than just that.

Manny - How so?

Peter - Well, on the drive back from Glasgow he sat and expressed his gratitude over me keeping my lips closed on things. Told me how he'd already done the due diligence on me before working together so had known that I'd never been arrested in my life, until the raid. As you can imagine, he was a touch nervous about how I would fare with a team of seasoned DS officers who would undoubtedly do their best to run rings around me and have me tied up in knots, with all the angles they'd be coming at me from.

The fact that at no point did he receive not so much as one tiny piece of blowback over my arrest had went a long way with him and so much - in fact - that he wanted to be the one to, personally, come and collect me from Barlinnie and express a personal thank you to me for all that I'd done, or not. Depending on which way you look at it.

He was grateful but was also frank and candid. Informing me that I was now too hot to deal with. Even if I was to build back up and get myself another bakery. The council wouldn't give me a license now, anyway, and even if by some miracle they did. The moment that law enforcement learned that I was operating another bakery, I would be back under the microscope.

'Don't take it as if you've been or you're being sacked here either, Pete. It's your position that's been made redundant due to 'restructuring and streamlining of the company business model,' your personal work within the company was never anything less than exemplary.' He told me in the back of the car as we cruised over the Forth Road Bridge.

I was a little perplexed, if I'm being completely honest. The *last* thing I was going to be doing - on release - was going back to drugs. I'd only got involved *because* of my bakery and well, now that I didn't have one. It was all moot. Hardly as if I was leaving prison to go back to my 'trade,' by any means.

He explained that he regretted having to cut me loose but there was no other way around it BUT that he *had* appreciated my work and, more importantly, my ability not to rat him or the rest of the crew out and wanted to hand me a 'little something for my trouble.'

A black Lonsdale sports bag was sitting on the seat facing me. He motioned for me to reach across and pick it up and look inside. I can only imagine what my face was like when I pulled on that zip and saw all the money inside of the bag.

Manny - And the money was for you?

Peter - Look, the man was capable of some very grim things and there were *many* examples to back that up with but he wasn't as twisted and sick as to show someone a bag of money - directly after telling them that they had something for them - and then snatching it back. *Of course* it was for me. I couldn't believe it. Ten grand he told me was in there which - I know, wouldn't even get me a watch in this day and age - was an unbelievable shot in the arm for someone just out of jail with no money and or real prospects. As we approached my mum and dad's house he asked me about what plans I now had. Fresh start etc. When I told him that I was thinking of heading over to Amsterdam to live and start again. That seemed to get his attention. The prospect of a potential connect over in a city like that. For him, priceless. As I was getting out of the limo he was handing me his business card, telling me to get myself settled over there and if there were any potential money making enterprises that I should come across then to give him a call. As it was to turn out. I did and - on and off, regardless of where I was living - we did a lot of business over the years in what was a fruitful relationship.

Manny - Did you head straight for Holland? What about family?

Peter - Well I *tried* to see the boy, once I'd been released. Doors were closing in my face left right and centre, though. The official line from his mum's side of the family was that if his father was someone like myself. A gangster, criminal, drug dealer (I'd say only one of those accusations was accurate) who had been in jail … maybe it would be best for Stevie if him and his dad didn't see each other. Can't help but wonder if he'd been involved in the decision making process? Blackballed, in such a way. What else *could* I do other than get what belongings mattered to me together and myself on that ferry to The Netherlands. I'd have loved for it to have all been different. Who knows? If I'd been able to see Stevie after being released, maybe I wouldn't have went to Amsterdam, at all?

Manny - Obviously though, you did.

Peter - Oh yes!

Manny - And how did you find the Dutch capital to live in?

Peter - I found it to be the greatest city in the world, and through my subsequent travel for Eddy and German Ramirez, I'd seen pretty much every major world city there was to see. It was - for someone like myself and my tendencies - the greatest playground I'd ever stumbled upon. At first I was so exhilarated that I didn't want to go to bed each night. There was just so much to take in. So much that I didn't want to miss a single thing. The concept of making a joint for yourself in a coffee shop and not be arrested for it, one that this ex drug charge criminal found hard to wrap his head around, but was embraced all the same.

The Red Light District and all its delights. The bars, coffee shops and women. The neon lit sex shops with some contraptions in the windows that I didn't even know *what* I was looking at half of the time. It was a world away from living in a small Scottish town. The characters that you would come across at all times of the day, and in all kinds of scenarios. It was - put simply - my kind of town. I just didn't know it until I got there. The city itself all pure chance and down to the location of Ocho's brother and nothing more than that. But my, did 'Zippy Broon,' owner of 'Zippy's Bar' on Oudezijds Achterburgwal have a good taste in where to set himself up in business.

I'd been slightly worried that maybe big Ocho was just giving it all the talk when I'd been inside with him and that when I got to Amsterdam his brother would not be as accommodating as his big brother had told me he would. If there even *was* a bar called Zippy's in the Red Light District, that is. Ocho was as good as his word, however, that he had even given his brother a heads up of sorts that chances were he was going to have a visitor from Scotland, namedropping his bigger brother in a cellmate kind of way.

Zippy was a character and one that from the very off I knew we would get on. Crazy but well, I'd already met his brother, so. There was evidently something in the genes with the male members of the family. Due to being slap bang in the middle of the Red Light District it had taken me an age to find the bar. Way too many distractions for someone who had been in jail and without sex in years to be fully focussed on their mission.

When I entered the bar, almost putting my back out due to the extremely low entrance, I found - who would turn out to be Zippy Broon - a man brandishing a pile of darts. And someone who appeared to have done a handstand against the wall - with playing cards strategically placed around them, held by drawing pins - and despite their face staring back at me from upside down, you could see the panic on it. There was a crowd all milling around while the guy with the darts was holding court.

To prove his darts prowess, the 'arrowsmith' - telling the bar's inhabitants - said that he was going to throw darts all the way around the person, hitting each individual card. And that if even one dart was to hit the poor guy against the wall. Then the bar's deeds would be signed over to him.

I held back to watch how it was going to turn out. One card after the other, pierced by a dart. A bigger cheer produced than the card before for each throw. It was the last card, the one perched just above the guy's head? I couldn't even watch that throw. It goes badly and he's going to have a dart sticking out of his eye. Oh and did I mention that the darts thrower - despite it being mid day - was half drunk when 'throwing' the arrows? Sometimes alcohol can be the difference between taking an eye out or not. Look at that Canadian snooker player. Can't even pick up a cue to hit a ball until he's sunk half a dozen 'warm up' pints. The cheer from the crowd confirmed that he had, indeed, hit the last playing card. The guy against the wall, literally collapsing into a relieved heap where he lay still for a few seconds until another drinker helped him back up.

The darts thrower headed, victoriously, behind the bar and - in doing so - completely taking me by surprise that *this* was who was running the place. I'd already heard the Scottish accent from him and - now that I was getting a better look at him - I *could* see the similarity with and big Ocho.

I introduced myself and - to show that I wasn't just some chancer - threw in that he didn't need to introduce himself as I could already tell by his similar looks to Ocho. He reacted to this like *I* was Ocho, released from prison, not some stranger that he'd never met before.

He wasted no time in showing me up to the room that he had spare. When Ocho and me had discussed things *this* was before I'd had my sudden windfall. It had been based on me not having a pot to piss in and that Zippy would help me out in that area so - sensibly - I elected to adopt - in the short term at least - the attitude that the ten grand I'd been given would be saved for the rainiest of days and for when was most needed. To Zippy, I was a penniless ex jailbird who would be willing to do 'jobs' for him - running errands and what not - in return for a crust and somewhere to live. And for all intents and purposes, that's *exactly* what I did.

Manny - And was this business related to the running of the bar?

Peter - Yes and no. Almost the first thing upon dropping my stuff in the room above the bar was for Zippy to ask me if I'd ever pulled a pint before. Telling him no, he then leapt into a tutorial on how to perform such a task. After half an hour I had him muttering ' F**k this, I'll get you to help out in other areas' before he mopped up the beer that I'd managed to have spraying all over the bar from my 'tapwork.'

The money that Zippy brought in, however, was not made 'exclusively' through the selling of alcohol to thirsty Red Light District tourists. Another way of putting it would be that 'Zippy's Bar' was nothing other than a front for to launder the money that he was making *outside* the bar. Something I can say without impacting on the man himself with him being put out of business after I'd stopped working for him.

Manny - Was it drugs that he was involved in? Leaving you right back where you'd started off?

Peter - Yeah, of course. Amongst other things.

Manny - What else was he involved in?

Peter - PORN! You should've seen the amount of hardcore porn VCR tapes that he was shipping over to Scotland each month. All of that Scandinavian triple x stuff. Those were the days where you couldn't get your hands on that type of content too easily in Britain. I think Zippy probably made as much from the porn than he did from the drugs that he was sending back in bulk. I used to call him Larry Flynt, the amount of porn that he had flying around.

It was through Zippy, that I ended up meeting Hakan. Considering Zippy's operation was months away from coming to a crashing end. It was probably for the best. It would *not* have been a good look to have been in a Scottish prison and then, upon release finding myself slap bang in a Dutch one. Not a good look, at all.

Manny - And this would be Hakan Yilmaz, the Turkish mafia crime boss of Amsterdam?

Peter - The man, myth and legend but - to me - was, and always will be, simply a good friend and associate.

Manny - You ended up switching sides, and working for Yilmaz and his enterprise. How did this come about? The Turkish mafia are extremely and notoriously guarded about outsiders. How did you find yourself, as a Scot, being accepted by them?

Peter - Probably *because* I was a Scot. You won't know this - because you're American - but being Scottish comes along with the very peculiar ability to get you through doors that you wouldn't do otherwise. I'm not even sure most Scots even realise this but the ones who *have* have prospered and made their mark over the world? I don't know what it is - or where it originated from - but in all of my travel across the world, with a few notable exceptions - I have generally found that when someone finds out you're Scottish. You're already on-side with them. Nationality aside, however. Hakan and me, we just had an instant rapport with each other from the first day that we met. Of course, it didn't exactly harm things that Hakan's introduction to me involved myself helping him out of a tough spot.

I had only been tasked with delivering a couple of hand guns over to one of the sex shops that Hakan owned, on the other side of the Red Light District. Zippy telling me to ask for Hakan when I got there and to give them to him and him only.

When I arrived at the 'Sex Emporium' I was met by this Turk with slick back hair (Think Michael Corleone in Part 2) and a goatee beard. The mere mention that Zippy had sent me over to deliver the bag sending the man into overdrive.

'Oh, no no no, not now, my friend. I have just had phone call. Police raid, this place soon. No guns, no guns. Understand?'

He took me outside - into the street - while he explained further to me. First of all, making sure that me and the guns were *off* his premises before he did, though. Telling me that he'd just had a tip off from another sex shop owner that there had just been a raid on his shop to recover some illegal porn and that if Hakan, himself, had anything under his roof that he shouldn't have done then he better act fast because the specialist police unit had been overheard discussing further targets for the day, and the Sex Emporium had been one of the names heard mentioned. Understandably, it would've been advantageous had there not been two handguns found sitting inside the place when the police arrived.

Stressing out about things I tried to calm him down. Telling him that I would just take them back to Zippy and how we would sort things out for another time.

'No no no no no. Do not do that. He will f**king sell them to someone else instead, surely you know him as good as I? I *need* them for something that is already arranged.'

'Ok, then. Here's what I'm going to do. You're going to give me the number of the shop and I'm going to go for a nice and innocent ride around the city centre on my bike, away from any police. And *then* I'm going to call you in a few hours time and make sure that things are clear before I return.'

It wasn't exactly rocket science but that I suggested it to him it had appeared as if I had just split an atom, there in front of him.

'YES, GOOD.' He said, relieved as he fished into his jacket and produced a card.

While in Amsterdam I'd been a complete sponge. Soaking up all the kind of information that you needed to if you wanted to know how the criminal side of things worked. *Who* was in charge, and of what. Who you needed to go see when you needed something arranged or taken care of or who - simply - you needed 'permission' from. I'd heard the name Hakan mentioned before by Zippy, in the general scheme of the Turkish Mafia inside Amsterdam.

It would not have been much of a leap to have come to the conclusion that this very same Hakan - owner of the sex shop - was the one connected to the Turkish criminal underworld. And if so - despite his clear stress and worry displayed to me - most *definitely* a man that it would not harm you in any single way to do a favour for.

Manny - So this job - of delivering the guns - this was where you began your relationship with the Turks, which then - directly - brought you into the world of the Colombians?

Peter - And, in fact, *directly* ending my working and or personal relationship with 'Zippy Broon.' These were the days where life was - depending on which way you want to look at it - simple (or harder) due to lack of cell phones. In Zippy's mind. He had only sent me over to the other side of the district. Estimating that I'd be back within the half hour. When I didn't return until the end of the day - high as a kite from sitting smoking with Hakan - him and I ended up having a heated argument that just stopped short of laying hands on each other. Apparently, I had cost him thousands of pounds with my disappearance act. So pissed off he was that he threw me out into the street that very same night, along with my belongings.

Manny - Why did it take so long in returning back?

Peter - Well, as I said. I suggested to Hakan that I'd come back in a few hours, which I did. It was a day where you lost track of time. We've all been there.

Manny - We sure have.

Peter - After finally getting the all clear from Hakan to return - which ended up being *longer* than the initially suggested couple of hours - and after a long and picturesque ride around the Pijp district. I returned back to the Sex Emporium to find the much more chilled and colourful Hakan Yilmaz - free of any law enforcement stresses - waiting on me. I'd no sooner handed him the bag with both guns in them and he had then handed them to another Turk who exited the shop straight away.

As I stood there. Surrounded by dildos, vibrators, penis enlargers and a whole wall filled with VCR tapes. Hakan - having never met me up until that day - started to quiz me on myself. What my story was and how I'd came to be in Amsterdam doing bits for someone like Zippy Broon. The fidgety and panicky man with the sweat patches under both arms had been replaced with the aura of a cool, authoritative and steely looking man. Someone that you could clearly see how he could give an order and it would be followed to *every* letter of the law. Despite someone who had such power behind them. He was charming and funny. I saw a lot of myself in him so, obviously, yeah, I liked him.

When he suggested that the both of us go out for an early dinner - and him batting away the raising of the topic of me getting back to work again for the rest of the day, saying that Zippy would understand when I told him - I was powerless to resist. As I was when he suggested that we go to a coffee shop called 'Toke don't Smoke' that his cousin from Trabzon owned, up one of the side streets coming off the Damrak. Once we started smoking that Thai Stick. It all got a little hazy from there.

Funny how Zippy telling me that I now no longer had accommodation open to me fairly straightened me out, though, and no mistake.

I didn't realise it at the time but it was just another one of those moments in life that was meant to take place. One could argue that I was *meant* to land up in jail so that I could meet Ocho. All so that I could be put in touch with his brother to facilitate myself and Hakan Yilmaz becoming friends and business associates.

Manny - So you went to work for the Turks, following the events of that day?

Peter - Well, first of all, I had to find somewhere to sleep for the night. Figuring that it had been *him* that had got me the sack from my job - as well as losing me my room - that he would, hopefully, be able to put me to work. I decided that I'd go and pay the Sex Emporium a visit in the morning and find out.

Chapter 8

Peter

'You're taking the piss. You expect me to believe *that*?' I laughed into the intercom. 'I'm a story teller and my stories must be told.' I then sang to him. An animated show that used to be on TV when Stevie was a kid, popping into my head where the opening credits had a man singing that very same song.

'Well, are *you* going to tell me how you and I, prisoners inside a fucking American supermax prison are sitting here in the dead of night, just having ourselves a casual conversation … via an intercom system that is used *only* for communication between the guard command centre and a specific prison cell. You think they just wired it up so that all the prisoners could just sit and natter to each other, when they were lonely and needed a chat?'

Now it was *him* that was laughing.

I didn't know *what* to think.

One second I'm lying on my, quote unquote, bed and the next I'm sitting on the cold floor by the intercom listening to a Cockney called Garry (although you've to call him Gal) filling my head full of stories about Republican governors, MI5 and a narco father and son who had previously enjoyed a stay in the same prison cells - that myself and this Londoner were now stuck in - until the Mexican government had struck a deal with its American counterparts which saw both father and son extradited back to Mexico where, quelle surprise, they were eventually broken out of the prison that they were in by some spectacular show of strength from their cartel.

I had every right to call bullshit on his story but he was right, though. How *could* you explain the fact that we were able to communicate back and forward in this way? I mean, you wouldn't be allowed a system like this in *any* prison or detention centre. So a remote prison like the ADX where the actual name of the game is to 'isolate?' Not a chance would prisoners be able to communicate with each other in such a convenient fashion. The thought of such so outlandish that even a prisoner would not even begin to entertain it.

It must've taken him a good hour plus to take me through his tale, where he told me that he was a - now very much retired - MI5 agent.

Something that he - normally - would not have been able to disclose but with him now ending up in Colorado, it didn't really matter anymore.

Up until the year before. He had been on a bi - nation led cross agency case between the American ATF, CIA and our own MI5. Trailing a weapons dealer from Moscow who - through his donations to the National Rifle Association - had bought his way into the kind of rooms that United States senators and congressmen would be found frequenting. As part of this investigation, the American and British alliance had uncovered that a prominent Republican governor had been found to be part of an ongoing child sex trafficking ring.

When this was brought to the attention of superiors? Well that's when the agents - investigating the Russian - all started to come by 'unfortunate' accidents. The girl on the ATF side had 'fallen' from her Pittsburgh apartment while cleaning the windows. The two CIA agents who were covering the case from outside of the States. Their jeep in El Salvador blown up by 'someone' with an RPG when they were on their way to their pickup, following a field op. The official line being put across that El Salvadorian rebels had blown the two agents up. Even the Russian mole - in Moscow - who knew nothing about the governor, disappeared. Last seen walking into a Moscow underground station.

They messed up when it came to Gary, however. Well, according to him, of course. Their attempt at *erasing* him from the record book not going so smoothly as the others had. Someone lost their life over it, just not Gal.

He'd already learned of the misfortune that his cohorts had fallen to so was, understandably, on his guard. As is sometimes the case, some poor innocent takes the bullet in place of the intended victim. Or in this case, replace bullet with 'bomb.'

Of all the times that 'they' would choose to plant a small bomb underneath Gary's car. It would follow the night before where he'd attempted to drive it across the city to speak with a contact who - he believed - was going to help him disappear, only for the car not to start. Carburetor issues or something. Gary, then deciding that he'd get a mobile mechanic out to look at it the next day and see if they could get it back to life. Meanwhile, he used public transport to get himself across the city. Mechanic booked with the instructions given that Gary had left the key on top of the drivers side front tyre and to leave it back there after he was done with it.

Later that day, when Gary returned to his apartment, he found a crime scene waiting outside. Police officers, detectives, ambulance, bomb detection squad. He also found that where his car had been parked that very morning now lay a burnt out shell. Being MI5, he couldn't pull that card out in any way. Instead having to be nothing other than a member of the public who has returned back to find that someone has blown up his car, along with the mechanic who was repairing it. The irony that it was his repair skills which brought the car back to life being the very thing that killed him. Something that I couldn't begin to wrap my head around. The moment he turned the key. It was all over for him.

'Hey, at least it would've been quick for the poor bastard.'

As Gary so eloquently put things.

This all leading to some unwelcome attention and questions from law enforcement over *why* someone would wish to place an explosive device underneath his car. While the attention was something that he hadn't sought, at least he was alive *plus* he was now going to be able to turn this failed attempt into his advantage.

Well, if you can class ending up inside the ADX for the rest of your life on some fabricated charges as *playing things correctly?*

With - whatever shadowy agency, the types that even the President probably doesn't even know exists … because technically, they don't - their attempt on Gary's life not going to plan, this along with the other deaths and how it wouldn't have exactly been impossible for a journalist to start joining dots. Gary himself said that he knew that they wouldn't make another attempt on him. The previous one, too public. If they tried - and succeeded - again they'd have been as well taking out a full page ad telling everyone that they had killed him.

They couldn't have allowed him to run free, however. Not with what he *knew.*

As a result of this they, instead, framed him. Creating a series of fake pictures which showed him receiving money from Al Qaeda second in command, Ayman Mohammed Rabie al-Zawahri, inside a tent in Kandahar, Afghanistan.

'I mean, yeah. I've done work in Afghanistan. Of course I have. Working *for* the fucking Taliban or The Base (Al Qaeda) though? Where do you even start with that. Never met al-Zawahri in my life but if I ever do I'll put a bullet right between the specky cunt's eyes. I sure would've liked the suitcase of money that they showed me in the pictures to be receiving, though, I have to admit.'

'Done me up like a right fucking kipper, though, and no mistake. Tapped right into all of that anti Muslim feeling across America - following last September - and turned me into someone who - as part of protecting my own country - had helped protect America, into public enemy number one. You'd think that it had been fucking *me* who'd brought those two fucking towers down, the way I'm now looked at.'

If it was the stitch up job that Gary claimed that it had been - and I had absolutely *no* way of verifying 'anything' that he'd told me - then the Americans played things perfectly. The wave of Anti Muslim feeling swarming the country as a whole, as if *every single* person of that particular faith had flown those planes that September morning? It was something that could be weaponised into a dog whistle of sorts. Being implicated as someone who had been dealing with Al Qaeda was not something that you wanted to find yourself being accused of in the United States of America. Well, once the Yanquis finally heard of 'who' they were, as a terrorist group.

Not that it would have mattered to my sentence, in any case, but luckily I had managed to get my trial over and done with - along with my sentencing - *before* September the Eleventh. Yeah Al Qaeda was mentioned in the trial but no one was paying attention, not then. They wanted to know about the boogie men that they already *knew* about. The 'rock stars' from the world of narcotics, terrorism and third world country civil wars.

'Is that rock and roll enough for you?'

I said out loud, to myself, the day we all watched the towers fall in Manhattan.

By the time Gary's trial came around, however. It was Al Qaeda mania and the poor fucker was sucked up into the machine. Exactly like the set up would have planned for. Here you had Gary, in a picture with one of the men who America had invaded a country to go and find, and they *still* hadn't found him. All of the might of the American military on your case - and with one hell of a point to prove following the attack on their country - and they *still* can't find the men they're looking for. And yet a British MI5 agent, living out of South Beach Miami just happens to manage to be bosom buddies with who was, is and will forever be until death or capture, one of the world's most wanted men.

Fake pictures or not.

'I'd seen a lot of fake pictures in my time of service. Some good, some laughable but *these* photos of me and him? I honestly didn't know that the Americans had the tech to pull something like that off. I mean, when I was shown the pictures for the first time, I had to even stop for a second and try to retrace my steps because - as far as I could see - I *was* looking at a picture of myself. Lawyers can argue back and forward for months, mate. Pictures tell stories though, don't they. I knew at the start of the trial that it was a formality. One look from the jury at those pictures mixed with the rabid viewpoint *whenever* The Base are brought into things and I was a convicted man even before the opening statements.'

Yeah well, he didn't need to look far to find a dove crying about that very same treatment, when it came to the United States legal system.

So that all explained the *why* Gary was inside the ADX along with yours truly. But *how* were the two of us speaking, via the intercom, and under the radar of the guards?

Narcos. Doesn't it always come around to those bloody guys in the end?

At Gary's sentencing and when he was in his holding cell awaiting to be called back in. He said that he'd had a visit from a suit. A *friendly* who had taken the liberty of telling Gary what he already knew. That he was going to spend the rest of his life in prison. What Gary *didn't* know though was *where* he was going to be carted off to. His visitor telling him that he'd already been assigned a place at the Colorado ADX supermax facility. The most harshest of 'on record' holding facilities that the country boasted. While that had made sense to Gary - with all of the Al Qaeda baggage - it was still a blow to hear.

The suit, was someone who had inside knowledge of Gary's work and how the fix was in, with regards to his terrorism indictments and I'm not sure if it was through sheer sympathy towards what was coming to him but he'd not so much specifically came to visit Gary to tell him what he was soon about to find out fo himself but, instead, something that he most definitely was *not* going to hear, said up above in the court room.

'Make no mistake, this place is *designed* to break you. Strip you down and leave you as half a person. Because you're MI5 don't think that you'll be better prepared for it. You *will be* but that doesn't mean to say that it won't get you in the end. The facility was literally designed with the aim of the brutality of isolation inside there responsible for breaking down the human spirit. And you're meant to spend a lifetime in there, huh?'

'Now while I can't do shit about the bullshit charges that you've had dropped on you. No one can. You know that yourself. What I *can* do is provide you with a small piece of intel for when you get there that *might*, and I say only might, just save your sanity, for a few years at least. Call it a small thank you for your work that you did that, incidentally, has now been erased. Thanks to you - and the other guys I've got that bastard in my sights. It won't be easy but I'm going to bring down that Republican paedo son of a bitch.'

'Now I was a bit underwhelmed, Pete. You know? When he *finally* told me what he was going to give me. In return for my service. I get it now, though. Big fucking time do I get it.'

Gary said as he then went on to tell me about how this suit was coming to him with the intel that - inside the supermax - there were two cells (out of the five hundred or so in there) that were connected to each other, via the intercom, unofficially. The only 'official' acknowledgement of any recognition of this coming in a heavily redacted CIA cable that left everyone no further forward for reading it. This suit *knew* what the black lines had hidden, however.

That Manuel Almeyda. Cartel boss of the state of Jalisco, Mexico - along with his son, Emilio - *despite* being captured and detained at the foot of the Colorado mountains inside the ADX had *continued* to talk, from their cells. To an extent helping to run their business down south *from* inside their cells in Florence.

So how does a father and son - in separate cells inside America's most secure prison - continue to have daily chats back and forward with each other, when they were meant to be isolated from the rest of the world for twenty three hours a day, you may ask.

In that initial chat and as much as what he'd told me, I'd questioned. What he'd said about Almeyda and son was the most believable of all. Then again, he could've told me *anything* about the Mexicans and I'd have believed each and every single word about those loco motherfuckers.

While both the Almeydas were locked up in those early days at the ADX. The operatives on the outside - stateside - were getting to work. You can levy all types of accusations at the Mexicans. That they're cold blooded sick murderers who don't care how many bodies they leave behind them in their pursuit of money and power. *That* being something that they wouldn't deny. Hell? They even *broadcast* that fact with some of the staged macabre point making murders that they commit.

One thing that you will never, ever be able to say about cartels down there is that they are never not resourceful.

This an example in how they went about creating a - sort of - two way radio system between cells. Without a single guard even aware of it. No bribes, no blackmail (well, towards any guards, so to speak) no pressure whatsoever. *That* was all going on *outside* the prison.

Operatives for the Jalisco Cartel found out the security company who had secured the tender - when the facility was still at the architects stage - contract to 'secure' the ADX.

'Calcio Security' from just outside Denver (and it was the small details that Gary gave in his story which made you doubt your own doubts about him) soon finding their C.E.O paid a visit to his family home one night by two sicarios. Delivering him a letter where it was made clear that while he may not have known who the Jalisco Cartel were, they most definitely knew who *he* was and, evidently, where he and his family lived.

The letter was offering him two 'opportunities.' To either inform the FBI of the letter and to take his chances what came next or to call the number provided, which would connect him to who was going to explain what it was that they needed from him. The letter included along with obligatory photos of his kids, taken from a telescopic lens camera. The nice little touch being that the pictures were of his two kids being dropped off at school one morning.

If true, it was a beautifully scripted piece of extortion.

I don't think there's a single person in the world who would judge the man over taking the decision to call the number on the letter, as opposed to informing the authorities.

I've seen what the Mexicans can and *will* do. The smart play was to call the number on the letter. It's what I'd have done, for what it's worth.

From there, the green light. The suit who visited Gary at his cell didn't know the ins and outs of what had happened but the owner of Calcio Security had - in some way - generated a 'reason' for his engineers to pay a visit to the ADX. This obviously meaning that he'd had to take some of his staff into his confidence, over the situation he was facing in terms of his family. Once again. Basic human instinct would and should kick in where - of course - you'd help in such a way. Who gives a flying proverbial if two narcos can talk to each other in their cells if it means that a family is saved from being flayed by some sick bastards of sicarios. It would not have been out-with the realms of possibilities if the C.E.O had received his kids heads in boxes one morning, delivered to his office by courier - when they should've been in school - had he not complied.

He did the right thing. And in doing so had gifted myself and this Cockney some form of respite from the sheer crushing loneliness of the best part of a whole day of imprisonment.

According to the suit, who shared all of this with Gary. When the Mexican father and son were moved back to a Mexico City jail. The two way intercom system that both cells enjoyed had never been disabled. This down to the fact that *no one* knew that it existed in the first place. Hardly as if Almeyda and son were going to mention it on the way out.

The nameless agent telling Gary that while he couldn't control which prisoner (or their nationality) was going to be inside the cell that Manuel Almeyda had been placed in he *could* guarantee that - after calling in a favour - Gary would be placed in the cell previously used by Emilio.

After that, it was all in the laps of the gods. *That* was why Gary had been so obsessed with whether I spoke English or not, at the very start of the conversation.

Whether it was real, half real or a hundred percent fake. It had been - hands down - the *best* time that I'd had since arriving at the ADX. Whether he was a bullshitter or not he was entertaining, knew how to tell a story and - already - I was looking forward to speaking to him the next again night.

Chapter 9

El Corazon Valiente - The Ballad of Peter Duncan cont

Manny - Ok, Peter. So you've shared with me *how* you landed yourself in Amsterdam Netherlands and how you subsequently managed to get yourself fired from the job, and accommodation, that you travelled from Britain in the *first* place to take up. What came next for Peter Duncan. Please take me through the rest of Eighty Eight.

Peter - Well it was an exciting year, period, Manfred. Lyle won The Masters, for one thing.

Manny - Huh?

Peter - Golf, my friend. Sticks and balls. Big thing for Scotland, that one of our boys was the first Brit to win the green jacket. Of course, there were a lot more important things going on. Noriega getting indicted by America and the Russians pulling out of Afghanistan. Two 'areas of play' that I didn't know it at the time but I would be going into, in my future. I'd have laughed right in your face if you'd told me - as I watched the mass pull out of the Soviet troops - that years down the line I'd be flying into the *same* country to do business with the locals who were left in charge after the war.

Manny - Yes but there were several other things that all had to fall into place, if you could put it that way?

Peter - Yes, mainly me getting put to work by Hakan Yilmaz. Once I began working for the Turks. My own natural combination of charm, personality and a survivalist instinct looked after things from there. After starting working with them, I never really looked back after that. Duncan mused from his American maximum security prison cell. *Duncan laughs down the line at his own misfortune* You can put that line in if you like!

Manny - And how receptive was Yilmaz towards taking someone from Scotland and making him part of his crew there in Amsterdam? Were there any issues. Some of the Turkish mafia gangs across the world notoriously operating at close quarters and, understandably, suspicious of outsiders.

Peter - Well the main issue that I encountered with regards to this was the next day when I returned back to the Red Light District to visit Hakan's sex shop and found someone else behind the counter. Luckily they had actually been in and around the shop the day before so had recognised me. Through this they were a lot more open than I'd have normally expected. Telling me that Hakan had left for South America earlier that morning on a business trip and was not expected back in Amsterdam for the best part of a week.

Manny - And in the meanwhile?

Peter - Well, thanks to the nest egg that I'd come over to Holland in possession of, along with additional scratch I'd been earning with Zippy, (while rarely ever being left in a position to spend most of it) I wasn't exactly struggling for money. I took the decision that I'd take a week's holiday to *enjoy* Amsterdam. From the moment that I'd arrived I had searched for Zippy's bar and - upon finding it - from there was as good as 'on the clock.' While I'd had some amazing experiences since arriving. They had been random and short lived, with no actual pre planning. Knowing that Yilmaz wasn't going to return for a while. This I felt, was finally a chance to *sample* the city.

Manny - And did you?

Peter - Yeah, I never really covered myself in glory that week but, undoubtedly, I had a f**king great time throughout it.

Manny - Care to elaborate for our readers?

Peter - I think some stones are better left unturned. Like I said, I didn't exactly cover myself in glory. You know? That city can really get you twisted. I had no idea if Yilmaz was going to *offer* me a job or not but the way I'd been behaving - as well as spending money - it was going to be the mere formality that it actually turned out to be.

'Peterrrrrrr my frrrrrriend, what is up?'

He greeted me - with that over exaggerated use of his 'r's' - as he spied me coming into the shop. Almost taking an eye out with a strap on dildo that was dangerously hanging down from the low roof in front of me.

When I explained the short version of 'what is up' he called out something in Turkish through to the small back room and this young girl - early twenties - emerged straight away.

He continued to speak to her in Turkish but from the body language that was taking place. She was moving to behind the cash register right as Hakan was vacating it.

'We walk.' He said warmly, grabbing my arm and steering me around the strap on and out of the shop and back onto the small uneven and cobbled road.

He took out and lit a Marlboro Red. Offering me one which I declined. At the time, I wasn't much of a smoker although - as I found my career choices unravelling - as time would go on, that would change. It wouldn't be my only vice either.

Now taking the chance to give Hakan the full and unabridged version of the story of what had taken place before he had left Amsterdam, cautiously reminding him that it had all stemmed from him. I wasn't stupid, either, though. I'd been in Amsterdam long enough to know that you didn't push a man, like Hakan Yilmaz.

Thankfully he was decent enough to remember, and admit, that I had been the one talking about going back to work that day and him telling me otherwise, along with that whole 'Zippy will understand' stuff. The fact that I was back to visit Hakan a sure sign that Zippy had not, in fact, understood.

'Ok ok, I speak to Zippy, on your behalf, yes? I will get you your job back.' He announced. Out of all scenarios I'd assumed possible, all the way to me packing my bags and returning to Scotland. I hadn't gamed on the possibility of Hakan offering to get me my *old* job back.

This not exactly agreeable to me. Not with how Zippy and I had left things. While Amsterdam was full of bridges. The one that existed between Zippy and myself was no longer in operation. Bulldozed the night we had our argument.

'I'm a man of pride and honour, Hakan. I cannot work for this man, now. Not after the way he insulted me.' I appealed to the basic functionalities of someone like a Turk. Knowing that pride and honour was a big thing to people from such cultures.

'Without honour, what really is a man?' I embellished things further as I spoke passionately, pleading my case while we walked along the street through the throng of tourists, pushers and pickpockets.

'I'm a hard worker and *very* loyal - people will testify to that back home in Scotland - but without any work here in Amsterdam, I will have to go back to the U.K.'

I left it hanging in the air. Didn't *outright* ask him for work but wanted him to know that I now didn't have employment *down* to him. There also was the advantage that already existed which was Hakan taking a genuine interest in 'my story' the day we went out to lunch. Wishing to know why a Scot had ended up in Amsterdam - and doing the kind of work that he was doing for Zippy - I took him through the more recent years involving the bakery and how it all ended. None of it was lies and it wouldn't exactly have taken a private detective to verify all of this. Shit, half of it was in the newspapers, for one thing.

'You know? I might be able to help. Do not go home just yet, my friend. I will need to speak to some colleagues. Some - who do not know you yet - will be against it because you are not a Turk but I will talk them around.'

He said, putting an arm around and bringing it hard down onto my shoulder in a way that I wasn't sure if he had meant it to be as forceful as it felt my end.

I appreciated it, greatly. Wasn't naive enough to think that just because Hakan was the boss that he would just go ahead and make the decision to bring me into the fold, there and then. Just because you're the boss doesn't mean that you can be doing with all the grief you may get from your associates when you mention bringing in a new member to the crew. One that no one knows and then on top of that, someone British. It would've been easier for him to have just hid behind the Scottish thing and telling me that I couldn't work for them for that reason alone. Not like I would've been able to do or say a single thing about it.

I told him the name of the hotel that I was temporarily staying at and he agreed to call me in a few days time with regards to matters. The man as good as his word. A message waiting for me at reception with a number for me to get in touch with. Hakan on the other end of the line when I returned the call.

'Come down to the shop and see me. I have a job for you.' All he said before putting the phone back down again.

I was down there within fifteen minutes.

'I'm impressed.' Hakan said - upon my early arrival - as he explained to me that his crew were prepared to give me a trial run, so to speak. I was told that, like any new employee to a corporation, I would have to show that I was up to the job in hand and should I prove as much then the trial would move to a more permanent kind of a fixture.

'I want you to take this bag to Rotterdam, early tomorrow evening. Your return train tickets are inside the front pocket. You will meet a man called Erwin outside Centraal Station in Rotterdam. He is going to give you back the same bag in return. Bring it back to Amsterdam and come straight to the shop.'

He said as he reached down below the counter and produced a red and black rucksack on his way back up again.

I didn't need to ask what was inside, and anyway. I was going to take a peek inside once I had it back at the hotel. Of course I was. Who *really* would carry a bag for a criminal gang - from city to city - and not want to know *what* was inside it? I wasn't surprised to find that it was, what looked and felt like, four kilos of either Heroin or Cocaine. With the grey electrical tape that was covering the four individual packages it was unclear what was actually *inside* them.

It really was the only serious tone that Hakan *ever* took with me - for the rest of our friendship - but his tone changed as he gave me the bag, asking if he was clear how imperative it was that I completed the task at hand. I didn't and I could kiss my chances of any long term work for Hakan goodbye, in amongst any more pressing problems that not completing the task might have also brought my way.

I set off for Rotterdam the next day telling myself that this was all nothing other than the exact same kind of errands that Zippy had me doing for him, all be it taking the package a slightly longer distance. Station to station was less than an hour. Barely even had enough of a journey time for me to start to overthink things before I was getting off the train again.

Hakan had told me that outside of the main entrance to the station was a small hot dog and burger stand. Sat to the side of that would be the Rotterdam connect called Erwin who would be waiting for me on a bench. With the same style of red and black rucksack as me, sat in front of him for my assistance.

Things didn't entirely go to plan. Do they f**king ever, though? It was just gone eight o clock - and rush hour now passed, - I made my way out of the station, following the 'way out' signs helpfully placed to assist navigating my way through a place I'd never been to in my life before.

As I was walking through a small underpass. A couple of teenagers, talking to each other in Dutch, came walking from the opposite direction. Due to what I was carrying I was on a heightened state of alert for anything that might appear off. Sometimes it's the paranoia that *keeps* you alive. I had noticed them due to this but they were so deep into their conversation that they didn't look like it was reciprocal. The two of them were loud, a bit rowdy and excitable but hey, they weren't harming anyone, right?

This allowing them the element of surprise when - just at the point we were due to pass each other - one of them wheeled around and started shouting in Dutch at me. It took me a few seconds before I'd even noticed the knife as the shouting - and the fact that I couldn't understand him - had caught me off guard.

Of course, while I didn't know *what* he was saying. The translation wasn't fully needed. He wanted the bag. The *one* thing that I could not give him. *Would* not give him.

'You're not getting the f**king bag. I screamed back at him, half frightened that this was going to result in me feeling the sharp and shiny blade that he was holding, plunging into some part of my body. Shouting in English, for a second, at least, stopped him in his tracks. His friend trying to move to the side to help box me in while I nervously looked from side to side at them as I frantically tried to cover myself from attack. Two against one is always difficult, though. *Especially* when they have a weapon, or weapons.

'Oh we're f**king taking it you stupid prick. All that's to be decided is if we take your life along with it.' The one with the knife said, confidently, in good English. Now appearing to decide that this 'transaction' may go through a lot more smoothly if he spoke in the same language as the person who he was robbing.

I almost went into a full blown panic and anxiety filled attack as I tried to 'negotiate' with them while at all times felt that I was only ever a moment away from being stabbed.

I'd taken this as nothing other than a random mugging. The kind that happens every single day where a robber will sense a moment of opportunism and go for it. Through this, I felt I should try and reason with them. Give them a brief 'overview' and bring them up to speed with regards to why they should really decide *not* to steal my bag and how it would be better for them if they just steered clear of the whole situation.

'You *do* know who this bag belongs to? Hakan f**king Yilmaz! His men will hunt the pair of you down and put your heads on kebab skewers.'

Like punk little kids tend to react, if they don't know something you're trying to warn them of. They both shrugged their shoulders.

'Do we look like we care? Give me the f**king bag.' The one with the knife shouted while edging himself slightly closer to me while we all kept constantly on the move around each other there in that tunnel, in a strange kind of dance.

I was praying for another passenger to arrive in the tunnel - from either direction - anything that would spook the pair of them and with the rucksack still firmly around my shoulders. Nothing or no one came, though.

The one with the knife eventually losing patience and making a lunge for me that saw my coat sleeve, and arm inside of it slashed with the knife as I moved out of the way. The fact it was the forearm a lot less serious than it could've been. Did it smart, though. Even after finally finding the knife coming into contact with me - which had been my prime motivation to avoid from the very off - I wasn't for handing the bag over.

Hand it over and my 'employment' was going to work out being for as long as the first job I'd had as a kid as a paperboy which had begun - and ended - over the course of a single paper round one cold wintery

December morning. *Also* hand over the bag and the last thing you'll really be worrying about is whether you 'have' a job or not. Through having to keep my eyes fixed on the one with the knife, now that he become a lot more 'stabby,' it led to me paying less attention to the other one. The kid in the black Adidas tracksuit top with the Ethiopian colours running down the sleeves. Which was regretful as it would've been highly advantageous for me had I been able to see the punch from him coming, which sent me crashing to the floor.

Even then, I struggled. Dazed from the blow to the head I was literally seeing stars as they held me while they slipped the rucksack down my arms. Constantly reminding them that they were making THE biggest mistake of their lives and there was still time for them to make a life altering change of mind.

I was getting desperate now. There was a real chance that if I pushed things even further then I *would* find out if they were going to 'take' more than the bag. Even so, I didn't feel like I could meekly surrender it to them. There was too much at risk to just hand it over.

And I was the furthest thing away from a 'fighter,' too. While I felt that with my skills and strengths I could be of use to a criminal organisation like Hakan's it would most certainly be *not* in any violence filled capacity. Let people play to their strengths, that's what I always say and having me roll around a filthy tunnel inside a train station while trying to avoid being stabbed was definitely not an example of this.

Overpowered. Eventually, they ran off with the bag shouting and jeering while I lay there. Blood coming from my arm and still a little swayed by the punch that had left me on the floor. If anything, I'd given a good account of myself. Not that it solved any of the issues that involved me arriving in Rotterdam for the exchange and no longer being in possession of the bag.

I got myself to the mens and 'freshened' myself up. Stemming the blood from my arm from the cut that - now that I had been given the luxury of removing my jacket - on reflection could have been a *lot* worse. He had nicked me and no more but that it had penetrated both my jacket and skin only highlighted how lucky I'd been.

A little worse for wear, I left the station in search of the man I was supposed to meet up with. I'd never been involved in something like this and felt that - before I returned back to Amsterdam to god knows what kind of problems - the decent thing, at least, would've been to let 'Erwin' know that he probably should now stop sitting around with a bag of money at his feet waiting on an exchange that wasn't going to take place.

If I'd had any thoughts that there may have been any sympathy from him in my direction, while I stood there explaining things to him, showing him my slashed jacket sleeve as evidence, I was sorely mistaken.

Instead, all I got was a volley of abuse from him in Dutch before he grabbed the rucksack sitting in front of him and stormed off down the street. I'd found - very quickly - that English wasn't used as frequently in Rotterdam as it was back in the capital. Then again, when the locals were as expressive in their own language. They were still able to easily make their point to someone like myself.

I stood there with a mind racing at a thousand miles a second. What do I do next? Against all instincts that had an interest in any kind of survival. I called Hakan from the train station to tell him what had happened.

As you can imagine, he hit the roof. I had to take the phone away from my ear for a moment until he'd calmed a little as it genuinely was too loud to listen to. The fact that it could be this way while I was stood in a large and noisy hall with all kinds of announcements going out over the tannoy, something that was perversely impressive from him.

Reminding me just how much I had blown things and that I was now going to have to answer for it. He told me to get myself back to Amsterdam and await further instructions in the morning.

The next thing that he said to me. Out of *all* of the small steps that I would have to make that would eventually lead me to Colombia, and all of the crazy that followed as a result. I have always felt that *this* was the defining moment out of everything for me.

'Now Peter. I understand that everything right now is telling you to disappear as fast as you can. I am asking you not to do this. If you *do*. I cannot help you anymore and we *will* find you. Come back to Amsterdam and we will talk, ok?'

Defining because that really was the choice. Run and hide, unsuccessfully, or show that I was someone willing to account for their own actions and responsibilities.

I never was any good at hide and seek. Well, the hiding part. No patience for that game. I returned to Amsterdam.

Manny - Didn't you worry that you were walking into certain death. You were in Rotterdam. You could've easily hopped onto a ferry and back to Britain.

Peter - Oh I was *extremely* worried, Manfred. I mean, I think I can say this with a relative degree of experience when disclosing that drug dealers don't tend to embrace the news of losing drugs and or money that fondly. A Turkish mob that I hadn't yet managed to experience how they reacted to such news? Yes, I was *very* scared about things. As much as Hakan and I had hit it off, personally, we did not have a 'history' and as such it would've been easy for him to agree with the rest of his men that I was 'expendable.'

On getting back to the hotel that night, sleep did not come easily and when I say that. It did not come at all. I was still lying staring at the wall, contemplating my fate, in the same position that I'd got myself into on the bed when I returned to my room, when the room telephone rang and brought me out of my almost hypnotised state that had me almost boring a hole into the wall with my stare.

'Yes, Peter. Can you come to Ankara Grill in Leidseplein. We are all here waiting for you.' Hakan's tone completely neutral. No warmth and friendship, as I'd always seemed to receive from him, but neither was it the tone of someone who you have just lost thousands of pounds worth of drugs for either.

I made my way up to the Leidseplein via the number two tram from just outside my hotel. In my time there, I'd always enjoyed either biking or walking around the city. There was always something that you'd end up seeing that you wouldn't normally if you were on public transport. That day, however. I had the impending feeling of doom that leaves you wishing for nothing other than to get it all over with. Even death. Part of me - with my destination a restaurant - was convinced that I wouldn't leave the place again. That I'd be taken through to the kitchen and that would be the end of the Peter Duncan story.

And it was even more ominous when I entered the place and found that it was deserted, apart from the table in the corner at the other end of the restaurant. *That* was where Hakan and around another dozen others all sat together at a large table. Them all looking up and over towards the front door when hearing the bell above the entrance ringing.

Their gazes fixing on me instantly.

Hakan did too and with the slightest move of his head, let me know to approach them. Talk about dead man walking? The others started to talk in hushed tones between each other but it was clearly apparent that I was the topic. Once I reached the table a clearly irritated Hakan roared out for them all to be quiet. With it being such early days in our relationship, I hadn't had a chance to see an angry Yilmaz in action. It was quite intimidating and with one sentence you could see the respect that the man commanded amongst his group. Silence what was asked for and instantly received.

'I, we, all of us, actually, trusted you, Peter. We trusted you with our product and we were intending to trust you with our money. It was not a difficult job to do. Just take a bag to Rotterdam. Bring another back with you to Amsterdam. Just one small, tiny job. A job that a baby could do, a child.'

The intimidation of not just his words - or where he was leading with them - but his eyes staring through me. Not just *his* eyes. ALL of their eyes. I felt the need to instantly introduce some breathing technique to help cope but didn't want any of them to see just how scared I was.

'Now, about that, Hakan 'I tried to offer some kind of a defence even though I wasn't sure what it was that I was going to attempt to even say.

'SILENCE' he shouted back at me.

Like with his colleagues, he demanded, and got it. I wanted to do *anything* other than look at him. If ever there was a time for noticing a spot of dirt on your shoe, it was then. The respect that he commanded, however, meant that I was left with no choice but to keep looking in his direction.

'You came to me looking for a job. I gave you one. An *easy* one, just to begin with. And do you know what, Peter? Never in MY LIFE have I EVER seen anyone, without a weapon, fight and defend themselves, when outnumbered and where his attackers are *with* weapons.'

He was now sat there with a smile forming on his face, they all did. Then came the laughter, roars of laughter, actually, while I stood there trying to bring myself up to speed with everything.

Wait a f**king second, I finally thought to myself. I hadn't *given* Hakan some of the details that he'd sat there and said.

Of COURSE! It was a test and the fact that the 'fake robbers' had actually managed to stab me during the *selection process* showed that the Turks didn't play around when it came to 'feeling you out' to establish if you were, in fact, someone that they could trust.

But hey, I'd passed it and - as Hakan would go on to explain to me over the course of 'my' welcome to the crew dinner - the way that I had passed it had meant a lot more than simply going on a hundred run of the mill and uneventful 'drop and collect' trips to other Dutch cities.

That trip to Rotterdam would prove to be the launchpad for a very happy and rewarding relationship between myself and the Turks, if a little shorter-lived than I'd have ever expected.

Chapter 10

Peter

It had been a long day. Longer than usual, if that was even something that was possible for to be left able to feel. When you reach saturation point of *anything* I'd always believed that it was difficult to experience things even more intensely, from there on.

If you're cold. Then you're cold, aren't you? How much *more* cold can you possibly get?

The ADX had the ability to push things further and in all ways, though. I mean, it was practically *designed* as such.

Over the day I'd thought a lot about Gary - and the conversation we'd had - from the night before. While - at the time - I'd initially pushed back at his story. Didn't call him an outright liar, of course, but neither had I been shy with some of the comments I'd put back in his direction as he'd told me all about himself.

Once the cold light of day had surfaced, and I'd had a bit of time to think things over, I was more responsive to his claims.

I mean, I was exhibit fucking A, there.

Then I took a thought over the fact that the ADX only housed the most notorious of prisoners. You really had fucked up in a very large way for you to find yourself in there, as Gary had.

THEN my train of thought took me to my own personal experiences on the outside and *all* that I knew when it came to the power that the United States of America could deploy, when it wanted to. Jesus? You, your life - and those nearest and dearest to you - could be completely dismantled on account of one phone call between a couple of suits, whether you're guilty or not.

I say 'when it wanted to' because, of course, America wasn't against dealing narcotics, <u>when it wanted to.</u> Unfortunately, I'd only ever experienced things from the point of view that drugs equalled bad but, fuck me, it must've been some sweet deal for those that were 'allowed' to flood the country with narcotics. Yeah, I was one of the *bad* drug importers and, as a consequence, had to always look over my shoulder for any 'Yanqui' looking to bring my beautiful, if bumpy at times, ride to an abrupt end.

I knew what they were capable of and *because* of that. It was child's play for someone to see to it that an innocent man - like Gary claimed to be - would spend the rest of his days behind bars and it would be incredibly naive of anyone to suggest anything to the contrary.

Every country has its dark side to 'national security' though so you would never have had me pointing the finger at America as such. I just wished that I'd been able to go about my business free of their intervention, like others had been, is all. Jealousy. Not a good trait although I'm not sure it was even that. More a case of someone looking for an open and level field of play, more than anything else. I'm pretty sure that there are rules for 'unfair competition in business' and if there was ever an example of that, it would be the country of America deciding on *who* they allowed to ship narcotics into their country. American dream? Land of the free? Yeah, ok then, if you say so.

I did what I could to pass the time over that day to get to the point where lights out would go out and Gary would make that first move. The second chat we would have, Gary telling me the specific code - **558367** - that required pressing on the keypad to link the two of our cells to each other. I'd been so engrossed by his story the first night that we hadn't actually got round to discussing the intricacies of *how* each cell contacted the other.

I'd passed the time either dealing with my own mind - which at times I would not wish on my own worst enemy - and then to blank it out, some TV.

When it came to recreation. You know? I really didn't feel like going through the whole strip search just so you can go outside into a small cage for a walk, that day. So I declined my invitation to do so. Choosing to just stay in the cell. I mean? What's an extra hour inside a cell when you're already in there for as long as I was going to be for over a day?

It's a dangerous road to be slipping on when you start thinking that way, however. *That's* when the depression can start to take hold. Before you know it. It's not just recreational exercise that is being skipped.

Next you can't even be bothered to switch on the TV, or open up a book, or even eat.

And the moment that you stop feeding your brain and your body. The jig is as good as up from that point. That's what the Americans *want* you to end up like. Practically mission accomplished for those bastards if they can reduce you to a shell of the man that you were when you first walked into a maximum security centre like where I'd landed up in.

As a matter of principle I sat there in the cell and made a pact with myself that I wouldn't give them the satisfaction. Not only would I commit to going outside for exercise (on the days that such a luxury was afforded to me) but I would seek out some self help books.

The Yanquis weren't exactly interested in 'helping,' that's for certain. They didn't *want* 'help' for you. They didn't want you to see the error of your ways as part of your rehabilitation. Where's the need for rehabilitating when you're never going to see the outside world again to *prove* that you're better, anyway?

No. All they wanted to do was feed you three meals a day until you eventually died. Even if it was through nothing more than spite on my part. I wasn't going to give them that particular pleasure.

When the lights finally went out on another day at the ADX, Gary didn't mess around. Almost as if he'd been loitering around the intercom waiting on the lights being cut. The second that they went out, the green light on the intercom started to flash, in the same morse code type of way that it had done the night before.

'How was yer day, treacle?' the Cockney accent enquired, following me 'picking up.'

'Oh, fun filled and action packed, Gal. Went for a Twelve K run up and around the Rockies. Skydived back *down* the mountain range, landing at one of the region's more exclusive restaurants - that I frequent - for a spot of lunch with some friends and associates before retiring back, with a few girls, to my private residence for some of the most filthiest of sex. It's been a good day, all in all.' I laughed back at him. ' I mean, I've had worse.'

'Yeah something similar my side, fella. You really just need to change the part about running up mountains to running in an exercise yard, scrap the whole part about the skydiving altogether, amend the favourite restaurant to very fucking worst restaurant in the Western world and returning back to my private residence with Pam and her five fingers for an extensive sex session.' He said with amusing self depreciation.

'Uncannily similar. Spooky, really.' I laughed back at him while recognising that - even in those few moments - it had been the happiest that I'd felt that whole day.

All plans of me reversing things from the night before and telling Gary *my* story were usurped when he said

'Ok then, Pete. What's your karaoke song?'

'What?' I replied. I'd *heard* what he'd said. It was just such a random thing *to* say, however, that all I could respond with was a dumb 'what?'

'Karaoke, Pete. You are aware of the phenomenon of drunken members of the public thinking that they can sing and, as a consequence, subjecting the rest of the bar that they're in to them completely murdering one of their favourite songs?'

Obviously, I was.

While my own personal life had not exactly been one of those who would work Monday to Friday and then let the hair down at the weekend by going out to get drunk and have a sing song or a dance to shake off the rigorous demands of the working week. I was still aware of what the general public, the others, were getting up to.

While - in getting into the narcotics trade - I had taken myself down one hell of a rabbit hole and one that had spanned decades in trying to get myself back out of. I wasn't so detached or insulated from what was going on in the real world. The area of life where the 'others' existed.

Even so, I *had* taken the mic on a few occasions, due to circumstance more than any actual desire to do so.

When you're in Tokyo - pretty much the spiritual home of the concept of someone who cannot sing picking up a microphone and belting out their favourite song with gusto - to do business with the locals and the head of the Inagawa - Kai Yakuza family passes you the mic and says its 'your turn' you really *do* take the microphone from them.

This all hardly made me the king of karaoke, however. For the record, though. That night in Ninety One - inside 'The Big Mouth' when Yamamoto Kenichi passed me the microphone. I thought the best policy would be to choose a song that I knew *all* the words to. This not only logical but - through having an accident with one of my contact lenses - an absolute *necessity* through my inability to read words on a TV screen.

'Cocaine Blues by Johnny Cash,' I replied to Garry. I'd chosen that particular song - that night thousands of miles away from home - in an attempt at having a laugh at myself, there in town to close on a shipping route that the Yakuza had offered us as a way into Japan. Plus, obviously, it's a great fucking song. That I knew the words, also beneficial to the situation.

'Nazareth, Hair of the Dog.' Gary followed up with before I could answer.

It made me smile over how small the world could truly be. And I reckon I'd seen more of it than most to know how *big* it could be, also. I'm sat in a supermax prison in the middle of Colorado speaking to a mystery voice through an intercom, connected only due to the power of a Mexican cartel, and the person on the other end is telling me that their go to karaoke song - out of the millions of songs they could've chosen from - is by a band who originated just along the road from the town I grew up in.

'NOW YOU'RE MESSING WITH A .... A SON OF A BI-IIITCH'

Gary treated me to a touch of his less than dulcet tones.

'Less of that, pal, or this conversation is going to be a very short one indeed. You not think being in here is torture enough?'

He just laughed back.

'Where did that question randomly come from, anyway?' I asked.

'Well, it wasn't exactly 'random,' Pete. Call it the start of our induction period of getting to know each other.'

'None of us is going anywhere anytime soon so I thought it would be good to get to know each other a bit better so I've spent the best part of today thinking of questions to ask each other.'

'Bullshit!' I replied. 'This is the patter that you use when you're chatting up girls online, isn't it' I joked.

'You fucking love it.' He laughed back at me without any form of denial.

This first question setting off a flurry of back and forth Q and A's that took us right up until the pair of us needed to pass out and grab some sleep before the custodians and the residents of the ADX would be making it their business to make sure that you were going to be awake.

Gary would ask a question. I'd answer - some back to him in the next breath, others after more of careful consideration - before he'd then go onto tell me *his* answer.

In an almost clever way. The questions that he was asking was helping reveal a bit of myself, without actually *telling* him. The rest, and all the stories connected to it, could then follow afterwards.

Who's your hero? I answered Louis Winsthorp - the third - from Trading Places on account of the man being put in the gutter to the extent that he'd been in only to show the resolve and fight to drag himself both back out but also get himself back on top, while managing to put those who had betrayed him *into* the gutter in his place. Fighting to improves ones fortunes with the added quality of dishing out some retribution to those who have wronged you. A true life success story. Qualities that I couldn't help but admire in a man. Gary's hero? Well it was a bit of a sore point and possibly just as well that he hadn't yet discovered all there was to find out about 'who' he was talking to but when he said Kiki Camarena I didn't really know what to say back.

YES it had been Mexicans who had brutally tortured and killed the DEA agent. Shit? All of that stuff had happened when I was still a nobody shifting drugs out of my bakery. The death of Camarena had had nothing whatsoever do to with me. Just hearing his name, though. It always touched a nerve with people from my (ex) line of work over how much that changed things, for everyone, through one moronic decision by those fucking maniacs in Guadalajara.

The questions, apart from that particular one, were a lot easier to negotiate.

What was your first job? Mines - Running to the bookies with my housebound grandad's betting slips and asking a stranger outside to put the bet on for him. Gary's - Working on the milk and roll van in his area.

Who was your first crush? Mines - Twiggy. Gary's - Maggie Benson, in second year at high school.

If you were the ruler of your own country what would be the first rule that you would introduce? Mines - If anyone wanted to be a politician in my country they would have to agree to be polygraphed every single day. Gary's - If a professional football player misses a penalty they will automatically be banned from playing professionally. Gary's reasoning behind this almost Nazi approach to being authoritative due to 'no professional football player should ever miss from that distance with what they have to shoot at.'

What do you do to keep fit? Mines - I substitute lifting weights with masturbating. Gary's - Five hundred sit ups a day.

Are you related to anyone famous? Mines - Regrettably I'm probably the most famous person in the family although I'm sure that the boy would argue against that. Gary's - An old uncle of his - and someone whose name was instantly forgotten by me the moment that he had told me it - had played a few seasons with Newcastle United before suffering from a career ending challenge in an FA Cup match against Leeds or 'Dirty Leeds' as Gal had referred to them as.

Where do you see yourself in ten years time? Mines - Here in the supermax. Gary's - Here, in the supermax providing he didn't come by any 'accidents' before then.

It was an appropriate time to end things for the night - due to what the answer led to - with his question of

'Have you ever had a nickname and if so what is it?'

'Yeah, when I moved to Amsterdam I started being called 'The Scotsman' and I guess it just kind of stuck because it followed me when I left Holland. It was only changed, amended really, - when Braveheart - the movie - came out - to El Corazon Valiente. Through time, I believe, it is now used in an ironic sense.'

'Wait a fucking minute. The Jock? Corazon Valiente? You're? Jesus fucking Christ. Peter Duncan?' He replied. 'I suppose it doesn't matter 'what' I say to you, or anyone, now. National secrets are right out the fucking window but over the years I've monitored you in Istanbul, - on both the West and East sides of The Bosphorus just so you know I'm not just guessing here - Rotterdam - anyone with such a keen interest in ports really should look to get a job there, fella - Kabul, - and with the greatest of respect, me and the rest of the crew were *astonished* when you left the city without a hair on your head being touched, never mind being fully decapitated, considering who you were there to meet with - and, if my memory serves me, Miami. That South Beach hotel couldn't have been cheap. Your employers must've paid well, eh?'

He was the most excited I'd heard him since we'd introduced ourselves to each other on the first night.

I was there on the other side, mildly freaked out over such a coincidence of the gods placing the hunter and the hunted on either side of a less than on the level intercom, in such a way. If anything, however. In me confirming who I was it automatically gave validation to *his* story because without question. I *had* been to all of the places that he'd mentioned. I wish that I'd stayed somewhere else in Miami but the facts were that I had stayed on South Beach at the SLS, in the penthouse. Even Istanbul. Weirdly I had only ended up on the East side of the city's river because my driver had taken the wrong road before correcting things and driving back across the bridge to take us to my destination on the Western side of the Bosphorus. This pretty much confirming that I'd been tailed that afternoon.

It created a bit of instant confusion and a case of trying to second guess things. Should I trust him from now on in, knowing who he was, and just put it down to a crazy coincidence and something you could just laugh about. Or was there *another* reason that he was speaking to me? Had he been put in there as a plant and was, in fact, still very much in employment? There to get me to incriminate myself further? I was frantically trying to produce some logical and clear thinking for those seconds, instead of submitting to the paranoid default state that had kept me a free man for all of the years that I'd worked for the Turks and Colombians.

Incriminate myself further? Oh yeah, what was going to happen there, even if I *did*? Careful, Peter, if you don't watch out, those pesky Americans might throw another few life sentences onto the ones that you've already got?! It took me a few minutes of searching for some sense out of things but I got there in the end.

'Yeah, bit of a small world, Gal, isn't it?' I eventually replied.

'I want you to know that it was nothing personal, just my job, fella. If I'm being honest, from all that I knew and picked up through case reports and intelligence briefings, you seemed quite a likable cunt. Everyone that we interviewed in connection to you and the Ramirez Cartel had nothing but good things to say about you.'

'I'm pretty fucking sure that if you go and ask Eddy and German Ramirez *their* opinion on me you'll manage to break your one hundred per cent record.' I butted in and laughed with an in-joke that I was certain he would get.

'My were you a slippery fucker, though, fella. Like you had the ability to know when you were being simply surveilled with no threat of arrest and when it was time to disappear from the radar completely and leaving us trying to work out what had just happened as if a magician had just performed a trick.'

'Talk dirty some more to me. I especially like the stuff where I don't get arrested.' I whispered back with a jokey bedroom voice.

'Listen, fella. Fuck me, we've got a *lot* to talk about, you and me.' He said, calmed down somewhat.

'Well the one thing that we *do* have, in here, is time for talking. For now though its only a matter of hours before those Al Qaeda bastards on my wing will be starting with their fucking morning prayer.'

'Same over here, annoying fucks.'

'We'll pick things up same time tomorrow. Allahu Akbar, pal' I said, signing off for the night. Left with a bent mind in much the same way I'd been the night before, all be it due to a completely different matter.

'Allahu Akbar, to you as well.' He replied with a few giggles to go along with it before the intercom went dead for the night.

His nickname, just in case you were wondering, was 'Bloodhound' on account of how extremely skilled he was at tracking his targets across the world.

Well he couldn't have been *that* good at tracking, I thought to myself later - thinking about some of the questions and answers - as I lay on my bed trying to catch a few hours sleep.

He didn't catch *me*, did he?

Chapter 11

El Corazon Valiente - The Ballad of Peter Duncan cont

Manny - The Turkish Mafia? How did you find things working for, perennially, one of the world's most well known and notorious criminal organisations?

Peter - Well, Manfred, If I was to put it into one single word it would be 'short.' I was only really *with* them for around six months or so before I was on the move again for pastures new.

Manny - This, especially, intriguing to me because, generally speaking, people in the line of work - that you were in - tend not to leave their current employers, even if they want to. Understandably, when you're given access to certain types of information. It can stop you from simply, as you said, seeking new pastures. What you 'know' is pretty much what keeps you *tied* to a gang. So what made *you* so different, Peter?

Peter - What makes anyone 'different?' What makes you want to take leave of your senses and investigate narcos who, with one phone call, can put a massive great price on your head?

Manny - Touche, amigo.

Peter - I guess things happen that are meant to and exactly when they do. Opportunities provides chances and chances are what, if you're brave enough to meet them head on, takes you places in your life. Obviously, I had to play my part along the way. You find it relatively easy when all you have to do is act naturally and instinctively, like I did when working for Hakan.

Work wise it wasn't really any different from the work that I'd been doing for Zippy when I'd arrived in the city, only it was with a much higher risk, alongside the greater rewards. Taking drugs and money from A to B. Collecting the same in return from elsewhere. Making sure certain members of the city council and police received their 'monthly payments.' That kind of thing. Helping to guard our product on occasion. Hakan also soon recognising my value in the sense that I didn't appear 'as' a Turk and that this could be utilised to the gang's advantage by sending me to places where I could go undetected. And, more pertinently, ones where the Turkish mafia could not. A skill set that would be used to its fullest by the time that the Colombians 'decided' to hire me. I was just happy to help out in whatever way that I was useful to the crew.

You should always use people to their strengths and it did not take Hakan long to realise that I was not someone who was ever going to be much good as some kind of 'enforcer' type so, as much as he could, kept me away from the more violent sides to the business. F**k me, he had enough of *those* types to keep things covered for generations. Whilst I, in no way, was ever going to be value for money as a hired goon he got a lot more out of me by letting me simply be myself where the lack of physical menace on my part was shrouded by my charisma and personality while mixing in such circles as the Dutch underworld.

Manny - And it was - through the work for Hakan - that you came onto the radar of the Bogota Cartel. What was the story there?

Peter - The Turks and the Colombians had been doing business, from what I had learned, for a number of years before I came on board with them. While Cali and Medellin were flooding America and Europe with Cocaine in the early days. The Ramirez brothers set about making their own contacts outside of South America. To undercut the 'big boys' Eddy and German offered less than favourable terms (to the brothers) to proposed buyers under the strategy that they would make a lot more back in the long run. I think it's what is called a 'loss leader' in the business world?

Someone who took a chance on the brothers - instead of going with the tried and tested Cali and Medellin routes - was Hakan Yilmaz. The Amsterdam Turkish Mafia and its Bogota counterparts ended up enjoying a long and mutually beneficial partnership where copious amounts of Cocaine would be sent, periodically, over the year and millions of US Dollars sent back the way to the Swiss and Cayman Islands bank accounts of the cartel's choice.

Then *I* came into the equation but even then - and as much work as I'd been tasked with in connection with deliveries from Bogota - I'd never came into contact with any of the Colombians, who, on the whole, were shit scared to leave their country in case any Yanquis grabbed them. That all changed, however, when Roman Ramirez flew into

Amsterdam on business on behalf of his father, Eddy, as a VIP guest of Hakan.

As Roman had explained to me - the night before he flew back home to Bogota - Eddy had felt that he had proved a big disappointment to him and was not appearing to step up to the plate, as far as being the son of a narco boss. Very family orientated, the Colombians, so someone like Roman was never going to get away with growing up and doing anything other than working for the family business with his father and uncle German. This didn't exactly suit the plans that Roman had, however, which was mainly to be a playboy and live off his dad's mass of wealth, without actually getting his *own* hands dirty.

This not something that was going to fly with his papi.

One day in Bogota things eventually coming to a head. A city centre nightclub owner had requested to speak to Eddy which - being old acquaintances - led to the club owner being granted a visit to Eddy's ranch. Here the man had the unenviable task of informing the cartel boss that Roman had ran up quite an extensive bar tab and upon being refused any further credit - the night before - had threatened to shoot a bartender. The owner of the club was there to plead with Eddy to do something about things, before they escalated further.

Eddy was heard on the ranch in an expletive filled rage where he spelled out that this layabout son of his needed some personal responsibility handed to him. Something other than sleeping until the afternoon and partying until the next morning. Drinking, sniffing and f**king women.

Coincidentally, the same day - and before Eddy had been given a chance to take Roman to task over his behaviour the night before at the discotheque - Eddy received a call from Hakan Yilmaz, this following a recent successful delivery of two tonnes of Cocaine into Rotterdam. This had been the Turk's largest amount imported yet and was a purchase that more resembled a power move rather than just a case of buying and selling. The more of the Cocaine that you have the more *control* you take of things. Hakan knew this and to celebrate, he wanted to make a grand gesture of thanks towards Eddy, who out of the two brothers Hakan had always done business directly with.

Hakan doing this through the medium of a rare bottle of 'Macallan Fine' scotch. The rare single malt setting Hakan back an eye watering nine hundred and seventy five thousand dollars. I mean, *this* was the level that everyone was operating at - and the money being generated - that they could spend the best part of a million dollars on a bottle of liquor as a 'thank you.'

Upon learning of this magnificent gesture, Eddy saw an opportunity out of it. Telling Hakan not to send the scotch by any courier and that - given the extremely rare and valuable element to the cargo - he would send someone personally from Bogota to collect it, Roman.

Eddy figuring that if his son could not complete a simple task such as collecting a bottle of scotch from the Netherlands - and safeguarding its passage back to Colombia - then there really would be all hope lost for the kid.

Upon us learning of Roman's visit, Hakan asked me to put the arrangements such as where he was going to stay overnight and which restaurant we would go out for lunch into place. With this, I took the opportunity to have the kid booked into 'The Grand.' An establishment where I was good friends with Gert, the hotel desk manager. The pair of us had a good thing between us where if I directed business to the hotel, I would get a small percentage of the booking kicked back to me. It also, from an even more personal gains point of view, allowed me to make sure that both my guest was being given the VIP treatment and, even more importantly, them being informed (low key) that their all star treatment was through *me* asking for it.

We had Mursel - one of our goons - drive out to Schipol to collect Roman on the morning that he flew in on the Bogota flight. The instructions for to bring him back to The Grand to get himself checked in. Soon after that we had the kid picked up and driven over to the restaurant that I had us booked for lunch. Hakan sitting there with the almost ceremonial bottle of scotch to present to Roman on behalf of his father sitting taking pride of place on the table.

It was there where Hakan launched into a big speech about how the Turks and Colombians - as business partners - were only going to go on from strength to strength and that they were destined to make a mutual fortune. I couldn't help but feel that a large percentage of it had been completely wasted on Roman because from what I had already picked up, through both his choice of words and body language. The kid was no narco or gangster. Sometimes though, when you have the fearsome reputation of a South American cartel, all you need to do is send a member of the family and they will be awarded the maximum of respect, on principle.

Regardless of this. With the bottle of Macallan being presented to Roman and a never ending series of handshakes and back slaps dished out, following the transfer of bottle from Hakan to Roman. The object of the young Colombian's mission had been achieved. As had been my remit from Yilmaz. Roman was to be extended a warm welcome to the city of Amsterdam and be treated as if royalty. With him having flown to Europe overnight he was understandably a little tired so - as part of my charm offensive task - we agreed that he'd be taken back to his hotel for a sleep and that I would take him out to dinner in the evening, in addition to showing him a little of Amsterdam's nightlife. Roman himself expressing during the lunch that he had never actually been out of Colombia until travelling to Amsterdam for his father and how he had been excited to see a different part of the world.

Unfortunately, while we were lording it up in an Amsterdam bistro eating lobster. Mursel was telling the police - in his role as an informant to the Amsterdam Serious Crimes squad - that, as part of his role of driver for the Yilmaz organisation, he had been sent to Schipol Airport to collect a South American kid fresh off a Bogota flight.

Now I'm not sure what name Roman Ramirez had flown into Amsterdam under but - knowing as much as I do, personally, about the Ramirez Cartel operation - I'd have been astonished if he had travelled without a fake passport. Even if he *had* flown in as Roman Ramirez, however. Mursel wouldn't have known about it. Hakan - with all the comings and goings that the business would see in a busy, cosmopolitan and easy to get to city such as Amsterdam - had introduced a clever coded way of collecting people from the airport.

Having a driver stood there with the name of who he was there to collect, written in large felt pen, was not exactly what you could call discreet. Instead, he would have his driver, wearing a red Turkey football shirt, standing to the side of the nearest set of payphones to international arrivals. With no names given whatsoever. The traveller would be instructed to approach the man in the red shirt nearest to the payphones and ask him 'how much would it be for a friend of a Turk for a ride to the city centre.' This confirming who each were and seeing them both leave the airport for the waiting car.

Whatever Mursel had told the Amsterdam police had been enough to get them excited, even if they weren't entirely sure why. With everyone and their dogs in possession of the knowledge that the Turkish Mafia moved a *lot* of product into Holland and then into the rest of Europe. Add that Hakan was entertaining someone from *Colombia* then you could see why the Serious Crimes Squad were interested in having a closer look into things. You could understand *why* they would assume that this visit was narcotics related, even if, in reality, they were miles off the mark.

Of course, we were all oblivious to it, sat there filling our faces and drinking champagne and toasting to all the money (and power) that the recent shipment that had arrived was going to bring. In all honesty, it made Hakan's bottle of scotch out to be chump change.

Manny - So how did you find out about the police coming into the intelligence of the Colombian visitor to Amsterdam? You will know every bit as much as I do. Whether Roman Ramirez was committing a crime or not in Amsterdam - which he appeared not to be - it really would not have mattered. Just through having Eddy Ramirez as his father and living under the same roof? The amount of conspiracy indictments that *alone* could bring a person, if the U.S authorities so desired.

Peter - Which you also know they very much WOULD desire.

Manny - A-ha.

Peter - Well it was through my sheer good fortune that I had booked Roman into the one hotel in the city where I was on good enough terms for them to phone me the moment that they noticed something was up, inside in the hotel. Any other hotel in the city and I'm certain that the story would have had a completely different outcome. Shit? There's a parallel universe out there where Roman gets booked into another hotel other than The Grand which sees Nineteen Eighty Eight to today play out in an entirely different way altogether and, ironically, one that would've seen to it that we would not even be holding this conversation today.

The first I was aware of any issues was when I received a call at my flat from a concerned Gert. Telling me that there was quite a bit of police presence inside the hotel and how - in his role of desk manager - he had been asked to sit down with a plain clothed officer and answer some questions regarding visitors who had checked in that day and, more specifically, which ones were of a South American description matching the appearance of Roman. He told me how they were now setting up some kind of sting operation in the hotel bar and lobby with plain clothed officers sitting around, as if they were guests.

I was scrambling and trying to limit damage in my mind before he had even finished speaking.

The chances were that they didn't know who it was that they were even staking out and were doing nothing other than taking a punt on the possibility of it being someone with a value to them. Since Roman wasn't in on any drug dealing business it certainly wouldn't have been a case of them acting on any kind of intel of an exchange taking place. This seemed nothing more than a case of someone taking a shot at goal, just in case they scored with it. If they'd *actually* known who it was that was sitting in an upstairs room. They'd have skipped the sting part and went directly to the warrant to bust into a guests room. That they hadn't done so already was probably the only saving grace and the thing that convinced me they didn't yet know the prize that was literally sitting on top of them.

Roman simply could *not* be arrested by the Dutch authorities. If he was there was a high probability that he wouldn't see Colombia again until he was in his forties. There was also the very large issue that, I'd been given the task of looking after the kid during his stay and had been given carte blanch when it came to carrying it out. There wasn't exactly much that I could've done about the fact that we had a rat on the team but - while Mursel's traitorous ways would be dealt with - that was something that I felt neither Hakan or Eddy Ramirez would be too understanding about when it came to Roman being arrested by the Dutch and then, as assumed, extradited swiftly to America.

Thanking Gert for being so quick witted as to let me know of this development I then sparked into some quick problem solving. With him painting the scene of a police unit setting up a sting down at ground level of the hotel I imagined that the police mentality towards this was that the person they were looking for was not looking for *them* and would be going about their business like any other visitor to the hotel. *Not* someone who would be inclined to use alternative exits from the building. I asked Gert if there were any fire exits to the hotel which he confirmed that there were some exterior stairwells, close to where Roman's room was situated.

I wrote down the directions which would literally take Roman from his room door to street level of the hotel on the rear of the building.

Next I asked him to transfer the call through to Roman's room, where I would explain matters to him.

Manny - And how exactly *did* the Ramirez son take to the news that there was a squad of Federales downstairs waiting on him?

Peter - Well Roman hit the roof when I told him and reacted in the *opposite* way to what I needed him to, in that high pressured moment. He kept shouting about how - funnily enough given what you just said - the 'Federales' couldn't get him and that he didn't want to go to America, and how he didn't have a gun to defend himself, amongst other pressing concerns.

'If you listen to me, Roman, and do exactly as I tell you to you're not going to *need* a gun.' I urged him before ordering him to grab the obligatory complimentary notepad and pen that would've been on the hotel room table and to write down my instructions.

'F**K F**K F**K! MY FIRST TIME SETTING FOOT OUTSIDE COLOMBIA AND I HAVE FEDERALES LOOKING FOR ME. F**K.'

He shouted, in no way at all appearing like he was calming down.

Man, those Colombians really do get psyched out by the prospect of being snatched by the Americans though and no mistake, Manny, eh? *Duncan laughs* He was no good to anyone during the call and I wasn't even sure if he had taken down my instructions in the way that I'd felt necessary for him to get out of there, without being arrested. He'd been a panicky mess during it and - from the start of the phone call when I'd broken the news to him - I'd felt it ironic that if Bogota had sent a *real* narco he'd have been as cool as a long green vegetable, in dealing with the situation.

There didn't appear any logic to me physically going down to The Grand to collect him - and with its locality being in the centre of

Amsterdam - I was spoilt for choice of places to pick him up. Taking no chances with that, though, I elected to direct him towards Centraal Station. Basing this on the thinking that if he couldn't find the massive train station, minutes from where he was then yeah, Eddy Ramirez would've been correct. There would've been *no* hope for the kid.

You know? It's funny how wrapped up you can get with your own stuff if you go too far into it because there I was, living in Amsterdam, and yet at times I barely noticed what the Amsterdammers were up to, as in the general public. This was highlighted that night when I jumped into my Audi and tailed it down towards Centraal. Well, crawled, actually.

Holland had been playing in a major football final, The European Championships, in the afternoon. I'd been aware that the team had made the final due to the celebrations around Amsterdam when they beat - of all countries, given their previous history - West Germany in the semi. I switched off again after that, however, with all thoughts on making sure how well Roman Ramirez would be treated on his visit to the city taking on much higher importance.

I was back at the flat when the full time whistle was blown and the city was sent into the most extreme version of party mode it had ever witnessed. Post war, anyway. Looking out my window and down onto the street filled with orange clad revelers I even had the thought that it was going to be quite an experience for me to take Roman around Amsterdam during this madhouse outside.

The drive through the - at times packed - streets filled with Amsterdammers drinking, blowing horns, whistles and chanting songs took more than double the time it normally would've on any other day. There was a moment where - considering the time that I had told Roman I would be there to collect him, coupled with whatever paranoid thoughts the kid would've possibly been entertaining - I began to panic that he wouldn't even *be* outside the station by the time I belatedly arrived.

Thankfully he was still there. I doubt he would have been able to make himself look more shady if he'd tried. It was a relief to get him into the car and out of harms way.

He was safe now. Literally anywhere other than being placed inside The Grand and the kid was safe. You could see how shaken he was by what had just taken place, though, and I decided that it would probably be a good idea to take him back to my flat, until things settled.

He eventually started calming down on the journey out of the city centre. Actually beginning to laugh, with relief, over just how close things had been for him and how I was an absolute hero for getting him out of there without being pinched.

As we were pulling up into a space outside my flat, his mood unexpectedly changed from relief to one of panic and frustration.

'You're safe as houses now, Roman. That's my flat up there.' I said pointing up to it. 'You can stay in there all night until your flight tomorrow if you like?' I said, trying to reassure him on things.

'No, it is not that. I have realised that after you called. I quickly grabbed my things. Passport, you know. Now that I have calmed down. I realise that I forget fathers gift. It is still in the hotel room.'

I'll admit. My first inclination was to tell Roman that he had been extremely lucky to have evaded capture by the authorities in the hotel and that the bottle of scotch was going to have to be put down as collateral damage. I mean, what would Eddy Ramirez have preferred? A rare bottle of scotch or his son? Yeah, preferably both but if he had to choose one I know what he would've chosen although then again, from what I had been informed, the way he felt about Roman was sketchy, at best.

'My father sent me here to collect the bottle, as a test. If I go back to Bogota *without* it. It will not be good for me. I will have failed. Who even fails going to collect a bottle of alcohol from somewhere, anyway?'

If you'd been able to predict my future - over what would happen due to my next choice that I made - then I'm pretty sure I wouldn't have done what I decided to do but first of all I got Roman up into my flat before launching into a plan of action. Telling him that I was going to get Eddy's bottle of scotch back from the hotel. His face lighting up at this.

Despite telling him this, inside, feeling like someone who had just rescued someone from a burning house only for them to then ask if I wouldn't mind popping back inside again for their family photos.

'This would be a personal favour, Peter. If you can get the bottle back for me I will make sure that you are rewarded in some way or other.' He said with his hands joined together as if he was praying that I was going to come up with some kind of a result that was going to ensure that he returned back to Colombia in possession of his father's scotch.

I hit redial on my phone and was soon speaking to Gert on the hotel desk asking him for an update on things his end. According to my diamond of a Dutch hotelier friend. The plain clothed police were still stationed across the bottom floor but there had been a further development in that one of the officers from the team had squeezed themselves into a staff uniform and, it appeared, that they were going to perform a knock on Roman's door, in an attempt at getting an I.D on him under the falsehood of the hotel staff member getting the wrong door with a room service order.

'Would you like to be connected to your friend's room to warn him to put his "do not disturb" sign on the outside handle? Legally, if he does this we cannot knock on the door.' Gert asked, helpfully.

'No, its fine. Elvis has already left the building.' I informed him.

'Oh good.' Gert said with relief knowing that the job was now done and that the Amsterdam police could literally check themselves into the hotel now for all that he cared, with the danger now gone.

I then went on to explain that it wasn't 'that' good because I was going to have to come down and retrieve something that Gert's guest had left behind.

I only had one question for him. Was it doable?

'If you are stealthy and do not draw any attention to yourself then yes, but you must be quick. I do not know if there are going to be any further developments. If the police end up with a warrant to enter the room then any hope of collecting anything from the room will be gone.'

As much as I was friends with Gert I didn't know whether he was in the bracket of being trusted with the knowledge that there was a bottle of alcohol worth the best part of a million dollars upstairs in a room so I felt it wise not to disclose that kind of information.

'Ok, I'm going to be there as soon as I can. I'll come to reception and pose as a guest. Give me the key to the room and I will collect what is there and I'll drop the key back off when I'm leaving the hotel again.'

I explained the situation to Roman before leaving him there in the flat. The best place for him, given everything that had taken place.

Gert wasn't joking about the police presence. I guess it's possibly a case of knowing when to look for them but I had barely put two feet inside the hotel when I spied a couple of them sitting there in large armchairs facing each other - drinks on the table - engaging in some chat while posing as a couple of guests staying there, and failing miserably. There was another one at the bar staring at the lifts. You could almost *smell* them all, in there.

And as subtle as a brick. Upon walking into the place you could *see* the eyes diverting towards you, like they would have almost certainly done with anyone else entering or leaving the hotel since they'd arrived there earlier in the evening and setting up shop. Once they saw that I did not match the description of who they were looking for - along with me heading straight for reception, like any other guest would do - they all began to divert their eyes back to the natural position they'd been in before I'd walked in.

'Ahh good evening, sir.' Gert said to me with a warm welcome (playing for the crowd) and handed me the key to Roman's (now) old room.

It was more the paranoia than anything else as I walked through the lobby but it felt like I had several laser stares boring their way into me. From the front, back and the sides. There was no need for it, either. I hadn't committed a crime. I wasn't *going* to commit any either. Just pick up a bottle of booze and be on my way again. Easy.

Still, understandably, being around coppers was something that had always left me uneasy. When you've committed the amount of crimes that I'd had it's really just a natural reaction that can't be stopped and I felt infinitely safer the moment I stepped into the lift and the doors closed behind.

This feeling of undeniable relief to be out of their gaze literally drained from me the moment that the lift doors opened on Roman's floor and me coming face to face with *another* couple of undercover officers. One plain clothed while the other was stood talking to him, poured into an ill fitting waiters uniform.

They wheeled around on the door opening but - like before - after initially checking me out, and finding that I wasn't of South American appearance, they turned back to speak with each other once again. The both of them as close to each other in discussion as to be invading each other's personal spaces.

'Evening, gents.' I said as I passed them. Taking my index finger up to eyebrow and pulling it away again in a small way of recognising the pair of them.

'Good evening, sir.'

'And a good evening to you.'

They both answered back, friendly enough. The way that I was approaching things it was on the basis that I should appear like I have nothing to hide. Saying an innocent hello to two people in a hotel floor hall, that exact kind of deal.

I walked down the hall of the floor looking for the number fifty seven door to match the key with the large rectangular piece of hard plastic - with the yellow "57" branded into the mould on both sides - that was joined to it.

As far as I was concerned. The only issue I was going to encounter would be if any plain clothes officers saw me physically entering the room that they were waiting on someone coming out of. As I walked down the hall in search of the room it had been assumed that one or both of the officers by the lift would have been keeping an eye on me walking down and to ensure which room I was heading towards.

When I found fifty seven, however, and had a quick squint behind me to see if anyone was watching. There was no one looking back down the hall towards me. Gift horse / mouth, I didn't mess around in letting myself into the room and closing the door fast behind me again.

I was relieved to see the bottle of Macallan Fine still sitting there in the room, on the table in the corner by the window that looked out onto the Red Light District. Any other regular bottle of scotch and you'd *expect* it to be still there but you really could never have ruled out someone being in the room since Roman had made his retreat and well, all it would have taken was someone with a knowledge of high end alcohol to appreciate *what* was in front of them.

Put it this way. If you left an open briefcase filled with near on a million dollars lying in your hotel room. How confident would you be of it still lying there upon your return?

I grabbed the bottle and for the briefest of moments had contemplated looking outside the room window to establish if there was a way that I could leave the hotel without physically having to leave the room but soon remembered that the direction Roman had been given had involved leaving through the room door before he could exit via the fire escape.

I quickly scanned the room for any other items that Roman had possibly left behind with him because the one thing that I could have guaranteed you, him or anyone else who would listen to me, for that matter, was that I was *not* going to be making a return trip to the hotel again. Not on that night, anyway.

With nothing else coming into my line of vision I made for the door, took a massive deep breath, turned the handle and left the room while saying a Hail Mary that my leaving the room was not going to coincide with any activity outside. I gingerly stepped out into the hall and cautiously looked from side to side. Nothing. Not a sight or sound of anyone. Acting on this I pulled the hotel room door slowly and quietly enough for it to lock back into place again.

That was the only potential moment where I may have made myself a person of interest to the Dutch police and I'm not even sure myself how I'd have been able to explain myself away out of me leaving the hotel room of someone they were staking out. Regardless of being in possession of a bottle of scotch being legal or not. It was shit that you really did not want, them on your case asking 'questions.' I'd managed to avoid any police issues since I'd arrived in Amsterdam but as Hakan had told me from the off when I joined him and the crew.

'Just because you don't know the names of some of the police around here does not mean that they do not know the name of *you*.'

I calmly made my way back up the hall towards the lift area of the floor once more. This time there was only one of the plain clothed officers hanging around there. Sat at the set of two chairs and a table directly outside the lifts, reading a paper.

You really do question the intelligence of coppers at times, don't you?

Manny - How so?

Peter - How many people do you know check into a hotel for a stay and spend their time sitting in the lift area relaxing and reading a newspaper?

Manny - You do have a point, actually.

Peter - Damn right I do, Manfred. It's not exactly rocket science to pick up on small things like that but it's what kept me a free man for a long, long time. Police stupidity.

Manny - So you managed to get the scotch out of The Grand and back to Roman in one piece?

Peter - Well there was still a long way to go before me - and the bottle of Macallan - were what you could class as safe. Just like when I'd got into the lift at the bottom. When the doors opened, all of the plain clothed officers spread around all lifted their heads to look over only to see that it was the same guest that they'd seen earlier 'going up to their room.' There could only have been ten minutes elapsed since they'd last seen me. Like before, though. As soon as they'd established that I was not their guy, they turned their attentions elsewhere.

Well, everyone *apart* from one eagle eyed officer who possibly possessed some kind of an eidetic memory that had been enough for him to remember - out of all the guests coming and going through the place - that when I had arrived I had not been carrying a box. Now that I *was* in possession of one. He wanted a look inside.

I was almost out of The Grand when I felt the tug on my arm along with the

'Excuse me, sir. Could you come with me for a second.' As he led me back away from the entrance and asked me to put the box - I was carrying - down onto the table beside us.

'Why, of course, officer.' I said, compliantly, having seen a quick flash of his badge.

'What's going on? Is everything, ok?' I asked him as he turned his attention to the box with the scotch inside of it.

He didn't answer me, initially. Too wrapped up in the box that I'd been carrying. Considering the exterior to the box had the Macallan logo along with the usual Hallmark style sentiments written down. Telling you the rich story of the company responsible for what was inside, it was hardly a spoiler to the officer when he opened the box up and saw the unopened scotch bottle sitting there in all its beautiful presentation.

He looked the bottle from top to bottom and then to the back and made a face of approval before setting it down onto the table. I'd hoped that the face he'd pulled had been nothing more than an uneducated guess that - from its presentation box - he was looking at an expensive bottle of alcohol. NOT a nine hundred and seventy five thousand dollar bottle of alcohol, though. *That* would most likely have brought a lot more questions than I'd have liked, or been able to answer.

The police know that you're in possession of something *so* valuable? All it would've taken would have been them to ask 'where did you get it.' and I'd have been left in a bit of a spot. One quick look at my bank account and you'd have seen that I certainly hadn't bought it, anyway.

I don't think I had ever felt so frightened and scared over something that wasn't even illegal to be carrying. I'd carried enough drugs to put me in jail for half a lifetime and been immensely relaxed over it, compared to this bottle.

'Yes, it's for a business client of mines. I hope he shares it with the rest of us when he receives it tonight!'

I said to him which he only really managed to half acknowledge while he stood there examining the inside of the box to make sure that there were no hidden compartments, inside hiding anything. Once he was satisfied that there was nothing else inside. He picked up the bottle, once more, carefully placing it back into the box and securing the neck and bottom of the bottle to the velvet protective mould inside.

'I'm sorry for your inconvenience this evening, sir.'

He said as he picked the box up and handed it back to me with a smile on his face.

'Is everything ok, here in the hotel?' I asked. Regurgitating the initial question that I'd asked him, that had been ignored. I knew the chances were slim of him telling me anything useful but for the purposes of me filling Roman in on things when I returned back to the flat, I thought it wouldn't hurt to ask.

'I only ask, as a guest of the place, you understand.' I pressed home with only to receive the stock and standard reply of

'There is no need for alarm, sir. You can go on with your night now.'

Something I took him up on. Taking the box of Macallan back from him and swaggering out of the hotel without a care in the world and back to my car. It was still complete bedlam outside. The streets, a sea of orange. The sheer colour and noise, the vibrance in general. It was a beautiful sight to take in. Thousands of people in some kind of shared delirium. Walking to the car I remarked that it would have been such a good night to be Dutch, celebrating in the frenzied way that they all were. Instead, though. I - as always - was doing my own thing and instead of throwing alcohol down my neck was babysitting someone like they had been my own flesh and blood.

I didn't even get annoyed, understood more than anything, when I discovered two young girls - early twenties or around that - standing, both draped in the Netherlands flag, on top of my car roof singing. Which wasn't like me. Instead, I smiled at the pair of them and asked them to please get down from off the car.

I reached my hand up to help the two of them back down. Receiving a kiss on the cheek from both of them before they both grabbed hold of me and - in some kind of three person huddle - started to bounce up and down, taking me along with them, while they sang

'CHAMPIONES CHAMPIONES OLE OLE OLE CHAMPIONES OLE OLE OLE'

I was less impressed at this than I was on them jumping up and down on my car. I'm not one for tempting fate and I put my many years of freedom - while being hunted by all kinds of 'crime fighters' - down to how cautious and careful I'd always conducted myself.

I don't think you could tempt fate more by holding a million dollar bottle of scotch and then jumping up and down in the street. I'd been holding the box as if it was some unexploded bomb and here's these two pushing and pulling me all over the street?

Getting myself - and the Macallan - into the car. I made my way back up to the flat. Getting there quicker than it had taken me in the opposite direction due to me amending my journey and taking a kind of long way for a short cut so as to avoid the more smaller and compact streets on the more familiar route back home from the city centre.

I walked in to find Roman pacing the floors of the living room. I'd sorted him for drinks - and if the mood was to take him - and grass. South Americans love their football so I'd also put the re run of the Holland - Russia final on TV for him to watch so that he didn't get bored when I was away.

It looked like it had been a waste of time because his drink was still sitting untouched, there was no smell of weed in the flat and - from the position he was in when I entered - he wasn't even looking in the direction of the TV. It appeared all he had done when I'd been gone was pace around the flat stressing out on matters.

The look of relief on his face - when he saw that I was carrying the Macallan - was undeniable.

'OHHHH HERMANO HERMANO HERMANO, GRACIASSSSS'

He shot over in my direction and took the box from me.

It was all in his eyes. You could *see* how important this had been to him. Words were almost unimportant in that moment. How appreciative he was, it was written all over his face.

I'd never met his father. Had heard the stories and even without hearing them. It would be a fair conclusion for *anyone* to make were they to conclude that Eddy Ramirez - being one part of the head of a Colombian cartel - must've been an absolute cold blooded loco motherf**ker and, whether you were his son or not, someone that you should probably avoid angering them.

'I will NEVER forget this, Pedro. *Never*, hermano.'

The pair of us sat down on the sofa and had a drink while I told Roman how things had went down at the hotel. The police presence that was waiting around the lobby on him appearing, the planned knock on his door from a 'waiter,' right up to me being stopped on my way out with the bottle of scotch.

'YOU STOOD THERE AND TOLD THEM THAT THE BOTTLE WAS FOR A BUSINESS ASSOCIATE???'

He sat there with a huge smile, picturing the scene.

'AND I'M THE BUSINESS ASSOCIATE! THE PERSON THAT THEY WERE LOOKING FOR?! YOU F**KING LOCO, PEDRO'

He exploded into laughter.

'Well, it *was* the truth, wasn't it? I laughed back.

He told me that I had made a friend for life in him, through what I had done *for* him. Just being in possession of the bottle of Macallan lifted the dark cloud that had been hanging over the kid from before and it wasn't long before we were agreeing to go out and revert back to the original plan of me showing him around the city.

In a night that just wouldn't end I showed him the sights and assaulted all his senses with as much as Amsterdam could throw at him, something he took head on like an absolute warrior. There's been many a man defeated by that city and found themselves back in their hotel room earlier than they'd planned but Roman took all that it had to throw at him and was still standing there asking for more by the end of it.

I didn't exactly envy the kid having to fly back to South America the next again afternoon though, due to the state that we were both in from the night (and subsequent morning) before. While nothing had been confirmed to me. Hakan had told me - in a call the night before - that until all avenues had been explored, Mursel should now be treated as a potential rat. The only three people who *knew* Roman was staying there had been him, I and then Mursel, when he dropped the visitor off at The Grand. There may have been another reason for the police sting - and that was something he was getting to work on in finding out - but until we knew for sure, tasks like taking a narco drug lord's kid to the airport was now off the menu for Mursel.

I'd agreed that with Roman staying at mines over the night it would've made sense if I, personally, took him back to Schipol for his flight. Poor kid was still drunk when I dropped him off at departures although, and I'm not that proud to admit, his driver was not much better in that respect.

After multiple hugs and handshakes - alongside what felt was going to be an endless series of thank you's for ensuring that he wasn't arrested by the authorities and then after that, returning back for his dad's present - off he went. Saying he'd see me soon as he headed into the airport to check in.

Manny - And did you see Roman again soon?

Peter - Well, that's the thing. When someone says that they'll see you soon. You kind of take that as a general and non committal thing on their, or your, part. *Especially* when they're a person that you've never met before until a few days previously, and who lives in another continent.

Roman went back home and we got on with our day to day business. Hakan almost had himself a heart attack when he heard how close Roman had come to being arrested by the Dutch police. Telling me that with Roman here in the city - as our guest - *we* were responsible for his safety and wellbeing and that had the kid been arrested under our watch it might well have caused some friction with the Ramirez brothers. Still, alls well that ends well, eh, Manfred? Well, if that *was* the end, of course. Which it wasn't.

Following Roman going back to Colombia we - in Amsterdam - got back to business. Even had another shipment from Bogota arrive a few months after his visit. Not anywhere as near as the one that had prompted Hakan to splash out on the Macallan but a decent Maersk container delivery that was more than enough to keep operations ticking over.

It was at the end of this deal - once the container had arrived in Rotterdam and Hakan had arranged the final installment of the transfer - where the call came for me to travel to Bogota.

Manny - Who was it from Bogota that called you?

Peter - I never received one from anyone on that side. I was simply told by Hakan that the Ramirez brothers had personally asked about me and - through their talks - had requested that Hakan put me on a plane to Colombia to visit them. Most questions that I asked the Turk, in relation to this, were met with

'I don't know.'

I'd already learned of what a crazy, unpredictable and violent country Colombia was - due to the cartels - and how it was in danger of becoming a lawless narco state if things escalated any further there. I'll be honest. I wasn't exactly jumping with joy over the request.

And expressed as much to a Hakan not exactly too sympathetic towards my viewpoint.

Yilmaz, telling me that as good friends as him and I were and that he would always have my back, in all ways. *This* did not extend to standing up to another criminal organisation on my behalf. We ended up having what could diplomatically be classed as a 'heated debate' where I accused him of being my 'friend' only up to the point that he had to choose to *continue* to be my friend or choose to step aside and go with where the money was coming from.

He, instead, tried to put it across that the relationship between the Turks and Colombians was a lot more than just financial and - without actually saying the words outright - painted the picture of when Bogota says jump, Amsterdam asks how high.

There was no choice in the matter for me.

The tickets were booked, for the next day.

AMS - BOG

I was going, whether I wanted to or not.

Chapter 12

El Corazon Valiente - The Ballad of Peter Duncan <small>cont</small>

Manny - How did you find Colombia? This was late Eighty Eight, yes?

Peter - God, was it hot, stiflingly so. There's your first impression of Colombia. Hottest part of the world I'd been to had been Magaluf on a two week holiday but Bogota was another level of heat. The moment the doors to the plane opened I was almost scared to *leave* it, knowing what was waiting outside for me.

Manny - The meeting with the Ramirez brothers?

Peter - The heat, Manfred. Do keep up. Next to dealing with that heat the meeting with Eddy and German was a piece of cake.

I was dropped off at the Hyatt by the driver who had collected me at El Dorado airport. In his flat cap and Hawaiian shirt, he was hardly the stuff of chauffeured driver but was friendly enough and had much better English in his locker than I did Spanish. He dropped me with the instructions that he would be back for me around eight to take me to Eddy's ranch where there was a party taking place in the evening. *That* would be where I would meet the brothers.

He was as good as his word and was there on the dot to pick me up. On the drive there he explained that the party planned was Eddy's annual pre Christmas bash that he'd been holding since moving into the ranch. The one night of the year where Eddy Ramirez would shamelessly showcase his wealth - in full - to all of his friends, business associates and a select group who were on the Ramirez Cartel 'payroll.'

There was me thinking that it had been laid on for the visitor from Europe, as well.

After a while - on the drive - he took a turn off the main road which then had us travelling down a narrow dirt track with well worn tyre trails that he himself followed in his car. Eventually we came to a small gatehouse of sorts where around half a dozen guards with rifles strapped around them stood. Three on either side of the road. He slowed down for them so that they could get a look at him and I before - recognising the driver - waving us past. Lowering the gate back down again behind us after we had passed.

We drove on for around another mile or so before the sprawling ranch came into view. I mean, you could hardly *miss* the place. It was no farmers house, this. Reaching the entrance to the ranch we had to negotiate our way past another series of guards before the large metal doors swung open for us to drive on in.

The first thing that struck me was the amount of cars that were parked inside there, and the actual models themselves. Any high end Italian or German sports-car that wasn't there then I hadn't been able to spot. And I knew my sports-cars. There had to be another way in and out to the ranch as the cars parked up would've had no chance of negotiating the dirt road that we'd just came down.

Out the car now, the driver, led me through the 'car park' towards the direction of the sound of a mariachi band playing and up a series of steps, which took you directly towards the back of the housing complex. Looking down onto it, there was so much going on that I didn't know what should hold my attention the most.

In the middle of everything - and from the benefit of the aerial view from my position - was a kidney shaped swimming pool with guests either sitting, standing around or dancing in the warm night air. The mariachi band playing on a stage in the corner. Bottles of booze and cereal sized bowls of Cocaine sitting on each table. Revelers drinking and sniffing away until their hearts were content. Page three stunners in high heels, thongs and nothing more, dancing around the pool with anyone who would look twice at them.

It was *everything* I'd ever dreamed of.

I didn't know it - in that moment - but I was looking down on everyone and every *thing* that made the Colombian narco world go around. There were representatives there from Medellin, including the man himself, Pablo Escobar. Cali, too. Both the Rodriguez Orejuela brothers, along with Helmer 'Pacho' Herrera. With the exception of Escobar - who really hadn't heard of him? - I hadn't heard of any of the others, or the contingent that had come from Sinaloa, along with other Mexican cartels. *All*, however, turning out to be names that - while not impressive to me at the time, that first night - I would look back on and shake my head over them all being in the same place, without any blood shed. Pacho Herrera, however it must be said was the only one - considering the money that they evidently all had - who stuck out to me as 'stylish' and someone who befitted the image, my image, of a high level drug dealer. As my time with the Bogota Cartel was to progress, though. I'd soon find that clothes were not as important to cartel bosses as I'd have believed so.

Even later on that night, though - when I'd been introduced to most of the various cartels by Eddy Ramirez - I still hadn't grasped the realities of all of these groups being in the same building, having a good old knees up. By the time I did, years later, things had changed between all of the cartels. The stakes had been raised beyond all recognition of the earlier days when they were all on the come up and as a result those parties - extending past Eddy or German's own personal group of friends - were, by then, a thing of the past.

The driver had literally just said to me that he was going to take me to find Eddy when I heard a loud

'PEDRO, MI HERMANO'

And was grabbed by Roman. A bottle of Club Colombia beer in his hand and the biggest and warmest of smiles for me. Grabbing my hand up high and then pulling me in for a hug.

'So happy that you came. I told father all about you and he wanted to meet you.'

I was instantly at ease after that. I knew that I hadn't personally done anything purposely to cause any annoyance to the Bogota Cartel but you know? The mind can play tricks on you. Hakan had told me that this kind of a request had never been made from Colombia before so he had no real point of reference to provide me with. Part of me had worried that - without me even realising or appreciating - Roman had told me something, when he was in Amsterdam, that he possibly shouldn't have done and *this* was why I was now being requested to come and see them over. And that it would be the reason why I would not be using the return ticket for the flight back to Holland. It was irrational but so was the thought of a notorious criminal enterprise like the Ramirez Cartel asking to see you in person.

Roman told the driver that he would personally take things from there and for him to go ahead and now enjoy the night. The kid steering us away from the party down at the lower level and back in the direction of the large hacienda that looked down over it.

The insides of the place were dripping in garish gold and extravagantly large paintings. Whether the taste of things was questionable, - to say the least - as a display of wealth to any visitor, it was off the hook.

'Come this way, hermano.' Roman said, leading me towards a room with its door closed. Reminding me as we went that him and I were going to party 'like diablos' once my meeting with his father and uncle was over. After what I'd just witnessed going on outside. I'd been left in no position to disagree with that assessment.

Manny - What was your first impression of Eddy and German Ramirez upon being introduced?

Peter - Well I thought that they were *twins* at first, due to them having the same mustaches. When Roman opened the door to lead us into that side room. *That* was my first impression. Oh shit, twins. As if my life isn't any complicated as things are already standing, *now* I've got to worry about getting two narco bosses names right.

The smiles that the pair of them had on me entering the room with Roman were the stuff that could have generated Bogota's city grid for weeks. Completely putting me at ease straight away.

Manny - You *were* aware that these two men, with the warm smiles, were - by Nineteen Eighty Eight - responsible for the deaths of hundreds of people either directly or indirectly though, right?

Peter - Oh, yeah, of course I did but in that position sitting there in Eddy's office, what did you want *me* to do about it? Citizens arrest the pair of them and march them right out through the party, past their sicarios, steal a car and drive to the nearest policia station with them? Look, I *knew* their reputation before I travelled to meet with them. Knew it while I sat there and spoke cordially with them and certainly knew it when I ended up joining their operation.

The brothers could not have been any nicer, though, and I appreciate there will be others who cannot say the same, but this is about me so I can only tell you how it was, on a personal level.

Eddy poured me an extra large glass of scotch. I didn't notice or think to ask if it was *the* scotch although, it would've been pretty weird of him had it been and him not mention it. Given the history between me and that bottle.

Meanwhile German is opening up a cigar box which was filled with Cuban cigars.

'Bolivar Belicoso Fino. Muy muy bueno' he said, urging me to take one from the box.

Next, it was a marble ornament being pushed over in my direction along with the instructions to take some of what was inside out for myself.

I wasn't displeased by the offer of a livener of a line of Coke - following my flight out of Amsterdam and the jet lag it had caused - but to sit there, in the office of a Colombian drug lord, sniffing Cocaine. It was almost a parody of itself. Still, I took German up on the offer.

Following this, the brothers - German using either his brother or Roman to translate for him - sat and explained their reason for bringing me to Bogota. You know? Out of all possibilities, I'd never even *considered* that it would be because they wanted to offer me a job?!

Well, if 'offered' is what you could call the *correct* term, of course?

Through the mix of German, Eddy and Roman it was put across to me that - as a direction the cartel was heading in - the game was starting to change for them. They'd recognised that there was a lot more, billions more, money out there to be made if they were to spread their wings a little further. Look in corners of the world that their Colombian counterparts had not looked. This would mean a new strategy - along with restructuring - for certain areas of the business.

Eddy laid out - in great detail and with a large amount of Cocaine assisted passion - their plans which would see the narcotics side of things continue but with an expansion also into arms trading. German explaining that with the network that they had built up - in addition to arms and drugs going hand in hand together - they believed that there was a global market waiting to be exploited.

Their sources of arms from as diverse locations around the world such as the Colombian jungles to the American inner cities with the Middle East and Russia tucked in between.

But they needed a man on the outside of Colombia. Someone that they could trust implicitly to do business, on their behalf, with the Ramirez Brothers name behind them. Something that they didn't have, or even need, due to how their business was meticulously run.

If things were to run as smoothly as they wanted them too they would need to bring someone in, a gringo.

'We want someone who is not South American appearance. You understand? Someone who isn't already on the DEA watchlist from our organisation. A person who can move between countries without lighting up the alert systems of the agencies who already want to take us down. Someone who has the personality and the character to fit into any situation that they find themselves, and that we place them in but also someone European. Someone who people will look at and *not* think Colombian cartel.'

At this point German interrupted. Battering away at a frightening speed in Spanish.

'Si, si,' Eddy said

'My brother is saying that we did not invite you over just so that you could visit the famous Eddy Ramirez annual Navidad party. That - following Roman's story of what happened in Amsterdam - we have looked into you. And we liked what we saw. You're loyal. Know when and how to do your jail time, if it comes. Enterprising, our good friend Hakan testified to that. That despite being an outsider in the Turkish mafia that you worked hard, brought money in and are someone that he trusted from day one and had never seen anything to contradict those thoughts.'

I put my hands together in a praying sort of gesture and looked towards German, offering him a sincere 'gracias'

That was when Roman butted in for the first time. His inclination - probably wisely - to sit there and let his father and uncle hold court.

'What you did for me in Amsterdam, and my father, Pedro. *That* is the reason that you are here. You barely even knew me, had only met me briefly for lunch earlier on in the day, yet you saved my ass later on as if I was one of your boys. And after that, despite the heat that was lying back there at the hotel with all of the Federales, you went *back* there and risked bringing big problems onto yourself and got the bottle for father.'

'The rest of what father and uncle found out about you afterwards only confirmed to them that you were the man that I told them you were.'

Eddy sat there with a great big smile at the mention of the Macallan story. Giving me a small round of applause for my efforts that evening.

By the time that they were done talking me through the position that they wanted me to fill, and all that entailed which pretty much added up to be a fixer, mover and shaker who could conduct business on their behalf pretty much anywhere they needed me to be, outside of Colombia. All the money that I was going to make and the level of lifestyle that I was going to be moving into. The hacienda that they would put me into - in Bogota - where I'd live, when not out of the country working.

They'd thought of it *all*. Completely seduced by their pitch. By the time they were finished speaking, and I had done asking questions, the only further question I was left with was.

'When do I start?'

The answer coming only a few weeks later when handed my first business trip to Inglewood, California. A place that if I hadn't already heard of - I hadn't - I would *never* forget the name of it for the rest of my life - I didn't.

Chapter 13

El Corazon Valiente - The Ballad of Peter Duncan cont

Manny - You moved over, to Colombia, permanently. Following the visit to Ramirez's ranch.

Peter - Technically, I never *left* again, after that first meeting. It wasn't as if I needed to serve my period of notice with Hakan. I didn't have much in the way of belongings back in Amsterdam apart from my clothes but they were hardly pieces that you'd have travelled continents and thousands of miles to specifically collect to bring back with you.

Knowing this. Eddy had Roman take me out in the centre of Bogota to visit some of the tailors and boutiques that they would often go to, so that I could be taken care of for clothes. Everything going on the cartel 'company account' with instructions to get as much as I needed as well as some suits that I'd be requiring for when away on business. Any other clothes, I would pick up as and when - on my dollar - once my money started to come in.

The brothers had been as good as their word, in relation to the hacienda that I was to stay at. A beautiful and secluded classic old stone building with swimming pool outside. I almost had to pinch myself that it was all happening, to be honest about it all. The place was already filled with furniture. Even had food in the fridge and cupboards. Almost as if they already knew that I was going to say yes to their proposition which, to be fair, they probably did.

I spent the night of the Christmas party at the ranch. There wasn't much sleep going on across the place that evening - not with all the sex, dancing and narcotics going on, there wasn't - so a bedroom was barely required but one was supplied to me all the same.

The next morning. The mariachi band long gone by then but several party goers were still there mulling around the pool, all be it without the same levels of energy that they were radiating the night before. I was given a stack of dollars that would've choked Escobar's hippopotamus and told by Eddy that him and German would let me settle into my new home and be in touch soon with me regarding business but in the shorter term to expect Roman to come by and pick me up and help me with obtaining a new wardrobe for myself as well as giving me my first look at the city.

Manny - You mentioned Inglewood, California. For your first business trip. What was that in connection with?

Peter - Inglewood? Inglewood Inglewood it's all good. It was a bloody baptism of fire, that's what Inglewood was. While it was the first time for me to go out there and show the Ramirez brothers what I was capable of it was by no means some kind of a test that they had put out for me, like the Turks had done. There was *no* test with the Colombians. You already *passed* their test by being let into their secretive operation. They already *know* that you're their man before they put you in place, even if - sat there in that run down trap house surrounded by Inglewood Crips, questioning (with a mocking tone) me about what would happen if they didn't pay up any fees due to my bosses in Bogota - you're not even too sure of *yourself.*

I knew that it wasn't a test and that things - moving forward - were always going to have the potential to throw up the unexpected, dangerous and at times most frightening of turns of events. Eddy had more or less told me upfront that the role was going to bring this into my world.

The main crux of my duties involved representing the Ramirez interests, wherever they needed me to. Making sure that shipments were on track to arrive outside of Colombia, receiving and delivering payments, smooching politicians, cops and - vitally - our contacts at the various ports with the necessary bribes in addition to meeting with potential buyers and sellers of both product and or arms.

While Eddy had told me that the bribing, wining and dining of the politicians and top cops would be relatively easy - which it was - the other side of the coin would be that I would have to meet with other less than gracious people. The types that due to the level of illegal activity that they were engaging in they were suspicious of pretty much anyone outside their closest of circles. These people would make for - at times - challenging, dangerous and naturally hostile opponents in trying to see the job through to its finish.

'You may face anger, suspicion and antagonism from some. Deal with drunken Irish terrorists one day and unpredictable Dutch biker gangs the next. Los Angeles gang bangers who would shoot you dead without a seconds pause, to loco Mexicans who will chop you up and hide you in a mattress like money. But I know that you are the one to handle these people. Your strength of character, personality and the power of the Ramirez name behind you. You will not fail, amigo.'

Eddy had said, with a touch of the ominous to how much potentially lay ahead.

I had made sure to remind Eddy - in the initial meeting - that I was not a violent man in any sense of the word and that if they needed someone with those kind of skills then unfortunately I would need to pass. This, waved away by both Eddy and Roman - and then German after having this translated - on the subject.

'No no no, Peter. You are our fixer. Our man in a suit. Your mouth is your gun. Your personality the bullets. There is no need for violence from you. And in any case. With the work that you will do for us. If things were to ever turn nasty you will be in the room alone with our associates so, regardless of if you are violent man or not. You'll be killed in such a situation, anyway.'

Manny - Reassuring, isn't it?

Peter - Oh, very, Manfred. Very.

Regardless, I was glad to be put to work and earn myself some stretch. Plus, I was going out of my mind with boredom, stuck there at the hacienda. On the surface of it all. Being in a warm country with your own swimming pool. It seems a no brainer that you'd spend your days lazing by the side of the pool getting a tan, which I did, for a few days. It *does* get a bit boring after a while, though. TV was no good either due to none of the channels being English speaking. Even in those earliest of days though I saw that if I was to survive and exist in Bogota, in any meaningful way, I would *need* to learn Spanish. Something that I wasted no time in getting started with. I began straight away. Even even listening to self taught Spanish tapes on my Sony Walkman flying up from Bogota to LAX for my first business trip that Eddy and German sent me on.

Manny - Which was Inglewood, to meet with some gang members. What was the reason for that?

Peter - Bogota had learned of some 'technical difficulties' that had arisen between a gang of Crips out of Inglewood - called Imperial Village - and the Medellin Cartel. Something regarding a shipment that never reached LA but one that the Crips had paid the majority of in advance. Upon hearing on its non arrival Escobar had told them that he'd be happy to arrange another shipment to them, but that they would need to pay again. Skipping to the end. This had led to word coming out that the Crips were now in the market for a new supplier.

Through this development. I was dispatched off to Los Angeles to meet one of the Ramirez operatives, stationed over there, and collect a goodwill gesture of one kilo of Cocaine that I was to hand deliver to Inglewood. While there, I was to get them to agree for the brothers to become their new supplier of product.

Manny - On the surface of things, not too difficult a task. I've studied narco and inner city gang culture long enough to know that there wouldn't be many gangs out there who would say no to the offer of free product.

Peter - Well it wasn't, on the surface of things, anyway. *Under* the surface was an entirely different proposition waiting for me, altogether. Meeting Hector - the cartel LA operative - had been no problems. The Ramirez man meeting me at the airport when my flight from Bogota had touched down at LAX.

He'd been mildly annoyed - not at myself - over the fact that my United Airlines flight had been delayed by two hours due to engine problems that had been discovered in Bogota. *This* in turn led to him missing his flight to Las Vegas that was leaving from the same airport as I was arriving at. Now messing his plans to get the shipment from LA to Vegas he'd told me that he was now going to have to drive almost three hundred miles over night so that he'd be in Vegas for the meet that had been arranged by Eddy and German. Had my flight arrived - when scheduled for - he'd have had nothing other than a quick two minute meeting with me to hand over the briefcase containing the kilo of Cocaine and then be off on his travels to Vegas baby.

Through this, he was able to offer me a lift to my hotel before getting himself back on the 'freeway' and on his way to Nevada. An offer I snapped up as it meant that I would be able to quiz him on things regarding the brothers and the American side of the operation as well as ask if he had any tips with regards to the piece of business that I was in town to conduct myself. On the drive to my hotel. Hector told me that, like the other prominent Colombian and Mexican organisations, the Bogota Cartel had men positioned in all of the major American states and cities. *That* was why he was going to Vegas. To provide a re-up of supplies to the Ramirez men hustling in that particular state.

Manny - And did Hector - and I will go on and make the assumption that you are speaking of Hector Carillo, now serving a life sentence in Rikers Island through multiple felonies, as part of his own interstate role within the Ramirez Cartel's U.S operations - have any advice for you in terms of how to deal with the Crips from Inglewood?

Peter - You know? Even though I met him a few more times after my first trip to Los Angeles I never *did* find out his second name. Sounds very much like the man, though. As for any advice he might've had for me? No, not much. Actually he laughed at me - in the car - when I asked him if there had been any advice that he could provide me with.

'Listen, brother. These negro gangbangers are CRAZY. They shoot you dead in a second if they don't like you. They make Los Angeles look like, well, Colombia, with the way they treat the cost of life. I was surprised when German call and tell me that he was setting up a meet with the Crips, or Bloods, they're all the same whatever the colour they wear. Word on the street is that they stood up to Escobar and he don't do a thing about it. German is the patron, though, so what he says, comprende?'

I found myself becoming more concerned about my evening in Inglewood with every single word that Hector spilled out in connection with the gang I was scheduled to meet with.

'Your accent, Peter? It is different. I do not know it? Where from?' He asked as he pulled off the freeway. Telling me that the hotel wasn't too far away now.

'Scotland, Hector. I'm Scottish.' I confirmed back.

'Ahhhh I was so, so close. I thought you were Australian.' he laughed.

'Well you were only around nine thousand miles out, pal. Close enough, I'd say, eh?' I joked back in return.

'Scotland, though. Woo weee and now you're here in LA, working for the jefes and meeting with cold blooded killers. You're a long way from castles and lake monsters now, amigo. Well, maybe not the monsters part.'

Manny - Oh yeah, we have monsters here in America too, only ours are apparently amphibious.

Peter - Ah, I see you know your monsters well, Manfred. Hector really wasn't joking when he said about me being a long way from home. If I hadn't appreciated the change in environment when I was showering and relaxing in my suite at the Beverley Hills Hotel I most definitely noticed the 'change' in environment when the taxi was taking me down Nectarine Street, Inglewood.

Despite being in nothing other than a non-descript LA taxi, the whole street seemed to stop what it was doing when the car cruised slowly down the road, towards the house where the Crips were waiting on me. I thought I was seeing things at first when I noticed someone on top of a house roof, staring straight at the car and then making some kind of call-whistle. Around a dozen houses later I then saw - on the other side of the road - *another* gang member, on the roof, watching every movement of the taxi from his viewpoint.

The cab driver himself, a short and stocky Mexican called Raphael was, at first, reluctant to take the ride from Beverley Hills to Inglewood. Especially since I was requesting that he waited outside for me to return from my meeting. I'd already learned that it was not a place to be left hanging around outside waiting on transport. I had to bribe him with an extra large tip, in advance, before he would even pull away from the hotel. This, a concept, that due to some of the more questionable destinations I would ask to be driven to I would experience with cab drivers all over the world.

Him telling me that he wouldn't normally go to Inglewood.

Yes, me too, pal. Me too.

The brief that I'd been given was to go to 1413 Nectarine Street and - when asked - say that I had a meeting arranged with 'Shade.' This one name, I had been informed by Eddy before leaving Bogota, was the one that would open doors for you in the area of Inglewood. Same went for if I was to encounter any problems from anyone else in the neigbourhood, prior to reaching the trap house.

'Just tell them that you're there to meet with Shade.'

With a friendly reminder to Raphael the driver that I would have his 'f**king license revoked' if he was to leave me stranded there in the middle of Inglewood, I took myself the deepest of breaths and grabbed the briefcase from the floor and exited the car.

A couple of gang members stood at the bottom of the path leading up to number 1413.

'Are you the guy?' One of them - a young kid with no top on and the baggiest of jeans that were managing to stay up by the collection of magic and the kid's mind power. Hanging from out of one of the back pockets was a blue and white bandana which indicated that, at the very least, I was on the right turf.

'I'm here to see Shade.' I replied, lifting the briefcase slightly high enough for me to tap it with a few fingers.

They both looked me up and down a few moments more before - and without any further words being spoken by any of the three of us - the other one stretched over to unhook the gate, swinging it open while - at the same time - the two of them stood aside for me.

You could already hear the blaring hip hop music from inside. Double or triple glazing, this homestead clearly did not have. This, at least, gave me a minor window into what it was going to be like when the door opened. I'd already assumed that they'd had someone watching the outside of the house because there was no way that anyone inside was hearing my feeble door knocks. Even so, it opened almost immediately.

Standing there on the other side of the threshold was a mountain of a man. Blue bandana on his head with a pair of sunglasses covering his eyes. Red and white Chicago Bulls basketball top along with the baggy jeans and Timberland boots look of his man over by the gate.

'What you want, fool?' He said with a bit of arrogance behind it, pulling his sunglasses to the edge of his nose and looking me up and down from over them.

The two of us looked and dressed like polar opposites. On my side I was wearing a light cream Hugo Boss summer suit along with a pair of fresh out the box leather Gucci loafers that I'd picked up in the centre of Bogota during my spending spree and like him, a pair of shades, even if the light had started to go down on the city and they were technically no longer in requirement.

'I'm here to see Shade.' I repeated the same simple sentence that had granted me entrance from the street.

There was then an awkward silence. The magic sentence that had worked so well the first time did not appear to be working.

'I'm here from Colombia.' I said, once again, tapping the briefcase to indicate that there was something inside for Shade.

'COLOMBIA? N***a you aint from Colombia. Stood there in yo fancy suit with yo wack Irish accent. Smell you a mile away, n***a. Five O motherf**ker.'

It was in this moment - despite never having faced such a situation, well not in that exact way - that I realised that I was going to have to give a bit back to earn even the most remote piece of respect from men like this. Sure if it went wrong I'd have ended up being shot in the face but if it went the way that I was hoping it was going to go, then it would've been worth the risk.

'Look, pal. I don't know who Shade *is* but I was told that he was at this address. I've f**king flown here from Bogota to come *specifically* to 1413 Nectarine Street. Now from what I understand, Shade *also* knows that I'm coming to meet with him, along with a free kilo of product. Like I said, I don't know who he is but if I was him I would be enormously pissed off if I was to find out that one of my men had turned away the guy who was bringing me twenty grand's worth of product for free. I don't know, you'll know him better so maybe I'm wrong and he'd be completely chill about passing up the chance to make some extra paper, free of charge to him.'

This threw him for a moment until he decided that he might want to take a different approach.

'Yo best step your ass inside, and bring that briefcase with you too, fool.'

He ushered me inside. You couldn't even hear yourself think with the bass that was banging off the walls. He, walking behind me, took me down the small hall - in the direction of where the music was coming from.

'In you go.' He said nodding his head towards me and the partially opened door ahead.

Gingerly, I pressed it slowly open, enough for me to see into the room, before walking in myself. There looked to be around half a dozen more gang members sitting around inside what appeared to be the living room. It wasn't what you would class as 'homely' but for a trap house - used only for the purposes of storing and moving product - then I guess, it served its purpose.

As I walked fully into the room, with the bandana man closely following behind, I could now see that there were a couple of Crips playing what appeared to be an American Football video game on TV. The pair of them sitting on a sofa that had yet to have its clear cellophane cover removed from it.

'BOOM' One of them said, standing up and throwing a gang sign in his homey's face. The other dropping the console controller out of his hands in disgust at what had just transpired on screen.

A third gang member was sat on the same sofa, staring ahead onto the table in front of him while he sat preparing a joint. A mountain of low grade broken up Mexican brick weed sitting on a tray in front of him along with Zig Zag papers and roach books.

One stood stationed by the window that looked back out onto Nectarine Street, operating as a look out while the other two in the room were over in the corner. One sat in a large armchair messing around with - what looked like - the same Grand Sky Pager as Eddy had gifted to me before heading off to LA.

If he's managing to work it better than I've done so far then fair play to the man, I thought to myself as I watched him with it in his hand. The last man in the house was standing hovering over the man in the chair watching what was coming up on the pager.

Once my presence had been felt inside the living room. Sega Genesis, pagers, what was going on outside on the main street. They were all forgotten about when that first gang member - followed by the rest of them - looked up and saw me.

His first instinct on seeing this stranger in the house being to drop the pager and in one smooth movement - from the side of his chair - pick up a - from my brief and unofficial induction period back in Bogota I'd recognised as - Mac-10 submachine gun and instantly pointed it in my direction.

I thought he was going to pull the trigger, I really did. The look on his face, the surprise, the panic. *Everything* about his whole demeanor screamed that he was going to act first and question later.

'YO, WHO THE F**K ARE YOU COMING ROLLING INTO MY CRIB, FOOL?'

He shouted in my direction. In what was possibly a knee jerk reaction, another couple of the members inside the room had also reached for their guns and now also had them trained on me.

I'm standing there - still holding onto the briefcase - with my hands in the air screaming 'COLOMBIA COLOMBIA COLOMBIA' as if I was a soccer supporter and urgently telling them that I wasn't armed and not to shoot.

'YO YO YO YO, I LET THE N***A IN. HE'S THE *'MAN,'* SHADE. HE SAID YOU'RE EXPECTING HIM.'

The voice behind me screamed out, a little spooked by his man's reaction.

'Shade,' who I had taken to be the one in the corner with the pager - without lowering his submachine gun - looked over and past me towards the big mountain that had let me into the house.

'He's right. I've been sent here to give you a present from South America.'

I seized on the chance to continue down this road while it appeared that the guy with the Mac-10 was possibly now *not* going to shoot me.

He gave me that same suspicious look that I'd been given at the door when I'd said I was there on behalf of Bogota. It was enough, at least, for him to lower his gun and remove myself from its line of vision. He looked to the side towards the others who had guns drawn and motioned for them to lower them too.

'Phew, that was a bit exciting, there, eh?' I said, trying to make light out of the fact that I had come closer than I'd have liked to have been left with holes in my body.

It wasn't until I'd ended up back at the hotel that night - when thinking back over what had happened in Inglewood - that I'd realised that it had been the first time that I'd ever had a gun pulled on me. Sure, as part of working for Zippy - and then Hakan - I had *seen* guns but had never seen one actually used and certainly hadn't had the misfortune of having one pointed at me. Having now experienced it. I was able to say with a degree of authority that it is truly frightening what goes through your head when you are seconds from death. It's not the thoughts that you would *like* to be thinking of in that moment, which may be your final thoughts.

In a perfect world you would be able to think of those - in those last moments - that you love and the things that made life truly worth living. Instead, though. You end up with the most irrational and unexplainable types of thoughts like what will happen to your belongings back at the hotel after you've been killed and whether Coca Cola will ever put Cocaine back into its recipe again.

'N***a, I can smell you from here. You aint from *Colombia*, officer. This motherf**ker here thinks we all tripping up in this place.'

The one in the armchair said, looking around to everyone who all began laughing along with him.

Again with the copper stuff?

'I never said that I was *from* Colombia I said that I was here *for* Colombia. I've been sent with something for you, which I believe you know about?'

He sat there looking me up and down, stroking his chin and appearing deep in thought.

'Yo, Gumbo, search this motherf**cker for a wire cause I aint saying a damn thing further until I know if this n***a is on the real.'

I knew the drill, spreading my arms up and out while parting my legs. If ever he wanted to get out of the drug business there would certainly have been a career with the TSA waiting for him because that search was the most stringent that I'd ever had in my life. If I'd been wired up. He'd have found it.

'He's clear.' Gumbo said, taking a few steps back away from me again.

'Yeah, I knew I had a, what was it your man put it down as?, A gesture of good faith towards doing business together in the future? What I *didn't* know was that I was going to have some FBI or DEA looking fool in my house 'bringing' me the good faith.'

'And yet, here we are, eh?' I said with a bit confidence and swagger which completely masked the fact that I was a nervous wreck. You don't recover from coming that close to being riddled with bullets from some unpredictable psychopaths in the blink of an eye. Even now that the guns had been lowered, there was no certainty towards how the rest of this was all going to go.

'So would you like to see what I've brought for you or not?' I said, shaking the suitcase in my right hand.

'Hell yeah, n***a. Break out that shit.' The one in the armchair who - by then - needed no formal introduction as 'Shade' responded positively. Appearing to be a lot more relaxed than he had been on my entrance.

'Yo, B, move you ass up and let the man sit down.' He barked over to one of the teenagers - that had been sitting playing Sega - for him to move over and allow me to sit down and put the briefcase on the table in front of me.

There was still an uneasiness to the room but - as I was soon to go on to learn - there would generally *always* be an element of uneasiness to proceedings with the people that Eddy and German would put me in touch with.

I sat down beside a kid wearing a Cleveland Cavaliers cap with a flat bill that I swear could've carried a couple of pints of lager on it, a white vest and Calvin Klein boxer shorts to match.

'Here, hit this.' He tried to pass me the joint that was in his hand. With absolutely no clue what was even inside it - in my mind, grass was not a one hundred percent cast iron guarantee - I thanked him but told the kid that I needed to do business on a clear head and turned back towards Shade. I wanted to be out of there as soon as possible and that wouldn't be achieved if I sat around smoking *whatever* was inside the kid's joint. Grass, Cocaine, PCP, whatever. Despite the Mexican brick that was lying out, I hadn't seen the teenager actually touch any of it.

'You know that if you're Five O you aint leaving this house alive. We clear on that, fool?'

Shade said to me - as I was fumbling with getting the case open - as if it was the most natural thing in the world and akin to telling someone that they're going to the shops.

Even the merest suggestion that I wouldn't leave that house again had me fighting heart palpitations.

'I'm not the police, pal. I'm someone whose done a piece of jail time in Scotland, decided to move abroad and through some improbable turns of events over the years has ended up with an employer in South America. Which has seen to it that I'm stood here in your house this evening. Trust me, you don't appear to want me here but, and with the greatest of respect to you all, I don't really *want* to be here in Inglewood either.'

He just sat there and looked across the table at me, measuring what he was going to say or do next.

'Telling you, Shade. This n***a is the po-lees. He aint no motherf**king product dealer.'

The one that had been standing looking out onto the street broke his silence. The whole of the room turning to him.

'N***a SHUT THE F**K UP. I'm thinking here.'

Shade shouted, shutting the man down, leaving him visibly scolded as he stared down at the floor to escape everyones gaze.

'Well, here's my problem. What's your name?'

Shade asked. Shit? No one had told me about whether I was to mention *my* name to who I was doing business with. Common sense dictating that I should probably *not* use my real name, just to make sure.

'Steven.' I replied, while finding myself with a sudden sweep of sadness over the fact that my mind had tried to pluck out the last time that I had saw Stevie's face, and, in that moment, came up with a blank.

'Well. Steven. Here's what I'm bugging out on. Someone contacts me out of the blue. Offering to give me a key to do with as I please. That's already a bit of a red flag because who in their right mind gives away thousands of dollars worth of Cocaine? And *then* a bacon smelling motherf**ker like *you* shows up, with the product. If something seems too good to be true. Well, I'm sure you know the end of how that goes?'

In a way, I could understand his point of view. Had an operative - straight from Bogota - walked into that same house with the briefcase with the Cocaine inside it I'm sure the transaction would have went down a lot smoother. Either that or they would have all shot each other to death there inside the living room long ago. Still, Eddy and German said that they had done their homework on me - which when fully disclosed, I was staggered to see just how far their tentacles spread when it came to obtaining information on someone from so far away as Scotland - and that I was the type of person with the personality and the charisma to see these *exact* kind of jobs through to the finish, and get them over the line.

'I can't actually blame you for looking at it in that way. It *does* seem to be an awful lot of Cocaine to give away to someone for free but here's the thing, Shade. What a kilo of product is worth to you here in LA is only worth a fraction of back in Colombia. Compared to the levels of stock waiting to be shipped or almost through the production process in the labs. A kilo to a gang of Crips in Inglewood is peanuts. Something you would lose, it is so common. Like a set of keys.'

He continued to sit and listen.

'Now *why* did you receive the unexpected call offering you the product? Well that was discussed in the call so I believe you know why. We would like to take up the business that you had with

Medellin until you encountered issues. Call this complimentary kilo a try before you buy.'

Opening the briefcase I picked out the taped up package from inside and handed it over to him. He reached over and picked a small knife up from the table and carefully pressed the tip into the kilo until he was able to pull it back out again, along with a small dab of the white powder and without any messing around whatsoever, placed it under his right nostril and snorted it straight up.

'WOOOOOOO YEAH' He screamed as the pure Ye-Yo hit. He hadn't even given me a chance to tell him that is was uncut before he had snorted it so it was just as well that he'd only tried the smallest of samples.

'Oh yeah, it's much better than that Medellin shit. More pure, higher percentage. We have cooks from Peru, the very *best*.'

I said approvingly to match the smile on his face and entering salesman mode. The part about the Peruvian cooks was completely made up on the spot but sounded credible, in addition to giving me more a look of someone who knew what they were doing and talking about.

Soon, everyone - including me - had taken a small bump out of the kilo I'd delivered and were all talking the biggest amount of collective Cocaine nonsense, *none* of it connected to the business that I was there to conduct.

I tried to rein everyone back in by asking about the split with Medellin which wasn't one of my better moves as the mere mention of the Colombians changed the entire tone in the room. The Imperial Village had lost a lot of money through the previous deal that had gone wrong and the subject of Pablo Escobar was still very sore with them.

'That motherf**ker ever comes to LA ahmma put nine bullets in the n***a's head.'

The kid in the white vest and boxers said to the side of me.

'There's a list of thousand who would happily supply the bullets, pal.' I replied, before looking back at Shade, figuring that there's nothing like a common enemy to bring others together onto the same side.

Just because I'd walked in and presented them with around twenty thousand dollars worth of Cocaine *and* we both had a mutual dislike for Pablo Emilio Escobar Gaviria and his crew. This did not make me and the Crips inside that room the best of buddies. Until I left, I don't think Shade was ever going to believe, one hundred percent, that I wasn't an undercover cop and I wasn't one hundred percent that they weren't going to kill me.

'So you like the product then?' I asked, trying to get back to basics and strike a quick deal with them and be back in the taxi on the way to The Beverley Hills Hotel and the safety of my room, which I had absolutely no intention of leaving again until my flight back to Bogota the next afternoon.

'Shhhhiiiiiit, there aint nothing wrong with the product, fool. The *product* is fire. It's this f**ked up situation involving strangers showering me *with* the product which is causing me the issue. I gots a cuzz in Pelican Bay right now over a sting by the police *just like this*.'

'Well I don't know what else there is to say, pal. You have this house watched from all directions, I take it, so you'll already know that I came here, alone in a taxi - which on that subject, the longer I sit here the more the bill's going to be - there's no back up waiting around the corner for some kind of signal that I'm going to send them from the hidden wire that I'm not wearing.

Like all of us, I'm just a man trying to keep his hustle going because when that stops, then so does the money. I understand your need for to be vigilant. It's that which keeps us out of jail at the end of the day. In this game, you go with your gut and if your gut is telling you that you can't do business with me and my organisation then we will understand fully. We felt that you would be looking for a supplier that you could trust, given how things turned out with your previous one. You're obviously going to need product and that is something that we *always* have in mass quantities. My bosses will not take it personal, I assure you.'

'DON'T LISTEN TO THE N***A, HE TRYING TO PULL THAT MEL GIBSON LETHAL WEAPON PSYCHOLOGY SHIT ON YOU, BLOOD.'

The other kid who had been playing Sega leaned forward to shout at Shade.

I reached over towards the kilo that was sitting on the table and picked it up. Shade sat there watching me in silence. It was only when he saw me flipping the briefcase back open again that it seemed to dawn on him what I was about to do.

'And where yo going with the motherf**king product, fool?'

I looked back at him and - while answering - continued with putting the kilo back in the case again.

'Well, I assumed that if you can't trust if I'm police or not then you'd have to be crazy to accept an amount of drugs that - if I'm undercover and am about to have this house's door kicked down and twenty DEA officers run in with guns - will put you away for years from me. Let me take care of it so it's not left lying around here.'

By this point I had placed the Coke inside the briefcase and snapped it shut again.

'Ok, fool. Let's talk business.' He said, after a piece of deliberation.

I sat and took him through what my bosses could do for him - drugs and weapons wise - the quantities that we could have shipped to them and the sliding scale of prices, depending on what they would look to take on a regular basis.

For the first time inside there I could honestly have said that things were calm and relaxed. Shade listened when I spoke and I answered whatever questions he had for me. Some I didn't know the answer to but had been able to keep things ticking along with various bluffs here and there.

That calm was broken, however, when it came to me laying out the ground rules for payment. Explaining to them that whatever amount they would buy within a calendar month, payment would be due by the last day of that same month and that should payment not arrive on time that would complicate things such as the - which Eddy had ambiguously put as - 'late payment fees' that would be incurred, as a consequence.

This seemed to rile them although this was - I'd felt - based on more of their previous dealing with Escobar than it had been about any future venture with Bogota.

'But what's to stop us from just ordering a shipment from you and at the end of the month turning around and saying F**K YOU, SUDACA? We almost did that with Medellin to make up for the missing shipment that we didn't get. So yeah, Scatlan, what's to stop the Imperial Village taking what-ever-we-like from you, while we watch you not do a damn thing about it?'

'That's right, homey. You know how we Inglewood Crips do.' Shade found back up through one of the others to the side of me. I wasn't taking my eyes off him due to the hostile tone that had risen up to the surface again, though.

Things seemed to be on a knife edge and a pivotal point in the discussions. I knew that whatever words came out my mouth next had a fifty fifty chance of either improving the situation or sending it down a path I'd much rather it hadn't.

I would have to choose my next moments *super* carefully. Not just my words but the tone and body language. If I tell him that if he was to do such an idiotic thing - to burn a South American cartel - he would have a death squad visit him in the middle of night and kill him and the rest of his family. I'm not sure that kind of threatening tactic would've had the desired effect. Not inside that room.

I'd have to find a way to put it across to him that double crossing the Bogota Cartel would not be the good move that he might possibly have it down as and that yes, should he try that then he *would* find himself visited by a team of operatives that he'd be much better off not, but doing so in a way where *I* wouldn't have to be the one to tell him so, directly.

Due to my continued silence, he sat there with a satisfied and arrogant look on his face, no doubt sure that I literally did not *have* an answer for him. That ripping off my bosses *was* possible from him and his gang. Which clearly was *not* the case. He needed educating on that first, though.

I don't even know where the moment of inspiration (or possibly madness) came from but looking towards the TV I noticed a video recorder sitting below it, with the Sega console then sat on top of the VCR.

'Ok, you want to know what's to stop you from double crossing my employers, as opposed to paying what you are due and continuing on with a long and trusting relationship where both sides make a shit load of money out of it?'

He sat there waiting for what I had as evidence but could never have ever predicted what came next.

'Is there a Blockbuster video rental around here?'

This threw him.

'Ummmm, yeah. There's one a few miles away on Nutwood East.'

'Good, then we're all going to sit down and watch a movie and, I guess, by the time it's over you'll know if you're ready to do business with a serious organisation like my employers, or not. Now who has a rental card?'

'Movie? N***a you clownin.' Shade laughed at me, the others joining in.

'I assure you that I am most certainly *not* clowning. If you do not have two hours of your day to spend receiving the message of the importance of keeping your word with a South American cartel. If you can't spare a measly two hours out of your time you do not deserve to make the *millions* that my bosses are going to make you.'

No matter what, when you bring the subject of money into matters, that can and will change the narrative.

The cab driver outside was dispatched off to Blockbusters to collect the movie - and also gather some more beers for the homeboys - and once back we all - surrealistically - settled down together for the movie beginning.

Two hours later and we're all watching Tony Montana's midriff being removed from the shotgun blast at close quarters, sending him crashing down into his fountain.

I think, by then, they were able to see the message that I was trying to convey.

Message aside, of not to take on a South American cartel. The gangbangers *loved* the film. Bouncing around their chairs at times. Throwing Cuban insults back and forward at each other to mimic the lead star.

'You is some CRAZY motherf**ker. You come here, almost get yo head blown off and instead of leaving here in the pieces, that for a while I thought you might be, have us all sat watching motherf**king Scarface. I like you, You's a funny n***a.'

Shade smiled across the table and raised his bottle of Olde English to me in respect. I picked up my own forty ounce bottle - which was so large it had lasted me throughout the duration of the film - in front of me and did the same.

'So you ready to get rich, amigo?' I smiled at Shade, looking for confirmation he was on the same page as myself.

'Helllllll YEAH, n***a. Money, power respect. For that paper I'll pop *whoever* in the neck.' He eloquently affirmed.

I left the trap house not only with everything intact but with an order for an initial ten kilos to go with, telling Shade that someone would be in touch with him in due course.

I didn't leave the place without exchanging some hugs and *very* confusing handshakes with them all. It was almost touching the way that - over the course of my time inside there - our friendship had blossomed.

Manny - And how did Eddy and German take the news that you'd secured some new business for the cartel, in the Imperial Village Inglewood Crips?

Peter - Well they took that particular news a *lot* better than they did over the expenses claim that was submitted for a four hundred dollar cab ride, that's for sure! Although, to be fair, once it was all explained to them the 'reasons' behind it - and my method of how I had persuaded the Crips to enter into business with us - it was all understood. Eddy even going as far as to say '*THAT'S* why we wanted you to come and work for us. You can't train someone that kind of life survival skills.'

Manny - So your employment with the Bogota Cartel was now officially underway. Were there any nagging doubts as early as that? Any regrets that you'd jumped in with them because I'm sure that you'd have already been made aware. You decide to work with people like Eddy and German. You won't ever work for anyone else again. Employment with a cartel tends to mean that you'll be with them until the very end. Whatever that ends up meaning.

Peter - Doubts? Regrets? On the contrary, Manfred. I felt exhilarated and - on that cab ride back to The Beverley Hills - as I replayed the whole scene back at that Inglewood trap house, I'd never felt more alive although at the time, I admit, I'd probably never felt more scared either. I had earned my bosses the exact type of new business that they'd brought me in to carry out. I'd proved my worth. I'd found out some new things about myself in the process, there doing deals with gang members. And to top it off. I'd earned myself a shit load of money through - in the scheme of things - not much in the way of effort.

Regrets? F**k, they could come later on.

Chapter 14

El Corazon Valiente - The Ballad of Peter Duncan cont

Manny - So at what point did Peter Duncan appear onto your radar, at the DEA?

Tommy Ambrosini: Drug Enforcement Administration 1984 - present day - Define 'Peter Duncan'

Vinnie Valencia: Drug Enforcement Administration 1987 - 1999 - *Laughs* I know, right?

Manny - What do you mean?

Tommy - I guess what we're both trying to say is that we knew who Peter Duncan was, *before* we *knew who Peter Duncan was*. As an unknown entity he came to our attention at the turn of the year in Eighty Eight. We had no idea who the hell he was but in that room, along with the Inglewood Crips, he sure stuck out like hell. From then on, despite not knowing who the guy was, he seemed like someone that we *needed* to be keeping an eye on.

Manny - In what way did you come across him? You mentioned Inglewood? Surely that would've fallen under L.A.P.D. jurisdiction?

Vinnie - That's the thing, Manny. We weren't looking for him, in any shape or form. How can you possibly be looking for something that you don't know even exists? He found *us!*

Tommy - Yeah, I was sitting in my field office in Miami doing paperwork when I took a call from an officer with the gang related unit in Los Angeles. They'd been trying to pin a series of drive by murders in South West LA on a member of the Village Imperial Crips and were as deep as to have one of the homeboys turn informant and wear a wire, trying to get some sort of an admission on tape from the guilty party.

Vinnie - And while that actual project was still proving to be a bust for the gang unit. While wired up, their infiltrator just so happened to be in the room when the leader of the Crip chapter - he was with - received a visit from some kind of middle man broker type. There on behalf of a South American cartel, delivering a sample batch of Cocaine while engaging in talks regarding setting up future business relations between Colombia and LA.

Tommy - With such trigger words as 'keys, Colombia, cartel, product, Medellin and Escobar' mentioned during the course of the 'lengthy' conversation. The tapes were immediately turned over to the Administration for evaluation.

Manny - You seemed to emphasise on the word 'lengthy' there?

Tommy - Well he *was* in there for around three hours or so. Most drug deals take ten minutes, max.

Vinnie - *laughing loud* Yeah, it wasn't a case of Duncan spending so long inside that Inglewood house that he could've watched a movie. The crazy f**k *did* watch a movie.

Tommy - *laughs also*

Vinnie - Listen, buddy. We both sat down and listened to the tape from start to finish.

Tommy - I thought he was English, initially. Meanwhile he (Vinnie) thought he was Australian. It took - believe it or not - one of the office juniors to put us straight. Telling us that his uncle was from Edinburgh and sounded very similar to the voice on the tape.

Vinnie - He walked in there with them all pulling their guns on him - The gang unit officer who was listening to it in real time told us that he was *sure* that they would pull the triggers - and within the hour they're all sitting down to watch freaking Scarface - with Al Pacino - and by the time he was leaving the house they were teaching him how to perform their gang signs. I'd never heard anything like it in my life.

Tommy - I kind of liked him. From the very start. When - in what had sounded like the most tense of moments - he came out with 'Is there a Blockbuster around here?' I genuinely spat out my coffee.

Vinnie - I can verify that this actually happened. Missed me and my monitor by an inch.

Tommy - As left field as it was, however. What he did, with the Scarface and the message - for the crips - to take away from it was a stroke of genius. Allowing the confident and raw film making of Brian de Palma to express to a gang of LA hoods just what *exactly* would happen to them if they didn't pay his organisation, as and when was required. It wasn't just the business with the movie. More the way that he interacted with the gang bangers. It was obvious that him and them were from two completely different worlds but the way that he engaged with them, even when they were hostile towards him. It sounded like he was always in control of things, even when things might not have appeared that way on the surface of things. Letting Shade, the gang leader, go on and on and on until he calmly lifted the kilo of Cocaine back off the table and put it in the briefcase, calling his opponents bluff.

Vinnie - Yeah, that whole 'do you want this f**king shit or not' move he brought out.

Tommy - Considering the high pressure situation that he was in, and dealing with either of the LA gangs has habitually never been anything less than a pain in the ass, I was impressed. Better men have wilted in those situations. Duncan, from the sounds of the tape, strolled through the meet.

Vinnie - Oh, me too, buddy. You couldn't help but like the guy. While we both liked him, though. We *also* recognised that someone like him was a danger, and one that would need taken out. From what had been picked up on the recording. Not only was this European offering to flood parts of Los Angeles with Cocaine and Heroin. But weapons, also. And if there was one thing that the Crips and Bloods in LA didn't need. It was *more* guns. A man - with ties to dangerous South American criminal organisations - trading in narcotics and weapons, on American soil? As much as he had given us a laugh back in the office, listening to his novel business approach. He was going to have to be treated as someone considered a threat towards our national security.

Tommy - Of course, though. We needed to find out who the hell he even *was*, first of all.

Vinnie - *Laughs* Well, yeah. *That* was the kicker, wasn't it?

Chapter 15

Peter

The relationship, and marriage, between Eva and me had never been by what you could ever have described as 'by the numbers.' And neither did I ever promise her that it would be. She could never have said that she hadn't walked into a life with me with nothing other than eyes wide open.

Things weren't conventional, like most other couples. Little 'date nights' out together to see a movie were as rare an occurrence as a comet in the sky. Movies? I barely had the *time* to sit down for a couple of hours and watch something from Hollywood.

I did enjoy going to the 'pictures,' back in Scotland when I'd been younger, as well. The Godfather 1 & 2, Scarface, Dog Day Afternoon, Mean Streets, French Connection. I saw them all at the old picture house in Kirkcaldy. Anything with gangsters in it and I was there.

When you take up employment for Eddy and German Ramirez, however. Finding a couple of hours of calm and peace of mind is not an easy thing to do. To truly *enjoy* a movie you need to throw yourself into the whole escape from real life that the story provides you for the hour and a half to two hours that it runs to.

Watching a movie in a hotel room while worrying if the CIA have bugged it or 'relaxing' at home on the sofa with your wife while you are receiving phone-calls telling you that you are booked on a plane the next day to go meet with some Middle Eastern terrorists to purchase the contents of their poppy field. None of this is much in the way of conducive to helping you 'escape' for a few hours.

Once, out of our whole time together, only once, did Eva and I actually go out to the cinema. When we were on a shopping trip to New York and she suggested that we should see what an American cinema was like and take in a movie. The exact reason *for* the shopping trip was down to me being in the dog house for leaving her back in Bogota for a week on her own longer than I had told her.

Of course, none of this was my fault. As much as I'd tried to ask her if she had really believed that I had chosen to be held back in Mogadishu by a local warlord, over an issue with a shipment of Kalashnikovs that had not arrived on time.

I'd spent the best part of a week locked up in a filthy cell without even a bed to sleep in at night while questioning if I was ever going to be released again and yet *she* - shacked up in our hacienda with all of her home comforts - was the one who was wronged in it all?

Anyway, due to how put out my detainment had caused her. I had taken her to NY to say sorry. Women, honestly?

While there, she suggested a movie and with me unable to say no to *any* request that she made on the trip. This, lead to us sitting inside a Midtown Manhattan cinema in Ninety Three watching 'Groundhog Day.'

A film that I had been thinking quite a lot about over recent days, stuck there, in the ADX. It wasn't so much the film 'itself' that I had been thinking about and more of the concept of it, and that I was literally living a similar but yet *much*, much shitter life than Bill Murray.

I'd even go so far as to say that had Groundhog Day been based on the life of Peter Duncan - the narcotics and weapons importer / exporter - while inside the ADX maximum security instead of Phil Connor the weatherman hanging around Punxsutawney, Pennsylvania like a bad smell, the plot would have went something like this.

6.00 am: Lights go on. And 'that' noise that accompanies the instant headache inducing brightness. A twin assault on your senses, and sanity. While I'm sure that the guards inside the facility think it's complete comedy gold, playing death metal at the most disturbingly loud volume you can imagine, almost giving you a heart attack each morning when it brutally snatches you from your sleep. It really isn't that amusing. Neither is it one of those things that you 'get used to.' I'd have gotten used to it by now if I was going to. I hate it and I hate the fact that I'm going to go through it the next day, and the one after that.

6.30 - 7.30 am: In the various wings of the prison. Each member is called on their intercom - cell by cell - over the course of the next hour. Notifying them that their cell water has now been turned on. I'd always been made aware about not dropping the soap in the shower in jail. That - at the ADX - was never an issue. Not when you didn't have to shower with anyone else, that was. Through the sheer ratio of complete and utter psychopaths that were incarcerated inside there. There really was no choice other than to keep everyone separated from one another. It's barely what you could give the name 'shower' to, either. With the large operation that involves getting everyone showered before the day has really began, you are literally given a few minutes to run around underneath the bloody thing to get wet before the water goes from hot to cold again.

8.00 am: Breakfast. Well, if you could call what the culinary talents of the chefs in the kitchen of 'Alcatraz de las Rocosas' serve up in the way of Danish bread, off-brand cereal and a glass of milk or water, that is. Most important meal of the day, they say? Just as well that I have the square route of nothing to do for the next twenty four hours then because that 'feast' would barely give you the energy to get your clothes on and out the house in the morning. After around two weeks of receiving breakfast - having been transferred from the detention centre in Brooklyn - inside the ADX, and noticing that there was no rotation to it, no change at all, in fact. I asked the guard, who had brought me the same tray, like every other morning, what the deal was with breakfast and if he personally ate the exact same thing every morning before coming to work, like the prisoners were being made to.

'Our meals here in ADX Florence may not be the best but, and according to law, they are adequate in terms of nutrition.'

According to American law it is also 'adequate' to put a whole chicken inside a tin can but that does not make it right.

There are a *lot* of aspects of life inside the ADX that is what you'd term 'utterly soul destroying' I mean, it was probably sitting in big bold letters at the top of the architects drawings before building the prison.

MUST BE SOUL DESTROYING!!

It really is peak soul destroying, though, to be sitting at a quarter past eight in the morning. Eating a breakfast that you don't want but know you'll *have* to eat otherwise you'll starve, and that you're going to be sat there going through the same thing in twenty four hours time again.

8.30am - 12.30pm: Leisure time. Which would, I feel, take on a lot more of a meaningful side to it if there was anything *near* to a semi extensive list of things to fill the time doing. Now at the cost of sounding ungrateful - while fully aware that there are some of the public who wouldn't be happy until someone like me was spending my days breaking rocks into tinier rocks all day every day - if you look past TV, books and writing to or reading letters from the outside. "Leisure" doesn't seem to extend past any of those activities.

For the initial period, when I'd moved into the cell - while I'd read every letter sent to me - I'd had no interest in writing back to anyone, apart from Manny from The Post, of course, but as the days passed. Each one practically the same as the day before, and the one that was getting ready to follow. The lure of writing back to a select number of 'fans' grew. Not through any kind of interest or desire on my part but simply through giving myself something to do that would take care of getting rid of an hour or two stuck in that cell because, at times, an hour would have the tendency to feel like double or triple that.

'What's it going to feel like when you've endured ten, twenty even, more years of living this same day over and over again?' I'd often asked the question to myself. Unsure of whether I'd even *want* to know the answer to that particular poser. It wouldn't take a qualified doctor to conclude that ten years of that, day in day out, was never going to be good for someone's mind body and soul.

'You can't ever worry about tomorrow,' though. Eddy Ramirez used to tell me, whenever the cartel was experiencing a piece of heat coming down on them from somewhere.

'Not while today hasn't finished with you.'

Living in that kind of lifestyle, like Eddy and me, he was one hundred per cent correct. Tomorrow never owed any narcos a single thing. If we reached it in one piece then god had looked down on us once again. The day he stopped looking down on you. You would know.

12.30 - 1.30pm: Lunch time. This, and the very fact that we are given a rotation of different lunches over the week, only serves to highlight how bland and unadventurous breakfast is in that it never, ever changes. Lunch generally consisting of a sandwich with different filling each day of the week, along with a piece of fruit and energy bar.

For an example, yesterday was turkey on wheat bread with lettuce, tomato and cucumber. Some days are better than others. Their egg mayonnaise is up there with anyone else's but in contrast, the tuna salad that they provide, and whatever the hell they put inside it, gives me the runs anytime I eat it. and I'm not ever left with the choice *not* to. Exactly like the ninety second morning shower, all meals are also taken inside your cell.

I'd never known that jails, in the West were so sophisticated with their sense of security. If you'd told me that there was a Siberian gulag where the worst of the worst were all put and shut off from ever being in contact with each other I would have believed you without any question. I'd have pictured them all being left in some dark hole left to rot, though.

A country like America, however? I didn't think that them, or any Western country, would have been capable of the lack of human rights to build such a facility that could only have ever mentally damaged a person for having been inside of it. Sure it was clean, as opposed to a dirty and dark Siberian hole in the ground. Just because it's a sanitised version of separation from the world does not remove the torture of the separation part to it.

The place was *so* security conscious, in fact, that you didn't even know *who* your neighbours were on either side of you. Due to the secure way that the cells had been built. Having a conversation with the cells to either side of you was impossible but - apart from the extenuating circumstances of how Gal and me were in contact with each other - across the cells there *were* a few chinks to the fortress of the inside of the ADX such as pipes and drains that could help carry a voice to another cell. Because of this, the noise was unbearable at times with all manner of conversations being held across the wing.

The only way that you could listen to the TV and radio supplied in your cell was if you plugged in headphones. This system, I assume, was put into place so that there was not the sound of hundreds of TV sets all playing in the cells at once but that all becomes a moot point when - even with a pair of headphones on and the TV at full volume - you can *still* hear convicts shouting all kinds of unimportant noise back and forward to each other.

1.30 - 5.30pm: And by the end of lunch time each day. You go *right back* to whatever the hell it was that you were doing between half eight in the morning up to lunch time. The only amendment to the afternoon portion of prisoners' leisure time, for me personally, is the possibility of recreation time out in the Rec Area. Not that you could ever place any money with any certainty on me doing so. The Colorado winters really don't take any prisoners so I'd found that recreation time tended to last as long as the turn of year it was. Well, it did if we're talking taking your rec outside in 'The Kennel' and the way that I viewed things. Rec was your *only* opportunity to get outside of your cell and breathe some fresh air, see the sun (if you were lucky to be out at the correct time of day) the clouds and sky. Out in the sun? I've seen prisoners allowed as much as up to three hours outside recreation time but on a freezing December afternoon ten minutes outside is more than you'd generally ever want before asking to go back to your cell.

5.30 - 6.30pm: Dinner, and coming from someone who - up until his untimely arrest in the Netherlands - had always liked to enjoy the finer things in life, food being one of them. Whether it was from one of the world's most fancy and famous restaurants when wining and dining businessmen while on the Ramirez dollar or grabbing a quick bite to eat from an undiscovered gold mine of a Taco stand in the middle of Tijuana. I knew what decent scran was. And the ADX ranked higher than I could ever have expected it to on that front, once you got yourself to dinner time.

Chicken, burgers, tacos, hot dogs, burritos, lasagne and fish empanadas.

Not too shabby.

There was also a 'retail food service' available to prisoners which allowed the purchase of additional items such as rice, tortillas, refried beans, that kind of stuff. 'Available to prisoners' was something that was a bit more subject to debate because since moving into the ADX I had been informed that I was *not* entitled to qualify for said food service but that my file would be updated accordingly at the suitable time which still had not come around.

Dinner wasn't exactly a royal banquet by any means but as your last meal, to see you through the night to breakfast time, it did the trick. It was hard to ever feel 'lucky' stuck inside there but on the occasions where you may have let your emotions get the better of you. Leaving you with the nerve to complain about the food that you were given you were, and more often than not, reminded that unlike the other penitentiaries across the United States, here in the ADX you were provided with *three* meals a day, not the standard two across state lines.

Oh yeah, spoiled we are in Colorado. You know? Some days I honestly wonder if the pampering will ever end.

6.30 - 10.00pm: Evening. Here, what you do is, you go all the way back to between half past eight in the morning and half twelve lunch time, for the second part of the day, and do it all over *again*. Whatever you did then, chances are you're doing it between those hours once more. Whatever you choose to do with your time, it'll take you up until the lights go out. Not that the lights going out equals silence across the wing although, from the standpoint of Gary and me, were it not for all of the prisoners spread across the wing making their own individual noises we would not be able to hold our nightly chats back and forth without being discovered.

And before you know it … **6.00am** once more and you get to re-live the same day *all* over again.

That shit will take my mind, I know that it will. For now, though. All you can do is keep doggy paddling because, fuck me, there's enough bad vibes inside the ADX to drag you under the water, if you let it.

I hadn't been able to speak to Gal for a few nights in a row which only served to highlight just how lonely it really is inside that tiny cell. Barely even knew the guy. Shit? He was one of the people on the outside who were trying to put me *in* a place like ADX Florence and yet, talking back and forth with him meant more to me than I would or could ever have believed. A man that I'd have hated outside a jail setting. Fuck, he was the enemy. I would simply have never believed you if you'd told me that talking to someone like 'that' would be the best part of my day.

The first night, he'd risked a quick buzz to me on the intercom to tell me that there had been a major incident on his side of the complex and that the place was filled with guards and sirens going off. He said that he'd buzz me back later. I eventually fell asleep so if he'd tried to get in touch then I'd slept through it.

The next again night I heard nothing from him and any attempts from me to buzz through to his cell were met with stoney silence.

The absolute key part to speaking with Gary at night was that I did not have to sit alone with my thoughts. I sat alone with them enough during the long days inside that cell. Gal was like some kind of escape for me. Without him on the other end of the intercom for another night, however. It was just me and those thoughts. Normally in the darkness of lights out on the wing, that's when the darker ones visit you.

Instead, my mind took me back to something that I had been talking to Manny the reporter about, in a recent phone call.

That first year, with the Bogota Cartel and how much of an eye opener it had been. Watching how the brothers operated as crime bosses and how - through their network of mass bribery inside Bogota - it generally meant that they had been able to run such an enterprise, with minimum bloodshed. Not to make the mistake that Eddy and German did not have their ruthless side ready to come out when someone needed an *example* made.

How they would fly in ex special forces from countries like Russia, Israel, America and the United Kingdom. Spteznaz, Mossad, Delta Force, S.A.S. *All* flown in to train the brothers' sicarios how to be more effective at shooting, as well as killing in general. I mean? These men were *trained killers*. What else were they coming to Colombia to teach the sicarios?

Eddy and German's ethos of ' We're not in the narcotics business and nor are we in the arms trade business. We are in the being *billionaires* business.

It was an experience to see in action, and be an integral part of.

While I'm sure that the American, and the British authorities would beg to differ but what I achieved in Nineteen Ninety, along with some help from my friends in Colombia, not only propelled me into the big league but - and without blowing one's trumpet - changed the face of how things were going to be in the United Kingdom, until the end of time.

It had been great, therapeutic even, revisiting those heady days in the conversation over the call with Manny. Days where I felt like *something*. That *I* was important and - whichever the side of the fence you were on, and whatever your politics - that I was making a mark in the world.

Despite all of the mistakes that I would, no doubt, go on to make all over again. Looking around my seven by twelve palace. I'd have revisited those days, again, in an absolute heartbeat, if given the chance.

Chapter 16

El Corazon Valiente - The Ballad of Peter Duncan cont

Manny - As far as your work in those early days of the first year working for the Ramirez brothers. How happy were your employers with the choice they made in bringing you on board with the cartel? What was the feedback you received on how things were going?

Peter - Ummm, yeah. You know? Eddy and German weren't too big on 'feedback,' as such. I think that the only - work related - feedback that they ever dished out was when someone ended up with a bullet in their head. I mean, you can't get any more clear of an 'appraisal' on how you've been doing than if you found guys like Jorge and Gilberto coming to pay you a visit.

Manny - Lozano and Martinez, El Jugador and La Cobra, the notoriously feared head enforcers for the brothers?

Peter - Yeah, the very same. You've heard of them I see.

Manny - Who, without even the tiniest degree of knowledge about narco culture, hasn't?

Peter - Well unfortunately you can rule me out there. You want to know how well things went in that first year with the Ramirez expansion plans? They had to bring in some genius of an accountant, just to help me manage the amounts of money that I was pulling in from whatever corner of the globe that they cared to ship me off to in a business class passenger jet seat.

Stop me if at any point you feel that I am in danger of sucking my own appendage here but that first year, especially inside the first six months when I was intent on giving a good account of myself, - in terms of in the eyes of Eddy and German - making a *name* for myself, along with a huge pile of money. I was an absolute tour de force. Wind fire and water could not have stopped me.

Following Los Angeles, and my evening with the Imperial Village of Inglewood. I returned back to Bogota the very next day to a round of congratulations from Eddy, German and those inside the inner circle. All of them cracking up at the dinner table - at the high end Ushin Japanese bar and grill in downtown Bogota, where my driver had whisked me to upon my arrival at El Dorado - as I told them about events the night before.

'You see, you see!' Eddy roared across the room jovially while looking directly towards Don Eduardo, Eddy's uncle and who from that one exchange, someone who I had taken as being objective towards me coming and working for the family. He would not have been the only one who had possibly thought that way. Why, after all, would Eddy have one of the 'gringos' come and work for the cartel?

Inglewood, (and the money that this new LA connect was going to bring into the cartel) at the very least, went a little way towards paying back Eddy's enormous sense of belief and trust that he had showed in me. After that, things only went from strength to strength.

It wasn't long before the two brothers had me on the move again. This time over to Ireland to broker a deal with some high ranking members of the Irish Republican Army involving weapons that we were shipping via an intermediary with F.A.R.C that - to make things more confusing - the Irish rebels were *then* selling onto some freedom fighters in Chechnya.

The trip after that, a multi stop outing, back to the Netherlands to meet with both Hakan (my head hurts at even the thought of how sore it was the morning after the night we went out in the city, for a much needed catch up) and a Serbian family - Stojanovic - who oversaw most of the supply of Cocaine in the Southern city of Eindhoven.

Then? The *very* sketchy 'diplomatic envoy visit' to Culiacan to try and smooth relations between Sinaloa and Bogota - which had been relatively tranquilo over history with both cartels having helped the other on occasion - due to a Bogota sicario killing a Sinaloan in a nightclub through some stupid argument over an accidentally spilled drink. The Sinaloans apoplectic that neither Eddy or German had showed face and that, instead, they'd sent some gringo who they had never heard of, and did not respect.

The situation was dealt with accordingly and whether I had their respect by the end of the meeting or not, they left the meeting *knowing* who I was.

That I did not end up left in a Sinaloan ditch with a bullet in the head - something that Eddy and German said, afterwards, was always a possibility, due to how loco the Mexicans are - *and* that the Mexicans were happy with the resolution to things was all that really was important. From that one meeting with the men from Culiacan. I was hoping that I would be kept away from them as much as possible. Something about them just rubbed me up in a way that psychotic gang members in LA or terrorists came even close to doing.

The trips kept coming. Eddy and German, it seemed, were intent on world domination. It was quite ingenious, really. Medellin and Cali generally enjoying all of the glory - and headlines - for being held responsible for the influx of Cocaine that was flooding into America and Europe and having been known to do so since the mid Eighties with both reputations now set in stone. Despite them being two completely different business models operating out of either of those cartels. The Orejuela brothers being a cool, smart and incredibly inventive set up while Pablo Escobar was, well, he was Pablo, an absolute f**king crazed lunatic.

While everyone - and more importantly the Americans - were looking in the direction of those two areas of Colombia, we in Bogota were allowed to make hay while the sun shone. And we were in Colombia. The sun shone an *awful* amount of the time. And as a result, we had a *lot* of hay to make.

But even so. The brothers knew that they could push things further. They weren't predominantly known for being Cocaine suppliers, on a grand level. That was left to Cali and Medellin. As a result, why *limit* yourself to just the supply of Coke when you can make millions of dollars simply by moving a cargo from one destination to another? Sometimes without the cargo even being in your *own* country and something that you won't actually see with your own eyes?

Enter the need for a 'me' to join the team.

Manny - And then - following this - an accountant?

Peter - Well he wasn't just *any* accountant, Mikael. He was all things to all men. Women wanted to be with him, men wanted to BE him. Well, if you listened to half of the bullshit that came out of the man's mouth. I know you shouldn't speak ill of the dead but for the record. I used to tell him - on a daily basis - to his face what nonsense would come out of his mouth. All jokes aside, though. He really was a good guy, Miki. Not that I had been receptive at first to him being hired as some kind of 'help' for me, mind.

I'm not sure what the hell it was. Ego? Arrogance? Possibly the fact that I had been sticking some of the best Ye-Yo known to man up my nose, I don't know, but when I found out that my solo operation was being changed to a double act, I was against it.

Confidence wise, I'd went from strength to strength, job to job. For the first time in my life I had truly felt *good* at something. While I may have completely bluffed my way through that very first trip to Inglewood I'd soon began to find that it had been that *exact* ability to bluff - the type of thing that can't be taught, someone either has it or they don't - that was my strength. The one key component that had been the difference between getting the job done or not.

Those who would not describe themselves as a 'people person' need not apply.

It had been going seamlessly - my lone wolf kind of operation - I mean, obviously there were various occasions where I'd be flying into a city and immediately meeting up with a Ramirez operative based there or to arrange for some back up for whichever meeting I was headed to. It really all depended the circumstances. If you're meeting - and conducting business with - someone at a nice restaurant to break bread with each other then, of course, there's no need for any hired goons to have your back. Midnight meets at the local port with people who you have never met before, however, *is* one of those moments where you would rather someone had your back, even if only for appearance purposes.

On the whole, though. I'd been more than successful just doing my own thing. Representing myself *and* the cartel by 'doing me.' And the results - in the money that I was bringing back to Bogota - didn't lie.

That was what was so surprising the afternoon - when I'd been enjoying the relative novelty of some extended downtime having received no jobs for almost three weeks following my return from what had been a most enjoyable trip to Casablanca. Rubber stamping a Cocaine shipment with a Russian mafia boss who had been forced to flee Moscow and was now running his business in exile and out of Morocco until things had been smoothed over with the authorities back home for him to return - when I had been asked over to German's mansion, on the outskirts of Bogota, one afternoon.

When either of Eddy or German would - out of the blue - call and ask you to come visit them it was always done in the briefest of ways before hanging up again. Putting the message across without providing any extra details in the process. It was Eddy and German Ramirez, they didn't *need* to provide details. Telling you that they wanted to see you should've been, and was, always enough to get the desired effect out of someone.

Being let into his office by Jose, one of the guards stationed outside. I entered to find Eddy and German along with Roman - who had more and more began to show that he was a lot more cut out for the narco lifestyle than maybe even he possibly had thought - and then to the side of Roman someone who I didn't know or had ever seen before. One glimpse at him, though, and you could tell that he wasn't South American.

He was a gringo, like myself.

What is it that they say about first impressions though?

He was sat there. Shoulder length unkempt straggly curly hair in a middle parting. Pair of aviators covering his eyes. Guns n Roses 'Appetite for Destruction' black t shirt with a couple of holes in it. Shorts that, even though he was sitting down, still went way past his knees and a pair of flip flops.

It wasn't a fashion contest - by any means - but if we're talking first impressions and the man that the scruffy younger guy in the chair was looking back at. It was someone with freshly combed and lacquered hair. A pair of Armani shades. Crisp white Gucci polo neck shirt along with a pair of summer Valentino chinos and Gucci loafers, no socks, obviously. I know which one out of the pair of us - considering we were destined to be working together - looked 'business like.'

After the introductions between me and Mikael - Garin, half Finnish half Colombian, a kid - who Eddy sat back and informed me had been some kind of gifted child back at school. National scholar of the year kind of deal where even when put up against all of Europe's best of the same age he wiped the floor with the lot of them. This - through his remarkable genius - had led to an honourary place at Princetown

University where he was shipped off from his home in Helsinki to study accountancy.

He returned back to Europe following gaining his degree. Through his impressive C.V, even at that early age. He could have had his pick of pretty much any of the world's greatest financial institutions to go and work with. No door would've been closed to this ex child prodigy with an Ivy League college degree in his sky rocket and someone who had been called the greatest mathematical mind of his generation.

Manny - Sky Rocket?

Peter - 'Pocket,' Manny. Pocket. Rhyming slang, I don't think you do that much over here? Anyway …

So where does he decide to go work for? Out of all the options open to him. The bloody Sicilian 'Ndrangheta! I suppose, in a way, he *did* choose to work for one of the world's greatest financial organisations.

As Eddy sat and told me the story behind Mikael and the 'Ndrangheta. The Finn nodding along at various intervals. I was informed that there had been a bit of a recent issue involving the cartel and the Italians over in Sicily. Payment that had been due to Bogota had not arrived and while normally that would spell trouble. The Ramirez brothers had always enjoyed good relations with the Italians and there was a lot of goodwill extended between the two gangs. This being the reason for Eddy and German's novel opinion that there would be no need to spoil what had been a long running relationship, over a late payment.

The Italians, with that whole honour thing that they at least *tried* to keep up in the public eye, were extremely *dis*honoured over the issues in them getting the money to Colombia by the pre agreed time had offered a 'gift' towards the Ramirez brothers, while they worked on getting the money for their shipment together.

That gift being Mikael Garin. Traded, like he was literally an object. One minute he was working out of an office in Paris on behalf of a shell company created by the Italians simply to facilitate the moving of the copious millions they would bring in per month and the next he'd been put on a plane to Bogota and told that he's working for someone else now.

Not too dissimilar a story to someone else I know.

'Hey, bro. I'm happy to work where-ev-er, you feel me? My boss, Don Salvatore, or *ex* boss I now suppose, he told me that Señor Eddy and German pay top dineros for the best people. With me, he has the best. I'll make their money disappear as if I was David f**king Copperfield.'

He sat there looking back at me and said in the strangest of accents. A mix of his native Scandinavian - or at least, that's what I 'assumed' to be, - American and a touch of Latin although I wasn't exactly sure if that Latin part was being adopted because he was in a room of predominantly Spanish speakers.

Despite the glowing reference that Eddy had announced the man with - and the very not so minor part where whatever Eddy said, went - I was against it. I'd had a good six months of getting myself ingrained into what it was like to be a core part of the inner workings of the cartel. I *knew* that whatever Eddy and German decided they wanted, then it would happen. I *also* knew, however, that - to those who were considered close to the brothers and someone whose work and opinion they valued - they were not so unreasonable as to not listen to others, even if it was largely, and ultimately, considered a waste of everyone's time.

The kid's credentials seemed impeccable. There was no debating on that. It was his whole appearance and - from what words he managed to speak in amongst Eddy's, practical, presentation minus slides on his new recruit - his whole vibe and attitude.

I'd taken *my* move to Bogota serious. Knew that I'd had some lofty promotion of sorts, especially considering a year or so before I'd been running around Amsterdam doing errands for the owner of a bar. And I treated it as such. Following the original 'rig out' that I'd received from the Bogota boutiques when I'd arrived in the city without any clothes. I'd spent triple, quadruple that in those same boutiques, with my own hard earned money. Why? Well apart from my own sense of pride in how I looked (while, admittedly, having the funds to facilitate things to my requirements) I wanted to show professionalism. I represented one of the biggest criminal enterprises in the world. Was required to play a pivotal part in that cartel and I would *not* be able to do that - win the respect of my associates across the world - if I was to turn up to meetings with them dressed in a Beastie Boys tour t shirt along with some beachwear.

The real irony with my exception to the slack way that Mikael was dressed was that - in general - despite having more money than they would ever know what to even do with. Both Ramirez brothers dressed like shit, most of the time, with their cheap market bought jeans and ill fitting polo shirts - with the big collars - that belonged to a previous decade and filthy vintage Adidas trainers that were more vintage as in they couldn't be arsed getting themselves new pairs than by any actual design.

I'd listened to Eddy. Shit? I agreed with some of what he'd said regarding managing the finances because *that* wasn't my biggest strength, - and nor did I ever claim it to be - especially with the complicated and convoluted ways that certain buyers preferred to funnel the money to Eddy and German back to Colombia or wherever the money was 'technically' going to. It certainly was never a case of handing a briefcase filled with unmarked bills to me, like you see in the movies. But him? This younger cocky Finn? He screamed 'liability' to me before he'd even opened his mouth. I'd initially - when walking into German's office - thought that the guy was a new sicario simply through his choice of clothes. An accountant - whose talents were known of and highly sought after across the world - and my soon to be assistant?

Nope, never saw it.

With Eddy finished. I decided to chance my own input.

'Look, no disrespect to you, Mikael but Eddy? German? Look at him? He looks like he's going to sleep in until the afternoon most days, go surfing, smoke weed the rest of the day and then forget the f**king passwords for our banking systems when we need them the most. And *this* is the man that you want looking after our not inconsiderable amounts of money that we have coming and going across the world?'

'Excuse me, and who are you again?'

The Finn, reacted to this

'Who am I?' I responded. Taking a step closer to him.

'I'm the one who single handedly stopped an all out war between Bogota and Sinaloa. Could sell Cocaine to Inglewood Crips. Ice to

Eskimos, if asked, and, if they were all still alive, manage to reunite The Beatles. *That's* who I f**king am.'

'TRANQUILO TRANQUILO, HERMANOS.'

German butted in making the international sign for 'time out.'

Then Eddy offered some words of wisdom.

'Remember now Pedro. The *key* part of our operation is the money. Who has it, how much they have *of* it, how much they want to give us and most important of all … how they're going to *get it* to us.

This man here. He can have our money bouncing around different parts of the world and eventually into Switzerland or The Caymans before you can say 'Control Alt Delete.' How he *looks* is unimportant. He is not you and you are not him. While you do the talking with your mouth *he* will do the talking with his fingers.'

'The jefe is correct, amigo'

Mikael said, looking at me, and, from his tone, a lot more friendlier.

It wasn't a case of jealousy, that there was another European on board and, subsequently, reducing how novel I was, being with the cartel. Although, some may have seen it that way. It really was more a case of me having eased myself into a nice routine. I mean, no two jobs were *ever* identical but still, all the same. My routine, if you could class it as that, involved - no matter how dangerous the situation - never being both killed and or captured by the authorities. Adding someone else to my operation was something that I feared might've altered that. If I f**k up and make a mistake leading to my death or arrest, fair enough. Only myself to blame there. Adding someone else, and additional room for human error. *That* was what worried me. That, as nice a guy, if a little full of himself for sitting in a room with cartel bosses for the first time being as chill about it as he'd appeared in German's office that afternoon, *he* would be the reason for it turning sour.

While my line of employment would've been what a lot of people would've deemed questionable. I was *proud* of how successful I was at it. It wasn't a working playground for everyone but I excelled in that arena. I just didn't want anyone, or anything, to come along and flip over the applecart.

Manny - Did the rocky start between yourself and Garin improve?

Peter - Miki? The kid was a diamond of a guy and by the time him and I were done he was without a shadow of a doubt my biggest confidant and right hand man. Shit? He was my best friend, which was just as well considering the time that we had to spend with each other when out of Colombia on business.

Following that meeting in German's office, it didn't take the two of us long to strike up a friendship. Especially with me landing up with him kipping at my pad while his own similar themed work related perk was being finished for him moving in.

Once we'd then had a couple of business trips under our belt and I had actually seen how beneficial he was going to prove. Even just to have him on hand to answer the financial related questions that I'd sometimes have fired at me that were so technical they may as well have been spoken to me in Mandarin.

And of course, all of that about Miki to the side. Were it not for him being brought into the fold by Eddy and German?

Well *who knows* how things would've turned out and when I say that I mean not just for me, him or the Bogota Cartel but life in general for the average British kid, as well as helping evolve a completely new musical movement.

It was Miki's intel but in sharing it with me I decided to take it to the next level and turn it into something, providing we could secure the Ramirez brothers' blessings on things.

We first discussed the matter towards the end of spring in Nineteen Ninety when we found ourselves in Detroit as part of a three stop trip in the States. Taking in New York, New Jersey with the final meet in Detroit, Michigan. With our flight back to Colombia not scheduled for the best part of twenty four hours, the two of us were left with some rare free time to see a bit of downtown Detroit. Visiting all of these cities around the world wasn't as exciting as you'd possibly imagine as 'travelling' to a city is far, far removed a concept from actually *visiting* one.

Even so - given a little downtime over the course of a trip - my inclination would've always been to have remained in either my hotel room or down at the bar and enjoying a bit of peace and quiet in those rare opportunities to stop and breathe and not feel like you had to be 'on.'

Miki's younger exuberance came from a different angle. Like me, he'd already seen most of the world but with youth on his side he had the bigger sense of adventure to explore *outside* of a five star hotel.

Through this, he'd managed to convince me to go out with him for a few drinks and to experience some nightlife. The 'nightlife' that I'd experienced over in the 'Eight Mile' area of the city had been enough to make sure you'd return to your hotel, triple lock the f**king door and never come back out again until your taxi was waiting to take you to Wayne County Airport for your flight out of the place.

Mikael was infectious, however. Plus, possessed the ability to get what he wanted through my search for an easy life wherever I could find one.

We jumped into a taxi outside of our hotel with Mikael's instructions of 'take us somewhere lively' handed to the driver and ensuring that he - after a fifteen minute drive or so - was dropping us outside a run down looking venue called The Soundboard which was situated near what looked like a traditional Scottish industrial estate.

From the lines of clubbers all waiting to get in you could see that the place fitted the description of 'lively.' Scores of people all standing patiently waiting on the line going down. Some girls - through the choice of what they'd worn - were standing there shivering their asses off, Their partner's jacket draped over them not coming close to protecting the exposed flesh from their short dresses.

I could already see that - I personally - was not dressed for the kind of place that it appeared we were heading into. Ironically, Miki - and what he had on with a pair of jeans with holes in them and an Armani t-shirt that - through its design - looked like it had been lying in a filthy ditch for a few weeks before he'd found it and put it on - was dressed *exactly* how he should've been.

It didn't take long inside the place - I mean, I'd barely handed my jacket into the cloakroom - for me to notice that things about the club were, different.

The music, for one thing. An electronic repetitive beat with noises like you'd hear in a computer space game. No vocals to speak of, whatsoever.

Then there was the crowd, or more specifically, their collective behaviour, as a group of people. It had been a few years since I'd really went to nightclubs with any kind of regularity. And this was not like a 'nightclub.'

There was no DJ announcing which records they were playing. No talking back and forward with the crowd at all in any kind of striking up a rapport with them.

No couples filling the dance floor having their own one on one dance with each other.

No groups of men sat at the bar chatting away nor girls on a night out dancing around their handbags. No lone wolf, out trying their luck and sat hitting some poor girl with his one liners with the aim of trying to get her into bed at the end of the night.

None of this.

What struck me - most of all - was that, bar the odd one or two, every one inside the place were all dancing. Not just dancing. I'd seen people dancing hundreds of times. This was a completely different thing all together. It was as if everyone in there was dancing alone, yet in the weirdest of ways, as if every single one of them were all taking part in the same dance. The screams that would go out inside the room when it appeared that a track had come on that they all knew. I'd never witnessed anything like it. The energy and togetherness that you could almost *feel* flowing through that hot dark and sweaty room. I - sitting there watching it all go on - was fascinated.

'This is unbelievable.' I said - wide-eyed - to Miki as we looked down onto the heaving dance floor from the VIP area of the club that I had bribed the two bouncers on the door into putting us in.

'Get yourself down there and into the mix and have a dance, brother.' He joked back. Well, I say 'joke' but with that crazy motherf**ker, Mikael, you never ever quite knew.

As we sat there - separated by the unwashed by a purple velvet rope - I'd began to notice that we were in the company of a fellow contraband provider. Someone, by the looks of things, several rungs up the ladder. Sitting there sipping champagne along with three women. Only really giving the game away - to the trained eye like mines - over the course of the night when, periodically, someone - and without being snobbish, someone who did not look like they belonged in VIP - being let past the velvet rope so that they could go and speak to the man in the corner sat with the women. There - in what was always the quickest of exchanges - would be the exchange of money in return for a bag of pills. If you weren't looking for it you wouldn't have even seen it taking place.

This was an obvious case of dealers having sold out and needing to re-up. The fact that the security were letting them into the VIP area so that they could go speak to the man sitting with the women showed that this was obviously an arrangement *with* the security, to allow for the dealing going on inside the place.

The biggest take away from it all was just how much product was being sold inside the walls of the club, due to the regular visits that the guy received, from three separate dealers.

'This is going to be massive. It's going to change the world, my brother.'

Miki said, cryptically as he leaned over the balcony and pointed down towards the crowd and the DJ, who had still not spoken an utter word since we'd arrived more than an hour before. It took me fifteen minutes of being in there to realise that he had even changed the record. Remarking to Mikael about how long the track was and him laughing his head off at me before explaining that he had been mixing different tracks. Because none of them contained any actual singing I hadn't been able to distinguish the difference from one track to the next. I admit, I was out of my depth.

'What's going to change the world?' I asked, genuinely.

'This, all of this. The music, the drugs, the scene. The people that are going to emerge from this lifestyle, once it finds them.'

I think it had been clear to him - just from the blank look on my face - that I hadn't the first idea of what he was going on about. Helpfully, he elaborated further.

Telling me about how for the previous two summers - in Eighty Eight and Eighty Nine - he had been to Ibiza for some much needed time away from the intense work of looking after the money of one of the world's most feared and powerful mafia gangs. There, he told me about all of the open air clubs, the power of the music played there, the collectiveness of the clubbing community ... and Ecstasy.

He ordered another bottle of Dom P to be brought over to our table and then - over the course of the next half an hour - took me through a crash course in how Ecstasy - known in the correct circles as simply 'E' - while relatively little known by most was going to change the face of the narcotics world.

'It will not affect one single gram of Cocaine sold over the world, brother. No, this is a *new* market out there. It is year zero. A customer base that does not even know yet that it either *wants* the product or that it is, in fact, going to even ever *take* it. This is going to be a drug that people who have never taken an illegal narcotic in their life will clamour for.'

It was hard *not* to let my business brain and unshakeable desire to make as much money as I could as *often* as I could not run wild.

'Just look at them down there.'

Mikael pointed again over the balcony and down below to the moving sea of shapes, caught in the light for a second before falling dark again.

'They look like a bunch slaves, drones. Hypnotised by what is coming out of the speakers but look at the smiles on their faces. Look at how *collectively* happy they are.'

'This, this is not the behaviour of a room full of people who have had Cocaine.'

He was correct. Had everyone down below been sniffing over the night the entire room would have had a completely different complexion to it. Half the place dancing, and thinking that they were the absolute *best* dancer in the place while the other half stood around talking the biggest amount of garbage you would ever wish to listen to.

There was a passion and an energy inside The Soundboard that Cocaine - as wonderful a drug that I think it may be - simply would not have been able to facilitate.

Mikael explained that Ibiza in the summer had been a perfect mix of holiday makers from around the globe but the majority of accents or people he would speak to himself were generally British and that some of them had been so impacted by the scene in the Balearics that they had now imported it back to the U.K by way of opening up their own clubs, playing the same tracks as heard out in Spain and, of course, sticking to the same formula as Ibiza in the way of Ecstasy being a staple part of the night.

While still semi underground in Britain. Miki told me that things were on the verge of exploding. Large scale legal festivals were going to be the future as opposed to the illegal ones that were held and constantly shut down by the police. Illegal was going to become *legal* but the one aspect that wouldn't change, couldn't, in fact, was the Ecstasy element to it.

'The music doesn't work without the Ecstasy and the Ecstasy doesn't work without the music. Unlike Coca - which we can all agree has its time and a place and that is generally whenever the f**k someone wants a line - Ecstasy is *directly* linked to something specific, such as this DJ playing records to a crowd of people.

Up until that conversation. The only three drugs that *really* mattered, Cocaine, Heroin and Marijuana, I knew *all* about. Knew where they were manufactured or grown and who was responsible for shifting the majority of it, and to where. Ecstasy was a new thing altogether. Obviously I'd known *of* the drug but it had been so far off my radar and - if pressed on things - I'd have probably classed it as one of those 'hippy projects' that some mad professor had messed around with in his lab and come up with. It was one of those many narcotics that simply weren't marketable.

Or so I'd thought.

Mikael explained to me that it had been the English leading the way with getting the scene going and that - largely - most of the moving and shaking was going on inside the British Isles although - as was evident from the scenes there inside The Soundboard - this was not a thing exclusive to the confines of the United Kingdom but, as Mikael put it and appealing to me like it had been someone trying to pitch me an idea.

'Once this takes off. There's not going to be a corner of the world that isn't popping pills and dancing all night long to House Music.'

I continued thinking about it as I made a trip to the mens. The VIP had kept us separated from all of those below but even from a quick trip to the bathrooms I'd encountered a couple of guys - stood talking - inside there who, judging by the looks of things, had potentially taken a pill or two themselves.

Either that or they were just two *extremely* friendly chaps. Reacting to the sight of me - someone they'd never seen in their life - as if I was some long lost friend that they hadn't seen in decades. Wanting to shake my hand - something I'm not too much a fan of doing with people inside public toilets, for obvious reasons - along with asking with such depth and warmth how my night had been going. One of them standing in there dancing to the relative muted sounds of the beat filtering up from the dance floor and into the bathroom.

'Ohhhh these Doves are POPPING tonight, though. One of them replied to me following the question - just to be sociable back - of how 'their' night had been going.

'Oh you *knows* it, dawg.' The other one smiled and gave his mate a fist bump in recognition.

Out of market research purposes more than anything else I asked them to elaborate, which they did, in explaining to me that the two of them had taken Ecstasy called 'White Doves.' Apparently these were the gold standard of pills. The original and best. The sheer passion that the two of them described and spoke about the pill that they had taken, though? I mean, people love drugs. It's why they take them, it's why they can't STOP taking them. It's why I became the wealthy individual that I was.

That aside, I had *never* seen anyone. Any user - or abuser - speak with such fervor, love and passion about a drug, as those two men inside the bathrooms that night.

My cogs began to seriously turn.

I guess Mikael's had *already* been turning because after I'd returned from the - due to the conversation held inside there - extended trip to the bathroom and took my seat back at our table, there was a freshly poured glass of Dom and a small white pill sitting beside it.

'Tonight, Pedro. You go to school, yes?'

More out of instinct than anything else. I turned and looked over in the direction of the man sitting with the three women. Catching eyes with each other at the same time, him lifting his glass and slightly tipping it in the air towards me. It all falling into place - right there - and me lifting my glass and returning the gesture.

'I had a brief conversation with our friend over there when you were in the bathroom. The short version being that I talked him into giving us both a free sample.'

He finished this by lifting his, popping it into his mouth and washing it down with a drink of champagne.

It was silly but I was scared to follow him. As hypocritical as I'm in no doubt this will sound, how could I trust a stranger to give me a pill to take? That's what doctors are for. Being with Mikael, there was never going to be an option of *not* taking it, however.

Shit? With Mikael's ways even if you *didn't* want to take it you'd have taken one just to stop him from tugging and nipping away at you.

I mean, I *did* want to take it. I was intrigued by it all. It was just a piece of the unknown though and sometimes you venture off into that with a degree of wariness.

One hour after I'd taken it. I was telling Miki that I'd thought the guy had burned us with duds as I wasn't feeling anything. *Two* hours after that I'm sitting there apologising to Miki as if my life depended on it. Feeling the most high I'd ever done in my life and oh, was I hot. Not a single hair on my head that wasn't soaking. Such a feeling. I felt content and without a care in the world as I sat dealing with the most intense of rushes running over me. Some so intense that you literally had to stop talking to let them pass before finishing your sentence.

I apologised to him profusely. Getting it all off my chest. Telling him how sorry I was for being against him coming to work with me and how I'd thought that he was a cocky and arrogant upstart who was surely going to get me arrested, and that I'd been wrong about it all and how just spending time with him - in the close quarters that our work sometimes dictated - I'd been able to see just what a good guy that he was.

It was all stuff that I would never have dreamed of saying to him under any other circumstances but - with those chemicals inside of me - it felt *really* important that I tell him, at the time.

Miki, himself, batting all of my words away and giving me a big man hug and telling me that he loved me anyway and that him and I were going to rule the world together. Something I agreed with although - even under the influence of this new wonder drug - I would never have been so stupid to say in front of Eddy and German, even in jest.

And another thing. I wanted to dance. As in *wanted*. I'm about the furthest thing away from a dancer. And didn't even know, or understand if I'm being brutally honest, the music, never mind actually *dance* to it, or know how to.

That feeling, though, Manfred? I couldn't have had *more* of a feeling if I was in Flashdance. The heat? I mean, the club - as you'd expect - was hot anyway but once the pill kicked in my hair was wringing wet. Hands clammy. All fingers and thumbs. Each and every time I'd pick my glass up it would almost slip from between my fingers.

The conversations that Mikael and I sat and had. Topics and depth that I'd never experienced with anyone in my life. It was an experience and a half, if a little long term in the way of the commitment that you make with yourself the moment you neck that small pill. A man, like myself, couldn't live by those rules. With Cocaine, you know where you stand. Knock a line of that back and you can take on the world at anything, and at anytime. By comparison take an Ecstasy pill and what good are you going to be to anyone?

Considering I could've, at any point, day or night, received a page from one of the brothers with some form of instructions, sometimes immediately requiring attended to. I needed to be ready to go *then*, not in eight hours time after I'm done through with telling the world that I love them.

I could see the fascination with the drug, though, and having had the luxury of witnessing the crowd in action, there inside The Soundboard. I'd seen its effects for myself.

Midway through the night - and where I was at the point where I was as high as I had ever been in my entire life - I pulled Miki in towards me and told him that the two of us were going to get involved with Ecstasy. That - if all of what he had told me was true - there was going to be millions, no BILLIONS to be made out of the stuff, once the snowball was pushed down the hill. And that *we* were going to be the ones to give it one final push.

All my own personal experience had been with Coke and - with its relatively high price - *that* had meant that it was a more exclusive clientele that would look to purchase it, - what the gangbangers did with it was their business but Cocaine, in its original form, was *only* for the rich - this being the complete *opposite* of the target customer base of Ecstasy with its price tag of around twenty pound per pill, if the conversion of the price of one in Detroit was anything close to the equivalent to the British pound.

My mind had been way beyond performing any kind of actual mathematics, there inside the club, but the one thing that spoke sense to me, high as a kite or not, was the simplicity of the revelation of the pills being *much* cheaper than a gram of Coke. And that this equalled a much *bigger* customer base that a net could be thrown over. A completely *new* market of customers. A target audience who were so young they probably couldn't have even afforded Cocaine if they wanted it.

They didn't though. They wanted to take tiny pills that kept them up all night so they could dance until their hearts were content.

And, tapping into my never far from sight entrepreneurial spirit, over the course of that night out with Mikael. All the sights, sounds and feelings I had encountered.

I'd decided that this was an opportunity too great to miss.

First of all, however, I would have to receive the green light from the jefes in Bogota.

Chapter 17

El Corazon Valiente - The Ballad of Peter Duncan cont

Manny - The Ecstasy project? How did the Ramirez brothers respond to this business idea that you went back to them from America with to pitch?

Peter - Enthusiastically so, Manfred. Of course, though. My planning had extended much further than some back of a cigarette packet stuff that had been planned *while* I was out of my mind on the stuff that night in the Motor City. No, I was able to go to Eddy and German. Fully in possession of facts, figures and projections. With Holland being the country widely responsible for the manufacturing of the pills in Europe I was able to make a call to a familiar and friendly face in Hakan, seeking further intel. The irony not lost on either of us that it was someone *from* Bogota asking him about the availability and price of a particular drug rather than the *other* direction.

Hakan, telling me that up until more recent times one solitary pill had been selling for around thirty five to forty pounds back in the U.K but - as is the case with supply / demand and how it can effect street prices - of late they were now going for the reduced price of twenty in London and Northern England.

'Aye but, most importantly of all. How much will *I* be paying for them?' I asked the golden question.

'Well, you know the nature of this business, Peter.' He responded.

'It all comes down to how *much* of them you want?'

Now *that* was the question. How much *did* I want? Given this was a brainwave, epiphany almost, that had taken place when I'd taken a pill for the first time and was sat in a Detroit nightclub. Hardly the road to Damascus type of stuff. However much I decided to delve into this new venture it was always going to be done with the element of taking a punt. There was no point of reference to go before things. No success stories whose method could be repeated. This was the unknown and as such. How much *did* I want to buy? How much would Britain *need* was the more pertinent of questions. The answer - it would turn out, decade upon decade - was an absolute mountain of the stuff. F**king K2 made out of MDMA. It's fair to say that the U.K youth took to the drug, with gusto.

Manny - So you were able to work out a deal with the Turks suitable for everyone?

Peter - Well it took some number crunching back and forth and even by the end I wasn't sure if I could've managed to have got a better deal out of Yilmaz. Simply through me dealing in a product I had no experience in I didn't know enough about matters to speak on with any degree of authority, or confidence. One thing I was confident of, however, was that Hakan would not fleece me on the deal. If not on the strength of him and I being old friends but because if he fleeced me then he fleeced the Ramirez brothers.

I came away with a provisional agreement to buy fifty thousand pills at four pounds a pill including shipping to my choice of destination. With a street value of twenty pounds I'd quickly scrambled in my mind that if I was to sell them at ten a pill it would leave the dealers in the U.K with a decent level of profit margin. These margins could always be amended to suit but in a rough guesstimate I'd seen a chance to make a quick three hundred thousand for little or no effort on my part. Of course, part of that would be going directly back to the brothers. Who, incidentally, I was not only seeking their go ahead for me to extend our operation into Ecstasy but would be looking for them to cover the start up costs, which they would receive back upon the first payment from the U.K.

I put it across to them in the most basic and clear of terms. That it was a way we could make money, and wouldn't even have to lay a single finger to facilitate any drugs from leaving Colombia. All sorts of middle men taken out of the equation with the arrangement.

I'd even been so far as to suggest to Hakan - following him filling me in on the kind of details that a drug importer / exporter really would like to know. Things like how the U.K authorities *knew* that practically all the Ecstasy entering the British Isles was coming in from Holland and - as a result - scrutiny was heightened when it came to lorries and boats arriving from there - that he have my shipment of pills re-routed to another destination *before* shipping to the U.K, so as not to have it coming into the country from the *one* place that the authorities were looking for Ecstasy arriving from.

'Fifty thousand pills is just a test, to make sure it is something that we should move forward with on a bigger scale.' I sat there and told the brothers while not even sure myself if fifty thousand was an amount that we'd never shift or if it was going to be gone within the blink of an eye. Resembling the second option a lot more than it ever did the first, in actuality.

I pitched things to Eddy and German like a kid trying to persuade their mum and dad to get them something in advance of their Christmas - while telling them that it could be their next Christmas *and* birthday combined - if they'll give them what they want.

It was a venture that Eddy and German didn't *need* to get involved in. They made more than enough - in a drug sense - from the Cocaine that would leave the country each week. I'd had the feeling that they agreed to it not just because of their love of money, wherever it came from and for whatever reason. It had felt that they were also going along with it because it was *my* idea - well me and Mikael I suppose, considering it was him that put the idea into my head in the first place - and that after the work that I'd put in for them since joining the organisation, maybe I deserved a little shot at making something happen as opposed to carrying out someone else's orders to *make* something happen.

The outlay that I needed from them - while still a lot of money - was, in reality, pennies to them. I needed a couple of hundred thousand to buy the pills and another hundred to facilitate things with all of the palms that would need greasing along the process. Ahead of visiting with the brothers, and following the conversation with Hakan to talk prices, I'd then made a few speculative phone calls back to Britain. Mainly to an old friend in Edinburgh (whatever name you might have for him) whose reach, I knew, spread far enough to be able to distribute the kind of numbers I'd be looking to send over.

My phone call back to Scotland had been as surprising to him as it had been welcome.

'Well, you did tell me that if there were ever any business opportunities in the future to give you a call.' I laughed, as he eventually got over the shock of who was on the other end of the line.

'What have you been up to since you got out?' A question that I literally could not have answered inside the space of a short phone call and, most of it, he probably wouldn't have believed anyway.

Over the call I - almost in the same vein as the one to Hakan - sought out what he knew about the drug and what opinions, as a wholesaler, he currently had about the stuff.

'I started to hear about it last year but it was such an underground thing that I didn't even give it a passing thought. You know what these things are like? Fashionable drugs means that - like fashion - they're not going to be around forever so as far as I was concerned there was no point looking any further into it. Only, a year later there's even more people speaking about it than there were the year before.'

This was all music to my ears. And then came the negotiating side of things, which was challenging. Well, it is when it's a completely new market place that you're sat at the negotiating table, anyway.

Having the street price of one pill was all that I had to go by. Obviously, there would be occasions where someone would buy more than one at once and land themselves a discount so this would have to be taken account of. So would the factor of my man in Edinburgh buying from me for one price and then punting them out to the next level down at a specific price too.

My rough calculations, based on nothing other than how things would work if *I* had been making up the rules, I had estimated that selling them at half of the street value while - ourselves - making more than double what we would pay would be a good enough deal all round. Obviously, I tried for more than that. Not that it was ever going to go anywhere with my friend in 'Auld Reekie.'

For obvious reasons, I hadn't told him on the phone who I worked for, or what I did for a living. Through that, I was able to bluff away that I was just the same old Peter Duncan. The clueless f**ker who got caught in his bakery with gear and then got out of the game after that before anything else happened to him. I'd just been 'the guy' who helped store the stuff. That was my level. Years on from that he could never have known that I literally made drug deals happen for a living.

I played the fool by asking for fifteen pounds a pill. 'Innocently' saying that with them going for twenty each there was a decent fiver profit per pill and he laughed right back at me like you would do with a fool who has just displayed their stupidity.

'Not even close, Pete.' He said, dismissing the derisory opening offer from me.

I'd went into things looking for ten pounds per pill. As long as we didn't go under that I was going to be walking away happy. I still wanted to have a little fun along the way before we finally shook hands. I went to fourteen and was knocked back. When I said thirteen, that was when he said ten. Naturally, I counter offered with twelve, expecting that he would agree to meet me in the middle at eleven and hand me an unexpected one pound per pill extra.

He wasn't for budging from ten pounds a pill, however. I was happy to shake on it, like with Hakan. In a provisional sense. Everything stood and fell on the colour of light - green or red - I'd receive from my paymasters. While the salary that I'd received since joining Bogota had been what most would describe as 'handsome' it hadn't been anywhere close to something that you'd have been able to finance a major drug deal with, and besides. Even if I *had* the scratch to facilitate things alone. How would you think that Eddy and Roman - drug kingpins - would've reacted if they'd found out that one of their closest of staff was off arranging his own little side deals, without their knowledge?

No, it would either happen with their say so or it simply wouldn't happen at all.

Pitching it to them in the most basic of ways. That being, they wouldn't have to barely lift a finger other than to transfer me the start up funds and from then on all they would do would be sit back and watch the money flow in. They wouldn't need to manufacture it. They wouldn't need to ship it from South America to Europe via some elaborate way of disguise. We would just need to pay someone else to do it for us, while making a profit. The kind of profit - as things were to turn out - that I could not have possibly imagined and one that I doubt Eddy and German would have believed if I'd told them in that very first pitch following Mikael and I returning back from our mini tour of America.

They believed enough to agree to front the money to start the ball rolling. The Bogota Cartel were now in the MDMA business and the best part of all was that not a single person *knew* it. The Dutch took all the glory when it came to the U.K and the explosion of Ecstasy. No one had taken it upon themselves to think that possibly *other* organisations were doing the same thing, by alternative means. Like we were with - through the sheer might of Hakan's enterprise - our pills going to Seville and then packed up with fresh oranges headed for England. While practically anything with a Dutch postal stamp on it was being put under the microscope, on principle, our thousands of pills - with Spanish imported documentation - were smoothly entering without any issues.

The brothers loved the idea, the easy money that was there to be made and the whole set up that I had come up with to get the pills from the supplier all the way to Mikael taking delivery of the money and doing his thing with it. Plus, it was an area of narcotics that neither Medellin or Cali had ever dabbled in. Eddy saw this as a little f**k you to both cities.

I'd never believed that it would be a case of 'my' business and that Eddy and German would have been responsible for fronting me the money to begin with that would then be paid back. No, the minute that I brought the idea to them - and found it to be one that they liked the sound of - Ecstasy then became a part of the Ramirez Cartel portfolio. I was just happy to be the one to take the glory for it.

And I would be rewarded for it, too. Apart from my general salary - of which, Ecstasy related work would now be a part of - on account of the idea and literally whole operation being my idea, the brothers agreed that I would be paid a percentage out of every shipment. This alone - through the demand which increased as much as tenfold in the end - would see to it that I would become a *very* rich man.

I felt a tinge of guilt that I would receive this percentage and Miki wouldn't. That it had been *me* who had went to the brothers with this whole new business venture and the truth is. Had it not been for that night in Detroit, and Mikael's knowledge on the subject, there wouldn't have *been* any new business venture to speak of. Still, though. It wasn't as if I'd 'stolen' a business idea from him. Simply taken something that he had told me and processed it in an entrepreneurial way that would engineer a facility to make money out of it. I still felt a little guilty though as we'd very quickly formed a bit of a team mentality together. I got over it, like everything else.

Telling the brothers that, logically, the summer was coming up soon and the pills would be in demand more than ever. We acted fast.

Hakan had shipped off fifty thousand pills (along with some complimentary samples of MDMA crystals which he had told me were pure Ecstasy and could, if the market was there, fetch even more than the twenty pound a pill that we had discussed) to Spain to be then re routed to Stranraer, Scotland where my Edinburgh connect would arrange for collection. The U.K side - I had been informed - would see Edinburgh supplying the whole of Scotland and parts of northern England. He'd said that the majority of them would, initially, be going to England as demand was not as high in Scotland but 'knowing Scots' he was positive that once they actually *did* start to take them, in large numbers, they would make the English look like lightweights.

I didn't care *who* took them. As long as they did. As long as I wasn't the one who was left staring up out of a three hundred thousand pound hole with the Ramirez brothers looking back down at me.

Manny - You'd have had to do a serious amount of overtime to pay back that amount to your employers.

Peter - *laughs* Well yeah, if you were lucky. You know? As good guys as Eddy and German always were with me. I'm not really sure if I'd have been comfortable enough as to be in debt to them, to such an amount of money. I think the only real thing that would've kept me alive would've been the fact that I was probably of more worth to them alive than I would've been dead. Then again, when you have as much money as they did who the hell knows *what* goes through their minds, or where their motivations come from?

Things moved so fast, in fact, that the 'oranges' were in Scotland within three days of the order being placed to Amsterdam and the money received our way inside two weeks. Once it had been a case of all systems go I had been left with no real choice other than to tell my associate *who* it was that shipped the pills to him, and that it wasn't just some chancer from the Kingdom of Fife, Scotland who thought he'd seen an opportunity to try and make himself a few bob.

Knowing that he was dealing with the utmost in professionals and ones that came with a 'rep' *did* have its advantages. The willingness to pay on time being the main feature.

It's funny but I didn't suffer from nerves. Technically I couldn't have done the job that I did for Bogota had I done so. One week of working for that mob would've turned the average man in the street's hair grey, if he'd managed to keep it, that is. Wow was I nervous over that first deal with the pills, though. Maybe it was because it was too personal for me. Like I was too close to things, too invested. Normally if something was to go tits up in my work for Eddy and German, providing I hadn't been the actual cause of any issues, then things would be put down to business.

This time around, however? If there were 'any' issues, my fault or not. It would be my fault. The epitome of the buck stopping with someone.

It went flawlessly, though, and as far as brownie points with the jefes? Immeasurable, truly priceless. Employee of the month stuff and while I may not have taken home a gift voucher for JC Penney and a family sized ham I *did* take home an extra zero on my paycheck so you could've rammed your glazed ham right up your derriere for all that I'd have cared.

Edinburgh was back on the phone way quicker than I could ever have anticipated. This time around asking if I could send *four* times as much. Telling me that the fifty thousand had sold like hot cakes with the feedback from all corners of Scotland and the North of England that the pills that had been sold had produced a resounding MORE PLEASE.

Things spiralled from there on. It was estimated that - and yeah, while technically the pills were *made* in the Netherlands - at one point in the rise of the House Music party scene in the United Kingdom that seven out of ten pills that people popped at the weekend had been supplied by the Bogota cartel. It was a fact *never* mentioned in the press. Mainly because no one *knew* we were doing it. Regardless of *where* the pills entered Britain. They were Ecstasy pills and that equalled Holland. No one in their right mind would have suggested that a Colombian cartel - with access to endless amounts of Cocaine - would be interested in dealing Ecstasy thousands of miles away. And *that* was the beauty of it all.

The Netherlands had the scrutiny heaped upon them. They had made their name for being the ones responsible for people dancing from Saturday night right through to late Sunday morning.

Why would we, in the Bogota Cartel ever wish to do anything to dispel what everyone had accepted as common facts and, in the process, have people looking in our direction more than they already did through our Cocaine production and export gig? Nope, our friends in the Netherlands were invaluable, in that sense.

We were - predominantly - a 'Cocaine' cartel. What would *we* have to do with a drug like Ecstasy?

It was beautiful.

Only really seeing the full potential of this new venture when we received that much larger order back from Britain. The brothers asked me to visit the U.K following it, in some kind of diplomatic state visit of sorts. Meet with those who were benefiting the most out of the shipments and do the introductions to put faces to names while ensuring that this arrangement was just the start. With the larger quantities we were being asked for. That, of course, would need to lead to us drawing up new terms. We'd get them cheaper from Holland but that would need to be recognised, also, in the reflection of the terms that our U.K buyers would naturally expect to be procuring at.

Mikael and me were shipped off to Britain for a series of meetings in England and Scotland scheduled over a three day trip.

This included a trip to my very first - and last - illegal underground rave.

For a whole raft of reasons. That visit to the filthy disused factory in Blackburn was something that was to change a *lot* of lives.

Chapter 18

Read on - as part of our Post exclusive on the life and crimes of a cartel 'Mr Fixit' to find Manny Ruiz chatting with not only Peter Duncan but Eva, Peter's estranged wife, along with Steven, his son. Two 'innocent parties' who found themselves directly impacted by El Corazon Valiente's dreams of being the U.K's prime importer of MDMA, in their own separate and very individual ways.

El Corazon Valiente - The Ballad of Peter Duncan cont

Manny - Hi Eva and thank you for agreeing to take part in the article. Would you like to introduce yourself to the readers of The Washington Post? I've offered all participants - across the article - the chance to show who *they* are in *their* words. As good a journalist as I am. If you don't tell the readers a bit about you I'll only end up going with the 'trophy wife of drug cartel associate' line that, being fair, is crying out to be used. *laughs*

Eva - *laughs also* Yeah, that old chestnut? If I'd had a pound for every time I've heard or read that description of me - that, or 'narco wife' - Fort Knox would be outsourcing me for where they should keep their gold. I'm sure you're better than that though, Manny. Not as if it's The Sun you're working for. *laughs* *You* work for a highly respected publication, for one thing.

Manny - The Sun?

Eva - It's a newspaper. A tabloid. It'll be gone eventually and nothing to worry about. It's something not to be taken seriously and *exactly* the type of publication that would've - and most likely did - called me a 'trophy wife.' I'm literally speaking to you *because* you're not from one of those excuses for a newspaper. I'd never heard of you, no disrespect, but I *had* heard of The Washington Post so when I received your letter I was happy to be part of the article. Since Peter's arrest, and all of what followed that, I've tried not to read the newspapers or watch the news. Some of the things written about me? Shameful really.

Manny - As you'll see, with the finished article. There is no 'stitch up' here.

Eva - Yeah I trust you, especially since you agreed to sign the document from my lawyer - ahead of our phone call - agreeing to use direct quotes from me as part of the article! But you asked me to introduce myself to whoever is reading this article? Well my name is - soon to be - Eva Pearson although the world, I guess, will probably *always* think that my name is Eva Duncan. I'm thirty one years of age and reside in a one bedroom apartment in the centre of Manchester, England. I'm just like any other average English woman in her thirties. I love shoes, soaps, zoomba, shopping and nights out with the girls. I also - and I guess, the reason I'm sitting on the phone to an American journalist in Washington D.C - had the displeasure of meeting, and marrying, a member of a South American drugs cartel, Peter f**king Duncan.

Manny - In my vast research that I did on the very same man. It appears that he impacted on pretty much everyone that he came across. Good or bad.

Eva - You're bloody telling me, Manny. Oh how very true. I was smitten with him that first night we met. Thought that he was the knees that belonged to bees, inside that VIP room in Blackburn. How could I not? A rave that was packed with thousands of sweaty and smelly ravers, eyes popping out their skulls. And then there was Peter. Sat there in the VIP area, inside that old factory, with a bottle of champagne sat on his table and sat in what looked like a very expensive looking suit. Not a hair out of place or bead of sweat dripping from him. He didn't just look cool but from his exterior it appeared that he *was* cool. I'd never been attracted to an older man in that way. Visibly you could tell that - while probably just in his early forties - he was older, a lot, than me but there was just so much that drew me in.

Manny - How did you and him first begin speaking?

Eva - He offered me a line of Coke.

Manny - That figures.

Eva - I know right. My friends and I who had travelled the short distance from Manchester for the night had found ourselves invited into the VIP section when Jez, one of my friends, had been invited in by one of the people who was running the rave and probably wanted some extra 'eye candy' inside the room. She said she'd come as long as her friends could tag along with her, which saw us all inside there that night.

We'd all had a pill and living our best life. Hair down completely with all inhibitions left behind in Manchester. I'd noticed him - first of all sitting in discussion with another man on the sofa who appeared to be his friend although the pair of them couldn't have looked any more different for being 'friends.' Peter, in his navy suit that was more appropriate for a business meeting rather than an illegal house party while his mate had a completely different vibe going on with this whole, open buttoned shirt and enough ivory draped around his neck and wrists that Peta would have him dragged to The Hague over, thing going on.

His friend disappeared, leaving him alone there on the sofa. This led to us chatting for a few minutes and me joining him and that mountain of Charlie that was sitting on the table.

We literally exchanged a few words between us, just the usual small talk between complete strangers.

'Are you having a good night?

The standard fare. *Standard* and Peter didn't really mix, though. After the hey how are you and are you having a good night part he skipped straight to the pointing towards the ounces of Cocaine there on the table, asking me if I'd like some.

We did a few lines and sat speaking for a while. His mood changed, however, when his friend returned back to the room, along with another two kids with him. Well, I say 'kids' but they were probably only a couple of years younger than myself but - in the wrecked state that they were in - they looked even younger than they probably were. Something about them seemed to spook the man who had introduced himself to me as Peter. Seeing them, his mood changed completely, and instantly.

In a way that almost seemed appropriate for someone sitting in the middle of an illegal rave wearing a suit with a bottle of champagne and mound of Cocaine sitting in front of him. He snapped from being the charming, smiling and attentive man he'd portrayed from the start to someone who was now dismissing me with the simple wave of a hand. Cutting me off mid sentence and curtly informing me that he now wanted me to go. He seemed so fixed on the three people that had entered the room that I don't even think that my 'F**k you, you ignorant f**king c**t' even registered with him before I stormed back across and rejoined my friends. First impressions, they say? I should've ran a country mile, I really should've.

Peter - As was often the case, it was Mikael. I'd never have even set foot anywhere close to that filthy factory in Blackburn, Lancashire, - You might have heard of it? If John Lennon was to be believed there were four thousand holes in the place, even if they were only really small - me sharing a Saturday night with thousands of goggled eyed and spaced out kids *not* exactly what I would choose to do. Michelin rated meal, a few glasses of a choice vintage red and - if in the mood although it has to be said, very rarely - possibly taking one of the regular hotel bar prostitutes back to my room with me. Not being stuck in such a hot, filthy and noisy environment. That music? It appeared that - back in Detroit - the pill had somehow empowered me into being able to find the music palatable.

Blackburn and me in business mode with the company head on and nowhere near *taking* one of the same pills that, for the majority, was making everyone out in the main room's night, left my head hurting with that monotonous and repetitive thumping beat that never, ever seemed to stop. Literally for even one second.

We'd been scheduled to meet with one of the heads of a family that, give or take, pretty much ran Manchester, earlier in the day at our hotel, in the city centre. Instead, we'd received a call to notify us that their flight back from Malaga had been delayed due to striking French traffic air controllers and were given the choice of meeting with him later that night at an alternative address or we could reschedule for the Sunday where they could come out to meet with us at the hotel. I was happy for the latter. When Mikael learned that the 'alternative address' had been an abandoned factory where a rave was taking place. One where our Manchester associate had a vested interest in having a stake in the actual staging of the rave as well as - naturally - the complete run of the place when it came to selling drugs.

'We go for one or two hours, only.'

Mikael said in the way which meant that we would both be going but there for a lot longer than two hours.

'You sure, mate?' The taxi driver who had been sitting outside our hotel in his cab asked straight up when I'd given him the address of where we wanted him to take us to.

A Saturday night, ten o clock or so. A bustling and vibrant city like Manchester with all of its pubs, clubs and restaurants. And he's got two men in his cab - dressed to go out - asking him to take them on an hours drive to Blackburn to an address that is on an industrial estate.

'Is this proof enough that I'm sure?' I replied - still less than excited about where I was going. I'd always preferred to do business in a professional sense and this kind of scenario was *not* what I looked on as business like - as I shoved two fifty pound notes into his hand before telling him not to worry and that they were real.

We arrived to the blackout like industrial estate. An area which looked like better days had been and gone, when it came to any kind of flourishing business sectors. I mean, when the council can't even be bothered to provide street lighting around the place, that's never a good sign.

We'd been told to mention to the first security we came across who it was that had invited us along for the night, and that we were there to meet with them. Letting them know that we'd been told that we would be looked after from there on. This confirmed when we arrived at the entrance and - to the audible displeasure of the lines of people waiting to enter - walked to the front to speak to security and were immediately led around the side of the building where we were let in a separate entrance to the building and taken directly to the VIP room.

A place that was another world compared to the sardine like way that everyone was packed in outside in the main hall of the factory. Sofas, a free bar and with the various types of drugs that were neatly placed out on a table to the side of the bar, it wasn't just alcohol that was complimentary.

We'd been told that our man was now back in England and approximately an hour away or so away and in the mean time to just enjoy the place and feel free to take advantage of all of the home comforts that had been made available to us.

Putting on the Ramirez Cartel head on for a second. I'd been annoyed that the man from Manchester had not made the original meeting which had been scheduled. I know, I know. French air traffic controllers. Evil incarnate, them. *And* the baggage handlers. When the summer rolls around you can be sure one or the other is going to go on strike. Like clockwork. Still, as far as appearances go. There was a meeting scheduled between Bogota and Manchester, *in* Manchester. And it had been the South American representatives who had been the ones there and available. That stuff, on a level of respect, didn't play well with us.

To then have the feeling that not only did they not show for the meeting but that now *I* was having to go to *them*. That, obviously, wasn't the case but it felt that way at the time. I should've been relaxing back at the hotel ahead of travelling up to Scotland later the next day and, instead, I was somewhere completely different to that.

A couple of lines helped perk me up and bring me more into the party spirit, as always does. Mikael's and my reaction - to the actual party that was going on there inside the factory - could not have been more stark. He had a look on his face that suggested he couldn't wait to get himself down there and into the mix of things where, for me, it appeared like some kind of a living hell and one that I was going nowhere near, thank you very much.

It only took us to partake in the free Coke that was laid out for us for Mikael and me to go our separate ways for a while. Me politely declining his offer for us to go out and have a walk around and check the place out. Telling him that I felt that at least one of us should hang back in the room for when our Manchester connect arrived. Reasoning - and with quite a bit of weight behind it - that if we were to go out into 'that' who could predict when we'd make it *back* to the VIP area again.

Like some dad with his kid at the park who just wants to sit and read his paper while their kid plays, I urged Miki to go out and do the exploring that he so obviously wanted to do and that I'd sit tight and wait in VIP. I mean, following how things had gone so far, a big part of me kind of wanted *not* to be sitting right there waiting on the arrival of our Manc associate. Just to make a point, if anything. The thing was, an even BIGGER part of me didn't want to be stuck inside that heaving and swaying room of sweaty and loved up dancers.

While sitting tight, having a glass of the complimentary Dom Perignon and really just minding my own business - I wasn't there to party, socialise or mix. I was there on business - I ended up striking up a conversation with a girl that was in there. I'd noticed her sitting with her friends when Mikael and myself had been shown in but by the time I was sitting alone she had found herself just kind of drifting around the room, having a kind of semi enthusiastic dance to herself in her own world, sunglasses on - despite the relative darkness in the room - holding a tall drink, occasionally taking a sip through a straw.

'Looks like someone's living their best life.'

I was surprised by her right as I was lifting my head up from the table and the line that I had just taken.

'Me? I'm working right now.' I said with a laugh as I thought of how stupid the words must've sounded despite how true they actually were.

'Yeah, you look it.' She said with a teasing suspicious look on her face.

'So are you going to come and sit down and have a glass of champagne with me or are you going to make me sit and stare up at you until I end up with a sore neck?'

I said to her, not really knowing why - as the furthest thing in my mind was trying to chat the girl up. For god's sake, the girl could've been in Stevie's year at school for all I'd known - other than it feeling a natural thing to ask on account of how friendly she had appeared and that I was sat there with a whole bottle of champagne to myself. It would've been rude not to, really.

She jumped at the chance and within minutes we were sitting with a glass of champagne talking back and forth at speed following some more lines. It wasn't going to go anywhere - her and I - but she was fun to talk to in the kind of way that I'd not had the pleasure of in years. At the very least, it was an ego stroke of the best kind to find - out of all the people milling around the room - that she wanted to sit and speak with *me*.

Even though it was only the shortest of time that the pair of us sat speaking for, it had felt like we had already known each other. A cliche, I know, but how else can you describe an instant rapport with someone that you've never met before?

Then, of course, Mikael came along and spoiled what had been one of the rare occasions where one could have described me as relaxing and enjoying myself.

Manny - Spoil? How so?

Peter - Well if I could get a do-over with that because 'spoiled' isn't really the word to be used. I mean, he reunited me with my son after having not seen him in almost ten years. Spoiled would be a harsh word for it and for the benefit of my son who may or may not read this article, 'interrupted' was the word that I was searching for.

Manny - Mikael? Steven? How?

Peter - Well yeah, exactly. Mysterious ways, Manfred. The world works in the most mysterious of ways, my friend.

I recognised the little bastard straight away. Obviously he'd grown a bit but he had the one dead giveaway in that he was blessed (or cursed, you'd have to ask him) with the same good looks as his father and I mean the *exact* same. Basically a younger and more dysfunctional version of myself. When called him - and his friend - one to join us at the sofa. I couldn't take my eyes off him, my heart racing faster than the entire contents of what was lying on the table in front of me could've come close to achieving. Once he saw me, his eyes never left me either.

We both kept quiet for as long as was required. For an enthusiastic Miki to make the introductions of Stevie and his friend to me.

It's the funniest of things but the only reason that Mikael was even introducing these lads to me was *because* Stevie had caught his attention, wearing a t shirt with the words 'Narcotics Officer' emblazoned on the front, in some kind of private joke amongst ravers.

Manny - That is some irony right there, Peter. Your son - who you haven't met since before Bogota becoming part of your life - wearing a t shirt stating that he's a narcotics officer while he has a dad doing the work that he did and in fact *there* in the same building as part of his remit of facilitating the flow of narcotics from country to country. That's actually quite amusing.

Peter - Funny? You want to know what's *not* funny? Seeing your son, after several amount of missing years, out of his tree on Ecstasy that you can't give him a hard time over because there was a high probability that it had come directly from *yourself*. In the years that we'd been apart - without anything remotely close to 'contact' - I'd imagined what it would be like, the day that we finally came face to face again. I'd played this out in my mind time and time again, in different situations and settings.

Not *that* setting though. I could never have come close to imagining *that* would have been how our reunion would ever have went down. Me trying to show how remorseful I was - regarding the relationship or *lack* of that the boy and I shared - while he was incapable of even finishing a sentence never mind fully appreciating the deep and sincere words that his father was sat trying to convey to him.

Sitting there, Exhibit f**king A of what I, personally, had helped bring to the U.K. Jaw swinging like a gate left open in the wind, manic perma-smile fixed to his face during a situation that most would *not* sit and smile through. It was an amazing feeling in the world - to see him again - bit it had been extremely weird, as his dad, to see him like that compared to the last time I had which had been nearer the start of the Eighties than Nineteen Ninety. I'd missed out on so much of his growing up. The changes in him. There, in Blackburn, I was given a more updated version of the not so much finished product but the very much work in progress and, from what I saw in front of me, the kid had *much* progress yet to make!

It was a strange and conflicting feeling, meeting again. I mean, if you needed someone to call a spade a spade and say their piece then I was your man. I'd practically built a brand out of it. It's how you *needed* to be in my game. No room for the shy and silent types, I assure you.

Yet even so, there with Stevie. Even if I'd hadn't had the suspicion that, - playing the odds, there was a good percentage of a chance that whatever pill he had (evidently) taken it had been supplied by the Ramirez Cartel masquerading as just another one of the pills that the Dutch distro were responsible for - I wasn't exactly the most innocent of parties. I think it would've been still difficult for me to have bent his ear over the drugs. It almost felt like too much water had passed under the bridge for me to be given the *right* to order him about, or give him "fatherly" advice. That ship was well out on the water by then.

Naturally, I had hidden the finer details of who I worked for - and what kind of job it was that I did - from him. I mean, who would broadcast to their son or daughter that they worked for a criminal cartel out of Colombia? Hardly the type of thing to be proud of - even though on a personal level I was *extremely* proud of myself - between parents and their kids. Plus, and with no offence towards that son of mines, *who* I worked for was a topic that I didn't tell anyone and those who I did tell it was only because of it being a case of a *need* to or that it was unavoidable due to work reasons. In hindsight, looking back at that night. The condition that my son was in. I could've told him all of the Bogota Cartel's biggest secrets and he'd have forgotten them again after five seconds, anyway.

I'd settled for 'importer / exporter in South America' with Stevie taking all of this at face value even though what I had termed it - on the spot and without any planning - was literally the most blatant euphemism you could have possibly come up with for someone who worked for a Colombian cartel.

That he didn't follow up with 'what kind of business' when I had told him that I was there - inside the factory rave - as part of my work was a clear indicator that the boy's mind wasn't at the races.

Stevie - How did I feel? At the moment where I saw my father again, after all those years? Well in a word, Manny. TROLLEYED! Those White Doves, back then? They didn't take any prisoners, mate. Of course, myself and my friend, popping our MDMA crystals cherry a wee bit before I was to be reunited with the man himself. Well, that didn't help matters. My mental state literally deteriorated there in front of him in the short time - what was it? An hour? - that we chatted.

Manny - I meant emotionally. How did it feel on an emotional level to meet your father again?

Stevie - Manny? I'd had a f**king White Dove how the f**k do you think I felt 'emotionally' towards him? *laughs* I LOVED the guy. Plus, he gave me a wad of guilt cash - that would've choked Red Rum

- over not having seen me for a while which, now that I think about it, my girlfriend had made me hand over to her because 'I would lose it' and that she would give it back to me later which now that I recall, I don't think she ever did. Not that I'd had a chance to count it anyway so no real sense of losing of whatever it was I'd lost, there.

Emotionally though? In that moment and with how I was feeling, well the loved up with the world version of me? That whole business of completely disregarding the whole being my dad stuff? Oh all that - during that moment, at least - was simply all water under the bridge.

Obviously, had I met him in the street or some other mundane setting the chances are I'd have punched his lights out for being such a deadbeat dad but well, what can I say? He chose the optimum time to show his face. It was literally a practical open goal for him.

I could've sat there all night speaking to him and I think you'd do well to find a better way to describe the effects of MDMA. This was a man who - over the years due to his inactivity when it came to being a dad to me - I had developed a deep dislike and distrust towards. I had travelled all the way down to England for the biggest House Music party that I had yet to experience and despite this - instead of being out there dancing and soaking in, what I can now look back and class as history, - there I was, quite the thing, sitting chatting away with my pops. The man who - and I may be paraphrasing myself here - I once said that I wouldn't pee on if he'd been stung by a jellyfish. Obviously, peeing on a parent, or anyone for that matter, is just plain weird but you know what I'm saying, eh?

Manny - Rrrrrrrrrrright.

Stevie - So how's the interview going so far, Manny? According to plan now that we find ourselves talking about jellyfish stings and urine? *laughs*

Manny - Did the Manchester associate arrive on the night?

Peter - Oh yes, I'm not sure there's many out there who would be as suicidal to stand up the Ramirez Cartel twice! To be very fair, until he arrived I really *had* been looked after and made to feel like a true VIP and it's touches like that which can go a long way. I'd actually felt a little guilty but having just met up with my son for the first time in so long - and with how fast time can really go in such moments - but near to the end of our chat I'd began clock watching, knowing that any moment he was going to walk into the room, most likely shadowed by a couple of heavies and completely radiating 'gangland' and looking directly to speak to me.

I needed Stevie to be gone before any of this took place. I felt like - what some would *actually* accuse me of - the worst father in the world. Hadn't seen the boy in the best part of ten years. Him and I should've been inseparable right there but no, I'm watching the clock and making sure that he didn't overstay his welcome. Just words, I know but had I *not* had prior business that had already been arranged to attend to I'd have happily sat there on that sofa and spoken to him until the final record had been spun. In *that* kind of a situation, however? I just didn't want the boy to see me 'at work' and what the optics may have looked like to him.

The Manchester connect - and really, the only reason that I was even there - could not have been more nice and accommodating, once we finally all sat down to talk. In his eyes, Mikael and me were GODS. We were the ones who were responsible for all of the pills that he had sold across the night and in the days leading up to it. We were there to see real time evidence of his customers in action. As some do when they think that they're dealing with some kind of - in their mind - cash cow, he looked on us as if we were royalty.

He had plans for some major expansions, which would benefit us in turn. That's all I wanted to hear. As nice as it was to receive the kiss ass gestures along the way that you would receive simply through people's knowledge that you worked for the Ramirez brothers. I didn't want my ass kissed *or* wiped. Never *asked* for to be treated as royalty. I just wanted to go back to Bogota and shove a list of orders onto the table and bask in the kudos - and eventual money - that my endeavours had brought. That's *all* I ever wanted to do whether that was through Ecstasy, Cocaine, Heroin or a bloody Panzerfaust 3 rocket launcher.

Manny - It would be stating the obvious to say that despite Peter Duncan dismissing you in the way that he had - there inside the VIP room at the illegal rave - this was not the end of the story of Peter and Eva. What happened?

Eva - First of all, I need to say that I'm not one of those highly strung types but I hadn't been happy with how he had practically waved me away with a hand. One moment we'd been sitting chatting and laughing. He'd been charming and enchanting in the kind of way that you don't normally find in men. Some could accuse this of being the effect of the E that night but well, I lived with the man for years, married him. It wasn't the Ecstasy. In the blink of an eye, though. He went from that charming and affable man to shooing me away like he was some ancient king sitting one hundred steps above you on their throne. Like I was some peasant who had come looking to them for assistance with a problem, only to be dismissed with the casual wave of a hand.

Following me standing there - before I left the table - and giving the man who had introduced himself simply as 'Peter' a piece of my mind - which considering the buzz I was on that night was quite remarkable as I hadn't had an angry or hostile bone in my body - to which he hadn't even given me the time or consideration of even listening to, I thought that would've been that. Putting him down to just another one of those cranks that you - as a girl - would meet on a night out.

Sometimes a diamond in the dirt but the majority of the time. Well, someone like how Peter Duncan had treated me.

I'd looked over his way a few times more, when I was back with the group, having a dance and a chat. It had been mainly him just sat there with one of the kids that had walked in. The pair of them could not have appeared more different. Peter sitting there in his suit with a serious expression to his face as he spoke while the teenager - who was clearly rolling - sat there looking like he wasn't taking the conversation in anywhere *near* as much as the other.

Eventually the teenager - along with his mate - left Peter and his friend after what felt like ten minutes of hugs, handshakes and loud laughter. In what was almost a WWF wrestling tag team move. The two young guys walked - I'm being complimentary when I attribute them as walking. Bumbling, would be more accurate, out of the room. In the same moment a man - with what looked like a couple of bodyguards hanging slightly behind him - swaggered past them and made straight for the same table and sofa that I'd been sitting at earlier in the night.

There, Peter, his friend draped in the ivory jewellry, and the man in the cream suit all sat in close discussion. As high as I was, I wasn't daft either. *This* was not normal scenes for a rave. Men in suits sitting drinking champagne and looking like they were heading to do business on Wall Street rather than raving in Store Street.

I gave them not much more thought than that. Obviously they were dodgy and up to dodgy doings. It was none of my business. I got on with my night. Even spent a good two to three hours outside in the factory dancing and having the time of my life. Out of everything about the scene, in those early days. The clubs round our way such as The Hacienda and Quadrant Park over in Liverpool. They were biblical places to visit and 'participate' in. The 'afters' in Blackburn, though? *They* were my favourite place to party. The fact that there was no airs or graces. It was a Saturday night and you were standing inside a dirty and derelict factory for god's sake?! Even in the early days of those all night parties in Blackburn. As illegal as you knew everything all was - for me, anyway - they were enjoyed like each and every one was going to be the *last* one before the police closed them down.

With an attitude like that. I wasn't going to let someone as insignificant as a Peter Duncan spoil my fun.

It was hours later and, like I said, after around three hours of straight dancing that I landed myself back in the VIP area. More to create a bit of space for myself compared to the zoo that was going on outside in the main hall. Almost as if he'd had his arse superglued to the sofa. He was sitting there in the exact same position as he'd been when I'd first set eyes on him to the last.

He was sitting there with his friend with the open shirt, long curly middle parting and the ivory. Seeing me walking in and in his direction towards the bar his face lit up. This alone confusing me. Why would he be happy to see the girl that he had so arrogantly brushed aside hours earlier?

'Eva, thank god you've come back in here. I've been looking for you but was never going to find you out there. Do you have a few minutes? I'd like to apologise.'

Now *this* I did not expect and rocked me in that kind of way where you've already decided that you're pissed off at someone only for them to do or say something - that doesn't suit the idea that you've already formed about them - which completely throws you. Stopping you from going through with the actions that you already had in mind.

'Ummmm, yeah. Let me get a bottle of water first.'

I replied only for him to tell me that he'd get someone to bring one over to me and asking me to sit and join him. His friend seemingly taking this as his cue to make himself scarce. Offering me a small smile and a hello as he got up out of the sofa before leaving us to it.

There, Peter sat and apologised to me for what he had done earlier. Telling me that he hadn't even really been fully aware of *what* he had done as he had been acting purely in an autopilot sense.

When he explained to me the *reason* for why he had suddenly resembled Jekyll and Hyde with me. I understood right away.

'You appeared as if you'd seen a ghost.' I said to him in agreement when he was talking to me about how one second he was sitting having a joke with me and the next left in a trance like state looking at his grown up son walking into the room.

What a headf**k *that* must've been for the guy. And as for poor Stevie, if we want to flip things around. There can't be many kids think that they're going to bump into their mum or dad when on a night out raving. If they did, deejays would be standing there playing to an empty hall.

He didn't have to but he told me the history between him and his son and how - for various reasons - he hadn't seen him in almost a decade. As much as he had been happy to see him again I was left with the impression that the 'setting' had not been one that either him *or* his son would've chosen, for their own individual reasons.

That aside, we spent the rest of the night together. His friend, Mikael, ended up getting chatty with Sarah - one of my friends in our group - which meant we barely seen him for the rest of the night, leaving the pair of us to chat and - when I was able to twist his arm - have a dance with each other.

My plans for going back to a friends pad in Manchester for our usual Blackburn afters was swapped for taking Peter back to mines, with a doggy bag of the free Charlie that was inside the VIP, where he stayed with me until having to call a taxi to get him back to his hotel in the city centre. The most ambiguous 'more business' the answer when I'd asked him why he was travelling to Scotland on a Sunday afternoon.

When it had come to the 'business' side of things. Like I told you, Manny. Yeah I'd had one and a half pills that night when I was inside the VIP room in Blackburn but had still picked up enough - from what I'd seen - to know that Peter Duncan was no double glazing salesman.

Lying on the bed - talking in general - the subject of where he lived inevitably came up. I'd really enjoyed the night and then the following morning with him. He *was* older than any man I'd ever been with but with his sense of style, attitude and way that he obviously took pride in himself, it made you almost forget that he was double your age. This being confirmed when he'd told me that he was forty one. Him almost cringing when hearing that I was nineteen. The fact that he was officially old enough to be my father and putting that to the side. He was someone that I'd wanted to see again.

Manny - And what was your reaction when you learned that he lived in Bogota?

Eva - I almost dropped the two mugs of tea that I had just made for us and was carrying when he'd told me but, apart from that, I'd thought Bogota was in Argentina so when he'd told me where his official place of residence was, I didn't even have the *correct* country in my head. Only that it was thousands of miles away. That much I *did* know.

Learning of that. It pretty much deflated any kind of plans that my 'comedown frazzled mind' had been forming of seeing the man again. It's a little difficult to forge a deep and meaningful relationship when you can't even see or touch the other person, never mind enjoy the basics of a 'partnership' with someone else. After the night of sex, drugs and House Music that the pair of us had enjoyed. Going from that to pen pals - writing across continents - would've felt like an extremely big drop off.

Of course, though. At this point, Peter hadn't given me *full* disclosure in that - for him - the fact that he was in Bogota and me in Manchester was all merely a minor factor. That morning - lying in bed recovering from the night out in Blackburn - I didn't know the level of finances behind the man *or* that he had the ability to make *anything* happen, if he desired it so. I never realised the power that he possessed and how - if you let him in - the ability he had to change your life for the better, or the worse.

Or both.

He left mines a little after lunchtime with a peck to my cheek and my phone number in his personal organiser. Telling me that he'd call me.

Yeah, we've all heard that one before but when its coming from someone who lives in Colombia you take it with the grain of salt that it should be taken with.

Manny - Peter, it would be hard to disagree that Nineteen Ninety was a defining year. Not only was it the year that you set up the Ramirez Cartel with its Ecstasy expansion but - directly through this - met both your future wife *and* was thrust back in contact with your long lost son.

Peter - Well you could never have predicted it all but yeah there *is* a link there, Manfred. Merging together in the way that it ended up doing so. Some might say that had Miki and I not went out to that club in Detroit that night then *none* of it would've happened. I think - knowing what I know now - the only guarantee of what would've *still* happened, even if I'd kept my nose out of the Ecstasy game, is that my son would've *still* landed himself up in that Blackburn factory that night. *laughs*

But, yeah. Technically, that night - and how a lot of my life appeared to all come together in one neat little package with things like beautiful partners and estranged sons falling practically into my lap - it should've signalled the beginning of a new phase of life. Sure I'd be continuing on with my work for the brothers and living out of Bogota but I had a chance to do it while being on terms with my son and - potentially - creating a new life with a significant other. It should've been nothing less than a positive thing. Life's never that simple though, is it?

While - weirdly - both Stevie and Eva had been in the same room as each other that night back in Ninety, they never actually *met* each other. It would - in fact - take the pair of them another six years before they *did* meet and wow, were *they* less than ideal circumstances that it would be under.

Manny - You were given a fresh start with your father, through your chance meeting. A cleaning of the slate, so to speak. Did you and Peter embrace the second chance that you were given?

Stevie - Fresh start? *laughs* Oh aye. Me and pops embraced the new beginning that we were gifted. Grabbed the second chance like someone who has just beaten cancer and, to celebrate, goes right to the shop for twenty Regal King Size.

And look, Manny. When I say stuff like this I really hope that it doesn't come across as me being cynical and sarcastic towards my dad. I may not have understood it as much back at the start of the Nineties when I was younger but now I'm a bit wiser, in addition to having had the benefit of learning all about my father through American news networks and the internet. I appreciate that the man's life back then couldn't have been easy and *definitely* wasn't one that I would've wanted to have lived.

Did all of that stop him from putting in a wee phone call across the Atlantic to his son? Probably not. And I know it takes two to tango but with him you never f**king knew which country he was even in half the time and even when he was in Colombia - not working - he was telling you to call satellite phone numbers to get him on which I kept telling him that I'd need to rob a bank to even *afford* the cost of a call to a phone like that but he'd never, ever listen to me.

And as 'challenging' as it was to have a father such as the one that I was blessed with - and while we're on the subject of Nineteen Ninety - I can't really speak about this period of his and my life and *not* mention the fact that - following us bumping into each other in England - the man really came through for me in the second half of that year. I'd been having - without going too far into things - some personal problems that didn't really seem like an end was in sight to. One chat with my father about it and within a week. Problem solved. Of course, I didn't understand the moves that he could make just from a phone call.

It has been well documented by the electronic music magazines by this point but that year he also bought me my first set of Technics decks. It might have seemed insignificant at the time when he had them shipped to me. At the very least, it ensured that his son was set on a path much different to the one that he had started on at the same age.

While the man over the years has given me nothing but headaches I will always thank him for what he did for me. He's a father, he's *meant* to be able to help fix his son's problems, you'd naturally ask? Well my own specific problem wasn't just any simple one and *any* father who would be able to fix it would've needed to be one with a very special set of skills and resources in his locker.

Out of all the odds. Mines was of the very small percentage of men who fell into that bracket.

It was a good thing bumping into him, when I did. He literally gave me back my life which is ironic because the next time again that I would see him, it appeared that he was going out of his way to ensure that I had it taken *away* from me again.

Chapter 19

Peter

'So what meal would you have, if you could choose anything for one of those dickhead guards to deliver right up to you in your cell?'

'Are you sure talk like that is going to help things?' I responded to Gary, negatively. I'd already been stuck in the past. Filled full of the finest foods in some of the world's most famous restaurants - as part of my earlier phone interview with Ruiz - only to return back to reality, once the phone call ended.

I didn't want to fucking hear how good Gary's nan's home made Yorkshire Puddings were. I was never going to see one at the ADX. Shit? It had been so long since I'd even *eaten* a Sunday Roast that I wasn't even sure that I remembered what a Yorkshire Pudding even *tasted* like. I reasoned that they couldn't have been *that* spectacular - whether made by Gal's nan or not - if I couldn't even remember that.

I had absolutely no interest in hearing Gary's reminiscing about all things great and good outside the walls, barbed wire and - in would be no way surprising in the slightest - probable landmines. I was all out of reminiscing. It was a double edged sword. It allowed you to call upon some happier memories that you have tucked away in your mind but in doing so only serves to magnify just how shit your life has now become when you hold that mirror up.

Despite my protestations. Gary carried on regardless. Roast beef, roast and standard potatoes, carrots, broccoli, Yorkshire puddings (gran made, obviously) and Bisto gravy all over it. The list of things that he rattled off to me that he was never again going to see for the rest of his life.

I just wasn't in the mood for him, or anything. Wasn't even in the mood for having to live with my own self and thoughts, never mind anyone else's. Yeah, one of those kind of moments.

The chat with Manny, and - in particular - Nineteen Ninety and Eva and Stevie, had left me in an extremely contemplative mood. That summer, and all of the things that came together over it. It should've been the springboard for me. That was the summer where *everything* had fallen into place. My stock with the Ramirez Cartel had never been higher. The fact that I, personally, had brought a completely new product to the cartel and one that was already making them a lot of money through, it was something that had ensured that 'The Scotsman' would be taken a lot more seriously and held in much higher regard than he might've been when he'd first arrived in the country.

Aside from that. I had my son back and, in addition to that, - for the first time since splitting with Stevie's mum - something resembling a promising relationship with someone. What more could a man have even asked for? Wealthy, healthy and happy. Like I said, all of those components should've propelled me into a new phase of life.

I'd been left thinking about it all, when back at my cell. How if I could've taken myself back to that summer of Ninety once more. Met Eva, reunited with Stevie but then made a series of *different* decisions following that summer it may have led to a different outcome. One where I kept Eva and Stevie didn't end up turning his back on me.

Then again. Following that summer, I still had a *lot* of years worth of work for Eddy and German lying ahead of me. To have tried to have had a go at predicting how something was going to be in a weeks time was always a bit of a liberty taken back in those days. To try and play some Four-D chess and see how things would turn out years down the line for you, or those closest to you. An impossible task.

For the most part, I just let Gal rattle on for the whole of our chat that night. He, himself, so into things that I don't think he even noticed how quiet I'd been.

Manny - from the way he had conducted the interviews so far - had been working his way through things in a chronological sense - allowing for the unpredictable rambles that I would go on once a certain memory had been triggered - and this meant that we'd soon be getting into some of the inner workings of the Ramirez Cartel and the 'business trips' that Eddy and German had sent me around the world on.

Some dangerous, others farcical and a few downright scary as hell but none of them never less than lucrative.

Nineteen Ninety to Ninety Six.

Days that - as a cartel associate - I would look back on as the golden ones. The rise within the ranks, the money accumulated, the glitz and glamour, and respect earned and received. That beautiful period of time that someone invariably enjoys before, inevitably, it all turns to shit.

Chapter 20

El Corazon Valiente - The Ballad of Peter Duncan cont

Manny - So with all of the successes of Nineteen Ninety and having completed a full year of working for the Ramirez brothers. It was a case of strength to strength for you, yes?

Peter - Oh yeah, but that golden year was not something that you could just ride off into the sunset and dine out on forever. And Eddy and German had been quick to recognise - and remind me - this. Once the initial honeymoon period that our Ecstasy operation had enjoyed subsided, the two brothers telling me that it was time to get back to work. Well, the *work* that they had brought me into the cartel to perform. The Ecstasy - and all the money that it was bringing back to Colombia per month - had been nothing other than an unexpected bonus for them. They'd brought me on board to help make them money. Which I had, only - and mainly - in a way that they'd not estimated for.

Later than they'd anticipated. It was time to put me out into the world in a much more sustained way.

Manny - You'd had a few trips before the diversion that the Ecstasy deals provided, Inglewood for sure. Where did they send you to once things had returned to as planned and they put you back to work?

Peter - Where did they send me? Where *didn't* they send me would probably be a question that would save The Washington Post on their phone bill if put to me, Manfred. I had more Air Miles than Michael Palin.

The brothers took me out to lunch one afternoon - along with Roman, Gonzalo (German's son) and a couple of the capos, Lucho Sensini and Adrian Ortega - where, at times, it felt almost like a yearly work appraisal where they talked over some of my successes over the year I'd spent as part of the 'familia.' The way the two brothers gushed with praise over what work I'd done for them, the exact kind of thing that an employee would sit there and relish hearing. If they kept on talking my head was never going to fit through the front door of restaurant.

'Everywhere you've been sent, whatever the task, you get things done and over the line.'

Eddy sat there - at the head of the table along with his brother - saying to me. The rest of the table all sitting agreeing with him, nodding their heads.

'And the MDMA, senor? Well *that* came from nowhere, didn't it but already we see that it is a market that will net the organisation millions. Take this, Pedrito. You've earned it.'

He picked up a package that had been lying on the large table in front of him. It looked something to the equivalent of a five hundred page pack of A4 paper.

There 'was' paper inside it, right enough. A lot more interesting than plain sheets of foolscap, too.

I wasn't naive to literally count it out on the table in front of everyone - instead choosing to say a gracious thank you to both Eddy and German - but I was receiving a small thank you bonus for what I had brought to the cartel with the Ecstasy idea.

The term 'small thank you' bonus being something that should be used *very* loosely. Counting the U.S Dollars back at the hacienda later that afternoon I was to find that there was half a million inside the packaging.

You know? It's funny but you would have the idea that half a million dollars would look a lot more than it actually *does*. Regardless, it still all spends the same, no matter the size, shape or smell of the stuff.

'We, however, need to get down to some *real* business, Pedrito.'

German followed up my thank you to him and his brother with.

'Yes,' Eddy said, interrupting. 'The real reason that we brought you to Colombia. The money from Ecstasy, it's good but you will make us a *lot* more money elsewhere than you will ever through our Dutch pills operation.'

Manny - Cocaine and weapons?

Peter - Well, yeah. Along with the rest. The corruption, the bribery, blackmail and general shithousery that my role required.

Manny - It almost sounded like an employer telling you that they were very impressed with your work but, with a caveat.

Peter - Well anything that follows the word 'but,' as they say, Manfred. You're right though. I'm not sure if they thought that I had purposely hijacked my designated role with the cartel and that I thought I could pick and choose what to do *because* of me bringing the Ecstasy deal to the table, but this couldn't have been further from the truth. Yeah, I'd taken a piece of pride of making something big happen, all from my own initiative and bravery and yes, I had been enjoying the pats on the back that it had brought. In truth, though, I would go where Eddy and German told me to go. I mean, I was hardly likely to tell them that I *wouldn't*, was I?

This was them, I felt, reining me in a little. Which was fine by me. Well, fine up to a point. I hadn't learned of *where* they were sending me as part of 'getting back to business.'

Manny - That sounds all very ominous. Where *did* the Ramirez brothers send you?

Peter - Khartoum, Sudan. Where I was to negotiate and close a deal involving the purchase of the contents of several poppy fields in Kabul. I'd been told that it was a simple straight purchase - from cartel to seller for the opium - but that I had the freedom to involve any potential arms trades in addition to monetary. The meeting had been all set up for two days time, he was sitting there telling me.

Manny - Why didn't you just fly *directly* to Kabul to carry out the negotiations.

Peter - Well, I did have that very same thought myself when I was given the finer details of things but, you know? It wasn't exactly out of the ordinary for me to meet X in Y to discuss something that would happen thousands of miles away in Z. As I was to find out, though. There was a *lot* more to it than that.

Manny - Who was it that you were being sent to meet with?

Peter - Well it was the funniest of things, Manfred. Eddy had told me that it was some group of freedom fighters. Rebels, if you like. A group who had sprung up, you know? One of those religious types? Not being really a religious person, myself. I still knew enough to know how important some of those types took their faith. Eddy had told me that they were growing the poppies *specifically* so that they could help raise funds for their cause. Had almost painted them as having risen up against oppressors and that *they* were the good guys. That they had helped push the Russians back out of Afghanistan and well, the Russians *were* the bad guys, weren't they? If they had fought against the Soviet Union then they must've been stand up guys, eh?

Manny - I'm not sure I like where this is heading.

Peter - Well in my full defence. I had never heard of him, or them but yeah, I was heading to Khartoum to meet with a delegation from a group going by the name of 'Al Qaeda' and someone who they called 'The Emir.'

Chapter 21

El Corazon Valiente - The Ballad of Peter Duncan cont

Manny - You flew to Sudan to meet with the person who would go on to gain global notoriety and become the world's most wanted man. To sit down and do business with, Al Qaeda, the world's most sought after, and infamous, terrorist organisation. How did it go?

Peter - Even to this day, when I sit and think about that meeting, it chills me to the bone. To know that I sat in the same room as him. It's like, how people say that if they could go back in time they would kill Hitler. Well I didn't *need* to go back in time. I literally sat in the same room as Osama bin Laden for the course of one and a half hours. While I'm not saying that had I killed him in that meeting it would have prevented all of the attacks that the West have suffered at the hands of 'The Base,' as they were called. You never know, though.

Of course, I wasn't going to be killing *anyone* and certainly not someone who I needed onside to rubber stamp the deal for the Opium over. I'd never had to return back to Bogota empty handed with any task I'd been set but it was something - whether the law of averages dictated that it *would* happen sooner or later, or not - that I didn't wish to experience. To go back home to the brothers and tell them that I had failed and that the deal had not been agreed. It was something that, where possible, it would be best avoided.

The meeting almost never even took place and for a while - as I was oblivious to this and still up in the air in an Egyptian airlines passenger jet - it had actually been called off.

The issue had been over my interpreter who would be accompanying me. An Arab - who had worked for the brothers in an interpreting capacity throughout the Arab world when required - called Abdullah. Al Qaeda who, I'd been told, were *very* security conscious had insisted that I travel to the meeting alone and that one of 'their' delegation would translate back and forth.

This, obviously, not working for the brothers due to the obvious. I mean, you'd have to have had a screw loose to enter into business negotiations while letting the other party be the ones solely responsible for making sure each point was put across. Eddy and German certainly didn't stockpile their billions through letting *other* - non cartel - people do their talking for them.

Eddy had explained that - while I was taking the best part of a day flying Bogota to Panama, Panama to Istanbul and then finally onto Khartoum - the meeting had been cancelled and that I'd already had a page sent to me, which I found pinging me on arrival in Khartoum, followed by another one. Advising me to ignore the *first* page.

This was the first deal that the terrorists had attempted to set up with South America and were extremely cautious about the meeting. I honestly don't know what they thought I was going to be able to do with my briefcase, although I suppose those briefcase corners *can* be quite sore if you catch someone at the correct angle?

They did not trust the fact that they were having an Arab *and* a cartel operative meeting up to then come talk with them. *Why, how* did we know Abdullah? Paranoid wasn't the word from what Eddy had told me about them although, as the years would go by, I would understand *exactly* why they had been so security conscious and cagey with regards to what - in my mind - was just another illicit deal. Just another day at the office, how I viewed it.

That view was soon altered later that evening when I received my page - as I was sitting having a quick shot of courage in the way of the bottle of Absolut that I'd smuggled into the country with me, knowing I was heading to a country more dry than Ghandi's sandals - to tell me that the car was outside to pick us up.

Abdullah, who had come to the hotel to wait with me on the arranged transport, had almost reacted like I'd whipped out my penis and started to masturbate in front of him when he saw me pulling the bottle of Vodka out of my overnight bag.

'No no no no no no no no' he just kept saying as I poured some into one of the room glasses.

'Yes yes yes yes yes yes f**king yes.' I replied. His opinion, to me, only of any worth when discussing the procurement of the poppy fields, later on.

As a way of compromise, Al Qaeda - when climbing down from me attending the meeting alone - had tried to arrange things so that I and Abdullah would be picked up in different locations and brought to the meeting venue separately. With me having never met Abdullah until that evening - at the hotel - it would've pretty much defeated the purpose had I not met him in advance as any of Al Qaeda, who could speak English, could've then told me *they* were Abdullah and I'd have just had to take them at their word.

We sat making small talk in the room while I had myself a couple of quick fire glasses with him looking on disapprovingly. Years later, on another job together and reminiscing about that first meeting, he told me that he had freaked out so much because even though he was not drinking himself, just being in the room with me, *with* the alcohol, would've brought a lot more heat than he'd have been prepared to endure.

Crazy f**king country. Man loses his shit around a bottle of Absolut Vodka yet is completely chill about having a sack put over his head and driven out to a mystery destination that - depending on how things go - he might not come back from.

Manny - *Did* they put sacks over your heads?

Peter - And the rest. When we left the hotel we found three filthy Toyota Hilux pick-ups all parked in a row. Flag upright fixed to the rear. It's not like I had the time to count - before the blackout sack was pulled over my head - but there must've easily been around fifteen upwards who had travelled in their mini motorcade to collect us.

One of them, who I took to be the leader. This guy in a pair of Aviators and a black and white Keffiyeh wrapped around his head with an ancient looking Kalashnikov strapped to his neck and hanging loose barked something in Arabic at the two of us. I was never sure with Arabic. A lot of the time it tended to sound more aggressive than the actual words possibly were. Then again, when the person is shouting and gesticulating - in a kind of stabbing motion - with an automatic rifle pointed at you, how else are you *meant* to take things?

'He is telling you to get into the back of the middle truck.' Abdullah whispered to me. The hostility was there from the very start. I'd came in peace. I'd came to do business, to make them rich. This, however, did not stop one of them from coming up from my behind and - without any kind of warning - pulling the sack down and over my head, plunging everything into darkness.

Cue lots more shouting between them, not one single word of it understood by me and by then I didn't know where Abdullah was and if he was on the back of the same pick up truck as me or one of the others. Almost shit myself when there was a round of gunfire, from what sounded like a few different rifles. This accompanied by them shouting out the same thing and laughing.

Over the years I'd seen various cells and factions letting off rounds of gunfire into the air, just because they could. Just raising their guns to the air and blasting away. No different to the 'yee haw' Americans, in that sense. It had probably been just a case of that but just you try telling your blindfolded self that when you hear that first set of bullets firing off.

The sound of the Toyota engines starting up soon after, following what appeared to be doors closing and people jumping up into the backs of the trucks.

God, was that a hellish journey. It probably goes without saying but the standard of roads in Sudan were not exactly what you would call flat and freshly laid, back in the early Nineties. Hey, a lot of countries that I visited *didn't* have what you would class as first world roads. That, in itself, isn't an issue. I wasn't a snob, in that sense. What I *was* though was someone wearing a sack covering their eyes being thrown all over the back of the pick up truck and with no way to be able to protect myself because I would never know what the hell - or when - I was crashing into.

Never mind being the epitome of cool and business like swaggering into a meeting. At the end of that long and incessantly bumpy ride I could barely walk or breathe. Smashing my kneecap into 'something' and cracking my ribs into the corner of something *else* which had left me winded and wheezing for breath.

I'd actually been left in a considerable amount of pain - on arrival at the compound - but could not afford to show it. Could not afford to show *any* weakness inside there.

'Weakness is what we pray on. There is weakness everywhere. From other gangs, from police, from the politicians. Humans *are* weak. And weak makes *us* powerful.'

Something Eddy had said at one of our early sit downs when I'd agreed to join the cartel.

This could not have applied more when I - still sitting in what could have only resembled a crumpled up mess in the back of the pick-up - had the sack pulled off from over my head by someone who I'd recognised from outside the hotel and - for all I'd known - had possibly spent the journey there in the back with me.

We were inside the grounds of a compound. I had already heard the trucks stop followed by the sound of a metal gate opening before we had crawled a few yards and then stopped again. I couldn't believe what I was seeing, once I was granted the gift of sight again.

In the grounds of the compound stood literally *hundreds* of men. Milling around guarding the place, hands around AK-47's and PK machine guns. I mean, - whoever was on security detail - they even had SAM-7 and FIM Stingers laid out around the grounds. I'd met a few colourful - not to mention dangerous - characters in my time but *never* anyone who felt the need to have a collection of weapons that amounted to a portable air defence system laying around in their 'back yard,' just in case.

I really did not take to the way that they treated me and Abdullah. The barking of orders and pointing of guns. I'd been used to better than this, yeah, of course some hairy, scary and unpredictable moments along the way but at the end of the day. I was only ever there to make people, as well as myself, money. There was no need whatsoever to treat me as if I was a hostile, when I was nothing other than a friendly.

These Jihadists were a different breed, though. Just the general vibe that you can pick up when you're around someone, you know?

Looking around for Abdullah, I noticed him getting out of the Hilux that was parked two vehicles behind my one. Meanwhile, the man who had removed my sack was shouting at me. I didn't need Abdullah's help to tell me that I, too, was being 'invited' to get out of the truck.

Abdullah and me were then paired up again and marched over in the direction of a small stone cottage that was built to the side of the much larger main building to the compound. When we reached the front door to it, you could already hear the shouting going on inside. This time, though. It was the loud sound of prayer.

Through this, one of the men who had led us up to the cottage stood in front of the door and explained to Abdullah that we would need to wait outside until The Emir - and associates - had finished prayer.

After the sound from inside had eventually stopped and a few more minutes had passed, the man turned around and knocked on the door. Hearing an answer from inside, he turned the handle with him, followed by the pair of us and a few extra Jihadists behind us, then entering.

It was the most basic of rooms. Like the outside, it was uneven blocks of stone for walls. There was a bookcase completely filled with old books at the far end and in front of that. Four men all with rolled up prayer mats to the side of them and an automatic rifle, each in front of them.

All eyes turned to us.

Mine were instantly drawn to the tall one, towards the centre of the room. Sitting there with a long salt and pepper coloured beard with a crisp white (which had been about the only clean thing I'd seen so far in such a dusty dry country) turban rolled around his head, dropping loose down to his side. Dark green camouflage jacket and what looked like a well used Kalashnikov sitting in front of him.

Looking back at me - and without taking his eyes off of me - he spoke in Arabic. Whatever he had said, it had been enough to get the men who had escorted us into the room to depart again. Leaving Abdullah and I with what appeared to be the elders of this organisation.

Then he - still looking at us - spoke directly to me and Abdullah. His gesture indicating for the pair of us to sit down on the floor.

Before doing so - as I would do at any business meeting - I attempted to introduce myself by way of a hand shake with the man in the camo jacket but he - not looking close to making an attempt to get up off the floor to meet me - waved this away as if he was waving me goodbye.

Even though it could have been down to nothing other than local custom - although in reality, when I would learn of the true extent of the man's hatred towards the West it would be made clear to me that he was *never* going to shake the hand of someone that he wished to destroy - it had put me at a bit of a nervous disposition.

This bringing itself to the surface by my attempt at a *very* poor joke. The kind of thing that you can only ever do *out of* nerves.

'Almost didn't see you there, with that coat on, mate.'

I said warmly, but also very stupidly.

Abdullah looked at me with a worried look on his face which was met back with a non verbal movement of the head which indicated that this was the part where he took something that I had said and turn it into Arabic. His job.

Hesitantly, he delivered my message.

It was what could be best described as an 'eggy moment.' First, the man in the camo jacket looked at me without any emotion, completely dead eyed before looking silently at the other members of the Al Qaeda delegation with an unimpressed look on his face.

I'd expected there to be a few laughs. This was how I played my game and did my job. Make them laugh. BE personable. Instead, the man - who had radiated nothing other than a quiet, serene almost, demeanor - exploded into noise. Just not laughter, though.

Looking at Abdullah, then me, then back to him again, pointing at me while shouting at Abdullah. It was difficult to take my eyes of him but I risked a look around the room and they appeared to be as unsympathetic towards my attempt at humour as their colleague.

Turning then to Abdullah - and the way that he appeared to be gulping while the man shouted at him - I had the few nervous seconds delay of having to wait and see what would be translated back to me, if we even got that far.

He finished shouting. He'd shouted so much - and for some periods longer than appeared possible without taking a breath - that it had left him reaching for the bottle of water that was sitting to the side of him.

'The Emir, he says that he did not ask for a comedian to be brought here. Do *you* think you are here to make him and his fellow men laugh, Peter? He has no interest in laughter. He has brought you here because your employer has expressed an interest in purchasing something that belongs to him. Are you here to talk about this or tell jokes because the Emir does not like having his time wasted.'

Abdullah putting across to me what could have only been some kind of amended version of what had been said to him. One of the others - who I had taken as the English speaker - nodded his head at Abdullah's words and looked at 'The Emir' as if to say, *close enough*.

I took the warning that I'd been handed to me and never made the same mistake twice in there, despite the nerves never really departing. I'd looked back to that popping of the cherry in Inglewood and how that had started even *worse* yet had ended so positively.

This didn't feel that way, at all. Sure, they had been courteous enough to offer us a bottle of water from the filthy looking fridge sitting in the corner of the room but that was as good as it got in terms of how their 'hospitality' went.

Wherever I had travelled on behalf of the Ramirez brothers, it had always been with a degree of 'insurance' of who it was that you were representing and how *that alone* would guarantee your safety.

With Al Qaeda, and the attitude that they showed in that first meeting, and the others that followed, however. They appeared that they couldn't have cared less *who* the Ramirez brothers were, or for their reputation. Obviously, we'd, in time, all find out that a terrorist organisation who weren't afraid of the might of the American Military of Defence were hardly ever likely to be concerned about one single cartel from Colombia.

The talks became long and drawn out and extremely stressful although I can only blame myself for that. I'd been told which price to go in at and which level I could go down to, when the bartering began. We also had the opportunity to swap weapons for the poppies and it was through this that things became messy.

When it had got down to my very lowest offer, and one that I was not prepared to go any lower on. This had inflamed things. Camouflage man, once again, raising his voice with the translation - and if I can paraphrase the man for a moment - coming across as 'do you think we're f**king stupid and that we don't know how much the poppies are worth?'

For a man, so silent and reserved. When he lost it, he lost it. It was quite remarkable how he would manage to instantly return to a state of calm and almost statue like appearance, following an animated outburst of opinion.

The thing is, I didn't think he was stupid but if he thought that *we* didn't know what the poppies were worth, well, then he *must've* been. It was *him* that was chancing his luck but doing so very much in possession of the knowledge that we were in *his* back yard and he was trying to make that apparent with the higher than market price for the poppies.

We'd only discussed money being exchanged for the fields worth of poppies, not arms.

That's when I - knowing that the deal wasn't going to be struck if he didn't lower his asking price, which the time had come and gone for him to have done so - said

'That's some nice, Stingers and SAM-7 air defence that you've got out there. Well, if you were able to go back in a time machine and use them from when they were new, of course.'

It was possibly too arrogant for people like that. Also, reverse psychology is a brilliant tactic but probably not so much with unpredictable terrorists, like were sat in the room with me.

Abdullah, gave me that same worried look as he'd done before when I'd made the wisecrack about the jacket.

'Just tell the man what I said.' I told him with a bit of impatience, having began to get tired of his second guessing about what I should and shouldn't say to these people. That's *not* what the man was being paid for. I could see that Abdullah was scared inside the room and - as a result - and it left him as almost a man short. You could appreciate that *he* had a much greater appreciation of the people that he was sitting there with than I did but once again, if you're going to let something like that get in the way of doing your job then you should step aside and let someone else do it.

Despite what Abdullah had thought, though. My comment had got their attention. The prospect of weapons lighting their eyes up in a way that the money hadn't come close to doing.

This kick started a stressful rerouting of negotiations where they were firing me their wish list of rifles, guns, surface to air *and* anti tank missiles that became so convoluted that I had to borrow the Emir's satellite phone to call back to Bogota to confirm what I actually could and could not supply them.

Eddy telling me that he would call back in half an hour to confirm all of this and get the deal closed. I wanted him to tell me that the answer was yes, there and then.

What were we going to talk about for half an hour? They didn't look the type for smalltalk and I was half scared to open my mouth for fear of saying the wrong thing and upsetting them.

It had been the longest of half an hours. Most notably because it took more closer to a full *hour* before the satellite phone on the floor sprang into life. I'd spent the time talking - in a limited way - with Abdullah. The English speaking member of the group also - for a short period - exchanged a few words with me. Asking me where I was from because I, evidently, wasn't South American. Me choosing to give him the smallest of answers back in return and without - unlike me when striking up conversation with someone - ever asking any questions back in return.

The fact that he did not translate any of my answers out for the group told me that he genuinely had wanted to know the answers himself or was actually someone who couldn't stand the silence and felt like they had to break it. After Abdullah had informed the group that we would need to wait on a phone call back from Bogota. This kind of signalled the group to fall into a period of silence, picking up and reading their Quran while we waited on Eddy calling back.

Far later than not a minute too soon. The Emir's large and cumbersome phone began ringing. Picking it up and looking at the front LCD screen, he casually reached over and with his long arm passed the phone to me.

There, Eddy told me that as far as rifles and guns. No issues. The only thing on their list that we would not be able to provide - put on the spot like this at such short notice - would be the RPG 27 Tavolga anti tank disposable one shot launchers. Mobile yes, disposable no.

I let Eddy go again and told him I would call him from the hotel when I returned. Then handing the phone back to The Emir.

The news that we could pretty much supply them everything on their list - apart from the disposable missile launchers - sparked a small discussion around the four of them, only after them ordering Abdullah out of the room. I was unsure of this at first but then I 'got it.' They didn't want Abdullah to hear them talk business in such a way and it was something that was easily understood, once I got over it. And anyway, once they'd finished speaking they had him brought back into the room again.

The small issue of the RPG 27's aside, they seemed happy to strike a deal and did not waste any time in doing so.

Now you need to understand, Manfred. I didn't know these guys or what they stood for, not a lot of people *did*. Regional struggles were something that had taken place across the world since year zero. There will always be conflict. Always be shit to sort out between people.

Manny - Forgive me when I say this, Peter, but it sounds a little like self justification.

Peter - F**k you, Manfred. You don't know *what* you don't know at the time you're involved in something, anything. Simply. You don't know *what you don't know*. Like I said. These fellows looked dangerous but you know what? So did the gangbangers in Inglewood or the Mexicans in Culiacan. When the English speaking member of their delegation - following the agreement of a deal which stopped short of us actually shaking hands, our words being enough - expressed to me with great delight that 'we will do great things with what you send us, great things indeed.' It didn't resonate at the time. Obviously they needed weapons to sort out their local conflict. When I look back at those words though, they're highly unnerving.

With the agreement in place that we would have the shipment sent in via the Red Sea into the East Coast of Sudan to them - the Opium from

Afghanistan to Colombia in another shipment arranged by us and a Middle East broker / shipping company - The Emir didn't hang around in then asking us to leave. Shouting something in Arabic that had been loud enough for the guards outside to come in and escort us back out and to the waiting Toyotas.

Manny - And did you ever see Osama bin Laden again?

Peter - No, well, not in the flesh, anyway. Soon enough you'd be sick of the sight of the man in your newspapers and TV. I never travelled to Sudan again to meet with the organisation although I *did* travel to Somalia and Kenya to do business with them, Afghanistan too. All of those other occasions with 'The Emir' absent from talks although with how much the Americans had been starting to look for him by then, he appeared to have other things on his plate.

I've actually thought of him a lot more recently, through the ongoing search in Afghanistan for him and how what a small world it really is. I'd told every single person, who would listen, that they will *never* find him in there. I'd heard the rumours years before regarding the network of caves that existed in the mountainous Afghanistani Tora Bora region that had been built as a base for the Taliban, as a stronghold location when fighting the Soviet Union. Ironically, this complex had been advanced into a stronghold financed by the CIA *especially* for the Mujahideen in the same war.

Manny - It will surely be only a matter of time before he is caught and brought to America.

Peter - Well you'd like to think so, pal, but when you've been looking for someone for ten years and *still* not found them then your people finding skills can't be up to that much of a high standard. *laughs*

Hey? Maybe if he took that jacket off for five minutes the Yanquis would possibly be able to see him a little easier?

Anyway, I digress, We were led back out to the motorcade of Toyotas that were still parked. Scores of men with guns all casually standing around them talking with each other before noticing us emerging and shaking themselves back into 'bastard mode.'

The sacks going over our heads again and bundled into the back of the pick ups before embarking on the same bumpy and painful ride back to the hotel.

It had been an extremely draining few hours.

I walked down the corridor with my hands on top of my head, almost dazed. Replaying what had just gone on and only then releasing that - for the first time in hours - I no longer had that nervous feeling of dread hanging over me. There was a Western looking man standing outside his hotel room door, trying to let himself in but having trouble with the key. As I got closer it appeared that he looked like he was drunk. Something, as far as Abdullah would've been concerned, that wasn't too good an idea in a country which less than ten years before had seen its president dumping whiskey into the River Nile.

'This f**king thing' the man said as I got closer while he struggled with his key and the room door's keyhole.

'You ok there, pal?' I asked, just trying to be friendly. The last thing the guy needed was to start making a scene outside his door and have security come and find him half pissed.

'It's this lock, buddy. It won't work.' he replied in an American accent. Turning around to me and shrugging his shoulders.

I asked him to let me take a look at it and saw instantly that the key number did not match the door that he was trying to get into. *His* one being the door opposite.

Showing him the error of his ways I went as far as to take the key and let him into his room.

'Come in for a drink, buddy. You look like you need one.'

He invited me in. Apparently visibly drained. As drunk as he had appeared to me, he hadn't been as drunk as not to notice how shellshocked I was returning from my meeting.

He had already lifted a bottle of scotch from up off the room table and began to pour two glasses out.

We actually sat and had another two before I left to go back to my room to provide Eddy with an update on how things had gone while - afterwards - hopefully catching some sleep. Having been awake for more than twenty four hours by that point.

He was quite a funny guy. You know, a funny drunk. Walt Branson from Delaware. Salesman for F&T Deas Electronics out of Wilmington and only in Sudan himself to try and win a contract for his company in relation to a textiles factory that was scheduled to open in the capital the following year.

Leaning on the fact that he'd, evidently, had more to drink than me I'd been a little less forthcoming. Lying that I had been there in Sudan to see my kids who were now living out there with their mum. It was as good as I could manage on the spot because I'd wanted to avoid talking about a line of work that I wasn't actually *in,* if possible.

I wished him good luck with the contract for the factory and let myself out and went back to my room for the night where I stayed until it was time to check out and get myself back to the airport for that long journey home. Coincidentally I saw 'Walt,' again, at Khartoum International Airport the next afternoon. Sitting in the same departure lounge as me. Reading a paper and - no doubt - nursing off a hangover from the night before. I decided that it would be better just to leave him to it so chose to remain in my own seat while waiting on the Bogota flight being called.

I thought nothing of seeing him, the next day. I had a long haul ahead of me. Khartoum to Istanbul and then an eight hour layover in Turkey before flying to JFK and then, finally, onto Colombia. Due to unforeseen circumstances - as I waited there in the Khartoum departure lounge - I wasn't going to be seeing Bogota as quickly as I'd thought I would.

Chapter 22

El Corazon Valiente - The Ballad of Peter Duncan cont

Manny - Something happened on the return journey from Sudan and your meeting with Al Qaeda?

Peter - A diversion, of sorts. Probably the best way that it could be described. My Istanbul flight had arrived at JFK - right on schedule - and I was trying to find my way around the terminal in an attempt at locating my gate - in the wired state I was in, all things considered - for Bogota when I heard my name called over the terminal tannoy. Asking me to report to the nearest American Airlines check in desk. Which I'd found strange. Especially, considering I wasn't *travelling* with 'American.'

Never the less. Figuring that there may have been some alteration with my flight, and the last leg of it, I went looking for their desk. Once I'd got there, and introduced myself as the passenger they had just called for, I was informed that there were flight tickets waiting for me, to be collected at their information desk at the other end of the terminal.

After stopping off for a quick glass of scotch - at one of the many bars and restaurants that lined my route across the airport - I reached the ticket desk where a beautiful Latino looking girl stood behind in her AA uniform. Looking more like she worked in the cosmetics section of Sephora than customer service for an airline.

'Ahhh you've arrived from your flight. Here you go sir. Here are your tickets for Miami along with a message from your employer.'

Manny - Message from your employer?

Peter - I know, eh? The way that she had looked *as* she said it and passed me the tickets - along with a white sheet of paper that had been folded in half to provide some kind of privacy to what was written inside - it left me almost fifty fifty over whether she was *in* on who I was or whether she really was just a friendly and innocent worker doing nothing more - in her own mind - than providing super great customer service without ever dropping the smile that she had for them.

Confused, I walked away from the information desk and opened the piece of paper.

'Switch your pager on pendejo!!!'

Either she really was just great at providing customer service to the point of repeating, verbatim, a phone message for one of their customers or she had taken the message from whoever back in Colombia and simplified things on the sheet of paper.

I got the message, regardless.

Once I switched my pager back on and it had been given a chance to work out which country it was in, Eddy's page appeared on the screen. It was informing me that when I arrived in New York I was to change plans and hop on a flight down to Miami - that the tickets were for - and that more details would follow once I'd arrived there.

I sighed with what felt like every single one of my bones aching. I wanted a few days out, for 'R and R.' Just to recover, I *needed* it. I hadn't been right since the first journey into the Al Qaeda compound in the back of that Hilux. And the return journey back again didn't exactly remedy things, either. I either had some broken - or at the worst bruised - ribs from whatever I had crashed into multiple times while having the blindfold over me on the double trip. Add the very real pain that my body was in next to the mental torture of the stresses of meeting dangerous terrorist organisations - as well as jet leg - and I was in no mood for surprise re routing of plans. Not that I was in *any* kind of a position to really voice any concerns about it, of course.

Don't take that as me being too timid to tell Eddy or German just what I thought of things on occasion but well, they were asking me to do my job. Sure, they were maybe taking the piss by keeping me on the go when I had done more than enough for a few days to earn my living but they'd probably have put it more down to logistics and them trying to save me from multiple trips back and forth to America from Colombia. They had a job for me. I was in America. Makes sense, I suppose, but doesn't have to be appreciated when you were completely on your arse, like I was.

Manny - So what, or more relevantly, *who* was waiting on you arriving in Miami?

Peter - A quarter of a million dollars shoved into a Miami AMTRAK locker and a dirty DEA agent with his grubby hand out, *that's* who, and what.

Manny - Name?

Peter - I think, by now, you'll *know* the name but sure, for your readers, it was Donnie Bannon from the Miami Drug Enforcement Administration. I don't have a problem naming him. He was a piece of shit and I never liked him from the very start and him and I weren't exactly strangers to one another, from that first meeting onwards.

I'd, possibly, put the first meeting between us down to me having travelled all that way to Khartoum and then back again and really not being in the mood for anyone, or their shit. I'd refused to believe that the man was as big an a**hole as he'd appear to be, when I'd diverted to Miami to carry out my orders.

Once I'd touched down I gave Eddy a call, to get some *actual* information. You know, Manfred? I really hated those pagers, with a passion. I mean, I practically had an erection the day that I received my first ever cell phone. *laughs*

During the call, Eddy informed me that he'd had a bag with a quarter mill - along with a kilo of product shoved inside along with the money - placed in a locker at Central Station downtown. Giving me the four digit passcode to gain entry to it. This, I was to take to The Mandarin Hotel where I was to meet with a man who would be sitting in the booth with a photograph of Muhammad Ali sitting above it. Here I was to give him the bag and - also - should he have any message that he would like passed on to my employers then I would be there on hand for him to do so.

I'd facilitated a few bribes since joining the cartel, some police but they were a lot lower level than DEA and even then, I never thought that he would be the BOSS of the Miami field office.

Like I said, I'd had a hard time of it. Flown twenty four hours to be treated like a piece of third hand furniture by the Jihadists and then *just* when I thought I was on my way home to some much needed peace and tranquility. Back to the pool, sun and an escape from the intense world that we all existed in, I was pulled back again.

If Donnie Bannon had been thrown by my appearance - like just about every one else when I entered a room and spoke up - he didn't show it.

'You got something for me?'

He asked as I slid my way into the booth and found myself facing him.

I placed the bag on the floor of the sprawling but barely even a quarter to capacity dimly lit hotel lounge and kicked it under the table in his direction. The bag knocking against his foot, making him reach down and pull it up. He brought the bag up to the side of him in the booth and had a quick peruse inside.

'Good, good.'

He said with a shit eating grin on his face. This unkempt and overweight man in a shirt that's buttons were working harder than I'd been doing for the past few days and a striped tie that had been loosened off to the point of it no longer being around his neck in any meaningful way. His looks did not match up to his attitude.

The swagger he had - which I generally don't mind in a person, if their looks, words and actions can back it up. You know? Like a trash talking boxer who talks the talk all week leading up to the fight to the point of almost turning the public *off* them only to get into the ring on fight night and completely take his opponents head off - did not win any friends in myself.

Sitting there telling me just how much of a god he was to us 'narcos in Bogota' and that if we didn't worship and praise him in the correct way and issue him with gifts then he would have the ability to hit our cartel with all kinds of 'plagues.' For a while - and with how he'd got so into this speech, which I'm sure he'd prepared in advance - I thought that with the words he was saying he really did believe that he *was* god.

'I'm not a religious man, myself.' I said, non plussed and definitely trying to make a point that his words were wasted on me.

'Well lucky for you, you found god today. Some go their whole lives waiting to find him and here he is. Sitting in the lounge of The Mandarin hotel in Miami, Florida.

'IT'S A MIRACLE' he shouted out loud enough for to have other patrons of the hotel looking over in our direction. Him sitting there with his arms up in the air waving his hands.

It would've been very much a case of stepping outside my boundaries but he kept pushing and niggling me to the point where I was ready to tell him

'Look, Eddy and German Ramirez could have you and your family wiped out inside five minutes, wherever they are in the world at that moment, and you f**king well know it so pipe down.'

I bit my tongue, instead. Choosing to sit and take everything he had to say while taking *every* opportunity to insert a passive aggressive reply or comment that I possibly could.

Threats are for the appropriate times, and anyway. If there was anyone that would *know* the capabilities that the Bogota Cartel possessed, it would have been someone within the American Drug Enforcement Administration, especially a gaffer.

His 'fronting' - I'd decided half way through - was more about how scared *he* was than anything else. Trying to put out there just how powerful people like him were than the actual bad guys, like my 'jefes.'

'Just you make sure that these bags keep coming. End of the month, every month, same amount.'

I nodded my head, sure that this was already an arrangement that Eddy and German were aware of but something I would mention to them, regardless.

'*Now* you can go.' He said, dismissively.

I was surprised that - apart from all of the unnecessary 'intimidation' that he had come out with - there hadn't been more to the actual 'bribing' of him. Sure, I'd bribed police and politicians but they had been a lot more clear cut. *This,* though was different. He was the boss of the DEA in the most vital of American cities to a Colombian cartel and someone with - I could only have guessed how many - a team of agents under him whose direct remit was to *stop* the flow of drugs coming in from South America *into* the state of Florida and the United States in general.

If 'his' boys were on the team, so to speak, then he hadn't mentioned any of this. *Just* that he wanted the same bag delivered at the end of the month and that - in return - he would see to it that any of our 'business dealings' in Miami would go on without us having to endure any heat from local agents.

It wasn't up to me to decide the finer details but I'd thought that to buy the *whole* of the Miami DEA? That was an absolute SNIP of a price. Are you kidding? Miami? Tell me a more important area of America when it came to importing narcotics into the country back in those days? My guess was that he was taking it all for himself and that he had his own ways of making sure that none of our deals were unexpectedly busted. Placing agents on other cases when he knows that we're about to ship a load of product, Stateside? I don't know. That wasn't of importance to me. What *was* of MAJOR f**king important was that he did what Eddy and German were paying him for.

From a selfish point of view. It would make life *infinitely* easier for yours truly if I was to be able to walk the streets of Miami with an almost diplomatic immunity air about me. Free from any kind of anti narcotics activity in a town that was extremely high on it.

So yeah, that was the first of me meeting Donnie Bannon. A man who I hadn't *wanted* to meet. Didn't *like* meeting him and was left depressed every time I was scheduled to meet with him *again*. But you want to know something, Manfred? Because of *what* we were paying him I will probably never, ever know how many times that man saved my bacon over the course of those five / six years. I mean, was I ever arrested in Miami, despite it being - most probably - the one city that I had done the most amount of repeat business and visits to, out of everywhere?

Makes you think, pal. It really does.

Chapter 23

El Corazon Valiente - The Ballad of Peter Duncan cont

Manny - Vinnie, Tommy. Nineteen Ninety Two. Record amounts of narcotics were entering the Unites States, despite the round the clock effort from American authorities. Is it fair to say that the war on drugs was being lost?

Vinnie Valencia - Well, with Tommy still being on the team, it's probably better for me to be the one to say that Reagan's 'war on drugs' was a war that was, is and always will be *un-winnable*. Shit, you'd think this country of hours would've learned about going into wars they couldn't win after Nam. What's that thing they say about the definition of madness?

Tommy Ambrosini - Well, I wouldn't exactly go along with my ex colleague with what he ..

Vinnie - *Interrupting while laughing* Yeah I'll bet you don't buddy. Look, what I'm saying is. It isn't exactly neurosurgery to know that if you want to pick a fight with someone then you do your homework on them. Work out what your adversary's weak points are, and where you can exploit them, so that you can win. You really think old Ronald would've taken America into a war if he'd been told that thirty years it would still be ongoing?

Manny - Vinnie, you sound a little cynical about your time with the DEA?

Vinnie - Oh, don't get me wrong, buddy. I *loved* my time with the Administration. It was as exciting as hell, worked with a great bunch of men and women that I would practically have given my life for and, in the knowledge, that they would've done the same for me.

Tommy - Damn right, bro.

Vinnie - We took down some big shipments - totalling in hundreds of millions of dollar's worth of product - and put away some *serious* players in the narcotics business along the way. Both Stateside and South American based. I, *we* made a difference.

Manny - So why the cynicism? You were making busts and putting criminals behind bars. That was quite literally your job.

Vinnie - Well, you know that there wasn't just a finite amount of drug dealer and importers that were on some kind of a file that could allow us to work our way through and - once the last one on the list had been scored out - then, voila, no more drugs in the world?

Tommy - As a kid. At the state or county fair. I'd always been good at 'Whack-a-mole.' Which was just as well as it gave me *plenty* of practice before becoming a DEA agent. Because that really is what it is like being in the position of stopping drugs from coming into the United States.

Vinnie - We both had pretty good analogies - in terms of being an agent with the Administration - if I can remember? Your one was Whack-a-mole while mines was that we were Mickey Mouse, the wizard, in Fantasia with the buckets of water and the brooms. What is it the narrator says in the film?

'He started something he couldn't finish'

Yeah well *we* started something that we couldn't finish. And we still haven't.

Tommy - Yeah well, your words, not mine, Vinnie. *laughs*

Vinnie - Look, Manny. The 'cynicism' from me is down to the fact that our job was hard enough as it was. Risking death every day going up against criminals who - with the high stakes the drug game had elevated itself up to - lived, and behaved, like they had nothing to lose. It wasn't an easy job to do. And that was *before* the, shall we say, *obstacles* that the Administration - and more specifically, the Miami field office - would have put in front of it. I think Tommy, even while still on the team would not be able to disagree with what is now widely known public knowledge.

Manny - Which obstacles are you speaking of?

Vinnie - Well, the CIA, for one thing. How the hell do you think us guys - busting our balls every day and putting our asses on the line - think when we see that the Central Intelligence Agency, who unless I'm mistaken are meant to be attending to matters *outside* of the country, are assisting flood the West Coast of America with Cocaine to help pay for one of their covert wars in a country that the average American couldn't even find on a map if their life depended on it?

Manny - Ah, Iran-Contra.

Tommy - As an agent, you see something like that and you'd only be human to think to yourself, what really is the point of all of this? We're going all out to stop drugs from entering the country, and to try and keep things safer on a nationwide scale, while *another* agency is bringing in copious amounts of product behind our backs.

Vinnie - What's the freaking point of having an anti-drugs task force if an agency - and one ranked higher up the food chain - are going to go ahead and do something like that, any time they're a little light on their greenback stack for financing 'foreign struggles?'

Tommy - Of course, the CIA had been a pain in the ass to us a *lot* more than just by flooding Los Angeles with Cocaine, over on the West Coast.

Vinnie - The way that they would tie our hands behind our backs at times. Pulling the plug on some of our planned operations in foreign lands. Disillusioning, it really was.

It's the main reason that I quit the agency. Some days feeling like you'd had your hands zip tied behind you and then asked to go off and catch the bad guys.

Tommy - Yeah, he done the whole Crocket and Tubbs end, exit. *laughs*

Vinnie - Only, just Crocket, pal. 'Tubbs' was still on the force last time I noticed.

Tommy - Yeah well you're not the one with six kids across three marriages and a girlfriend breaking your balls for cosmetic surgery!

Vinnie - Well it wasn't *just* the CIA placing obstacles in our way that had led to me calling it a day. There were *other* issues at play which kind of left me feeling like I was banging my head against the wall and, anyway, when you're put in a position that you don't even know if you can trust your own fellow agents - with the exception of this man next to me here, of course - then it's time to check out. I would like to say more on the subject but my attorney has advised that - with court proceedings currently ongoing - I may be at risk of being held in contempt of court* if I speak on my former head of the Miami field office.

*Insert

Due to court restrictions on reporting the trial. Vinnie Valencia - at the time of interview - had been prevented from speaking out on Donnie Bannon, ex director of the Miami field office of the Drug Enforcement Administration. Bannon, was subsequently found - as part of an undercover Internal Affairs operation - to be someone who had received bribes and gifts from gangs in both America, Mexico and South America over a period of over five years. Taking payment from criminal organisations in return for information and their shipments arriving into Miami, untouched.

Bannon is currently detained in an Idaho prison as he begins his thirty year sentence that was handed down to him in Miami-Dade County Courthouse last month.

Manny - So, Peter Duncan? How did things go in the hunt for the cartel associate?

Tommy - Well, I wouldn't say that we were 'hunting' him as such. More keeping a watchful eye out for the man for when he next popped up onto the radar again. Only, - as time passed - the Bogota Cartel operative was barely ever *off* our radar. You wouldn't have a week or two pass without something regarding him coming our way. Eventually we managed to get a visual on him, as part of a bigger operation, and - knowing from the original recording - after faxing the British authorities a photograph of him we were finally able to establish that he was one 'Peter Duncan' born in Scotland and jailed in the mid Eighties for a narcotics related offence and someone who had never been seen again in the United Kingdom, following his release.

How he had found his way to the United States - on behalf of a South American cartel - was anyone's guess and one that we hoped we'd get to the bottom of ourselves, sooner or later.

Regardless of being from out of town, he was making an impact *inside* it. The occasional high level bust and we'd have someone sitting in an interrogation room shouting about this 'foreign dude' in an attempt to try and save their own skin. Exactly like we'd hoped Peter Duncan *himself* would do, once we caught him. With the slick hair and expensive sharp suits and cocky swagger - that had been observed by many an agent - we'd all agreed - back at the field office - that he did not look like a man who would relish the prospect of some jail time and would snatch a Wit-Sec offer off you in a heartbeat.

It's funny but whoever it was that we had sat in one of the interrogation rooms trying to describe him, in their attempt at helping get out of their own trouble, they *never* ever said that he was a Scotsman.

Vinnie - Well we can't judge, there, can we? *laughs*

Tommy - The Irishman, the Australian, the Englishman. It sounds like the beginning of a bad British joke.

You know, though? You never, ever heard anyone saying a bad thing about the man. Well, while they were ratting him out. Of course, he was too smart to give them anything remotely close to an identity so they could've sung until the fat lady joined them for all Duncan would've cared, I imagine.

Vinnie - Listen, buddy. We weren't just sitting around the office with our fingers up our asses, obsessing about Peter Duncan. Cocaine was coming into Miami in record quantities, year after year. We didn't have enough hours in the day - or the required manpower - to fight the war on drugs as it was, never mind waste *any* of what we had available to us.

Admittedly, he - or just the mention of him - kept appearing now and again before we could get our shit together and do something about it. All we could do was add to the intelligence we were compiling on him. Places - and on which dates - that he'd been to. Which gangs he was known to have business dealing with. We just needed to make sure that we were ready for the day when he slipped up, as they *all* inevitably do.

Tommy - As things had progressed we finally got ourselves into a position where we had a potential bust of him in Ninety Three. Six months of dangerous - not to mention incredibly ambitious - undercover work had resulted in the set up for a major purchase that - through the sheer scale of the deal - Duncan was to attend personally, at a Miami marina, to oversee. The idea had been - simply - that we catch him and he was going to, automatically, lead us somewhere *bigger*.

Vinnie - *laughing* Yeah, what was it I was saying again about us having our hands zip tied behind us some days, though?

Chapter 24

Peter

'So what was the sex with her, that night?'

Gary asked me on what was a particularly chilly night which saw me beside the intercom with a blanket wrapped around me like I'd been rescued from a dinghy out in the North Sea by a search party.

We'd been sitting talking about old times - and more specifically - the times where our 'work' had crossed paths, all be it without my knowledge at the time.

Exchanging anecdotes from our 'previous life' to show what it was like on our own particular sides of the 'cops and robbers' fence.

His question hadn't made sense, though. Unless I had zoned out on things or there had been a dip in the connection with the intercom but the last thing we had been talking about had been about how annoyingly nice the bell boy at the Kabul Serena Hotel had been, in his quest to receive a tip when taking you to your room.

'I swear the guy would've given you a fucking blow job if you said it was part of the tipping process.' Gary had joked.

He *was* right, though. Well, not about the blow job. Well I wouldn't have thought so, anyway.

But *her* and *that* night? It certainly hadn't been in Kabul, anyway. Hardly a place that would ever be awarded the title of 'Sin City.' Anytime I visited I literally lived in my hotel, only creeping out to meet whoever it was that I had travelled to negotiate with and even then, if I could engineer it, I would have them come to the hotel to meet with me.

'Who?'

I said into the intercom.

'Ahhhhhh you know who I'm on about. Don't be coy with me' he ripped me over something that he clearly didn't appreciate that I had no idea what he was talking about.

'You've lost me, Gal.' I admitted.

'Christ, she couldn't have been *that* special if you can't even remember her. Looked a right sexy sort, too.'

I stayed silent, hoping that he might provide some kind of enlightenment on things.

'Fuck, she didn't have a dick, did she?' He said, almost as an afterthought.

'Gary, I don't have the first fucking clue what you're talking about here, mate, but I can at least clarify that I haven't been with any lady boys, if that's what you're saying?' I responded, a little impatiently.

'Istanbul, The Marriot. That little sort that you picked up at the bar and took back to your room. The one with the red hair?'

Oh. *Now* I knew 'exactly' who he was talking about. A point - and a person - that was still very raw to me.

'*You* were in The Marriot? Fucking christ. I should have you done for stalking you creepy bastard. I'm surprised you didn't have my room bugged with a video cable so you could sit masturbating in your own room watching us.'

I joked while taken aback that the man on the other end of the intercom - with us both underground at the foot of the Rocky Mountains - had sat in an Istanbul hotel and watched me negotiate with an escort to spend the night in my hotel room, and he was being *paid* for it.

'Fella? Like I've told you, I didn't see you very often and the times you came up was only because I was in the same area that you had been spotted flying into. But, yeah. I saw you pick her up at the bar. Part of me was pleased because it looked very much like you weren't going to be going anywhere for the rest of the evening which pretty much gave *me* the rest of the night off. So anyway, what was she like in bed. Get your money's worth? She didn't look cheap, mind. That handbag alone she had wasn't too far away from my years salary.'

I thought long and hard for a second before I answered him. Just thinking of her again - and the mixture of pleasure and sharp pains that her memory brought on - had knocked me off guard.

In what 'should've' been just a 'locker room' style talk between two prisoners. One living off the memory of something and the other, vicariously through the story teller. It was anything *but* just a tale of sexual conquest and all of the dirty details.

Any and *all* thoughts of Jenna Walters - Ross could not be without the reflection that it was - indirectly - her who had led to my arrest, and where I now found myself.

'What was she like? Well, apart from landing me up here in the ADX?' I said sarcastically.

'Wait? She fucking grass you up, fella?' He asked?'

It *was* something that I'd considered - following my arrest - but - in reality - she hadn't known *who* I actually was. To her I would've been nothing other than a customer. A businessman - most likely - cheating on his wife while in another country, when away for work. And besides, I'd hardly introduced myself to her as

'Hi, my name is Peter Duncan and I work for the Ramirez Brothers. Purveyor of narcotics and weapons since the early Eighties. Here, take a business card.'

'No, mate. If anyone grassed themselves up it was myself by even flying to Amsterdam to meet up with her. Was still a horrible piece of karma for someone to have forced upon them, though. I mean, most men who cheat on their wife get their clothes cut up or made to sleep in the spare room for a few nights. A lifetime in an American supermax prison seems a little harsh, don't you think?'

Gary started pissing himself laughing

'Yeah, fella. You know? I'm not exactly sure that you're in here because you couldn't keep your cock in yer pants.'

Touche.

He'd taken me back to that night inside The Marriot, near to the airport. I'd been in town to meet up with a Turkish contact that Hakan had thrown our way who was looking to move on a quick deal for selling opium, something that the Turks in Amsterdam had passed on but knew the brothers would be all over.

It had been one of the more straightforward trips that Eddy and German had sent me on. The man - a Syrian based over the border in Turkey who was brokering the deal - had stupidly appeared desperate to sell the poppies from the start. This was something that he had already expressed to Hakan who had, in turn, told me. Entering into the deal radiating such neediness, it had led to a quick and hassle free negotiation. Due to his desperation, we agreed on a deal that fell significantly lower than the market value but well, he shouldn't have come to the table reeking of so much desperation, shouldn't he?

If all deals had been like that I'd have slept a lot easier at night while - without question - managing to retain more of my hair, as well as having less international crime agencies on my case.

Eddy, unable to believe how cheap we had got the shipment for which was planned for to be sent up north to Sinaloa. The Mexicans - remarkably - in a dry spot for poppies due to a recent cross American and Mexican raid which had seen two billion dollar's worth of potential heroin destroyed by military with flame throwers. The brothers who had joked that they could sell sand to Arabs were now in the position of the next best thing.

Selling poppies to Mexicans!

I took the opportunity to enjoy the downtime that I was now left with and doing exactly what I would normally do on those trips, sit either downstairs in the hotel or relaxing up in my room.

That night - after sitting and having some dinner - I decided on a few drinks sitting at the bar. I'd been having some on off small talk with the bartender who had been semi distracted from doing his job due to the football match that was on the TV in the lounge. Two teams squaring off against each other. One in blue and yellow and the other one in predominantly all white with a hint of red. At least half a dozen times he had been in the middle of saying something to me before pausing - while looking at the TV - and then cursing when the team in the yellow and blue missed a chance.

I'd not long ordered - what I had decided - my last drink of the night down there before heading up and getting tucked into the mini bar in my room. The plan to then catch myself some sleep ahead of the Bogota flight the following afternoon when she came up and sat at the bar, One spare seat separating us.

She was trying to catch the attention of the man behind the bar but was having no luck due to the action on the TV.

'You'll be lucky' I joked with her. This man here is just a vision of yours. He's not actually here, behind the bar. He's in an Istanbul football stadium. Let me get you it, what are you drinking?'

I asked her, thinking I wasn't exactly getting much in the way of conversation out of the barman - and I'd always been under the impression that had been one of the roles of a hotel bartender in that they would *always* be on hand to talk to some bored customer who's there at the hotel on their own - so thought why not substitute that for a drink with someone who was happy to have their back to the TV.

She thanked me and asked for a glass of Cristal before sliding up and planting herself down on the spare seat that was beside me. She wasn't shy, was she? Someone asks you for a drink and *that's* what your answer is. Not just 'champagne' but champagne and none of that cheap stuff, remember now.

I got myself one, too, thinking why not. It had taken her the time that it took to drink her glass and for us to engage in the smallest of small talk for her to get down to brass tacks.

'Two thousand dollars, American. Into this bank account, in advance, will buy you the whole night with me.'

She said, completely off topic, after her taking a look at the barman - serving another guest - and passing me a card with her name, phone number and bank details printed on it. Not even waiting around for any response. She gave me a confident smile before picking up her Chanel bag and walking off towards the bathrooms.

I'd been in a thousand hotels across the world and had probably seen a thousand and one prostitutes inside the bars of them but - for some reason - I hadn't pictured her as one. Too high end to be someone that could possibly be with a different man from one night to another. Naive, I know.

I watched her every step of the way until she disappeared. I'm sure that she knew it as well. Could have probably felt my eyes boring into her back, ok, not just her back. She just oozed class, in every way. Then again, that's much easier to achieve when you're getting paid a couple of thousand dollars a night. Not that I could have sat throwing stones at glass houses, there. I'd like to have thought that I *too* had oozed class and style, and I was being paid a *considerable* more amount of money for my efforts than she was asking for.

She had really left me in a position. Had plunged me into a moment of weakness that I should've had the strength to walk myself away from had I not been so selfish. Like I'd said, I'd been around *many* escorts and prostitutes. I'd lived in Amsterdam for fuck's sake. I'd never had my eye turned, despite countless hotel bar propositions in all corners of the world. Yeah, I know it was a cliche, but there was something 'different' about her. Something that I would go on to prove - to anyone that needed persuading - through my idiotic actions later on in life.

'Just go up to your room, masturbate, have a few drinks, pay for a movie and fall asleep without even seeing the end of it.' I told myself over and over again while I sat there looking at her business card.

Those thoughts fell completely to pieces the moment that she emerged back from the bathrooms, freshened up, and with a mischievous look on her face.

'So, shall we retire? She asked me in that sexy American soft accent. Confidence personified. Four words that had me acting like a stupid fucking lapdog. Before leaving the bar, I had bought a bottle of Cristal to take up to the room with us, where we spent the rest of the night.

'So what does two fucking grand get you, fella?' Gary asked, now back in the moment himself, having had the luxury of sitting and watching me leaving - clutching the gold coloured bottle of champagne - with the woman in question.

'Whatever the hell you want, Gal. You'd bloody hope so for two fucking grand! *That* was what caused all the issues in Amsterdam. That your money did *not* buy you whatever the hell you wanted.'

Up in the room, there had been that brief awkward moment where - despite the whole natural easiness about how we'd sat speaking to each other downstairs - the fact that this had been nothing other than transactional between the two of us became glaring. This coming when - before we even got close to getting down to any *business* - she had insisted that I have the funds transferred to her bank account first of all.

Kind of a mood killer and not something that is hardly likely to make your dick hard, unless you happen to have a kink for paying an exorbitant amount of money before a women will let you touch her, of course.

I'd had the thought that this was possibly a scam. I transfer the money and then she suddenly gets a call telling her that it's an emergency and she has to go.

Thinking that a happy compromise would be that I pay her half up front and the other half in the morning and then thinking twice about it as that kind of behaviour would have made me out to be cheap. I decided to trust her, making the call to my bank to have the funds transferred.

Once she was happy that the transfer had been made *then* our night could begin.

'Details, mate. I want the gory details, every single one of them.' Gary shouted down the intercom like some pervert who has called an 0898 sex chat number.

'Shit, I'll draw you some pictures and have them sent over to your cell tomorrow and you can have a wank to them if you like?'

I joked back before then going on to give him *exactly* what he had been asking for. I'd been left a little disgusted with myself to find that - given all the problems that meeting her, for the second time had caused - as I told Gal about the events inside that Istanbul hotel room I was sitting there with a rock hard erection. Talk about "memory bank?"

As I described the night to Gary. I swear I could smell her perfume, feel the touch of her skin and the sound of her moans. It all reminded me of the spell that she cast on me that night and, from how I was in that cell feeling, I was apparently *still* under.

God, did I give myself a hard time, the next day in Istanbul. How full of hate and self loathing I was over doing such a thing with Eva - back in Manchester - completely oblivious. She didn't deserve it. The long distance relationship was hard enough and - for a young beautiful girl like Eva - the sacrifices that she'd made to make it work between us. And what does she get back in return from me? I felt sick with myself.

It was a difficult flight back to Bogota, alone with my thoughts. What if the condom had broken and I'd ended up getting the escort pregnant over the many times that we'd had sex the night before? What if she'd had some kind of an STD and I was now going to pass it onto Eva. *Confirming* that I'd been cheating on her, in the process. What if she 'hadn't' been an actual escort and had only been 'posing' as one and had in fact bugged something on my suitcase or my clothes when I was in the bathroom? My head had been filled with all kinds of scenarios and paranoid theories over the course of the seventeen hour flight, broken up with a couple of hours in Houston.

By the time that I was walking through the front door of my place back in Bogota I had - somehow - managed to come up with the calming and soothing placation that 'technically' I hadn't been having an affair, no cheating on Eva with the sexy American woman. There was no love, no getting to know each other over a period of time and becoming emotionally attracted to one another. It was all purely a case of someone telling themselves *exactly* what they want to hear. It would be enough to allow me to accept myself what I had done and move on as I couldn't afford to let it be something that I would dwell on. Not when my work required the sharp mind that it did to get through each and every single day alive and well.

Thinking more rationally, I was able to come to the reality that I could be tested at a local clinic for any sexually transmitted diseases before I next saw Eva. As for any potential electronic bugs? That was what we had security for and so much so that it was not uncommon for me to be scanned for bugs upon returning from foreign climes. Jaimie, our head of security, someone who had been turned by the fact that he could have earned ten times the money providing security for a narco as he ever could with the police or military. I would call him to come and visit the hacienda and scan everything that had been with me in Istanbul.

Despite the 'acceptance' in spending the night with Jenna Walters - Ross. The knowledge of what I'd done - whichever way I wanted to conveniently dress it up as - weighed heavily on me. Regardless of what some may have thought of me. My loyalty had been something that had never, ever been questioned. Not by me, not by anyone else. I may have been a lot, or little, of things but one thing that I *was*, it was loyal. *That* had been what I lost, personally, that night in Turkey. My own sense of loyalty. What a cost.

It hadn't been *expensive* enough to stop me from thinking of her, and the night that we'd spent. So much so that when the internet was unleashed on the general public, I had not been able to resist looking her name up. After ten minutes of searching, finding her services available on a high end agency which was advertising escorts available to hire all over the world, with various levels of packages to cater for the needs of their wealthy customer base.

And if the deep regret and remorse that I'd been left with - regarding how I felt about cheating on Eva - hadn't been enough to stop me from seeing if I could find her on the internet then it *definitely* hadn't been enough for me to not REGISTER my details on the escort site along with a request to be emailed for when the - listed as unavailable - Jenna Walters-Ross might potentially become *available* again.

Years down the line, when the email fell into my inbox. Informing me that there was a free weekend spot for Miss Walters - Ross?

What do you think I did?

Chapter 25

El Corazon Valiente - The Ballad of Peter Duncan cont

Manny - So tell me about the DEA and the submarine, Peter.

Peter - The submarine? You *know* about the submarine? It wasn't mentioned at the trial.

Manny - *laughing* Did you ever think that the Administration would have wanted *that* particular piece of dirty laundry aired in public?

Peter - *laughing back* What? You mean to say that you think they'd have had some issues with people knowing about them making a complete abortion of arresting me and spending millions of the public's purse in the process, leaving them look, well, like clowns. Circus clowns. We all had a good laugh at them, back in Bogota, I assure you.

Well look, I just want to go on record and say that I thought it had been a bad idea from the very start but had decided to keep schtump over it. I'd got to know the brothers well enough by then to know - with how enthusiastic German had been at the prospect of the cartel owning an underwater craft - that there would be absolutely no point in trying to voice any concerns over the deal. I mean a submarine? It was like something out of a film. Completely preposterous.

Only, it kind of wasn't. For a South American or Mexican cartel, they would take what the average person would class as 'preposterous' and then go *ten* levels above that. There had been whispers that the Sinaloans already had a network of underground tunnels. Set up with railings - welded to the floor - to push their product across the border into the States in carts.

German, like his brother, would always jump at the chance if he could usurp any of the other narco bosses. Anything that could possibly add to the folklore of the two Ramirez brothers they would be down for, no matter the cost.

Manny - I'm imagining that there aren't too many submarines in supply in the world? How did you come by the one that was for sale?

Peter - You would be quite correct there, Manfred. And you would *also* be forgiven for thinking. Hang on a second, the Ramirez brothers have more money than sense, can't they like, just go and *buy* one, right? From the manufacturers? *Wrong*. It's not like just buying a car with one of these things. You need to buy from official channels and - through that - this means that 'certain people' become made aware of said purchase. Certain people who you wouldn't want *knowing* that you were buying in the first place and if they were, indeed, in possession of such intel. Then obviously, it would render the whole *having* a submarine as completely pointless.

The thing is, I'd sighed when hearing about the deal, while saying 'here we f**king go again.'

Manny - Again?

Peter - This hadn't been the brothers' first foray into the potential purchase of an underwater means of transporting product to America, and money in the return direction. Wow, was that a proper headache, and a half.

Sent half way across the world to find out that there had been several wires crossed between Moscow and Bogota. Dispatching me to Russia, following the break up of the Soviet Union and the 'everything must go' fire sale that followed its split. *That* was a golden age for anyone who needed to get their hands on 'equipment' that they would otherwise not be able to do so. Guns, tanks, planes, submarines, uranium, plutonium. That not inconsiderable mass of land was a literal one stop shop for those out there who wished to do some serious damage to others.

The retired general was quite a character and the meeting between us had been quite enjoyable. The stories of all the madness that had engulfed the region had me hanging on his every word.

As we were making our way through the lunch, he asked me.

'So, would you like your submarine to have nuclear missiles equipped to it or without? The missiles, I'm sure you will understand, would incur a quite substantial additional cost?'

That was when the penny dropped. I'd never asked and Eddy had never told. Only that someone was trying to shift a submarine and that I was to go and buy the thing for him. Sometimes with the man, minor details like that didn't matter. Despite the hugely successful businessman that he was, though. He would have a tendency to act with impulse and passion first. Logic coming second.

This old man was trying to sell us a *full sized nuclear equipped naval* submarine?! The Yanquis would've shit bricks had they detected a Soviet Union submarine entering their waters. That would be just the thing that myself - and the Bogota Cartel - would do, though. Accidentally setting off World War Three when all we were doing - in reality - would be innocently trying to sneak some Cocaine onto the coast of America, under the noses of everyone.

Eddy and German paid me for a lot of things. One of them, I'd have liked to think, was my good business brain and the ability to see further down the line and try to see how things will play out.

A submarine with nuclear capabilities, I'd felt, did not have much promise when it came to what was written in the stars.

I did not even begin to talk money with the general. Instead, apologising and explaining that I needed to leave the table to make a quick call to my boss. Heading straight for the nearest phone in the hotel to call Bogota.

'So, it is a little big, what is the worry, Pedro? Bigger size, we can have more Coca per shipment, no?' German replied to my opening line of

'German, they're trying to sell us a f**king one hundred and seventy five meter length submarine. The general just asked me if I wanted it equipped with nukes or not?'

I instantly wished I hadn't mentioned the nuclear missiles. Negotiating or not, *that* was a hard no from me. I mean, not that German Ramirez would ever fire a nuclear weapon at anything or anyone but well, you know what the cartel bosses are like, Manfred?

Manny - I do

Peter - He'd have been waving the fact that *he* had a nuclear weapon in any Mexican or South American cartel's faces until they ended up purchasing *two* just to shut him up.

'No, German. That's not going to work when the American Military have blown our fifty million dollar submarine out of the water, while its citizens on the East Coast are running around dry land freaking out to the sound of air raid sirens.'

There was a pause before I then heard Eddy - on the speakerphone - reluctantly say

'Pedrito's correct. America will think they are being attacked. Muchos big problems, hermano.'

I will forever be glad that I was not inside the same room for what next came out of German's - who had evidently had his heart set on this submarine - mouth because I fear that there is no way that I would not have been able to gloss my way over such an idiotic thing to say without laughing.

'Cannot we just paint an American stars and stripes flag on the submarine, over top of the hammer and sickle, and make the American's think that we are just one of their own fleet?'

Standing there in the hotel, I face palmed while I waited on Eddy fielding that one. I definitely wasn't giving any advice on it.

'No, hermano, they have computers that tell them these things, remember?' Eddy replied and in doing so helping bring a close to things. German reluctantly telling me to thank the general for his assistance and to make sure that he was compensated for his trouble and for me to get myself back to Colombia in due course.

I did indeed thank General Kuznetsov and - through some of his stories and the very evident hardship that him and a lot of his countrymen had suffered and were destined to continue to - gave him a few additional dollars out of my own funds - on top of a token 'consultancy' payment from the brothers.

Joking with him that it was too bad that we would not purchase the sub from him but that if there was anything that James Bond films had taught me it was that there would be a super villain along any minute looking to buy it from him. He didn't get it - I could see that from his eyes - but, being the warm and friendly man that he had been, laughed along with me all the same.

I thought that had been the end of matters, as far as any purchases of underwater vehicles. Then came Miami.

Tommy Ambrosini - Over the previous couple of years we had been gathering intel in relation to South American cartels looking into investing in 'underwater vessels' which would be used to bring narcotics into The States.

Vinnie Valencia - *laughing* The Medellin Cartel had even tried to build one, it sank. The dumb f**ks. The one man sub being fished out of the Caribbean Sea along with the poor drowned captain and his cargo of several hundred kilos of Ye-Yo.

Tommy - You can see how attractive a proposition something like that would be for a gang of narcotics importers? That was when 'Operation Cousteau' was born. We had one of our agents - who due to national security his name can't be given - go deep undercover down in Central and South America. We'd had a credible background created for him that would stand up to any scrutiny that any organisation would potentially carry out. When I say that this agent went deep undercover he went ...

Vinnie - Sometimes we didn't hear from him for months and months to the point that we'd assumed that some cartel had chopped him into pieces after him asking the wrong question or straying down the wrong road, only for him to surprise our asses by breaking silence out of nowhere to give us an update on where things stood. Who he had met up with and where. Even if they had not been interested in buying the submarine. The value of him even getting in the door of some of these places down South had been high to us with pieces of intel being picked up along the way that - otherwise - we wouldn't have learned about the comings and goings in Colombia which, by then, had been nicknamed 'Locombia' through the mind boggling amounts of murders that were happening on a daily basis.

Tommy - Apart from actually getting a cartel to take a bite out of our bait and yeah, that *was* the difficult part, the rest of the plan was simplicity. Obviously, we didn't have the budget to just go out and buy ourselves a shiny submarine to try and use in an operation. We had the next best thing in the offer of a loan of one from the U.S Navy. One of the smaller ones that they use for training exercises compared to the fully sized subs that can take a crew on board. We only needed to have a submarine, for viewing purposes, for a potential buyer to see. The sub, itself wouldn't have been going anywhere other than right back to the navy at the end of the operation.

The agent, himself, didn't exactly have an endless list of buyers to work his way through. Mexico would've been a waste of time. With most of the major cartels being so far from the East Coast of the country they would not be in too desperate need for getting their product all the way over to that side of the country and *then* onto a sub and the coast of America. Not when they had their own tried and trusted smuggling routes that were seeing millions of dollar's worth of narcotics entering the states every single week.

Vinnie - No, the only *real* options were only ever going to be the Colombians.

Tommy - And you know? It's not like you can just walk up their garden path, knock on their front door and say ' hola, would you like to buy a submarine today per chance, senor?'

It took months before our man could even get *close* to any kind of a sit down with any of Escobar's people. Escobar, we'd felt, would have been the best bet for who would buy the sub. He'd already tried this method, and failed. We were giving him a fully working professionally made version, though. Surely he'd have bitten?

Vinnie - Well. he probably would've done, had we asked him a few years before. In fact, had we asked him in the mid to late Eighties he'd have snapped our hand off.

Tommy - Yeah, unfortunately by the time that we attempted Operation Cousteau, Escobar was hemorrhaging money by the millions while engulfed in the double pronged issues of his war with Cali, while the Americans, Search Bloc and the lawless Los Pepes all hunted for him. The man had a lot more on his plate than buying extravagant purchases like submarines. Submarine, aside. The intelligence coming out of Medellin was that it was now only a matter of time for Escobar. Sicarios had either deserted him or been killed and - regardless of how - were dropping like flies around him. The man was now in complete and utter survival mode. Technically by then he wasn't even *dealing* drugs. His operation completely shut down. Like was said, we were years too late with him.

Vinnie - Cali, for the similar reasons of being at war with Medellin, did not return any of the numerous messages that our guy - whose undercover name was simply 'Nuggy' - had left for them in connection with the sale. We'd thought the idea for the operation as an excellent way to bring down whichever criminal organisation cared to bite with us but - looking back - the timing was less than ideal.

When two cartels are in the middle of bombing the hell out of each other maybe just maybe it's not the time for *anyone* to be sticking their heads in between the two? Cali could not have been discounted on being interested - they were a smart set up and we were already convinced that they would be around after the Medellin Cartel fell - but it just wasn't the time.

That was what made it all the more amazing when - on the same day that Escobar had bombed *another* of the Rodriguez Orejuela owned 'La Rebaja' pharmacies in Cali - Nuggy came in from the cold and called the field office, telling us that he had a buyer for the sub.

Tommy - I almost fell off my chair when he told me. We'd barely even mentioned the operation by that point and - after receiving no's from Medellin and Cali - we'd have even had Nuggy called back in for debriefing, if we'd been able to locate the man.

'Yeah, Ambrosini? I got us a serious buyer on the sub. Operation Cousteau is go go go.'

Manny - So how did the arrangements go for the purchase of the submarine?

Peter - I'd been away on a trip out of the country up to Guadalajara to deliver a bag so had been gone while the seller had visited German's ranch. The seller himself having been checked, double checked and triple checked before getting as far as the gate to the ranch.

The information coming back that the guy was a Jake 'Nuggy' Lopez. A Floridian who was one year back out from a five year jail sentence in a Panamanian prison for gun running charges for a rebel group. Also a couple of felonies back home in the States for aggravated robbery and grand theft auto.

Not the type of person that you would imagine in a position to be offloading a submarine but this world we live in you should never be not ready for the element of surprise in anything. I didn't think that prior to moving to Bogota at the end of the Eighties but I sure as hell believed it afterwards.

Lopez answered all of the brothers' questions in a satisfactory way. When asked how someone like *him* had a submarine. He had been up front in saying that he was simply trying to sell it on someone else behalf so that he could make a fee for himself. When asked - by German - why the people did not just sell it themselves he had admired the answer that he had been given back.

'Because the people who are selling the submarine are too nervous to enter into a business deal with someone of your reputation, Don German. With the greatest of respect. I am *not* nervous to break bread with you and this is why they use me as an intermediate.'

It mattered not that I hadn't had a chance to meet with the seller - ahead of Miami - as most of my business involved me turning up and meeting with a stranger anyway. Eddy and German were convinced, that's all that ever really mattered.

I met with the two brothers the night before I was scheduled to travel up to Florida.

Eddy - at the prospect of closing the deal and our cartel becoming owners of a submarine - was in a jovial mood with the scotch flowing.

'Tomorrow, we set about changing the history of drug importing. Tomorrow we change the game and make up some new rules.'

Going on a long monologue of how - historically - from a smuggling narcotics between South America and America point of view, it always came down to Mexico and that we were on our way to completely flipping that particular script. We'd had to use them, Cali used them and - apart from the well documented Caribbean air route which he had used, with success, until the DEA brought it down - so had Pablo Escobar. The Mexicans - and their border to America - were a necessary evil.

You wanted your drugs into America? Then the high percentage of the time, you're going to have the Mexicans carrying the water for you.

Every time us, Cali or Medellin used them, however. All all it did was help them become even more stronger and powerful, in their own rights. Long since demanding payment in product over money. Sure, we had our own routes for all of our deals that *weren't* going in the direction of the Yanquis but on the whole, Mexico was important to us.

With their array of underground tunnels and routes for getting narcotics into the states. It was undeniable that the Mexicans were the very elite in smuggling. That was why we *all* used them.

'But what if we didn't *have* to use them, at all. Or at the worst, in a more limited capacity?' Eddy had said while in the middle of taking us all through - what we already knew but weren't for stopping him - the history of smuggling Cocaine from South America to Mexico and how it always really did come down to the Mexican cartels.

'We take *all* the profits *and* we can make as many shipments as we like *when* we like. We will not be on the Sinaloan clock anymore. Bogota time, pendejo. It is get rich o clock, si?'

German, chipped in as they both considered the difference this was going to make to our business.

'We will have our shipments driven up to Barranquila. There, it will be loaded onto the submarine and taken to Florida, we will do this once a week to begin with.'

Eddy said, appearing as if he had already began making the plans needed for what to do with his new toy.

All of this could not have possibly been more of a contrast to the two - much more famous - cartels who were destroying themselves with bombs and bullets. Cali and Medellin had been pretty much going at each other from since I'd arrived in the country. Either city - as beautiful as Medellin had appeared - didn't exactly look like much of a picnic to live in and its citizens never quite knew when the next bomb was going to go off, or the next person assassinated.

War is no good for business, unless you're *in* the war business, that is. Cali, the intelligent business brains that they possessed, would not have ever wanted to get into it all with Escobar but sometimes you get poked enough with the stick, the tendency to snatch that stick off the person - doing the poking - and shove it *right* into their eye. Something you could say Cali did the day that they made an attempt on Escobar's family.

I had always said to Eddy that it was a *good* thing that the other two cartels took the glory as it allowed us to get on with the business of making billions, without as many looking in our direction. Cali and Medellin fighting with each other in such a brutal and pubic fashion could not have been a better scenario for us in Bogota. A magician's slight of hand trick. Look over there at that shiny thing while you miss the *other* thing that is going on.

The first night that I had arrived in Bogota - and then to the party - there had been members of both Cali *and* Medellin representing at the ranch. That had been the last time that they had been spotted in the same room. Friction already having been created between both cartels by then and - I was told years later - that neither city had wanted to lose face by not attending Eddy's Christmas party. Things hadn't exactly been ideal though, to put it mildly.

In a ghoulish way, the more trouble they had between them would be a case of the more dead bodies the merrier. With Bogota out of the beef between the two. The weaker either cartel became, the stronger it made Eddy and German.

With the Ramirez brothers no strangers to doing business - on occasion - with either Cali or Medellin. Their relationship with both had been cordial. But when it's war time. If you're not picking a side, you stay out of things. This being the case with Eddy and German instructing both Escobar - as well as the Rodriguez Orejuela brothers - that Bogota would be cutting off any kind of communication with either cartel, until they had sorted out their little tiff and the bombings had stopped while - privately - saying that if they wanted to get themselves all killed or arrested then let them, but that we would be loco to put ourselves into any crossfires.

Eddy and German being held in such high regard with any of their business associates - I think in part due to being such affable and likable men - that Miguel Rodriguez called Eddy personally to say that he looked forward to doing business in the future with them again, once he had dealt with the small technical problem that the cartel were experiencing with Medellin.

As would turn out. That 'small technical problem' - Escobar - would be gone by the end of the year. Although that only really marked the *start* of the Cali Cartel's problems. Escobar did not return the brothers' call but - with half of the country now officially after him, alongside the Yanquis - it was not taken personally by Eddy and German.

Cartel bosses normally don't take kindly to having *anyone* tell them what to do but with Eddy and German, they had the ability to get away with it. The cheeky, massive cojones larger than life personality the pair possessed. Sure, you're a boss. You *deserve* respect. That does not mean, however, that you're not immune to pissing off those who are sitting at a similar level. Something which can cause 'issues.' Issues that can escalate in the blink of an eye and resulting in all out war. Go ask the Orejuelas and Escobar about it.

As crazy an idea to spend millions of dollars on a submarine was to me. I *did*, however find the limiting things with the Mexicans appealing.

Up to that point. The only two types that I had been left nervy around - when doing business - had been Jihadi terrorists, and Mexican narcos. The Mexican cartels really were in danger of making Colombia look like a children's soft play area, when it came to the brutal murders and the horrific 'spectacular' scale of them.

The one real issue for them was not managing to maintain 'The Federation' following things turning sour and leading to the arrest of its former leader 'Miguel Angel Felix Gallardo.' Whatever skills the man had in his locker they had included being able to control all the separate and volatile cartels and have them work as one, with limited blood being shed in the process.

It was said that - when he had been arrested - he had told his interrogator that

'Now you will see what happens when you open the cage and let the animals out. You're going to miss me.'

Judging by what I had witnessed - added to the stories that I'd heard about what went on up in Mexico - and all of the incessant slaughter of both the guilty and the innocent, they seemed to have been prophetic words from the man that they occasionally called the Thin Man' but in most cases, El jefe of jefes, The boss of bosses.

It had turned into a - to lend Gallardo's line - complete animal house and if we could limit dealing with them to get our Cocaine into America then it was a case of sub me *right* up.

Manny - The submarine, was sat in Miami. A seller in the region, right?

Peter - Yes, it was docked at Miami Marina. The story that Eddy and German had been fed - by the undercover agent - had been that the submarine had belonged to a marine exploration organisation who had been in danger of going bankrupt. The organisation, themselves, an actual non profit environmental protection charity, something that stood up to our security background checks. The sale of the sub was being forced to pay back some of the outstanding debts the organisation had been left with. The plan had been that I would be given a demonstration that the sub was fully active - from one of the staff from the organisation doing the selling - once I'd arrived.

"Nuggy' had - as part of the deal - asked for his cut of the sale to be paid to him in product, as opposed to money. Telling the brothers that - following his stay in the Panamanian jail - he was working to get himself back on the up again and the value of the Cocaine was of much more to him - a lot more - than the money would ever have been. This suiting Eddy and German even further as it would only mean that this would go on to make the purchase of the 'Ocean Pearl Mini' submarine even *more* economical than first anticipated.

I was off to Florida the next day with my orders of collecting what was waiting for me with my contact on the other end and to then meet with Nuggy at the Miami Marina at three o clock. Should things have been as they were *meant* to have been then I was to proceed with supplying him with the product - as his payment - with the money transfer already set up and waiting on the green light from myself by giving the word to Mikael at his location.

Manny - You had the sting all set up for that afternoon and Peter Duncan in your sights?

Vinnie - Peter Duncan? We didn't even *know* he was going to be a part of things until early morning - the day of the meet - when he had called our man to say that he had arrived in Miami and to confirm if everything was all arranged.

Tommy - We thought we'd won the freaking lottery, when Nuggy called to tell us that it was arranged for three, and that he was meeting with 'The Scotsman.' The plan had always been for *whoever* we busted, that we would lean on them, hard - then the standard offer for them to cut a deal - and move our way up the ladder and bring down their bosses. We could not have dreamed that this would be the same man that we had made an official person of interest several years before. Someone that we'd already decided that we would have no problems in getting to talk. We just needed to get *them* first.

Vinnie - When you work in the narcos business you're pretty much either a suit or you're a soldier and rarely is there ever any blurring of that. Ray freaking Charles would've been able to tell you which one out of the two Peter Duncan was.

Manny - You were in Miami and ready to do the deal with 'Nuggy.' How did things go at the marina?

Peter - *laughing* Well I never came away with the keys to an Ocean Pearl Mini submarine, that's for sure, Manfred. I mean, I *saw* the submarine, from the Julia Tuttle Causeway, as I travelled across it, in my hire car over from my Miami Beach hotel. If anything, I'm a punctual man. I think it was around quarter to three that I found myself driving over the causeway. I'd say that it was a beautiful day - which it was - but well, it *was* Miami. It was a day that had a letter 'y' in it so, yes. It was also a day where the sun was bright and the sky was blue. The yellow and blue sub was sitting there in the sea, floating beside a yacht that must've been twenty times its size.

Boats were not exactly a rare thing to see in Miami Marina, however. Submarines, not so much. Reaching the end of the bridge, I took the slip road off to the side and continued on towards the marina. Driving to the destination, standard black heavy duty case containing Nuggy's Cocaine, I got the familiar wave of nerves that I would *always* get when it was 'game time.' The nerves were a good thing, I'd always told myself. That if I ever stopped getting nervous *that* would be when I would get sloppy.

Due to coping with the nerves and - while fighting them - trying to gain some kind of focus for whatever lay ahead, inside the not too distant future, I almost jumped out of my skin when the phone inside the car went off.

I was just about to pull into the marina entrance when the ringing from it pulled me out of the focussed zen like state I was in with the job ahead in my mind. Still driving I reached down to pick it up and answer.

'DON'T GO TO THE MARINA.'

The voice - American - said before the line went dead again.

Manny - Who was it that called you?

Peter - Well, you'd like to have thought that it had come from Donnie Bannon. I mean, we were paying him enough. It was Miami that I was in. The call - reading between the lines - was telling me that there were DEA there. Who do you think would have had access to such sensitive information as that? Do the math, Manfred.

I recognised the voice, in any case. Of *course* it was Bannon.

It shook me, the call. I pulled to a stop directly outside the marina. A stifling hot afternoon had - in that exact moment - been made to feel *infinitely* warmer. I had to jump out of the car for a moment, feeling like I was in danger of suffocating. I got out and leaned against the front of the bonnet and, paradoxically, sparked up a cigarette, power smoking it in a matter of moments while I evaluated things and decided on the next moves I should make.

Them being for me to leave the immediate area as soon as I could. Return the product that was on my person back to where it had came from and then get Mikael and myself out of Miami as soon as humanly possible.

We could investigate - and we would - what had gone wrong, afterwards. All I knew for sure is that when - in the line of work that I was in - you were on the way to a business meeting - holding enough Cocaine to put you in prison for twenty years - and you received a call telling you that the Drug Enforcement Administration were likely waiting on the other end for you, you paid attention to whatever angel from above was trying to guide you.

I left town that night and was back in Bogota in time for supper.

Manny - You had everything all set up. The fact that Peter Duncan walked a free man until the year Two Thousand, and this all took place back in Ninety Three. What went wrong, guys?

Tommy - I watched the man himself drive *right up* to the entrance of the marina in a Mercedes. Looked straight at him through a pair of binoculars from my vantage point I'd been stationed. I had even radioed to the rest of the team that I had a visual I.D on our target and to be on alert. The moment that he passed over the Cocaine to Nuggy we were to move in on him.

Vinnie - And, not for the first time, or the last. Duncan left us standing around with our dicks in our hands.

Tommy - None of it made any sense. He's travelled from Bogota. Had called our man. We hadn't had to chase Duncan in any way. He had come as a *willing* buyer. Even when he stopped the convertible that he was driving and got out for a cigarette, I didn't see any problems. Just him appearing to take a moment out before he went in to do business. It was when he got back in the car and drove away though. I knew we were screwed.

Vinnie - All you heard on our radios, from Tommy, was 'No …oh, no. No no no no don't drive away ahhhhhhh DAMMIT.'

Tommy - We had no explanation for it. Why would someone travel from one continent to another. Go as far as driving *right* up to the meeting place only to casually stop, have a cigarette and then drive away again? Intelligence reporting that a man fitting his description - travelling with a companion - left Miami International Airport on a plane for Bogota early evening that same day.

Vinnie - We were left scratching our heads for a couple of days on the matter. Nuggy had tried and tried - without success - to get Bogota to answer his calls. Trying to keep up the appearance of the seller - as you'd have expected from someone - seeking an answer to why the deal had fallen apart. He had been stonewalled for the following forty eight hours from the day of the planned deal.

Tommy - Then we received the out of hours voice message, at the office, on the twenty four hour 'hotline' that we left available for the general public to leave any enquiries or tips that they may have had to share. Definitely not a fact that we shouted from the rooftops but something like around eighty per cent of our busts in Florida - in recent years - had come through tips from informants and suspicious members of the public. The phone line was always worth a listen to in the morning when we appeared in the office.

Vinnie - Yeah, we used to take it in turns who had to listen to whatever had come in through the night. It was always a mixed bag. Cranks, drunks, junkies and wackadoos, most of the time. You never discounted the *real* tips that were going to be tucked away in amongst the crank calls though and as such, *every single one* had to be treated as serious as the previous, until actually listened to.

Tommy - Yeah, it was Vinnie here who was on the rota for voice message duties that morning. I was in the middle of checking on a surveillance team that we had positioned out in North Beach when Vinnie shouted me over. Shaking his head but with a strange kind of smile to his face. Almost like he was smiling but didn't know *why* he was.

I told our agent that I'd call him back and got myself over to Vinnie's desk where he was hitting the play button for me on the answering machine.

'Hello, hermanos. It's your friend Señor Cousteau. Such a shame that we weren't able to do business with each other on the submarine. She looked a beauty too. That yellow and blue really gave it a nice finishing touch. I'm sure you'll agree, it would've been perfect to ship from Colombia into Florida? Oh well, some other time, perhaps? I would suggest that should there BE some 'some other time' that you may be better served trying to get up a little bit earlier in the morning next time.'

The call ended with him laughing down the line. From the accent, and how descriptive he had been in what he had said. We were left in no doubt *who* it was on the other end of the line. With that - by then - almost pseudo Scottish accent like that, it was highly debatable that his second name was Cousteau!

Vinnie - I don't know why he did it, make that call. In doing so, though. He had told us something that we hadn't known. That he had been tipped off about our presence at the Miami Marina.

Tommy - Yeah, buddy. You can only imagine our frustration and anger that all of those months of hard work. Our man Nuggy, putting his life on the line every single day. A gringo moving through South America trying to mix with cartels is not a walk in the park by any means. All of our efforts down the drain. Our network had been pretty tight. No more than ten people max, knew about the operation.

Vinnie - It was a hard thing to face up to but Duncan, while looking to do nothing other than likely taunt us out of his own sheer arrogance, had confirmed to us that the Miami DEA had a mole inside of it.

Chapter 26

El Corazon Valiente - The Ballad of Peter Duncan cont

Manny - With such a colorful and unpredictable life, where one week to the other was barely ever the same. How did you manage to carve out any kind of a 'life' for yourself. Privately, were you *happy* with your life?

Peter - Ooooooh that's a question and a half. Was I happy? A dirty Bogota cop once told me - when I had been delivering his monthly bribe to him and his team - that in narco culture *no one* is happy. I'll always remember the words, actually. They'd made me think about things a lot deeper than his off the cuff comment had probably been intended.

'In narco culture, no one's ever happy and *everyone* always wants more.'

He had a point. Look at all the drug lords from the region who got a taste of the lifestyle, and riches that it brought, and were they happy? Well, no. They wanted even more of it. More power, more money, more of the feeling of being able to do *exactly* what they wanted *when* they wanted. The pursuit of money so relentless that most drug lords barely ever got the chance to 'truly' enjoy the wealth they already *had*.

Me, though? Best I could describe things would've been that I could've been a lot happier but also, *far*, far worse than I was.

I was seeing Eva - in whatever random location that my work would take me to that was within a quick flight for her - relatively frequently. Well, for two people who live in separate continents.

The Spanish lessons that I had thrown myself into with most of the spare time that I had back in Bogota - along with the self taught tapes that I would listen to on my Walkman on flights - had paid off and I was, a few years into my stay, by then speaking relatively fluently. This seeing to me getting out and exploring the city of Bogota. A place that I had began to fall in love with, once I'd eventually got myself out and about to explore.

I admit, for someone from Scotland, I'd been a little overawed by the city. Felt that I'd have been better off just staying behind the gates of the hacienda and keep myself to myself. Wasn't so naive as to think that just because I was new to town - and here to work for the local cartel - that I'd have been able to walk around the city - while sticking out like a sore thumb - without attracting any attention, some unwanted.

Fast forward a few years, however, and anyone in the city of Bogota who knew about the inner workings of the Ramirez brothers cartel, knew my face. The fact that I could communicate with the locals - in their own tongue - helped enormously. Changed how I approached living in the city, once I could speak the language.

With a population inside the city of over what was even in the *whole* of Scotland it had been a culture shock at first. I'd never been one of those Brits who would travel the world and expect the locals to be able to speak English and that was how I treated Bogota. Got my head down and learned as fast as I could so I could enjoy the whole experience of living in such an exciting and vibrant city.

Before that, in the early days. Some had suggested that I get out in my car and go for a drive, to see around the city and surrounding area. Get to know my environment, so to speak. At *that* time, with the reputation that a European had come to Colombia with in his mind? No, thank you.

I'd have loved - I really wouldn't - to have seen how far this 'gringo' would have got had he ran into some F.A.R.C rebels - who I would go onto have a major 'run in' with as the years went by - or something of their equivalent. Early days, I stayed closer to home. A lot closer.

Apart from the times where Eva and I would see each other. My down time would be spent just relaxing around the pool. Simply trying to do the *opposite* of what I'd find myself doing when travelling out of Colombia.

There were also the parties that Eddy and German would regularly throw which - were I in town to be able to attend - were literally worth risking your life and liberty, working for the pair of them, just to be able to attend.

Manny - Some of them were spoken about across the whole of the Americas.

Peter - With good cause. How many parties have you been to where the drunken host crashes through the middle of it, strapped to a terrified elephant while swigging from a champagne bottle and firing off a clip into the sky from a Glock Nine M, leaving a trail of destruction in their wake?

Manny - None that I can recall.

Peter - The majority of the times I was out of the country so missed them but the ones that I *did* attend? Crackers, absolutely crackers. You know? Say what you like about Eddy and German Ramirez but they knew how to throw a party. Like I said, Eddy strapped to elephants waving to everyone, shooting and drinking. The hiring of a *very* famous singer to be flown to Colombia for German's birthday that resulted in the songstress - who out of respect I will not name but will leave it at that you know her songs, and so does whoever finds themselves reading this article - sleeping with German for an obscene amount of money - that had initially been a joke offer from German which had hastily been upgraded to a *real* one, once he got a sniff of her actually being 'open' to the offer - in a night that I cannot imagine she'll look back on with much pride or relish, even if her bank account does.

The expensive food flown in from all over the world for the night. The finest and rarest alcohol of which 'year' the bottles were, highly discriminated upon. Shit? So intent on their guests receiving nothing but the best *of everything* that the brothers would even ship in Cocaine from Peru even though they had access to an almost unlimited supply inside Colombia!

There were a *lot* of parties although I only saw a fraction of them. Hey, the brothers were party people. I mean, I went to my fair share of them and I was barely ever in Colombia most weekends. It wasn't just the parties, with Eddy and German, though. The men liked to have a good time and had the funds to facilitate it. Can anyone really blame them for going ahead and doing so?

Due to the sheer amount of acres spread across German's ranch He'd had a special pit designed which allowed him to hold Demolition

Derbies on the ranch. Him and close friends all driving around smashing the hell out of each other.

Manny - Something similar to Escobar?

Peter - Well, similar if you mean by how Escobar loved to race with cars - and bikes - while German loved to smash the hell out of them, repeatedly?

It was outrageous but a *lot* of fun. They never mention that side of narcos, always the bad sides to them. Not that they're just like the rest of us, at times. For a while the flow of used cars being brought to his fortress on the outskirts of the city was incessant. Good times, Manfred, good times.

Manny - So, Eva. You were living in Manchester, England while engaging in a long distance relationship with a man who was an associate of the Ramirez Cartel in Bogota. Do tell.

Eva - *laughs* I know right? Conventional, it was not.

Manny - You *did* know that the man that you were romantically involved with was someone who was an operative for an international drugs organisation and that - as an estimate, around a few years after meeting him - he was someone who was already on the watchlist of the DEA, ATF and the CIA?

Eva - Well yes and no, really?

Manny - I'm not really sure that was a yes *and* no kind of a question!

Eva - What I meant was, yes - I knew that he was not entirely what you would have described as 'on the level' - but no, I didn't know how *serious* or how deep he was into that world. Do you honestly think I'd have got myself involved in *that?* I liked him, then went one step further and fell in love. I'd have ran a country mile if I'd known what loving someone like *him* would've brought me.

I have to admit, it *was* exciting. The life that we had. With sometimes less than a day's notice have him call to notify me that there were tickets waiting to be collected at the airport and that he would see me at - insert whatever European city - on my arrival. Budapest, Madrid, Kiev, Frankfurt, Lyon. I saw so many cities that - otherwise - would never have had the pleasure. Of course, some times all I would see would be the journey from the airport to the hotel and then back again for my flight home. Hey, we missed each other like any other long distance relationship couple would! Other times however, we would go out strolling and discovering parts of whichever city we found ourselves in. It felt exciting, also romantic.

Some trips we would get the whole weekend together. Others, it would literally be the case of me travelling to somewhere like say Paris only *because* he was connecting there on his way to somewhere and would have an extended layover of six hours or so. Flying to see your boyfriend, in another country, for a total of six hours? I must've been crazy. It was an exhilarating time, though. Sometimes I would barely see him before he was gone again on his flight while others we would be holding hands walking along somewhere picturesque like The Danube as if we had all the time in the world before going to a nice cosy restaurant for a romantic dinner.

Manny - How were your employers with your last minute frequent jet setting across Europe? They must have been most understanding with your love life, yes?

Eva - I worked in a coffee shop when I met Peter. Through the relationship that we had together, and how last minute and unconventional it all was. Once we had become serious and had shown each other that - despite the clear challenges - we wanted to continue with what we had, Peter soon had me handing in my notice at work.

Initially I had been a little unsure about doing so. He was going to send me a monthly payment that would be a substitute for my salary. At first my thoughts were that I was literally being *paid* to be someone's girlfriend. And there's a name for girls like that.

Once Peter had spun it a completely different way to me - in that due to how unpredictable his working schedule always was - if the other half of our relationship was not in a position to drop what they were doing - on their side - then him and I were never going to get off the ground. It made sense.

After a few of our 'city breaks' he had started to ask me about whether I would consider moving out to Colombia to be with him. With it being such a big step for a young girl to take, my answer to him was that I wanted us to get to know each other a bit more before I would commit to that. Something that I eventually would do in Ninety Five, following his marriage proposal.

I was so in love with him, completely captivated by his charm and personality. The way that he loved *me* and yeah, the fact that he was in a position to give me a better life than I could ever have managed to carve out for myself on my own in Manchester.

So much so that I had been prepared to overlook things like him being away from the house and leaving me there on my own in a foreign country and me not knowing what he *really* did for a living. He - evidently - had money and he lived in Colombia. Describing yourself as an 'importer exporter' while you live in a major city such as Bogota. I wasn't naive. He wouldn't make any work related calls in front of me when we were in hotel rooms and then - as his Spanish got better - he *would*. Safe in the knowledge that I didn't understand what he was talking about.

I think I just conveniently put the blinkers on. I'd been seduced in mind and body by the man, himself. The red flags of the baggage that he was going to bring me further down the line, I preferred not to see.

Manny - Following meeting in England at the start of the decade you and Eva - despite the challenges of a long distance relationship would've brought, pre internet - continued as partners. Was it always the plan to have Eva move over to Colombia?

Peter - Well, to be fair, I had been trying to get her to move over to Bogota from about Ninety One and it took all the way up until Ninety Five for her to *finally* make the move. And even then, I had to propose to her first.

Oh you'd have been proud of me with this, Manfred. Took her to the Dominican Republic. You know? Working for the Ramirez crew. It's not exactly a case of writing your holiday dates down and submitting them to your manager for approval but you *can* get yourself a holiday from time to time. Everyone needs to go away and and get some sun on their backs while they recharge the Duracells, don't they? *Even* narcos. They work as hard as anyone else, probably even harder.

Well, it was around late Ninety Four and I'd had a good few wins - business dealings wise - for Eddy and German leading up to that. So much in fact that they'd given me an extra large bonus of a couple of hundred grand which had been, in reality, for very little work and told to take myself off for a break and come back energised and ready for the next piece of world domination that was being plotted.

I'd wasted no time in arranging the flights and hotels for Eva and I. With it being such a long flight I had made the small gesture of flying from Colombia to Manchester - a few days before our trip - *so* that Eva wouldn't have to travel such a long distance on her own.

What she *didn't* know, however, was of certain plans that I had put in place over in the Dominican Republic, waiting on our arrival.

One night while we were there we had sat having a meal and a few drinks at a beautifully set up candlelit private table, beside the swimming pool, that I'd arranged while back in Colombia. After dinner, I suggested that we go for an evening stroll along by the beach.

We walked and talked a little before heading to the stairs that would take you from the hotel and down onto the beach. It was from this vantage point that she was able to see all of the hundreds of tea lights that had been carefully arranged in rows on the sand to spell out a perfectly lined up.

'EVA, WILL YOU MARRY ME? X'

Eva - I had never seen anything more romantic in my life. We were in such a beautiful country as the Dominican Republic. I was with the perfect person in the world, and they had arranged all of this, *for me.* I cried and cried the best of tears that night. Wow, it was so very overpowering. So emotional. To feel *that* kind of love from someone.

Amongst my tears, I also said yes.

Peter - The moment she saw the candles, she was a blubbering mess. A beautiful sobbing snotty nosed mess. And she wasn't much better when she turned to find me on my knee with that box open. Showing her the twenty four carat diamond ring that was waiting on her.

She also said yes, though. The moment that she said that important three letter word, allowing me to signal to the hotel worker positioned down on the beach, waiting on the go ahead to light up the sky above us with as many fireworks as I could possibly find on the island ahead of our visit. Pink, green, purple, red, orange you name it, the sky was that colour. Her face - and the massive smile that she had firmly fixed to it as she looked back at me - changing shades of colour with each firework burst that exploded into the sky.

We were married before the holiday had ended. A beautiful beach wedding that had followed Eva going out the day before where - arranged by myself in advance - she was to meet with the island's most regarded wedding dress maker who, it was hoped, would be able to take Eva's description for her dream wedding dress and bring it to life. If a bespoke wedding dress made inside twenty four hours seems a bit of a stretch. It all really comes down to how much you are willing to 'pay' for one.

The holiday ended with Eva flying back to Manchester and me having to head straight to Bogota. Through a call to the hotel I had been made aware that something had come up for the brothers and that they would appreciate me back there sooner than later. I couldn't justify the additional time lost of flying to Manchester to then turn around and fly all the way back to Bogota. Not when I was under three hours away from Colombia, and the brothers knew it too.

Eva - I returned back from that holiday, head in a spin, high as a kite with that rock around my finger and new life plans now waiting to be made. My mum hit the bloody roof, over missing the wedding. I'd been so swept up in everything that I hadn't even thought about anything like that. Her *and* dad were furious, actually. Their daughter went off for a sunny holiday to the Dominican Republic and came home married and telling them that she is now moving to Colombia. Looking back, I can see their point. I didn't at the time, though.

Manny - And your son, Steven? With you and him reuniting as father and son. How did your second chance with each other progress? Did *he* ever come out to Bogota to visit his father?

Peter - Yeah, Stevie? Well, you know, Manfred. *That* was a bit of a sticky subject. I mean, if you worked for an outfit such as the Bogota Cartel. Would *you* bring your kid over to Colombia for a holiday? Under such circumstances? I'd have loved to have brought the boy over, take him to meet Eddy and German. They'd have got on like a house on fire and I already *know* that Roman and Stevie look like they're almost the same model of each other only one has *made in Colombia* stamped underneath their foot and the other *made in Scotland.*

Ethically, though. I'd felt that it maybe wasn't the most responsible of things to do, bringing Stevie to Bogota for a visit. That if - as the father of someone closely linked to the Ramirez brothers - I was to put him in any kind of peril then I would have to live with that for the rest of my life. I felt that he'd be safer *away* from South America.

Apart from that, though. It wasn't like Stevie and myself needed people to grab the phone off us because we spent all day long talking with each other. Yeah, never kept in touch in the way that we *said* that we would but I'd been settled with the fact that he had been keeping his head down - and out of trouble - with the playing records gig that he had going on.

Not that I'd ever believed that the boy would've actually *made* any money out of it but compared to what he was all wrapped in - prior to him and I meeting in Blackburn in Nineteen Ninety - it was good, as a parent, to see him actually making something of himself.

Manny - And what *was* your son Stevie mixed up in? The way you say it, it, it sounds like he was involved in something serious?

Peter - I'm afraid, Manfred. Out of respect for the young man that I'll say *that* particular story - about the goings on back in Nineteen Ninety - is not mines to tell. It's my son's. Tell you what? Should he ever wish to recant it, I'll pass on your details to him. *laughs*

Chapter 27

Peter

'I can't fucking take this place anymore, mate.'

Gal was shouting through the intercom to me. He sounded a frightened and completely different person to any other time he'd been on the other end of the conversation each night.

'Woah, pal. What's up?' I asked, trying to calm him a little *without* actually saying the words 'calm down' to him. If the words 'calm down' have ever worked for anyone else in the history of mankind then fair play to whoever it worked for. It had *never* went well for me so at an early age had elected never to say those words, when, paradoxically, they were the *exact* words that you wanted to say to the person.

As he rambled, vented and voiced all of his fears and depressions. It became clear that Gary had 'hit the wall' as far as his early entry to life at the ADX.

I mean, you can't exactly call living in a supermax prison - for the first time in your life - a honeymoon period, because it definitely isn't. Still, I think the change in scenery and the fact that you're now having to deal with the very real situation that you've found yourself in. It can keep you going for a while. Your mind leaps into self preservation mode and you do what you can to cope with your 'new life' in those early days of imprisonment.

I think it's when you allow yourself to ease off. Relax a little. *That's* when the gravity of it all starts to hit you, and from all directions. I'd faced it myself - after a couple of months of being there - and it wasn't a nice experience. Once I got past that stage, things began to lift again. I'd seen it almost like the stages of grief and once you get to acceptance - *if* you can get there, of course - then life improves for you, considerably.

I didn't want to risk diminishing any of his fears and worries by telling Gal that it was natural and that I'd gone through the same stuff as him. Preferring to let him get it all out and let him know that someone was actually *listening.*

'Mate? Where the fuck do you want me to start?' He asked

'You could try at the start?' I said trying to joke with him but should've known that he was beyond that.

'I don't even know where the start *or* end is, fella. Just lots and lots of dark thoughts that I want out my head but they won't leave. I've got two beautiful children back in the U.K that's never going to see their dad again. Fuck, I don't even know if they even realise *where* their dad is, never mind that they'll never see him as they grow up. I've got a mum and dad entering their later years. Dad's already had two heart attacks and the next one will finish him off. I can only imagine how worried they are about me. I've not received any mail yet so I don't even know if they've written to me or not.'

'They will have, Gal. You'll get your letters soon enough, pal.' I told him with not a single shred of evidence that I could possibly call on to back that up. Carrying on speaking - while I tried to calm him - I doubt that he'd even heard my less than certain reassurances.

'I'm stuck in this fucking cell - which feels as small as a cunting phone box at times - for the best part of every day. No contact with anyone. Just me and my mind and that's the *last* thing I need right now. The bastarding food tastes like shit, I can barely eat it. American TV is fucking shit. Those excuses for pens that they give us to write with are fucking shit. It's all fucking SHIT.'

'Yeah but, Gal' I tried, once more but, to be fair. I had encouraged him to get it all out and let me know what was troubling him. He had taken up this offer from me, gladly.

'And another cunting fucking thing. These raghead terrorists that I've got either side of me. They just won't stop fucking praying, mate. Either I'm going out of my mind - which is entirely possible, to be honest - or the two cunts are praying even *more* than Muslims are even meant to, just to fucking wind me up. They're taking the fucking rise, mate. Feel like I'm living in between two cunting mosques for fuck's sake.'

I mean, he wasn't wrong, about the Al Qaeda operatives and their prayer. We had them over my side too. Anytime they prayed you would have the cacophony of the noise *they* were making as they prayed to Allah and the - in response - jeering and cursing from non Muslims which pretty much translated as something along the lines of 'shut the fuck up.'

The time of Ramadan, the absolute worst for it all.

'I keep getting these thoughts, horrible black thoughts, Pete.'

I asked him what kind of thoughts he was referring to but it didn't sound promising, his mental state.

'That I'm not gonna make it, mate. I'm not going to go the distance in here and that, maybe I should just cut my losses and save the time. If all I've got left ahead of me is endless days inside this cell, like we all have in here, I'd much rather not. I'd never discounted that there would be another attempt on my life, some point down the line when the bombing of my car had left the public's memory. Some days, fella I swear that I would open the cell door and let them in, just to finish me off.

I'd been put in a plethora of different situations in my life and had been forced to use some serious people skills and in some very precarious of circumstances. Talking around someone who was displaying signs of suicidal tendencies was *not* one of them, though.

I - while I admit, completely winging it - managed it, of course. Took Gal through every single one of his worries and fears, and provided him with a solution to each and every one of them. Took his mind and all of the clutter that was lying around inside of it and gave it a bit of a tidy up. Made sure everything was put back where it was meant to be, so to speak.

Almost believed that I was a therapist myself - or something to that effect - the more I got into it and the results I was hearing simply through the change in tone of his voice. He was starting to sound less desperate which, for sure, was a very much welcomed step in the right direction.

I told him that - whether he liked it or not - he would be going out for as much recreation time as the guards would offer him the next day.

Reminding him that while no one likes to have to strip naked just to enjoy the basic human right of some fresh air, it was what it was and he was *where* he was. That he hadn't been out of his cell, at all. I told him that it wasn't healthy and was only further helping contribute to his extreme feelings of isolation and cabin fever. I knew I was being hypocritical on some subjects but that was kind of my point. I'd learned from some of my own mistakes and didn't want Gary to make them all over again for himself. He was a good lad and it was hard to hear him like that. As a mate, you'd do *whatever* it took to pull someone back out of that state, wouldn't you?

It took all night - and resulted in us staying up way past our usual 'bedtime' - but Gal was in a far better state of mind than he had been when he'd began the night, ranting through the intercom about how he was going to end it all. I don't even think that I'd have managed a paltry couple of hours sleep before my Jihadi friend next door started his shit for the day.

I was touched with how Gary had left things and how he'd said it. I don't think I had ever heard such gratefulness and sincerity in someone's voice when speaking in my direction as I did that moment, even over the crackly - and hardly Nicam Stereo like - intercom.

'You know, fella. I just want to thank you for tonight, and all you've done to help. You're a fucking good guy, Pete. You know that, mate.'

I'd been told that many times before but no, I didn't know *that*. How could you when you balance things out with the *opposite* of being a good guy? Plus, when the words come from sycophants who you suspect are only looking after their own interests, talk can be cheap.

For the first time in my life, though. Someone was telling me that I was a good guy, and I actually *felt* that I was one.

Chapter 28

El Corazon Valiente - The Ballad of Peter Duncan cont

Manny - Taking the events of Amsterdam Two Thousand completely out of the equation. Were there any *other* moments where you thought the game was up and that the authorities had finally caught up with you?

Peter - Well, to be fair, we could've done a specialised interview, dedicated *just* to the times that I had felt that I was being tailed or sounded out by law enforcement. Of course, though. Depending on the country that I was in, I may have been there specifically to *deal* with the police.

If you have ever held any fantasy filled beliefs that all police are the keepers of law and order then a week inside the drug business would knock that right out of you.

Following events in Miami and the failed submarine purchase. Every single time I returned there - and of which there were many returns, it was Miami, had *that* particular city been deemed a no go area, while working for a Colombian cartel, I'd have been as well handing in my notice to Eddy and German. A little like being a taxi driver but not having a license, or know how to drive, selling weapons and Cocaine in America and not being able to enter Miami - I would pick up a tail, or someone following me.

I'd absolutely been besotted with Miami, the actual city, and it was never, ever bad news to be told that I was heading up there, for whatever reason. The nightlife was the best in America. Huge open air night clubs with beautiful people. Cocaine fueling the party city from dusk til dawn to a soundtrack of infectious Latino music. I enjoyed the clubs, the people, the music and the general vibe to downtown, once the sun went down and people were out and ready to party. Most business trips I rarely ventured further than my hotel, recreationally. Miami, Florida was *always* the exception to that rule.

It was a playground that I completely adored from day one - and were it not for the obvious - a city that I would have happily retired to at one point. It, for me, had *everything*. If Miami didn't have it then, simply, no one had thought of it yet.

Following the complete bust of a submarine purchase - and the first confirmation that I was subject to a police sting that had been set up - I treaded a lot more lightly around the city. Trading staying up all night dancing, drinking and taking Cocaine in the city's hottest clubs instead, for parties of one, in my hotel room. Helping myself to the array of products from the mini bar.

Manny - But, you had the insurance policy in the mole that Bogota had gathered *inside* the Miami Drug Enforcement Administration. Didn't that offer you a certain level of 'comfort' moving around the city?

Peter - Can I ask *you* a question. I know that's *your* job but I'd like to ask one back in return.

Manny - Emmmm, sure. Fire away.

Peter - Just say one day you cheated on your wife with someone else who was *also* married. An affair behind both spouses backs, that kind of thing. One day you and your mistress decide that you're both going to leave your partners so that you can start your new life. How are you meant to *trust* your new partner? Shit? How is she meant to trust *you*? My point being that you have both already played your hands. You've both showed that you're someone that is untrustworthy. Simply through what you had both done to get you *up* to that point.

Manny - Your point being?

Peter - Have you not had your coffee this morning yet or what? What I'm saying is that Donnie Bannon was someone trusted by all of his team in the Miami field office. He was their *gaffer* for f**k's sake. How trusted does one have to be to reach the lofty position of director of an anti drugs task force field office? This man had a team of people who would quite literally take a bullet for him and look what he was doing behind their back? And *I* was meant to trust a man like that? By taking bribes from a drug cartel and - considering me questioning the level of money that he had received in the first place, coupled with the fact that his team had actually set up a sting to catch me - not kicking any of the illegal payments downstairs to any of his team.

I treated Donnie Bannon like someone would treat that spray that you cover your car number plates with to avoid being snapped by speed cameras. You'll *hope* that they'll do the business for you if ever required but as an extra level of security how's about you just look after your own shit and drive slower?

I'll never know just how many times - or as little - that Bannon actually *did* assist my work on the Miami side of things. I didn't like the man from the first meeting and there was no way that I was going to be cutting around Miami with impunity just because Eddy and German were topping up his pension fund each month. A guy like Donnie Bannon wouldn't hesitate to burn *anyone* to save their own skin. And I treated him accordingly. If he helped along the way - like he had done that afternoon at the Miami Marina - then so be it. I preferred to help myself, before accepting it from anyone else.

Sometimes I used to f**k with the DEA agents in Miami, when I was sure that there was nothing that they could pin me on during my stay, just for a laugh. Knowing how seriously they took their jobs and how someone like myself must've screwed with their heads at times.

Like, one time in South Beach. I'd left my hotel to go to meet with a client and discuss a shipment of guns - by this point we had an ongoing successful arrangement that was seeing us receive crates of automatic rifles from out of the former Soviet Union - that was being arranged for the following month. There was not one single element of our meeting that was actually criminal. Yeah, we were discussing payment and delivery but there was no money or weapons actually being changed hands. The DEA did not know this, of course. All that mattered to them was that I was in town and - as a result - they wanted to know what I was up to, where I was going and who I was meeting with.

I spied the two agents sitting in a rather nice black Ferrari soft top. It was comical how - on my leaving the front entrance - they both appeared to try and do anything *other* than actually look in my direction. I mean, I really had tried. Had literally *told them* in a voice message that I'd left on their DEA hotline that they would need to get up a little earlier in the morning if they wanted to get the jump on me.

And yet here's two of them, practically sitting *right outside* the hotel in a car that you couldn't help *but* admire, thinking that they were the ultimate in stealth. My taxi was parked two cars behind them and on getting in I asked the young Jamaican driver how eager he was to earn a tip larger than what he'd probably make all week long, combined?

Well, you can imagine that he was more than open to such a proposition. All ears, so he was. First of all, as we were driving away from the hotel, I told him to pull up alongside the black Ferrari for a moment. Complying, he stopped so that I could look out at the two agents from the back of the cab. Rolling down the window for a brief chat with the two of them.

Their faces had been a picture when they saw my beaming face looking back at them. I'd been informed that there had been two particular agents in the Miami office who'd had a particular hard on for me. Bannon even telling me as much at one of my drops to him. Saying that - especially - following the submarine deal going south they were like dogs with bones when it came to me.

I took a punt that the two agents sitting in the car were the very same pair that had been making it an almost collective crusade to catch me in the act.

'Senors Valencia, Ambrosini.' I said with a big smile while they sat there with faces visibly draining in front of me. Faces shouldn't ever look as grey as that, not in perma-sunny Miami.

'I like your suit, Tommy. Armani or Boss? The Administration must pay well, eh? Maybe I should apply for a position myself?'

They were literally catching flies. I guess they didn't usually have their tails come up and expose them in such a way?

'Well, on second thoughts' I said looking down at my Chanel suit, taking a a small piece of the fabric in my hand to indicate that no, in fact I was doing quite alright for myself in the suit and tie department.

'Anyway, must dash. You know what time is in Miami .. *money*. Step on it, Jeeves.' I ordered the Jamaican. Him doing as told, pulling away and taking off along South Beach. Predictably, the black Ferrari pulling out two cars behind. I mean, they *knew* that *I* knew of their presence. I found it funny that they still chose their 'stealthy' approach of hanging back. Estupido pendejos.

In reality I'd had absolutely *no* idea if the pair of them were actually the Tommy Ambrosini and Vinnie Valencia that their boss had spoken to me about - and even then, which one was which - but from the look on their faces when I'd stopped for the briefest of words it appeared that was *exactly* who they were.

'Ok, now to earn that tip, brethren.' I leaned forward from the back to tell my driver with the shoulder length dreadlocks and the map of Ethiopia hanging from his inside mirror, doubling up as an air freshener.

'That black Ferrari that we stopped beside is tailing us. I need you to lose it before you take me to our address in Venetian Islands.'

'You got it, man' He nodded while attempting to negotiate changing lanes to overtake a slow moving lager delivery truck before pulling back into our original lane again. The DEA agents following suit. What followed was a game of cat and mouse that took almost twenty minutes before the taxi driver had managed to lose them.

The fact that he - in his car as opposed to a Ferrari - had managed to lose them *at all* was commendable although in a city like that, especially during peak hours, 'torque' is no good to anyone, or their car. At one point it had felt as if I was part of a Hollywood movie. My driver running a red and taking such an extreme left turn that - looking out the back window - I could see one of his hub caps rolling along the road in the direction of a row of parked cars on the other side of the street.

Like I said, I had no money, product, documents or anything else incriminating on me. They could've had a roadblock with stingers laid across the road to stop the car. What would've been their reason? They had none. To make them *think* that there was a reason, though. Have them freaking out back in the Ferrari over why I had the taxi driving in a way that was clearly trying to lose them.

To leave them thinking that they had possibly struck gold and caught me in a compromising position, there in Miami, - when I was anything *but* - I found really, really funny. Thinking of them back at the office cursing losing me and speculating what kind of illicit behaviour they consequently missed out on. Hey, they f**ked with me so it was only fair that I'd do the same back to them occasionally, right?

Manny - Were you ever arrested?

Peter - Probably more times than you've had sex *and* eaten a hot dinner, incorporated, Manfred. No really, I was arrested a *lot*. Always abroad and had never been an issue that a bribe wouldn't fix or having the local drug lord put in a phone call to the station, asking what law enforcement were playing at by arresting someone who had flown in *specifically* to meet with them. Yeah, seen a few jail cells, even if they were - at times - only for an hour or two. Never America, well, until now. That's peak me, though. Nought to Sixty, eh? Can't experience a United States police cell or standard prison one. No, I have to go levels up and try out Florence ADX.

There *was* that scare, though, towards the end of Ninety Three, at JFK. *That* was a moment where I'll happily admit that I'd thought that it had all come to an end. I mean, does any good *ever* come out of a pair of suits apprehending you in an international airport, asking you to *please come this way, sir*?

I'd been to Bonn to meet with a banker from a major German bank with regards to a 'financing plan' that the brothers were in the process of arranging which would ease the flow of money generated on the European side of our business. As was generally the case. I'd have to connect somewhere in America to take me down to Bogota. The flight had been called and it was when I handed my ticket over to the attendant it had felt no more a case of her checking my name against her list and I was feeling the strong hand placed on my shoulder.

Through me consistently travelling across the world on behalf of Eddy and German. They had arranged for me to have updated passports supplied to me, periodically, with the previous one - used up to that point - then destroyed. Over those months, I had been Archie McAlpine. It had been a system that screwed with my head, to begin with. I was just getting used to my new moniker when it would be changed all over again.

'Please come this way, sir'? The one who had - in my opinion - overstepped the mark by laying a hand on me said. The other one standing there close by there as back up and waiting to see what my reaction was going to be.

'Is there a problem?' I asked, while the Avianca attendant attempted to have me moved to the side to assist with the flow of passengers trying to board the plane behind me.

'No problem at all, Mr McAlpine. Now if you'd please like to step this way with us.'

It wasn't hard to not feel the glares from all of the passengers over this departure lounge scene. Someone who gets stopped from boarding a plane by a couple of suits? Well there has to be something underhand about someone like that, surely? I mean, to be fair. They wouldn't have been too wide of the mark, there.

His words would have been a lot more meaningful had he not then slapped the cuffs around me before leading me down the terminal, through a side door and down a series of steps and into a room that was sat below terminal level.

It appeared to be a room built *specifically* for someone like me. The desk in the room had a specially inserted steel loop that could be handcuffed to. I was sat down there, tethered to the table while left to drink the coffee that the agent had supplied me with and smoke my cigarettes with my free hand.

The agent who, technically, hadn't been the one to detain me, advising that someone would be along to talk to me soon. All attempts at asking *why* I was detained, falling on the deafest of ears. I mean, I'm pretty sure that it's illegal to just handcuff someone and cart them off to a secret room in an airport without being given a reason?

The lack of procedure was fully understood when - after around a half hour's wait, while my Bogota plane had long since taken off - he walked into the room to join me.

Shit? How many places did I visit in a year. How many *faces* I would see inside that year? Some you pass in the street and they're gone again in seconds, others you stare are for hours on end talking to.

When the door opened and I looked up and the drunk from years before in Sudan - who I had helped into his hotel room - walked in, carrying a brown folder in his hand, I recognised him straight away. And another thing. I could now see that me meeting him in that corridor in the Sudanese hotel hadn't been the chance meeting that I'd put it down to.

'Hello stranger, 'sobered' up yet?' I said sarcastically to him while letting him know early doors that I remembered him. He kind of half smiled, almost impressed that I knew his face.

'Ohhhhh, Peter. What the hell are we gonna do about you, buddy?' He said with a sigh as he sat down in the chair facing mines and threw the brown folder down onto the table in front of us.

'Well, if you can get these cuffs off me we can go out for a couple of drinks and talk about it, for old times sake.' I joked. I don't know what the hell I had to joke about. I was sitting inside some kind of hidden room inside an airport where they take you to without charge and this guy - who was one hundred percent in Sudan when I was there, meeting Al f**king Qaeda - sitting with a folder in front of him which I was already guessing I probably didn't want to see its contents, but that he was going to show me regardless.

'And where did you get the 'Peter' from, anyway? My name's Archie. You literally have my passport in front of you.' I said, feeling that I at least better try and keep up the pretense that I was the person on my passport. In that moment I had been unable to recall 'who' I had introduced myself to him as back in Khartoum so tried to concentrate on the name that I was 'that' day, and see how things went. Generally if someone calls you by the wrong name you would correct them, though? So I did, for appearances. I was wasting my time, however. *Clearly*, he knew who I was.

'Cut the crap, Mr Duncan. We know who you are and all about you so please don't waste our or your time with any lies. You'd do well to understand that if I ask you a question then the chances are that I already *know* the answer to it. Sooner you take that on board and be level with me the sooner you'll be out of the cuffs.' He dismissed me as if it had been a charade that he had faced countless times.

Despite the seriousness of matters I couldn't help but laugh at the irony of him telling me to stop wasting their - and my - time while in the same breath admitting to the chances of him asking me questions that he already knew the answer to. Hypocritical, much?

I *did* like the part, however, where he mentioned the possibility of the cuffs coming off. I hadn't actually considered they'd come off again, once they'd been slapped on me.

'First, let me introduce myself. My name is Walt Branson and I work in U.S national security for a government count-terrorism task force and I feel that you and I may be able to scratch each others backs, so to speak.'

Well *this* was an intriguing development.

Manny - 'National Security?' Not DEA?

Peter - The more he explained things the more obvious it became which agency he was part of.

I told him to continue as he sat and told me that - following Khartoum - I had found my way onto their watchlist. Branson, himself, in Khartoum like me *because* it had been the base of several Al Qaeda members that his counterterrorist unit were trying to track and capture, notably the bearded fellow in the camouflage jacket that I'd sat in the same room as.

If I'd had any thoughts of denying things he pre-empted this by taking out photos of me outside the hotel in Khartoum. Standing with the Jihadists moments before they shoved the sack over my head.

'We'd heard intel chatter that kept speaking of 'The Colombian' who was arriving to meet with The Emir. We knew that you were coming, we just didn't know *who* you were, or that when we made a visual I.D that you *wouldn't* actually be Colombian.'

He explained that they had watched my movements over the next few years following Sudan and collected intel on me. The 'hot spots' that I always seemed to turn up in and more importantly, the people that I was there to meet with. The *exact* type of people that foreign U.S agents were trying to capture but could not get anywhere remotely *near* to. Branson, laughing at the irony of the finances and power of the CIA getting them nowhere while I was literally being picked up - in most cases - by a driver and taken right to the front door of these terrorists and notoriously hard to locate cartel and crime bosses.

Telling me that - with the doors that I, personally, found open that *they* had always found firmly closed - he'd felt that I had high value as a consultant for 'The Company.' Passing on intel on the whereabouts of mutual interests of both the Bogota Cartel and the Americans, planting state of the art listening devices around the vicinity of targets, that kind of deal.

The idea of me doing *any* kind of intelligence, for the United States of America? Given the relationship me and that country had enjoyed so far with each other? It was completely demented. Surely out of *anyone* that a nation should be trusting to do a job for them, it wouldn't be a person who was already kind of a wanted man in the *same* country?

As the agent spoke, it showed me just how naive I was about how countries approach protecting themselves. Obviously, everyone knew about Iran Contra but you kind of thought that it would've been a case of a slap on the wrist and that they wouldn't do anything like that again. Instead, I was sitting there in that room seeing how things *really* worked for myself.

'We've been waiting to move on you, building our intelligence. What happened back in February at the World Trade Center though? That changed things. We need to hit those bastards and we need to hit them *hard* because make no mistake, if we don't. They'll attack American soil again. Over recent years *you* have met more times with the organisation - in different countries - than anyone else that our intelligence has picked up. Your help in stopping the next attack on American interests could be invaluable.'

This was all *very* heavy stuff. You could see how spooked he was on the subject of these Jihadists and the potential they had to make life difficult for the West. Telling me how they would not be happy until they had destroyed people like me and him and the life that we all took for granted living in our democracies. I fully admit, when I saw the bombing of the World Trade Center on the news in February and the name of the outfit responsible for it, I'd felt nauseous. It was one thing to meet with them in Sudan and trade weapons for poppies but *this* was a lot closer to home. It put a face to things which never suited my agenda, when it came to the area of business that I worked in.

He, evidently, had not sat in a room with these types, though. Who have an eye on you every single moment that you're sat with them. That eye generally having a side dish of hatred towards you in it. And this agent wanted me to just sashay my way in there acting like Sean Connery double - o - seven. Out of interest though, I asked him.

'You said something about us helping each other? So far I've only heard it from the one point of view? What are the benefits that I would get out of things?'

He could've answered me a kajillion pounds and a penthouse on the moon and I'd have still turned him down down due to the idea of me working for them - and in such a dangerous way - was completely preposterous.

'Well we're not asking for much in return.' He lied. I mean, he'd already *told* me what the agency was looking for out of me so that by its very definition was *not* 'not asking for much in return.'

'But if you help us, we will see that your work for Eddy and German Ramirez will go 'uninterrupted.' You guys have been busy the past few years, very busy and doing business in ways that we wouldn't have believed a Colombian cartel would, although maybe that is more to do with *you* then anything, yeah?'

Clearly, what was all shoved inside Branson's file had been a run down on my movements over the previous years. They seemed to know everything and he took enormous pleasure in dropping in random pieces of intelligence - inside our conversation - to let me know as much.

'Your work, outside of the States, will go unhindered by our foreign agents and we will ensure that you have no issues *inside* America, from your friends at the Drug Enforcement Administration.'

Knowing exactly the type of man I was dealing with I didn't even try to lie or bullshit with him.

'You seem like the kind of man to know that DEA can be bought. There's probably agents on the payroll of Medellin, Cali, Bogota, Sinaloa and god knows who else.' I'd tried to say it as ambiguously as I could but while letting hm know that his offer of keeping the DEA out of my business wasn't as big a prize as he had put it across as. He just laughed at this.

'Who? Bannon? Listen, buddy. He aint the guy. I wouldn't rely on that corrupt piece of shit to go and get the morning coffee. If you think that someone like Donnie Bannon is going to be the difference between your ass staying out of an American jail or not then, good luck. You're gonna need it, pal.'

Yeah, he really *did* know everything. I hadn't even come close to insinuating that the Miami field office director was on the payroll of Eddy and German. Him, instead, just coming right out with it.

'There is also the one other thing that you'd maybe like to consider.' He added.

'Surely you know that there's gonna come a time where your jefe's days will come to an end. You know? The cartel won't go on forever. All empires fall sooner or later. Look at Escobar and how powerful he was, and look at him now? On the run like a frightened animal with his operation on fire. Now ask yourself.

When the Bogota cartel begins to be dismantled and the high value targets either killed or extradited here to the States. When *you* find yourself in the crosshairs. Wouldn't you be happier being left in the position of someone who has a *record* of having helped secure the interests of American national security? There's no telling what kind of goodwill *that* will bring you, when the time comes. And make no mistake, Peter. It *will* come.'

He was now starting to appeal to my own solid sense of self preservation, which was always dangerous. No way did I want to help them but *this* was conflicted by the very appealing prospect of helping *myself.*

I fronted things out by telling him that if I ever grew myself a moral compass that Walt would be the very first person I would get in touch with. Him releasing me from the cuffs and popping his business card into the chest pocket of my suit.

'Call me, Peter. And don't wait too long in doing so. You may find the offer withdrawn if you sit on your hands.' He threatened before wishing me a most passive aggressive safe flight back to Colombia, whenever that would actually *be* with my original flight most likely well over the Caribbean Sea by that stage.

It, in fact, took eight hours before I saw myself up in the air and homeward bound. While I was on the plane, though. all I could think of had been the exchange between myself and the man from the CIA and how possibly 'playing the field' might not have been as outlandish as I'd thought it of initially.

Manny - You mean? Work as a consultant for them?

Peter - Well if that's what you want to call it? First of all though, Manfred. We need to be clear about something. When I say that I had taken Branson's words from earlier in New York and - after careful consideration - began to think seriously about taking him up on the offer. That did *not* extend to burning Eddy and German and selling them out to the Yanquis. *That* was non negotiable. If Eddy and German Ramirez landed themselves inside an American prison at any point in their future, it would not be through me.

Sure, I'd been happy to take the payments from the brothers - and where 'their' money had been questionably coming from directly - but I had began to become a little uneasy with regards to some of the parts of the world I was being sent to and the 'choice' clients of the brothers. With unwavering loyalty I would travel to all corners of the planet for them. The World Trade Center bombing had been enough to make me really think about *who* I was assisting, and the impact that my actions alone might have had. You know? In a butterfly effect kind of way.

It had been a wake up call. These guys Eddy had once described to me as 'freedom fighters.' Shit? Pretty much described them as brave soldiers who were standing up for their region. Yeah, 'brave' enough to come to America and attack one of New York's most important financial hubs and a building that represented America in its entirety. People of all colour and creed working inside the same skyscraper. And Al Qaeda attacking it without discrimination.

Now that they were coming to the West and escalating their war with it. It had left me feeling that while yes, I had made a *lot* of money through the deals that I had arranged between the Bogota Cartel and the Jihadists. What was the point of making money *through* them if they were intent on murdering people exactly *like* me.

On a morally - and socially - conscious and responsible level, it was torturing. Did I plant the truck bomb underneath the World Trade Center? Shit, I didn't even *sell* them anything remotely close to be used as a bomb. Of course not. My conscience was clear as a whistle, there. Yet seeing the number of people that they killed that day. It left me with an uneasy feeling that I'd never had to experience while working for the brothers.

Manny - Did you decide to take things any further with the offer from the U.S Government?

Peter - As you can well understand, Manfred. Arriving at such a decision was not an easy thing to do. Like I already said, *whatever* I did - if anything - would not have brought a single piece of heat onto Eddy and German from the Yanquis. There *was* though the potential for that to still happen, should any of the brothers' clients learn of my 'side work?' There were so many variables. I already knew how many dirty cops - and agencies - there were across the world. How could I trust that everyone who knew about me could keep their mouth shut? The reality of it was, I couldn't.

If I'd been discovered then it would've been certain execution from either Jorge or Gilberto, the brothers' most esteemed sicarios and the ones who only came out for the *big* jobs.

No, it was a decision that I wasn't going to be rushed into over, *couldn't* be pushed into. Make the wrong choice and you would pay with your life, in one way or another. It really was that simple.

I spent the flight, and the following days trying to formulate a plan that would've been as safe but also as beneficial to my own self as possible. Hey, Manfred. If anything, I fixed things. It was literally my - unofficial - job description. I was a schemer by the very definition of my being.

I put my mind to work to try and establish if there would be any way possible for me to add several layers of self preservation - from U.S authorities for when the day came that they would become a problem, in an official capacity - as protection that I could have stored away for for a rainy day but in a fashion that would see me giving away as little in return back as I could possible.

Don't get me wrong, I wasn't under the impression that the Central Intelligence Agency were not stupid people but neither was I.

If there were a way that I could exploit things and string the CIA along - while being given carte blanch to travel the world conducting business on behalf of the Bogota Cartel - and take advantage out of matters - while providing the Americans with as little assistance in return as I could - then I, Archie McAlpine, would find it.

Chapter 29

El Corazon Valiente - The Ballad of Peter Duncan cont

Manny - So by Ninety Four. You were known to both the DEA and also the CIA. Clearly, you were a popular guy in the States.

Peter - Well, that all depends on who you ask, Manfred. It's funny how you list both of those government agencies as 'knowing' of me but the irony being that one wanted to arrest me and throw away the key and the other offering to *stop* them from doing so. It was extremely messed up although, I suppose, something that could be used as a metaphor for this batshit country I'm in. As long as someone's *own* interests are being met then they're happy and to hell with the cost towards others.

Manny - Regardless, you continued with your work for Eddy and German Ramirez?

Peter - Oh yeah, business was booming. Escobar had been assassinated by then and that had changed the landscape of things quite a bit. As Eddy had always said privately. The less Cocaine that Escobar sold, the more probability that *we* would. The more wars he started, the less power he would have. Power that would transfer to others waiting in the wings to benefit from. Well he wasn't likely to be selling any Coke from where he was now, that was one guarantee. The Mexicans had scooped up a huge chunk of things but that had not affected us one iota. At times it had been almost a challenge to keep up with the demand for both product and weapons.

The day that he was shot and killed - up on that Medellin rooftop - We'd been in celebratory mood. There weren't many left in the country who were seen to shed a tear, to be fair. Most of Colombia long since having given up on him and the blood that was shed in certain parts of the country through him. We all went out for a slap up meal and drink that night to the brothers' favourite restaurant in the city centre to celebrate Señor Escobar's demise. The brothers, familia, capos, even their most trusted sicarios. It was an occasion.

Later that night when I was back at the hacienda I watched how the BBC World Service had covered things. Reporter Bill Neely - live from

Medellin - telling the people back home in the U.K and around the world

'This killing is the single biggest blow to international drug trafficking in a decade. But it does not mean that fewer drugs will find their way onto the streets of Great Britain and America. Authorities simply accept that other cartels will take the place of Escobar's business.'

Yeah, US! *laughs*

Manny - You must not have been able to believe your luck? The focus had been pretty much entirely on taking out the Medellin Cartel in a joint country operation. Obviously the American government will not admit to it but it is widely known that the Orejuela brothers from Cali helped finance taking him down.

Peter - *laughing* Yeah and we all know what good it done Miguel and Gilberto. As soon as Medellin had fallen, where did the Yanquis turn their attention to? Hey, they weren't turning their attention to us in Bogota so what was the problem, right? I mean, it was obvious to anyone that once they brought down Cali they then had the choice of looking towards Bogota and focusing on taking down the last remaining big cartel in the country or looking at what was the *real* danger, Mexico. It was a scenario that we would just have to deal with as and when it came along. While cartels were either falling or downsizing in shipments - due to the heat that they were under - we were coining it in. At year end when Mikael crunched some numbers to come up with what kind of figures we had done over the course of the year, things had ran into the billions. It was the stuff of the Forbes rich list.

There had not been a single continent that I had not visited and we had not either shipped Cocaine and weapons to or, alternatively, that we'd had something sent over from that part of the world across the year.

I don't think that there could have been a better way of summing up that financial year than the trip to Sydney, Australia where I'd experience the juxtaposition of meeting with an official who worked for border control, specifically in the mail department at Sydney Airport and someone - whose role is literally to stop drugs from entering the country - who would be our main entry point for our smaller - but more frequently sized - shipments to Australia.

First meeting with him - the man meant to stop the drugs who, instead, will make sure that they get *in* - and then with a local biker gang, who were going to *sell* the product, once it had cleared customs.

The bribing of the customs officer had been the easiest two minutes work you could have ever wished for in your life. He was so nervous - over how serious he knew this all was, with grave consequences if caught - that he just wanted it over with.

My 'Now, remember. The brothers will be looking for results. If we start finding our shipments not going through, they will want to ask you *why*.' was not required but it was always good to remind these people of where they now stood with things, once they took that first tentative step.

'You don't need to worry about me, mate. I was told that you'll be in touch again in the future with my next payment?' He asked, taking the briefcase filled with Australian dollars.

'Well, yes. Providing we get our money's worth. What's in that suitcase should provide a lot of 'plain sailing' don't you think?'

'Like I said, don't worry about me mate.'

Picking up the briefcase he left as quickly as he'd arrived, in a hurry.

If that had been a walk in the park. The trip to meet with The Comancheros Motorcycle Club - at their official clubhouse - in the city centre, wasn't. I'd cringed when German had told me that part of the Sydney trip would involve meeting with a biker gang. I hated biker gangs with a passion. They were always so uncouth.

Preferably, I liked to do business with people that were more a bit like, well, *me*. There was a lot to be said for just sitting down in a hotel and having a civil and mature chat over a glass of scotch with a like minded soul. Someone who knows his remit and just wants to get the deal closed and move onto the next piece of business.

Biker gangs and me were not 'like minded souls.' And neither were they civil, or adult.

Even the taxi driver shook his head when I got into his car outside my hotel and asked to be taken to the street where The Comancheros clubhouse was situated.

'Flaming ell you wanna go to that part of town for, mate?' He said with that familiar Aussie brashness. Never mind the fact that he's the taxi driver and his passenger has issued him with a task to perform. Instead, he's electing to question the passenger *why* they want to go there.

'None of your business, now do you want the fare or not? You're not the only taxi parked out here.' I sniped. Already in a bit of a foul mood because I'd been nervous about going to meet with the bikers and had just had an argument with Eva on the phone in my hotel room. Whenever I was away on business I would always give her a call before I left my hotel to go and conduct whatever I was there for. It wasn't like I felt that she was my lucky charm or anything like that. More a case of, you know? You not knowing what you're about to walk into in some situations and well, I always wanted to hear her voice just one more time. Just in case.

Only, that early evening - I think it was around half five or so - I gave her a call and due to the time difference it was the middle of the night her side and she wasn't best pleased about being woken up. I'd never told her about the finer details of my work. I'd figured that she wouldn't have ever wanted to stick around if she knew how deep I was into that kind of world. Because of this tactic, she did not understand *why* I called her each time before going to work.

Instead, that morning at whatever time it was her side. I was just some moron calling her in the middle of the night to wake her up. And she let me know it too.

I ended up just putting the phone down on her. If it *was* to be the last time I'd hear her voice then it would not have been what any couple would have been able to class as an ideal parting of words.

'Well I never said I didn't want the fare, did I, mate?' he replied while putting his seat belt on and starting the meter, signalling that he was ready to take me.

I sat in silence in the back of the taxi as he took us into Western Sydney towards the clubhouse and headquarters of one of Australia's longest running criminal organisations.

Eventually, though. Being one of 'those' cab drivers - the kind that even though they absolutely positively know that you're not in the mood for any talking, they *are* - he couldn't help himself.

'You want to watch your step with these mad f**kers. They beat a rival gang member to death only last week inside a burger joint. All the other customers sitting there eating their meals having to watch it take place.'

It was hardly the stuff of 'revelations.' What motorcycle gang probably *hadn't* beaten a rival to death over recent weeks. That was *my* opinion on gangs like that. Which was, of course, *why* I was always on my guard when having to do business with these individuals on behalf of Eddy and German.

'Well, I'm sure that the rival gang will kill someone from The Comancheros back.' I replied, non plussed about things while trying to display to the driver that I knew *exactly* who I was sat in the car driving towards.

'Oh, no doubt, no doubt.' He agreed. 'So, anyway. What's a guy like you got with a gang of killers like them?' He asked, eager to know. I mean, once again, the natural reaction had been to tell him that this was none of his business. I was already stressed about meeting with the bikers, pissed off with Eva and the stupid argument we'd had. I could've done without a bad atmosphere inside a car between myself and a taxi driver, on top of things.

'I'm their insurance broker. I'm here to see about updating their policies.' I answered dryly. So dry, in fact, that he actually believed what was only a sarcastic reply, as opposed to the more hostile reply that I'd wanted to give him.

'Jesus christ, Bikie Gangs have *insurance*? Bloody ell, what must *their* premiums be like?' He chuckled to himself in wonder.

'Oh it would make your eyes water, pal.' I said, stringing him along.

While I'd been - more or less - duped by Eddy and German on the subject of Al Qaeda, and who they were and what they stood for. There was *no* duping me if I was being sent to meet with a 'motorcycle club.' Say those two magic words to me and I then already would *know* what I was getting myself into.

I'd decided to use the cab driver - and his motor mouth - to my advantage by asking him to tell me about the *other* gangs in Sydney. It is by no means an exaggeration to say that there are so many gangs in Australia's largest city that he had not finished taking me through all of the ones that he was personally aware of when we were pulling up outside the headquarters to The Comancheros. The rows and rows of black Harley Davidsons - alongside more modern styled super bikes - that were neatly parked up outside of the clubhouse leaving you in no doubt whatsoever that you've arrived at your destination.

Terry - my driver - had explained enough to me over the second half of the drive across the city though for me to know that the place was an absolute war zone. Countless biker gangs - although he seemed to pronounce it as 'bikie' like how a toddler would've said it while they couldn't yet say the word biker - and then you had the more traditional criminal organisations who conduct their business in suits or tennis leisure wear as opposed to a leather gilet. There were a *lot* of illicit outfits, all looking for the same thing, and a lot of scores being settled across the city as a result.

Reading between Terry's lines. I was already seeing that the product that the Ramirez brothers were offering to supply The Comancheros would be a lot more important to them than the money we would be receiving back in return would be to us. As important money is.

This completely highlighted with the way that I was treated by the gang, on arrival at their headquarters. The two bikers - doubling up as security at the front door - had been nothing but nice to me on me getting out of the taxi. Clearly appearing as being told to expect me from higher up, ahead of my trip over from the hotel.

'Just go up to the bar and ask for Clem and he'll fix you up.' One of them - with an array of mini patches on the front of his gilet that obviously all individually meant something but had been lost on me - nodded while opening the door to the clubhouse to let me inside.

Straight away I was almost knocked down by the aroma inside the place. I mean, it was Sydney so it was hot as hell obviously, I don't know what else really to have expected from a searing hot room filled with men in leather gilets over their - otherwise - bare bodies. The smell of the B.O mixed with the leather - something equivalent to the fake leather shops in tourist destinations when you first walk into them - made me nauseous.

It was the type of place that *no one*, other than their own would've been able to walk into without them being made, never mind the summer suited up me walking in there. I spied the bar on the other side of the room. A small pokey area that only held enough space for one person behind it. The wall - behind the spirit optics - covered in number plates, once you got closer to it you saw that they were from destinations all over the world.

'Can I get you something, mate?' The barman - who looked just like everyone on the other side of the bar and obviously a member of the gang - asked me. Neither friendly or hostile. With how hot it was in that small room I asked him for a bottle of Coke and when he was putting it down in front of me I asked him where I could find Clem.

Answering that Clem was through in the back with some of the other heads, he told me to sit tight and that he would get word sent through to the other room to let him know that I'd arrived.

Meanwhile, I sat nursing the bottle of cola. Keeping myself strictly to myself while trying to handle the level of noise that was going on inside there. The heavy rock music, the shouting from everyone *over* the music so they could be heard.

I was maybe around halfway through the bottle when one of the members of the club approached me. Shaking my hand firmly with a warm smile on his face while saying something to me that I never came close to understanding over the noise inside the clubhouse. I understood the international sign language for 'come with me.' though and was soon following him out of the bar and through a door, taking us into a new room.

There, sat a mean Maori looking motherf**ker at the head of a large boardroom like table. The kind of furniture that you would only ever see inside the chapter of a motorcycle gang. Guns and knifes carved into the slab of wood along with all kinds of symbols. The

Comancheros badge, a big scary looking phoenix with what appeared as fire around it, sitting in the middle of the table taking centre stage.

There were another five bikers sat around this large table. They all wheeled around at the sound of the door opening. On seeing me, the big man at the head of the table instantly shot up and made his way over. 'Clem Parata, good to meet you, mate.' He extended his arm out to shake my hand.

'Likewise, Clem. Peter de Mooy.' I smiled back and took his hand while bracing for what kind of a handshake he was going to have on him. With near permanent bone damage left to my right hand he let go after wildly swinging it up and down for a moment in enthusiasm.

'Sit yourself down and we'll get you something to drink.' He urged me. I took the seat nearest to Clem which I'd assumed had been kept free ahead of my arrival. The rest of the bikers - inside - all there to hear what I had to say.

To a man, they all sat in silence - asking questions where applicable - while I took them through the in's and the out's of what it would require from them to enjoy a long and successful business relationship with the Bogota Cartel, while confirming that we now had the infrastructure in place to get serious weight into what had always been a notorious country to do so with such tight borders control that it possesses - the key reminder to proposed new clients no matter wherever I was in the world ... pay your bills on time - with Bogota. As always - with new customers - I'd been in possession of a sample of product that had been waiting on my collection once I'd arrived in Sydney.

Parata wasted no time in sampling what I had brought him. Taking the kilo from me, then a hunting knife from out of the inside of his gilet and plunging it right into the packaging. Pulling out some of the product and putting the knife's edge up to his nose and promptly making it disappear. Taking a few seconds to appreciate the quality of what he'd just taken up his nose before smiling and saying.

'Ok, mate. We'll take two hundred and fifty keys. We'll pay half up front and the other on receiving the shipment.' He said, seemingly making the decision for the rest of the men on the spot. Sliding the package across the table to the next member who would repeat what

Clem had just did before sliding it on to the next one. This repeated until the kilo had found its way slid back to me again.

By this point, my Cocaine use hadn't yet spiraled out of controlled. It was very much *in* control. While I wasn't against using it - and it would've taken the discipline of a saint to work in my business and *not* take it - and there were some cases where I'd even *had* to take it, as a show of good faith that I wasn't an undercover policeman, it was not something that I'd found myself using on a daily basis, yet.

Them all now very much aware of the quality of the Ramirez brothers' product, their eyes all fell expectantly on me and what I was going to do with the snow sitting in front of me.

'Can I borrow that knife of yours please, Rambo?' I said, breaking the silence. A big smile forming on his face as he slid the large knife over that he had still to put back inside his gilet.

'Ok, I suppose I better make this official then.' He said looking around the room at everyone. All sat there dealing with the follow up sniffing that their bumps had brought them individually. The room sounded like a Scottish doctor's surgery in the winter.

'Right then, lads. All or against going into business with Eddy and German Ramirez.' Clem shouted to everyone. I assumed that it was a formality but I guess rules are rules to these guys. As far as I was concerned, their vote was written over all of their faces.

This vote went around the room, all the same.

'AYE' said the first biker to the right of Clem at the end of the table. A handy looking guy who looked like he needed a gilet just to deal with the muscles that he had on him as anything with sleeves might've been a challenge.

'AYE' the man next to him with the shaved head that was covered in tattoos.

'AYE' The one next to him, and so on.

Once the member to the left of me had affirmed his support for the motion. I couldn't help but say a loud 'AYE' next, before things had gone full circle and back to Clem. They all laughed, the one to the side of me bringing his hand up and down hard on my shoulder while announcing to the table,

'This f**king limey?!'

Once the laughter stopped Clem said one final 'AYE' before bringing his gavel down on the table and rubber stamping things.

'Right, celebration time. Give me that f**king gear.' Clem said reaching over and taking his knife to cut the packaging further open. Enough for him to tip some of the powder out onto the table in front of him and then passing the package back around the table to his crew.

With that, I was happy to sit amongst the other bikers that night and - while celebrating the concluding of a deal, this always something to celebrate over - have a couple of lines while we all sat talking back and forward. Sharing a drink, line and a joke with each other. I did business in many countries and saw a whole series of local customs that - from a perspective of trying to show respect when in someone's back yard - I was happy to go along with.

Sitting drinking scotch while having a few lines of the finest Coca that would come out of Colombia? Well there's been tougher gigs, I will readily admit.

As you tend to find when there is copious amounts of Cocaine being used in a room. A lot was said, at a fast speed of knots. Clem couldn't decide if he wanted to speak to me about my line of work or tell me about the various wars that the club were currently involved in. Mainly territory and narcotics related.

'This gear is choice, Petey, mate, absolute preeeeemo.' He said gleefully as he racked out two mammoth lines in front of him. 'Obviously, we get white here but Australia isn't an easy place to get product *into* which means that we're literally at times a case of beggars not being choosers. I've never seen Cocaine like this in my LIFE.'

It kind of showed. The way that he was going at it. Like a dog with a bone.

Taking a rolled up Australian twenty dollar note he - almost in the blink of an eye - hoovered a line up each nostril.

'WHOOOOOOO YEAH! F**KING WOOOOOO'

'Ok, we're all going through for drinks and to celebrate.' He shouted across the table to everyone.

Without trying to draw too much attention to it I tried to quietly tell him that I would be politely declining this invite as I had other business to attend to, namely sitting in my hotel room and out of harms way, away from biker gangs.

With those two lines hitting him right about the same time, I was told 'nonsense' and that if I did business with The Comancheros then I *drank* with them too. I didn't see any sense in arguing back against this figuring that - as loud and head splitting that it was outside there, not to mention *that* smell - it would at least appear 'respectful' if I was to be seen having a few drinks with the leaders in the clubhouse.

Some times you just have to hold your nose and get on with things, literally.

We moved through to the bar area to find everyone in there all - in unison - belting out the song that was coming out of the speakers. I tried to get an I.D on the song but it didn't seem a familiar one. It certainly was to them. The passion they were singing the words, testament to that. Punching the air all at the same time while they sung what appeared to be the chorus.

Parata led us to a series of two sofas sat facing each other. The bikers that were sitting there making no slouches of themselves in getting back off of them, once they'd saw 'who' was heading in that direction to sit there.

'We've got strippers coming down in a few hours, mate. You like strippers, Petey?' Clem announced and asked.

'Well that all depends on who's doing the stripping, Clem, my friend, eh?' I laughed back at him before being told that The Comancheros only had the *best* of biker chicks which I gave him a thumbs up over while - inside - was highly sceptical.

Instead of some seductive temptress I was imaging some strung out scrawny crack addled hanger on of a 'biker chick' that I'd seen at pretty much every chapter of motor cycle club I'd visited in the world for Eddy and German.

You could barely hear yourself think in the place. Anything that you wanted to say you had to say it at the top of your voice and even then - accents and all to be taken into account - it wasn't a guarantee on being successful. Some things were more easier to understand than others. Like Clem passing you a rolled up note while there's a line of Cocaine the length of the Great wall of China sitting in front of you or picking up his empty glass and shaking it while looking at one of the younger bikers - the prospects - to indicate that he wanted them to go to the bar and get us another.

Looking up from the table - having devoured the mammoth line that he had racked up for me - I thought that my eyes had been initially playing with me because on looking up I found myself watching the prospect walk over to the bar with our empty glasses, and with what looked like sprays of blood coming from out of him, fell to the floor, along with the glasses which shattered on impact. Then another biker - maybe a metre away or so from the young prospect - also fell to the ground.

'GET THE F**K DOWWWWWWWWN' Clem screamed while pushing me so far downwards - with his hand around the back of me - that it could've easily broken my neck, not to mention my nose which he had accidentally slammed hard and right down into the table in front of us. I'm not sure if someone intentionally stopped the music or if a stray bullet had taken out the jukebox but with the music killed you could now clearly hear the incessant rounds of automatic rifles being fired off as - what appeared to be a group of shooters - stood outside peppering the Comancheros clubhouse with bullets.

Bullets and glass flew everywhere while all bikers lay as flat as they could down on the floor. I just froze there, praying that once the gunfire stopped I would still be there, intact.

It's stupid, the things that you find yourself thinking of in those most extreme of moments, where your survival is at its most risk. I should've been trying to plan whether I could get out of all of this alive and well while - instead - was lying there, watching all the glass going flying and the bullets rip up the wooden paneling of the clubhouse thinking that they should give the strippers a call and tell them their gig was cancelled because the bar now resembled the centre of Beirut.

Eventually the firing stopped, closely followed by the amplified - through the now lack of windows to the bar - noise of motorbikes starting up. Taking this as the cue that things had passed. Clem rushed out the front, just in time to catch a look at the patches that the shooters had been wearing.

Running back into the bar and showing how the leader of a heavy biker gang would operate.

'Bandidos. Three shooters, they're going down Caddens Road North. They've killed Batesy and Silo is in a bad f**king way. **GET AFTER THE BASTARDS. I WANT THEIR F**KING HEADS.**'

This was all it took for to send around a dozen shaken but ready for action bikers to go charging out the place. The sound of the night soon filling with multiple bike engines all sparking to life at once and driving off.

Evidently acting on instinct. Clem - now back in the clubhouse - was seeing the extent of the damage that lay there, following the shooting. The clubhouse was torn to pieces but that wasn't the issue. That could be fixed.

'Jesus f**king christ.' He said, looking around at the devastation. Two men killed and six *very* badly wounded.

I was almost in a denial of sorts. I'd seen a lot of things in the years with the cartel - and *heard* of how brutal and sadistic my own crew would be on occasion, when pressed to show a sign of strength - but this level of atrocity was something that I was normally sheltered from. Sure, I'd supply the guns and the atrocities would take place *after* I was gone. Not during, though.

It was scenes that - as I sat there and looked around - I knew would live with me forever. Those bloodied and torn up bodies, there waiting for when I closed my eyes on a bad night.

'Petey, you gotta bounce, mate. The cops are going to be down here in a moment and you're going to stick right out to them. You probably shouldn't be here when they arrive.'

I wasn't about to disagree with Clem on this. Plus he was right. Say you were a copper and you attend a shooting at a notorious biker gang's clubhouse and you get there to find that there was a smartly dressed businessman sitting with the bikers that evening. You'd be failing in your duty of a copper if you didn't ask the question *why*.

Clem had one of the bikers get me out of there on the back of their Harley and - on a death defying ride across the city with me hanging onto the back of him for my life - got me back to my hotel before any of the Sydney Police Department had began to show up at the clubhouse.

It really hadn't been the time for it but I felt that it would be in Clem's own interests to know that we could also supply a wide range of weapons, not just the Cocaine. Telling him that, obviously he was busy at the moment but if he wanted to know any further details then I would be at the hotel until the following day.

Understandably, he had other things to attend to and didn't call me at the hotel although - further down the line as our Cocaine shipments became more and more regular - The Comancheros expanded into having guns, semi automatic and full blown automatic rifles sent to the city.

Ethics were something to be avoided completely when doing my job. To possess ethics would have simply not worked. That said, when you see the damage that a rival gang could have made inside thirty seconds to a minute during an attack like I had withstood that evening. You can appreciate a lot more *why* people across the world *wanted* the weapons.

I'm sure that it was Martin Luther King who said 'If we do an eye for an eye and a tooth for a tooth we will be a blind and toothless nation.'

With the greatest of respect to the doctor. He said that from the vantage point of being someone who was not working from *within* the underworld. A place where when one takes your eye, if you don't take one back they're then just going to take your other one as a result.

Appreciating just how close I came to being shot - inside The Comancheros clubhouse - I ended up asking the biker who was taking me back to the hotel to stop somewhere that I could get a bottle of scotch to take back with me. This leading to me drinking half the bottle there in the room while I surveyed just what had happened earlier. Drinking so much that I ended up passing out. Waking up the next day for my flight still in my suit. Hadn't even removed my shoes.

It was a less than fit as a fiddle state of mind body and soul that I found myself sitting in the Sydney Airport departure lounge, waiting on my LAX connection flight as I tried to get an extra large coffee into me ahead of the even larger flight, while I read about the previous night.

'Night of Horror: Six dead, multiple injured'

The article - crediting a dual pair of journalists - telling the reader of how the previous night in Sydney a gang war between The Comancheros and The Bandidos had been reignited following reported of shootings at the headquarters of The Comancheos where four members of the bikers gang perished along with multiple serious injures to others. Thought to be related. Two members of rival gang The Bandidos were murdered outside of a bar in the South Side of the city later in the evening. Their murderers fleeing the scene on motorbikes.

Despite the near death experience, it had been a successful trip and one that *completely* exemplified the Bogota Cartel's business model. Wherever greed, corruption, power and money existed. So would they, ready to capitalise on matters. Filling their deepest of pockets while fueling the flames of conflict thousands of miles from Colombia. Like I said. Ethics? There was no room for them in our place of business.

Chapter 30

Peter

I'd been pleased to see that Gary had improved since that night he was threatening to end it all. Just one of those low days that we all suffer from, I guess. Only, when *we* - at the ADX - have a low day it makes everyone else look like they're higher than Yuri Gagarin.

Still, I'd had a bit of a nervy night - following our chat - and had been worried sick that my words hadn't gotten as through to him as he'd displayed and that he'd have went away anyway and done something 'stupid' between the next time that we would (hopefully) speak.

Only really *sure* that he hadn't when I - relieved - heard his dulcet cockney tones through the intercom the following evening. This then followed a period of calm again. We'd speak most nights - the only times we didn't was due to 'activity' inside the ADX that would prevent us from doing so.

Speaking to each other at night had fast become something that I had looked upon as one of my basic living rights there, inside the supermax. I couldn't have even begun to imagine the implications - mentally - if such a means of communication had been discovered by the guards and taken away from me.

The sheer ability of being mentally challenged, asked questions by another person, urged to 'participate' in something (anything) by another human being. It was invaluable and most likely the difference between going off your head slowly and surely as each day passed and merged into the other while you sat there the very definition of 'alone.'

You never, ever knew what the pair of us were going to speak about from one night to the other. At times, just one throwaway comment from the other leading to a four hour discussion on a single subject. Hey, if anything, we had all the time in the world to go through all the subjects we liked, and as detailed.

He was an interesting, funny and engaging guy, Gary. I could've been hooked up in communication with far, far worse a companion. With how widely travelled we both had been - for our own individual reasons - we were never short of a tale to tell each other.

Other times we'd just sit and talk about our memories of back home. TV shows, fashion, cars and old girlfriends. There was never anything that was off topic for Gary and me.

We got into talking about our kids one night. Kid? Stevie? I guess that no matter *how* old your son or daughter is they'll *always* be your kid, I suppose.

Gary had been talking about his son and daughter and the regrets that he'd been left with over the things that he hadn't been able to do with them and - due to his personal situation - would now never get the chance to do. Just basic stuff. Feeding ducks and flying kites. Painting and rolling eggs down a hill on Easter Sunday. Gary had a virtual shopping list of 'things to do' that he'd, now, be unable to do that he was rattling off to me.

I couldn't help but notice that there was not a single thing that he'd come out with that I - myself - had actually done with my *own* son. You name it, we'd not done it as a father and son combo. That - in that moment and in the ADX even the smallest thing can hit you differently, if you allow yourself to think that way - and the realisation that it brought, saddened me.

Sure, I'd blown things with Stevie's mum. That wasn't the boy's fault though, was it? He was just a toddler at the time with no concept of what was even going on. As Gary went on I became more aware of my own shortcomings as a father. At least Gary had an excuse in that he'd been (falsely?) imprisoned while his kids were still on the young side. I hadn't, and I'd *still* not taken the opportunity to spend the type of time that a father should with his son.

Not that I'd been *unaware* of my own shortcomings as a dad. Oh I was aware. It's just easier though when you take things like that and bury them as far from your mind as possible. Gary started a flow, a flood actually, of thoughts that evening, though. A flood that once started couldn't be stopped again and turned to a tsunami.

I should've made more of an effort following his mum and I going our separate ways. Even while wrapped up in the drugs game - back in Scotland - I could've and should've made more time for him, while I had the chance. Instead, thinking that I could just blind the kid with fancy talk, even fancier cars and a few notes shoved in his hand before I'd disappear from his life again, until the next time I would show up completely out of the blue.

Following my spell in prison it had all changed. I'd lost my chance. I couldn't help but feel that had I been closer to the boy - in the years leading up to my eventual arrest and prison spell in the mid Eighties - then it would've counted for something, when I was released. I didn't have that kind of goodwill backed up, however. I can't say that I wouldn't have went to Amsterdam to work, regardless. I'll fully admit to having - on the whole - put myself first in life so even on good terms with my son there's no telling whether that would have altered the path I was destined to go down in life. Being cut off from him, however, only expedited matters.

'Any regrets, your side? Anything that you never did with yours that you'd have liked to have done?'

It was a hard question from Gary. Literally a question that held a mirror up to you for your answer. My days of lying, cheating and scheming were over. There was no more lies left in me anymore. And anyway, what good were lies now, where we were?

'What would I have liked to have done, with my son? That him and I never got a chance to enjoy together? How about *everything*?'

Seeing things from my point of view and then flipping them to how things must've been and looked like from Stevie's perspective. I managed to gain quite a piece of enlightenment.

'What do you mean by everything, fella?' He asked.

'By exactly what I answered, mate. *Every. Thing.*'

'Look at things from my point of view, Gal. On your side, your kids are so young they've not had a chance to build up any memories that they'll be able to carry on for the rest of their life, in relation to their dad and while that can be quite a sad thing to think about. In another way, it's not.'

I sat there and told Gary about how things could be, if flipped around.

'Take Stevie, and the memories that he has of his father, and how he feels about him. Sometimes, it's better if your kid *doesn't* have any memories. What recollections does Stevie have of me other than of visiting him in Italian and German sports cars like some fancy dan - only to find out later in life *why* he was able to drive all of these cars - then the next *again* memory he'll have of me is - inexplicably - sitting in the VIP area of an illegal rave. Next time? I'm bringing a wife to Ibiza - that he didn't even know existed - to see him with two of the most feared Colombian sicarios known to South American narco culture following closely behind me, putting my son and his girlfriend in serious danger. Something that he has *still* not forgiven me over. And then the *final* time that he would see me, following the Ibiza trip and years later? I'm being arrested by Dutch police right in front of him on a list of serious charges from drug importing to financing terrorist organisations.'

'Well, when you put it like,' Gary tried to add but I wasn't finished.

'It maybe doesn't feel like right now, Gal, but you've got the chance to have almost immortal status with your two kids, depending on how your other half paints things. I don't have that kind of a chance open to me. My son already *knows* what kind of a cunt I am. There's no rewriting of history there, short of Stevie receiving a full frontal lobotomy.'

I wasn't a man for regrets. I lived hard and was never one to point the finger at others for my own misfortunes or undoings. Karma was a bitch that would have to be *always* on my case, were the rights and the wrongs - that I was perennially involved in - to be addressed and with the life that I had been part of. I'd learned to take the rough with the smooth, as long as the rough was the rare exception to the rule, and not the other way around.

When it came to Stevie, though. I couldn't help but feel that the regrets were there. If only I'd have tried harder when he was still a kid. It's *those* days and the love and work that you put in to your own flesh and blood that forges the relationship that you're going to have with each other moving forward, and whether you're going to be close with each other or not.

By the time I got myself to Colombia - were it not for what was written in my stars - I had almost decided with myself that I pretty much *had* *no* son. We had no relationship, we didn't speak. Shit? We weren't *allowed* to speak, the family had seen to that. And now with me taking up work with an organisation such as a South American drug cartel. *Maybe* it was for the best - as well as possibly for the safest - that I did not recognise that I even *had* a son. What rival cartels - possibly even my *own* at some point down the line? - didn't know, it wouldn't have been able to hurt Stevie, if and when it came to it.

That's what was so ironic about the danger that I had put him in, out in Ibiza. I *knew* the dangers of how the lifestyle could be and the very *last* thing I'd have intended would've been to bring that *to* his door.

'What would you say to Stevie, you know? If you were to get a chance to speak to him again?' Gal asked.

Christ? He was really putting me on the shrink's sofa that evening? Sitting there, filled with all kinds of regrets over chances missed in life, with the truly *important* things.

This period of reflection hadn't all been born out of the chat between Gary and me, that evening. It had been something I'd found myself thinking of increasingly the more time that was spent inside the ADX. The one thing that you had - out of everything - was time alone with your thoughts. Reflecting over life and its successes - and failures - was unavoidable when you were left sitting there looking back on it as if it was *another* life. Now that you are there in a supermax with life - as you'd previously known it - now over.

'What would I say to the boy? You know, Gal? I fear that once I started speaking to him I wouldn't stop. After being banged up in here for as long, there's a lot of things that I'd like to say to him that I didn't realise I *did*, until coming here.'

'More than anything else, however. I would just like one final chance to speak to the boy and apologise to him. Tell him just how sorry I am for the fact that when it came to being given a dad, he kind of drew the shortest of straws.'

'Nah, don't say that, Pete.' Gal butted in, purely to try and make me feel a bit better about things but I knew it was the truth and there were no amount of positive strokes or platitudes from anyone that would have been able to persuade me otherwise.

'It's true, Gal and Stevie knows it. To suggest otherwise to him would be an insult to his intelligence.'

'You know what else I'd tell him, though? And this is something that I can't for the life of me remember ever telling him in his life?'

I said, taking a pause as I'd found my voice beginning to wobble as I was consumed by the thoughts of the chances in life that had passed me by while I was doing the things that I thought had been more important, when they actually hadn't.

'That just how proud of him I am that, *despite* having the father that he has, through his own character, strength and personality - not to mention the obvious creative skills - he's been able to get on with his life and make something of himself.'

I found myself with tears forming in my eyes as I spoke.

I wasn't a 'cryer.'

Hadn't cried when I was in my twenties and banged up alongside a murderer in a Scottish prison.

Or when I'd been threatened to have my hand chopped off by a Sinaloan Cartel member because I'd refused to shake his hand, having already seen the man take a piss and not wash his hands.

Or even when I'd been arrested on espionage charges in Vladivostok - which I had been told carried a life sentence - until a local mafia boss had the bogus charges dropped on my behalf.

Shit? I'd *laughed* when the Dutch copper had listed off all the charges that I was being arrested in Amsterdam.

It wasn't a macho thing. I was far from macho macho man. I just didn't generally cry about anything. Maybe I couldn't *feel* enough about things to be able *to* cry about them?

Was it even the subject of Stevie or was it just the ADX and how one thought had spiralled to leave me in this way? The only thing that I knew to be real, for definite, was the tears that I found myself wiping from my cheeks.

I decided - that night - that I would reach out to Stevie. Let him know some of the things that had been rattling around in his old man's head.

Would it make any difference? Probably not. I was going to try, regardless. Figuring that there would be no good in having moments of epiphanies like that - where I'd actually *really* felt the sadness and regret that a father *should* have in connection with his kids - if I wasn't going to follow up on them.

I figured that there would be no time like the present. Strike while the iron was scolding, so to speak. Assuming that any correspondence from prisoners would be triple vetted before working its way out of the system and out into the world. I began straight away the next morning after breakfast.

Hoping that, preferably, Stevie would be able to read my words to him while he was still young.

Chapter 31

El Corazon Valiente - The Ballad of Peter Duncan cont

Manny - As things progressed on your side - regarding work for the brothers - how did the DEA and CIA impact on you, in their own individual ways and with their - very obviously - different agendas to one another?

Peter - The Administration? *laughs* Those chumps couldn't catch a trick on the street with a hundred dollar bill tied to their dicks although, to be fair, it *does* tend to help when you have their office director batting for your side. The fact that you *also* have the CIA sticking their noses into their business and causing static? Well, that doesn't exactly harm things, either.

Manny - So you decided to take the offer that was put to you by Walt Branson, the 'Company' representative?

Peter - Well I didn't not not take up the offer from the CIA agent.

Manny - Were you as cryptic with the DOJ when you were extradited for interrogation as you are with me?

Peter - Oh you have *no* idea, Manfred. *laughs* But, yeah, the offer I'd been made? Following that unplanned meeting that I'd had with Branson - underneath JFK - I'd taken a good and long hard think about things. I'd been smart enough to know that he had been both telling me the truth with a side order that was high on bluffing. It had always been about my own self preservation and it was through *that* which told me that the best way to 'preserve' myself would be to stay *completely* clear of it all. I know he'd rubbished the idea of Bannon - and the assistance he was giving us from out of the Miami Bureau - being adequate protection for someone like me when it came to prosecution inside the states but I had elected to take the position that someone like a Donnie Bannon - while someone that I didn't feel could be trusted with complete implicitly - knew *exactly* who it was that he was in bed with. And what their expectations were and - more importantly, for Bannon - how they would react if they were not met.

Manny - Quite a bold move, Peter. It's one thing to have the DEA as an enemy but the Central Intelligence Agency, quite another thing.

Peter - I crunched the numbers and threw the dice while of the opinion that I was playing it the correct way. Who's to say that the CIA wouldn't have burned me in the end, anyway, right? That was the way I came to my conclusion. Understandably, the thought of trusting *any* American agency was a tough sell. How many times have you seen a movie or cop show where you see a Fed say something along the lines of 'you've just got to trust me on this' to some poor member of the public who - in the end - gets burned by the situation anyway while the cop is stood there saying it had been taken out of their hands?

Manny - Well yes but that's ..

Peter - Yeah I know it's on TV or in the cinema but once an idea gets put into your head it can be hard to get it back out of there again. And besides, Branson never called me or tried to reach out to me again in the immediate weeks following JFK and because of that I'd felt that he had been potentially fishing when it had come to grabbing me for the chat.

Manny - And was this the case?

Peter - I'd assumed to be so. Following our introduction, I got myself back to work. Traveling the world including the frequent Miami and New York trips in amongst them. I did so without any issues with my Miami Administration friends - save for the occasional bust that we would suffer from which was always insignificant compared to the shipments which *did* get through - *or* free from any meddling from The Company when anywhere else across the world.

I'd actually near enough forgotten all *about* Walt Branson until the November bombing of the U.S military training facility in Riyadh, Saudi Arabia. As soon as I saw *who* the bombing had been linked to I was left with that same sick feeling anytime I saw them mentioned on the news. This brought me back to thinking about Walt Branson and what he was out there doing in relation to stopping the Jihadists, other than propositioning random men and trying to get them to do his own dirty work for him.

The thought came and gone but it would only be another three weeks before he would magically pop up when I was sat enjoying a coffee in the warm late morning sun on the Casco Viejo, in Panama City.

Sitting there basking in the warmth - having spent the previous week travelling across Scandinavia and Russia - with my eyes closed, I did not even see him coming. Finding Agent Branson sitting down in one of the free seats at my table by the time I was opening my eyes to look at where the noise - from the scraping of chair legs - was coming from.

'We need to stop meeting like this, Peter, orrrrr what is it we're calling you today?' He chuckled, with a little arrogance behind it.

With someone like this - and all the evidence that he'd previously provided me with to illustrate how much he knew 'about' me - there was no need for even attempting any acts.

'No, Peter's good. We're amongst friends here, after all.' I let him know that I was not phased in any shape or form, even if - just like our last meeting - that wasn't strictly the true measure of things.

'Can I get you a drink, Walt? What you having?' I asked, already looking around and trying to catch the waiter's attention.

'Nothing for me, thank you. Or you, were leaving.' He replied, standing up and lightly grabbing at my arm to pull me up along with him.

'We're not in America, are we?' I asked, looking around and then over to the flag of Panama that was gently flying across the street.

'Humour me. Come on, lets go.' He said without anything in the way of patience and lifting me up, partly through my own cooperation in standing in compliance.

We took a walk down towards the beach end of the city where he entered into a similar sales pitch from last time in the airport when we'd spoken. His tone - this time however - was different. A touch more threatening and sinister than it had been previously - by comparison - friendly and cordial.

He asked me if I'd seen what had happened in Riyadh to which I confirmed I had.

'*And?*' he urged me.

'And what?' the follow up he had pressed me for.

'And what did you think when you saw it? That more American lives were lost?'

'Well, actually, funny you ask that but my *very* first thought was '*I take it Walt hasn't caught that bastard yet.*' While I appreciate that this would have just come across as someone trying to be sarcastic, it was the truth.

'This is not f**king funny, Peter. With every strike they make on us they grow bolder. Each time their actions go unchecked, they feel that they can repeat it again, only bigger.'

'Well I guess you better find them then' I replied, a little put out over why any of this was *my* problem. I mean, I'm pretty sure that they *paid* people to do that kind of stuff, and not an unscrupulous South American narco with a mounting Cocaine addiction.

He ignored this. Pulling out his packet of cigarettes and offering me one while taking another out for himself.

'You know, Peter. We *will* catch them. Some things just take longer than others.' He said lighting up his Marlboro, then passing me his lighter, allowing me to follow suit.

'The thing is, though. See when we *do*. When that Al Qaeda house of cards falls to the ground - and we *really* begin to investigate into them - it's going to be documented *who* it was who assisted and collaborated with their terror campaign. Which weapons they used and *who* supplied them. Technically these people could be *also* charged with terrorism. Do you see where I'm driving here?'

This was not the same tone that he had taken with me in the previous meeting. *This* felt a whole lot more like blackmail than it had back at JFK. Back then it had come across as a case of lets all scratch each others backs. *Now* it was feeling a whole lot more like help us or we'll put you away as if you were a member of Al Qaeda yourself.

Strolling down the street with an increased breeze now starting to cut through the air as we got closer to the beachfront, he reminded me that with the repeated attacks that American interests had been suffering from. The United States were going to be ruthless when it came to how they would go after anyone they felt were connected to the Jihadist group.

'Oh now, you're not suggesting that …' I tried to stop him from the road he was going down. Trying to class me as an Islamic terrorist was an outrageous leap. His wording was what worried me though. Almost like how a lawyer would put it to the jury.

'Now while the defendant may not *appear* to be as a member of Al Qaeda let us tell you some more background about him.'

'Who is making suggestions, here? I'm speaking in facts. Written down in black and white on the files that we already have on you. You know, Peter. Your role with the Ramirez brothers - and what the DEA intends to do with you, once they eventually catch you - might be the *least* of your worries, if you don't pick the right side.'

Everything what he was saying. The underlying tones of intimidation to it. It made me feel sick. I couldn't smoke the cigarette like that. Flicking it up ahead of me only half used.

Sides? I wasn't on *any* sides other than 'Team Duncan.' The way that Branson was putting it across to me, though? I wasn't naive enough to not know that some of what he was getting at may (once again) have been bluffs but - from my globetrotting over the recent years - it had been difficult *not* to notice that Al Qaeda and the United States of America had a bit of a *thing* going and they probably wouldn't stop going at it with each other until all the Jihadists were either dead or in an American maximum detention facility.

It definitely wasn't something that I needed - or indeed wanted - to be caught up in but if there was one thing I was sure of it was that being known as someone who had occasionally done business with the terrorists over the years with regards to Opium poppies and arms trades. It was that it did *not* look good on my part, whichever angle you'd have tried to approach it from. There really is *no* 'yeah, but I can explain' when caught in cahoots with a terrorist group.

We stopped at a beach front cafe where Branson ordered a couple of beers while we sat and discussed the finer points of things. I'd felt squeezed and shaken down. He'd probably already assumed that him and I would reach this phase of 'getting to know each other' and here we were.

I didn't *want* to help. Had I done so I'd have called him following his original proposition. I also, however, did not relish the prospect of being indicted on charges of helping a group of terrorists intent on killing the West and the values that it held. He explained to me that I would be free to travel the world - on business for Eddy and German - but if there were any destinations that I was going to - and they would *know* where I was travelling to and *when* so there would be no point in trying to hide my 'itinerary' from them - that were of interest to them then they would be in touch.

Specifically, though. They were looking for me travelling to any Al Qaeda hot spot in the world to do business with them. *This* was where my value would be of the utmost of importance to them.

I tentatively agreed that I would help. In return I would not be arrested in connection to any work for the Bogota Cartel, so much so I had been given carte blanch to do what I pleased in my role for them, free of any potential hinderances from any Yanquis. As had been mentioned back at JFK. Through helping the U.S - against an enemy of the state - I would be protecting my own interests should there be anything come down the line at a later date through the immunity deal that Branson had offered me.

'Obviously, I'll want all of this in writing. Forgive me if I don't take you for your word.'

He asked me *what* I 'all' wanted in writing.

'*All* of it.' I replied.

He laughed back at me as if this was every day stuff for him which who knows, maybe it was.

'Well if you're looking for *official* documentation from the CIA telling you that they will make sure that they or the DEA will not interfere in your illicit narcotics and arms trades then yeah, dream on, buddy.'

He found this quite amusing while on my side what *I'd* found amusing had been the thought of taking the Central Intelligence

Agency at their word. A group more shady than all the cartels in South America and Mexico combined.

'Look, Peter. You know that I cannot put into writing that we at The Company will 'officially' stop the DEA from doing their jobs, surely you realise that? Shit? Can you imagine if *that* was to get out, especially after Iran Contra? Look, I know you don't trust me but well, you're going to have to on this. If you know the history of the business that you're in then you'll know that we have a history of getting in the way of the DEA and their work. Of course, all completely in the interests of national security, you understand?'

'Oh, absolutely, Walt. I'd never have thought anything to the contrary.' I replied, with us both laughing at the things that hadn't been said as opposed to what *had*.

'Don't you worry, Peter. We have a habit of making sure that the Administration stays in their lane. Half the time without them even realising it. You'll have no problems from them, apart from the occasional bust that, I'm sure you understand, will by the law of averages happen from time to time? The proverbial collateral damage.'

I nodded, falling silent for a moment while trying to make sure that I had looked left, then right, then left again while using multiple use of my mirrors when it came to covering all angles on the road that I was about to turn onto and go down.

'And my immunity, my insurance policy, if you will?' This, I'd felt, the most important carrot of them all in terms of providing me with motivation. Well, that and the avoiding being classed and charged as an Al Qaeda collaborator, of course.

'I'll get you your certified rubber stamped immunity but I will tell you this one time, Peter. You ever lie to us, mislead us or - despite your promises - do not produce any examples of 'assistance' to The Company then that piece of paper won't even be fit for wiping your Scottish ass with never mind keeping that same backside of yours out of an American penitentiary. Do not f**k with us because, believe me, you really do not want us f**king with you, Peter.'

He sat there with a serious look to him, holding my gaze for a few seconds longer than normal in an attempt to get through to me.

'I'll get you your 'examples of assistance' Mr Branson. You make sure you get me my sheet of Andrex first of all.'

'Good,' he smiled as he finished the rest of his beer in one go before standing up to leave, me standing up to shake his hand as he left. Telling me that someone would be in touch. I'd had a mind to remind him that he didn't have my pager number before it, obviously, dawned on me that if he'd wanted it then he'd have probably gained the number long ago.

I watched him walk back along the beachfront while I ordered another beer from the waitress who had been standing around looking bored due to the lack of customers.

It had been the height of naivety - possibly arrogance? - to think that the C.I f**king A would have just 'forgotten' all about me but you know? They hadn't written, they hadn't called. It was very much a case of out of sight out of mind but there I was. It was a bit of a spot, Manfred.

Don't help them and the kind of indictments that I might be facing down the line were chilling, and the potential charges that I'd face through my Bogota work alone were hardly the stuff to provide you with the best of sleeps each and every night, I assure you.

Help them? Who knew - yet - the pitfalls that getting into bed with them and the metaphorical STD's that it could bring me?

The worst part of it all was that Branson had landed me in the *one* specific position that I had wanted to avoid at all costs, especially by the year Nineteen Ninety Five and what I now knew by then.

This being me requiring to do some more business with Al Qaeda. The absolute *last* thing that I'd have ever chosen.

Chapter 32

El Corazon Valiente - The Ballad of Peter Duncan cont

Manny - It would be fair to say that in a business sector - like yours - that would have resembled a pressure cooker at times. The CIA - and their pressing - managed to turn the heat up even further on matters?

Peter - Things were hotter than a pan of fried Ghost chillies in the devil's kitchen, Manfred. And yeah, you're right. There's already a hell of a lot of pressure in that line of work only to then find yourself with heavy duty people like the CIA all over you like a cheap suit.

You had to laugh at the irony of it all, though. Yeah, Branson had me by the cojones and while back in JFK he had left it hanging as if I had the *choice* in helping. He'd probably already have known that eventually he would have to turn the screw on me. That aside, however. I was travelling the world with the safety blanket of having the knowledge that the CIA were going to be some kind of a guardian angel, of sorts, to me.

I'd always made sure that I had some form of back up plan or friendly face in the area to help me in times of trouble should they occur but there's having a back up and then there's having the *CIA* take care of your interests.

The irony was that I was crossing the globe, doing the illicit deals that they already knew to be my choice of occupation, without any problems being presented my way. *This* while still never coming close to providing them with any kind of hard intel on any of their interests.

Actually no SOFT intel, either. Nada.

Eddy and German had sent me practically everywhere *but* to meet with Jihadists, Al Qaeda or any other outfit. Arms sales had never been so high but they had been going in different directions. Instead, to street gangs in the inner cities of America and Europe rather than to training camps in the Middle East.

You could only go where you were sent to. This I had told Branson when he had 'grabbed me' for a quick chat and 'debrief' at Schipol Airport one evening as I was waiting on my Houston connection on the way back to Bogota.

'You gots to steer things *in* that direction.' He tried to advise me.

'Are you f**king nuts, Walt? How am I *meant* to steer things in the direction of me meeting up with the world's most wanted terrorist organisation? I go where I'm sent and besides, don't you think that someone *asking* for to be sent to meet with those murdering Jihadists would look a little, I don't know? Out of place? Who in their right mind ASKS to meet with people like that? That's going to set off all kind of red flags on this, no?'

I admit, it was convenient to say but that didn't mean that it wasn't the truth either.

'You gotta do better, Peter. *Much* better because up to now you haven't given us shit and well, those boys in Miami. They're getting real itchy. Rumours are starting to gather pace about Bannon. Not sure how long he's going to be 'your guy' for and when he goes? Well there's at least two of the task force agents that I can think of that will be smelling blood. It's almost uncanny how an agent can all of a sudden find all roads blocked to their enquiries and then one day almost as if by magic. Road open, sorry for the disruption.'

He threatened. Leaving me in no doubt that he was referring to Vinnie Valencia and Tommy Ambrosini, two agents that - through Bannon - I'd found out more of and yeah, they had arresting me sitting at the very top of their pending tray.

Eddy and German had told me not to worry about them, and I hadn't. Brushing their obsession towards me off as something that would be easily dealt with, should that day arrive, considering all the personal information that the brothers now held on both agents.

'Anyway, you have a safe flight over the Atlantic, Peter. We'll speak soon. I'm off to London. God I hate that city. Crap food and even worse weather. The things we do for love of country though, eh?'

He walked away. Pep talk over.

Manny - And were there any further progression to this matter?

Peter - Well yeah, I received the official documentation stating that should I be committed as 'on record' and cooperating with the United States of America then, as a result, it would free me from any other charges that may have been levied at me in connection with matters unrelated to the capturing of Al Qaeda. Stamped and signed by the United States Attorney General. The Yanquis had been good as their word but there was the obvious caveat contained there. That I would need to *actually* provide them with evidence of helping them in their fight against an enemy of the state.

Manny - Did you come any closer to being put in a position where you *could* provide the CIA with any assistance?

Peter - Nope! Had it not been for the obvious I'd have - otherwise - been absolutely delighted with that status quo. I think the only way that I'd got myself through those previous meeting with the Jihadists had been down to my sheer ignorance of them. Yeah, I can pick up body language so had been always able to tell that they hadn't appeared to be much fans of myself but I'd never thought that they had been the shove a van full of explosives under a skyscraper and attempt to bring it down types.

I honestly felt like god had been mocking me or karma was having a little bit of fun to itself because from late Ninety Five and into early Ninety Six. Eddy and German had sent me practically anywhere *but* to an Al Qaeda hot spot in the world.

I visited and arranged for hundreds of millions of worth of narcotics and arms to be sent to all continents outside of South America. Met with more corrupt police, politicians and government officials than I could remember. Just no Jihadists.

Shit, I'd even taken a few days out - on behalf of the brothers - to visit Russia and attend the birthday party of Mikhail Kalashnikov in St Petersburg. The godfather of automatic rifles being someone that Eddy and German had enjoyed good business relations with for many years. Myself and Mikhail no strangers to each other and - following my first ever visit to the country to meet with him and his representatives where after concluding business we all got roaring drunk on vodka on what was by no means the most professional of business trips but one of the best laughs I'd had in a long time - he was a man that, upon learning that I was visiting the area on my birthday, the next again visit, had arranged for me to be given a personalised AK-47 with my initials and a small St Andrews cross painted on it. It was an amazing gesture from him, truly humbling. The fact that I would never shoot a single bullet out of it, or would even be as stupid to attempt to take it home with me in my luggage, did not change any of that.

It was a gun that I would never see again, after that visit. I had been told that it would be included inside the next shipment of rifles that would be sent to Colombia but if it had been then someone must have pinched it. The fact that the father of the AK-47 had one made - specifically *for* me - was good enough. You know what they say about the thought being the thing that counts?

Apart from all of that, though. It really was just a case of 'business as usual.' I'd made more money for myself in Ninety Five than I'd had in Ninety Four and from the way that the new year had kicked off, it looked like we were in for another record breaking twelve months.

Manny - Yet still no meeting with Osama bin Laden or colleagues from The Base?

Peter - Negative on that, good buddy. Of course, it didn't help that I was taken out of the game completely with that helicopter crash in the jungle. To be fair, it sounded like I was almost moaning about having to take some time out of work when - in reality - I'm lucky that I'm speaking to you today. Well, if you can class sitting in a side room of a Colorado supermax prison in an orange jumpsuit as 'luck?'

Manny - Yes, not to take you away from the topic we were speaking of but can you briefly tell the readers about that helicopter crash?

Peter - Of course, Manfred. I was in a helicopter, and it crashed. You know? I'm not even sure they're *meant* to fly, those things. The amount of time that they'd crash. Is that brief enough?

Manny - *laughing* Well, you can provide a little more depth than that, if you like.

Peter - You're the boss. I'm very much aware that you only have four phone calls with me. What I have to tell from over the years would take a *lot* more than four phone calls, my friend.

But yeah, short version is that German - as a personal favour - had asked me to fly out into the jungle to inspect a tonne and a half of product, that was in the finishing stages. Dealing with that type of thing *inside* the country was not usually part of my remit but due to the sheer scale of the batch, he had asked that someone fly out to keep a check on the team that we had working in the lab out in the jungle, while the final preparations were being made in anticipation of the batch reaching completion.

I hadn't been much a fan of going out there into the jungle. Eddy had personally taken me in there to show me one of our labs - as part of my induction period to the cartel - but I hadn't been back since. Being honest, the Colombian jungles scared me *way* more than anything that I would encounter away from it.

All those creatures, tiny insects that would go up your nose, or in through an ear, and before you know it they're burying themselves into your brain and laying eggs. And that's just the insects, I didn't even get to the poisonous snakes and frogs. Then you have the potential for stumbling across the *wrong* lab and once you see one of those you're never going to be allowed to walk away from it again. Throw in the potential to come across rebels hiding out in the jungle or the army who are out there and looking for them. Too many variables for things to go wrong out there, *without* helicopter failure.

I'd been around the lab to make sure all was as should've been. I'd been impressed. Not only was the batch almost complete but most of the keys had already been weighed and packaged up. Seeing all I needed to, I got Paco - our pilot - to take me up and back to Bogota. We never made it out of the jungle. That kind of environment out there can go from one extreme to the other. From humid to boiling to freezing at will. I'm not sure if it was down to this. I don't know? Precipitation messing with the electrics on the chopper or something but we were only up in the air a matter of minutes when the scariest of alarms started sounding on the dashboard of the helicopter, along with a red light flashing on and off.

Paco didn't have to tell me that we had ourselves a major problem. The sights and sounds on the dashboard of the chopper told me that. Well, this along with the panic stricken look on his face.

I suppose the fact that the helicopter had stopped moving forward in the air and had began to drop towards the trees below us was also a good marker, as far as where things stood.

There next followed the most frightening seconds of my life as the helicopter fell from the sky towards the thick jungle, the tops of the trees getting closer and closer to us as the helicopter gained momentum in its speed to reach the ground. Eventually crashing into the treetops which - thankfully - had been there to break the speed of the chopper's fall and save it from certain explosion on impact with the ground below.

The trees - so old and tall that they were enough to stop the helicopter from actually reaching the ground - seemed to open themselves up, snatch the chopper, and then close in on it again. Holding us up high and swaying at a precarious angle, with me staring out of the window but with the view out of it showing that I was looking directly at the ground below.

Getting my bearings I looked to the side to find that Paco wasn't in the pilot seat anymore. His screams below confirming that he wasn't far. The daft bastard having not had his seatbelt on, and paying for it. Apparently having fallen out and then down through the trees. Screaming up that he had broken his legs and asking if I was alive. I was in pain, everywhere, but alive.

I felt like half a tree was inside the helicopter with me. I was scratched to hell from all of the branches that had ripped into me and felt also like I possibly had a couple of broken ribs but yeah, I was alive.

Manny - A seriously close call for you?

Peter - Well, when its your time it is evidently your time. That wasn't my day although if I'd known that I'd have had to spend the best part of forty eight hours sitting up in that helicopter before Paco and I would be rescued I think I may have chosen to have crashed and burned in the helicopter. God, was that a long two days. Rationing the water that was in the helicopter. I think it took Paco almost a full day to drag himself to the bottle that I had thrown down to him which - in my own defence - I'd had no choice other than to throw out in that direction due to being unable to move freely stuck, there in the helicopter.

Sleeping, drinking shitting inside that small cabin until our rescue came via a group of hunters that were out in that area of the jungle and had stumbled across a passed out Paco on the ground, clothes coated in blood.

Had it not been for those two men then who knows if we'd have made it.

It provided a most unwelcome break from work. Eddy and German insistent that I take as long as I needed out to get the recovery that I required. The *last* thing I needed was time off work. I needed to be rubber stamping my freedom from the Yanquis and that was not something that I was going to be able to achieve sitting around my swimming pool.

And you know what? I came *this* close to meeting my objective, 'this' close.

Manny - With Al Qaeda?

Peter - The very people. Following my recovery from the helicopter crash. Eddy and German had been talking about my first trip - on my return - being me heading back to Afghanistan to conclude a deal for another poppy field. I'd been there previously - dealing with a Taliban warlord - to purchase the contents of a different field. They wanted me to go back there but this time it would be to meet with operatives of both Al Qaeda *and* the Taliban. The group now making their presence felt once more in the region of the world where they had originated, fighting the Russians.

Well, as you can imagine. Walt Branson was practically wetting his pants at the prospect of this. Advising that - once I'd learned more of the trip I was going on to Kandahar - they would provide me with what instructions they'd have on their side for me to carry out. This, my destination - Branson telling me - a veritable two for one for his counterterrorist unit.

When I think of it all. How near I same to having *something* tangible on my record as having helped the Yanquis. Would it have been enough to keep me out of prison? Possibly not but it *may* have been the difference between me spending my life in the ADX as opposed to a slightly looser sentence and one that would've provided me with better living conditions, in addition to the prospect of seeing the outside world as a free man once more. It's so, so frustrating. Agonising to think of, really.

In the end, though. I ran out of time. I'd always had that lucky knack of managing to stay one step ahead of everything. The authorities, the dangers of who I did business with and the chaos of the lifestyle. This that and the f**king third. I'd *always* managed to stay ahead of the curve, even if at times - I'd readily admit - that it was done in a way like that of a piano teacher who has, in reality, only had one more lesson than *you* have would've been able to pull off.

No more, though.

'You're out of touch, I'm out of time.' *Duncan sings*

Mikael - and the move that he was busy pulling off behind all of our backs - saw to that.

Manny - Mikael, your partner?

Peter - Partner and - in a world where they were extremely hard to come by - my friend. The *one* person that I knew I could've trusted. It's always the ones you least suspect though, isn't it?

When I walked into his apartment - in Bogota - that morning and found him sat there in his armchair - drenched in blood - with his throat slit and his tongue pulled down through it, I was heartbroken.

But nowhere near as heartbroken as when I was to discover *why* he had been left in that way.

Manny - Clearly, someone had wanted to make a particular statement. Sicarios simply do not go to the trouble of leaving their victims with the 'neck tie,' otherwise.

Peter - Well, you're right there, Manfred. They wanted it to be known that Mikael had been 'talking' to someone. Thing is, they weren't wrong about that.

Manny - Who was it that he had been speaking to? DEA? Rival cartel?

Peter - That was not a luxury of something that I was to know until a lot further down the line. I had more pressing matters. Mikael had been - without question - the one that was closest to me. Lived in each others back pockets half of the time, up until Eva had flown out to join me and live in Colombia.

Who Miki had been speaking to - in that moment - was not of importance. What *I* now did was of the utmost of importance. I didn't know who had killed him. It could've been a rival cartel or it could've been something much closer to home. As always, my sense of self preservation kicked in. Did I want to hang around Bogota and see which way the wind blew? It was literally a case of fight or flight.

I flew.

The morning that he'd been murdered. He'd called me specifically to tell me that he had left a computer disc in the side pocket of my car door and had asked if I could bring it to him. He'd actually sounded a little out of character that morning on the phone. Kind of edgy, you know? I just put it down to him having a little moment to himself, as we all did in the business. He'd been sure to remind me on four separate occasions - across the call - to bring the disc to the point that he had me wondering just what the hell was *on* it that was so important to him.

When I'd fled the scene of the crime - and, along with Eva, Colombia entirely - I'd instinctively grabbed the floppy disc and taken it to Europe with me. It was a decision that would have the widest range of consequences - not just for me but for a whole varied group of people - you could ever have possibly imagined.

Manny - What was it that was actually *on* the disc?

Peter - Well, you're asking the wrong person, there. I wouldn't have even known *how* to put it into the laptop the correct way. That was Mikael's job. Through time I would eventually learn that what was on the disc was the equivalent of the Bogota Cartel's 'little black book of secrets.' The kind of information that - left in the hands of either the DEA or the Mexicans - would bring down Eddy and German's operation.

Manny - But it *wasn't* in the hands of either of those. It was in the hands of one of Eddy and German's closest allies. Why the issue?

Peter - Well I guess we'll never know if there *would've* been one. When I decided to flee the country - and take the disc with me - I *created* the issue. The optics were horrific. I was as innocent as you could've got yet *looked* guilty as sin.

I'd seen and heard enough to know that when your partner is murdered in such a way. You will soon have questions to answer. Trying to anticipate what might follow, I had looked ahead to a point where Eddy and German - or more specifically Jorge Lozano and Gilberto Martinez - would be asking questions that I simply would not have had an answer for, with Mikael doing all of this behind my back.

And you know how gangsters can be when they ask a question and don't get an answer, while already assuming that the person actually *knows* what intel they're seeking?

It was a sad way for it all to end. That of all people. Mikael had done something like that, to *us*. The betrayal between two friends but yet done in a way that would leave *me* open to suspicion, after his death.

Whatever the reasons for his treachery towards his friend and his jefes in the cartel. His actions would set off an atomic bomb that would end up exploding over the White Isle of Ibiza, that summer in Ninety Six.

Chapter 33

El Corazon Valiente - The Ballad of Peter Duncan cont

Manny - So out of the cartel and on the run in Europe? Take me through things.

Peter - Well it was a piece of f**king shit, that's what it all was. Forced on the run, literally for my life - as well as my wife's - and all because of some rata move from someone who was meant to be my best friend? You know what though, Manfred? What do you do when life throws lemons at you?

Manny - Duck?

Peter - Pffffft, Yeah, you'd do that too, wouldn't you? Screaming 'journalist journalist.' *laughs* Well there lies the difference between you and me. You would duck from the lemon where as *I* would throw my arm right into the air to catch the thing and use it to my own advantage and make some lemon juice out of the situation.

Manny - I don't like lemon juice, anyway.

Peter - And neither do I and that's not the point I'm making and fine you know it. I wasn't making lemon juice out of the situation. I was going to make *cheddar* instead. Some seriously, *life changing* hand in your notice and ride off into the sunset kind of bank for a man to make.

Manny - You carried on Mikael's bad (sic) work with the disc?

Peter - Look, the disc was initially only ever looked upon as something that I'd felt would be a bargaining chip to help keep myself and Eva alive. I'd never envisaged that it was going to provide the 'windfall' that it did. I mean, like you already know. I didn't know *what* was on it so how the hell could I go off on some quest to sell it? I just knew that once I'd fled Colombia and pieces of the puzzle began being put into place. It was apparent that Mikael had been murdered *for* it and Eddy and German were most insistent that they got it back again. If you appear as desperate as that, from the beginning, then you have already given away your hand. Eddy and German Ramirez practically teaching me this, themselves.

Manny - Stevie? Your father had fled Colombia - along with his wife - and, indirectly, came to visit you, with two of Colombia's most notorious cartel sicarios following closely behind them. How was that for you?

Stevie - Obviously this is for The Washington Post and a certain standard and class of reader but I'm sorry, mate. My dad completely f**ked my whole shit up, in Ibiza. Have you heard of Space, Manny?

Manny - What? Like the universe?

Stevie - No, mate. *Space*, the Ibizan behemoth of a super club. Literally one of the most famous night-clubs in the world. You don't go out much, Manny, no?

Manny - Well, no. I, mean, my work and ..

Stevie - I could tell, Manny. Everyone and anyone who knows even a modicum of anything about clubs would know of Space Ibiza. Anyway, guess who bags a three month residency, guaranteeing themselves three straight months of partying, sun and playing records in one of the most famous buildings in clubbing folklore? Moi, obviously. You any idea how hard it is to land a gig like that? Of course you don't, you only learned about the place two seconds ago. Well I - through some part to my skills and another to my smooth silver tongued grind someone until they're completely worn down manager of mines - had managed to secure a spot for me on the terrace, outside of the main discoteca.

Of course, next thing. Enter Peter 'El Corazon Valiente' with a wife, that I didn't even know about who was almost the same age as myself and Bogota sicarios coming to Space looking for me as a way to get to my dad and this disc that they were after. As you can imagine, I wasn't best pleased. He - my father - almost got me killed, my girlfriend was taken even closer to that stage. It was around five years ago now but it's still a sore point, like. I wasn't best pleased with how it all started, went in the middle, and how it all ended. It was a disaster of a few weeks but, in fairness. Technically, a brilliant metaphor for being around Peter Duncan.

Manny - Following your marriage to Peter. You took the plunge and moved from England to Colombia, only to then abruptly be taken back *out* of Colombia. How did this feel, Eva?

Eva - There have been people facing ballistic missiles fired at their coasts given more of a warning than Peter did with me back then that day. One second I was lying by our pool wondering if we were going to have the Wagu Steaks that were in the fridge for dinner or if we would be going out somewhere to eat - what dilemmas, I know - and the next I was sitting in a seat of an Avianca plane from Bogota to Barcelona with little or no explanation for it forthcoming from my husband, other than that we had to leave Bogota. Not at some point down the line after selling houses and arranging all of that normal stuff when you relocate. No, we had to leave, *now*.

One of those scenarios in life that you always hear about but never ever think that you'll have to face yourself. I'm not even sure that the human mind has the capacity to even be able to deal with such a headf**k. Have you ever been told to 'grab what you need' and that you have ten minutes to leave your house, one that the chances are you won't ever be returning to again?

Manny - Thankfully, no.

Eva - It's not something that I would recommend. It would make you cry when you stopped to think about it. All of those clothes and shoes that were left behind. I still think about them from time to time. Literally *thousands* of pounds worth, who knows, possibly even into the hundred thousand mark? I'm not sure if they have Ebay in Colombia or not but if they do, someone probably made a killing. Well, not a killing, as such. Considering what happened to Mikael maybe I could've chosen a better wording. He was a nice guy. It was horrible what they did to that man. Well, once I *eventually* found out the full story of how he'd been found.

Manny - Your ex husband seems to have a different opinion on Mikael Garin.

Eva - Oh I'm sure he does. While married to the man I was not part of his 'lifestyle' so was not wired the same as he was. I know they all had their 'codes' to live by but at the end of the day. Someone I knew - and liked immensely, we all did - had been found with his throat cut and tongue pulled through it. *No one* deserves that.

Manny - How did you find Colombia to live in?

Eva - That's just it! I was only really beginning to get used to - and enjoy - the country and city. Moving from England to Bogota was - understandably - something that took a little time to get used to. It didn't help that half of the time Peter never seemed to even *be* in the country with me. I knew what I was getting into - when moving - so could not have pointed the finger at anyone when it came to being left there in that beautiful hacienda on my own.

Due to how much of a rush that we had left that morning I never got a chance to feel any sense of remorse or loss in us actually 'leaving' Bogota. No build up to things where you could sit and reflect about anything, as such. Being truthful. Life was so stressful at that point on the run that you didn't really have time to sit and think about things like that. It took many months down the line when we were finally given a chance to stop looking over our shoulders that I realised that I missed Bogota in ways that I'd have never thought possible when I'd first arrived there. What I'd have done to be back lazing by the pool in that warm sun. Reading my book without a single care in the world. I guess sometimes you never really know how good you have it until one day you wake up and it's been taken away?

Manny - Out of all places - on the run from Eddy and German Ramirez - you took your wife to Ibiza. Forgive me for saying but out of all corners of the globe that you could've chosen to hide in, why the island of Ibiza, in the Balearic Islands?

Peter - Convenience, more than anything else. Mind you, I'd imagine that my son wouldn't be so quick to categorise my appearance that summer as too 'convenient.' We couldn't hang around in Barcelona as Bogota had too many links there inside the city and I'd felt that to hang around town - while Salomon Sanchis, my European based lawyer, moved around the money that I needed access to before me and Eva could drop off the grid for ever - would've made the pair of us sitting targets. Jump in the wrong taxi or walk into a Bogota friendly restaurant and be recognised and it would've been curtains.

With the level of funds that Sal had to move around for me - and the complicated and convoluted 'tumbling' system that he would put the transfers through to avoid detection - it was not something that he would've been able to do at the touch of a button or stroke of pen.

Logically, while this was all being taken care of I thought it best that we get out of dodge in the meantime to hide out until all funds transfers had been arranged. Ibiza was just a coincidence. Had I not seen the beachside poster for a club in Ibiza with Stevie's name on it Eva and I would've probably ended up somewhere completely different.

Now you have to understand here, Manfred. At this point of proceedings. I was not aware of what was on the disc. Did not even know if its importance yet. Had not spoken to Eddy or German. The things that I, indeed, did not know about this very real situation that I'd been thrown into was frightening.

Obviously, I wasn't stupid. I *knew* that back in Bogota the inquest would have already began, from whichever angle it may have been formed from. I just hadn't realised that things had been escalated so promptly that by the time Eva and I were on the boat to Ibiza Town Eddy and German already had their two best sicarios on a plane in the direction of Barcelona, in pursuit. I mean, had I known that, *obviously* I wouldn't have sailed to Ibiza in Stevie's direction.

Manny - After a whistle stop tour of Barcelona. You landed up in Ibiza, party central.

Eva - I'd been twice before with the girls and absolutely *loved* the island. How on earth could you *not*. That summer, in Ninety Six? Not so much. Even on the plane from Bogota to Barcelona - when explaining things to me and why we'd had to flee the country - I could tell that Peter wasn't telling me the *full* story. Just his usual 'abridged' version of events. He'd *definitely* not told me that we'd end up in San Antonio that summer. Then again, I think there was an element of him making things up as he went. You'd have hoped so, anyway. Why would a father have ever brought - the storm he invited to Ibiza that summer - such heat onto his son, in the way that Peter did?

Manny - How aware were you of your father's 'occupation,' leading up to that summer?

Stevie - It was more a case of educated guesses when it came to him. Yeah, he'd let a few things slip on the phone that would give you a little glimpse of the world that he existed in but look, Manny. When you'd already discovered narcotics for yourself and then start to find more and more about them and that whole culture. When your dad pops up out of the blue telling you that he lives in Colombia and - most of the time - if you want to get hold of him you'll need to call him on a satellite phone. How much more blatant do you need things to be?

With a few gestures here and there, he had showed me the power that he had behind him, if he wanted something to be done. It wasn't a bad problem to have, if I'm being honest with you. The fact that he was thousands of miles away while *doing* it and not something that could impact on me worked out well. His business and my business were two things that it would've always been preferable if they were to never cross paths. Of course, though. He just had to, didn't he?

Manny - Your father - as part of this article - has claimed that he would never have travelled to Ibiza had he known what was to follow.

Stevie - Oh I've heard that story too from him but I've got a wee bit more up top to be daft enough to buy what he's trying to sell, there. Look, Manny. I've never been part of a narcotics cartel from South America and I can't see that ever changing but let's use our heads here. You work for a gang of murderers who - mistakingly - think that you have burned them. This scenario leading to you having to leave the country to escape them. Given those basic fundamentals. Where would you travel to? Oh I know, haven't seen my son for a good six years or so. Why not combine running for my life by stopping by his neck of the woods for a cuppa, a few Custard Creams and say hello to him?

There's *nothing* that he will *ever* be able to say to me that will allow myself to see any logic to him travelling to Ibiza that year to see me. Nicks, nada, nathan. You could literally see the headlines in some low brow tabloid.

'Peter Duncan in thinking of himself shock'

Manny - How did it feel - in amongst all that was going on over those frantic first few days on the run - to meet who was technically your son, Stevie?

Eva - I admit, there *was* an initial feeling of awkwardness between him and I, due to how similar of age we were to one another. Of course, I can't help but feel that Stevie's first impression might've been better if his dad had actually *told* him that he'd been married. To have your father surprise you that he's not only gone and got himself married but to someone practically *your* age? You can only imagine the impact that would have on someone. Once we got past that awkwardness, though. I'd have to say that Stevie - along with his friend Si and Flo, the girl Stevie met in a club over there in Ibiza - were the difference between me losing my mind over that period and not.

Had I been stuck with Peter and Peter only. Seeming - at times - to do nothing other than put Cocaine up his konk twenty four seven and the mood swings that it brought, as he felt the walls closing in on him. Well who knows how things would have turned out? The more pressure that he felt under, the more gear that he would take to try and get him through the days. He was a mess and was deteriorating in front of me as each passed.

I liked Stevie, though. He didn't deserve what Peter did that summer, he really didn't. Came close to destroying the boy's life and as for Flo - and what the Bogota sicarios did to *her* - that girl *certainly* didn't deserve what she'd had handed to her.

All of this lying firmly at the door of my ex husband. You know? Without trying to come across as some bitter and spiteful ex wife but. You know? He really was a selfish bastard, that man, at times.

Manny - Tell me how you hatched the plan to get yourself out of the precarious position that you were in? Eventually, you learned that Jorge Lozano and Gilberto Martinez were already in Spain and - with Sanchis or anyone else not answering calls at the Barcelona office - you were fearing the worst on both receiving the millions that Sanchis had been transferring for you *and* being found by the Bogota sicarios. How did you manage to turn things around in your favour?

Peter - It's a miracle that I didn't suffer from radiation burns those couple of weeks following us leaving Bogota. That phone was never away from my ear. You know how hard it was to run out the battery on one of those old style Motorolas? Managed to do it most days trying to dig myself out of the hole - or, shallow grave, if you will - that Mikael had dug for me.

Being realistic. There was no way that I was going to be able to return to Bogota again. That ship had sailed. Knowing how the brothers would've been viewing things - even taking sentiment into account - I also saw no possible scenario of any 'negotiations' being able to be held with El Jugador and La Cobra, should they have managed to catch up with me. When I finally spoke on the phone with Bogota and - without being directly told so - finding out that what was on the disc was complete gold (without me yet having had the chance to find out *what* was on it yet) I stashed the disc somewhere that Jorge and Gilberto wouldn't find and got to work on a plan to get out of Ibiza with Eva with the disc, sell it to the highest bidder and then for the two of us to drop off the map.

By then I'd found out about the brutal murders of Sanchis - along with his staff in his Barcelona office - and knew that my money was gone. The same *escape* money that I had gathered over all my years of working for Eddy and German. The *exact* same money that I had planned and had waiting on me for when a day like that was to ever arrive. I needed a new plan. There was no way that any of this would've been possible - and to remain a ghost to the Bogota cartel - without serious funds behind me to facilitate such a lifestyle.

Visiting an internet cafe in San Antonio and, after having the teenager in charge of the place help me with installing and opening the disc onto my terminal. I found that it had pretty much everything that you needed to know about the Bogota Cartel's operation. Politicians and police that they bribed. Their connections in all corners of the world that they dealt and bought arms and drugs with. Which routes were used across the world. Which methods deployed. With even my basic computer knowledge. What I had seen had been enough to show me what I was in possession of, and its likely worth.

It was only once I knew what I had on me that I able to plan myself a path out of the world of shit that I'd landed up in.

Of course, Stevie - in a show of what little regard family loyalty meant to him - did his very best to ruin *all* the plans that had been set up during my final days on the island.

Stevie - Family loyalty? Did he honestly say that, aye? *laughs* Did he mention *why* there was a question of 'loyalty' in the first place, per chance?

Manny - He omitted to mention the specific reason.

Stevie - Can't for the life of me think why not? Look, mate. Blood is thicker than water, I admit, but Peter Duncan is even *thicker* than blood if he thinks that his son is going to sit back and let an innocent girl be murdered - through Peter Duncan, someone she doesn't even *know* - while he has the *ability* to put a stop to it all at any time.

These Colombians *really* wanted to find him. To the point that they were abducting my girlfriend and coming to Space looking for me. I had to be snuck out the side door one night - after my set - while they searched for me inside the place.

When I discovered that not only had he decided not to hand over the one thing that the sicarios had been sent to Europe to retrieve but that he had *also* hidden it in my apartment. That was it, for me. F**k him and his family loyalty.

According to both the Colombian I spoke to on the phone and then Flo's account of things when I'd got her back safely, she had literally been seconds from death. The other hitman actually in the process of suffocating her when I'd called to tell them that I had the disc that they were so desperate to get their hands on.

Loyalty? Aye, good one, dad. If he ever gets out of that Colorado prison I'm sure he'll absolutely kill at the Edinburgh Festival with material like that, if he has a go.

Manny - Eva, tell me about those final days in San Antonio before - once again - you were on the move.

Eva - They were pretty real, I admit. By this point it was just Peter and I, along with the bodyguards from Liverpool that my husband had hired towards the end of our time there on the island. Stevie and Simon were no longer part of the equation. I'd loved spending time with them but then things got serious and we were back in survival mode, our exact whereabouts shrouded in secrecy. You know? Those couple of days with Peter - before we left Ibiza - were torrid. He was going through what I can only describe as his Ray Liotta Goodfellas helicopter phase.

Manny - *laughs* I'm going to trust that the reader gets what you mean!

Eva - All he seemed to do over those two days was either sniff patsies or make and take phone calls, most of them intentionally out of my earshot. We had a massive argument in our hotel the day that he - out of the blue - came back in from a phone call on the balcony. Telling me that we had to leave in a hurry. While he had been in a panic back in Bogota when telling me the same thing, he hadn't had the fear in his eyes that he had when looking at me inside that San Antonio hotel room. Something really bad was coming for him, us. It scared me. I didn't want to be part of this any longer.

Fast forward to the next again day and I'm sitting staring at two dead eyed Colombian assassins with their guns pointed at us, inside our dining room, while we sat eating dinner that evening.

Stevie - Look, Eva was well sound, like. We all loved spending time with her and that night at Space will go down on record as one of *the* great nights. I wouldn't have wanted a hair on her head harmed. Neither my dad, if I'm being honest. I'm possibly not his biggest fan but he's still my dad at the end of the day. *He* hadn't left me with any choice. Throw in the fact that the sicarios weren't going to hand Flo over to me *unless* I gave them my dad's new address. It was something that I *had* to do. I obviously knew that by handing over that address that I was leaving things open to the laps of the gods. I did what I did and I'd do the same thing again, if forced to.

Manny - You mentioned disloyalty from your son?

Peter - I had everything worked out. From the shit show that things had been to where I was going to pull Eva and I out of to? It was beautiful. Stashing the disc at Stevie's in a place that he was never going to find it. Knowing what it was that I had to tout around, I had two instant clear choices. Get in touch with a certain Vinnie Valencia and or Tommy Ambrosini and inform them of what I had on my possession and would be willing to take a WIT-SEC plea deal in return for exchange of one single floppy disc that would allow them to dismantle the Bogota Cartel brick by brick. Then there was option B, sell it to the highest bidder.

You can imagine how the latter option was the one - out of the two - which appealed the most to me. A life in witness protection was one that - looking ahead - I'd assumed would've completely sucked the life out of me. All that had went before in my life and for what? To end up as some blue collar schmuck, living in the suburbs in Arkansas or Delaware?

Regardless of that they - the Colombians - undoubtedly wanted me dead. I still could not deal with the thought of assisting those pricks at the DEA. Imagining some of their press conferences where they would be gloating about their triumph.

F**k them, let them do the spadework for themselves and not have things fall into their laps, I thought, as I decided that I'd have been crazy *not* to sell the disc to the highest bidder although, in reality, this was always going to be a smallish market of a select few bidders and - certainly - *all* from Mexico. So much so, I didn't even bother trying to sell it anywhere *other* than that part of the world.

I'd been surprised, heartbroken and simply sickened to find out - through my third party contact - that Sinaloa, on hearing that I had resurfaced trying to sell the disc, had confirmed that Mikael had actually been in the process of obtaining the information on Bogota *for* them.

Since finding Miki sat there with that Colombian necktie I had searched hard and deep for some kind of explanation that would've absolved him of any wrong doing and allow me to remain thinking of the guy as the diamond geezer that he was to and with me. Anything, case of mistaken identity, Mikael sticking his dick into the wrong woman and her husband taking exception? Just *anything* other than going down as the rat that he had showed himself up as. I couldn't work out the reason for the greed. We were exceptionally well paid for our work.

My contact in Culiacan told me that Sinaloa had enlisted in Mikael's help following the demise of the Cali Cartel after the arrest of both the Orejuelas inside the short same period. The Sinaloans sensing the chance to finish off the last of the big Colombian cartels with Medellin and Cali now taken down. The focus turned to Bogota.

Manny - How can you make a case for there being a difference to your actions - selling the disc - and taking the Bogota Cartel down and handing it over to the authorities, and the cartel *still* being taken down, regardless?

Peter - Oh I had my reasons, fifty *million* of them to be precise. The sad fact is, Manfred, that there was no way that I could pass on the disc to anyone *without* the Bogota Cartel falling by the way side. I mean, it was pretty much the disc's reason for existence. I didn't *want* Eddy and German in an American prison. I had hoped that the Sinaloans would have been gentlemen and offered the brothers a payment to step aside. You know? Out of respect.

Manny - Sinaloan cartel? Gentlemen? That's something that I don't hear everyday.

Peter - Whatever their plans were, they were offering fifty million dollars, American. It was not the level of money that I could have possibly turned down, in the position that me and my wife had been left in. I needed the funds that would provide new identities and the ability to disappear off to any part of the world that we wished to and live out our life. What the Sinaloans were offering would be more than enough to give us all of that.

I'd even gone as far as to arrange a preliminary meeting in Mexico City with Manuel Loerda, a Culiacan intermediary, to arrange terms and how the safe exchange of disc and money would go through. This agreed for a few days time after leaving Ibiza. Then Stevie went and pulled the carpet from under all of those plans by going and finding the f**king floppy disc. His timing? It could not have possibly been *any* worse.

You enter into discussions over something that is going to provide you with a life changing amount of money and then what happens? He finds the disc - which I'd taped underneath a kitchen drawer and had thought of as safe and sound - and starts running around trying to play the hero.

Manny - The Medellin sicarios were as good as their word? They gave your girlfriend back?

Stevie - As you know, this kind of situation was not a world that I'd been used to. I'd thought it as nothing other than common sense for us to meet and do the exchange in a busy place. Only - as we sat there inside Cafe Mambo - after they had looked at the disc on their laptop and then received the updated address where my father would be found did they let her go. But aye, they were as good as their word. The psychological damage that they did to her for the twenty four hours or so that they held her for though is something that can't be measured. She still suffers from PTSD over it to this day which - from her description of events - I really cannot blame her for.

It was a stomach churning feeling to hand over his details to them, knowing that it would possibly lead to his death. They now had the disc so they did not need him for that, which only meant that they had *another* job left to do before leaving Ibiza to go back to Bogota to their bosses. From the moment that they had been passed my dad's address it was a case of the long wait to find out from the police that my father - and possibly Eva too - had been found dead.

Manny - Sicarios, in your dining room? The Colombians tracked you both down?

Eva - They just walked casually into our cottage - that was in the middle of nowhere on the outskirts of San Antonio - and into our dining room. I just sat there with some salad still sat on my work as I held it in the air, mouth open catching flies. Shit scared to move a muscle for fear of one - or both - of them shooting me. I couldn't understand just how cool Peter was with it. They had come - specifically - to kill us. And he sat there quaffing red wine and speaking to the both of them as if he was catching up on old times with some familiar friends.

Five minutes later and one of them was lying dead on the floor from a bullet to the head and the other one was on his way to the same destination. Peter pulling the trigger on the second hitman and in doing so marking the beginning of the end of our marriage. I knew my husband was one who operated on the fringe of what the authorities saw as illegal and legal. This, however, was a line crossed for me.

Manny - The *fringe?*

Eva - Ok, that was more a figure of speech than anything else. What I'm saying is that I knew that Peter wasn't an angel but a killer? He wasn't one of them. Well he wasn't, up until Ibiza. He'd left me questioning if I even *wanted* to be with a person like that. Whether it was even *safe* to be with someone like that?

Having him tell me to leave a room where one dead body lay. Leaving him alone with the other barely alive one, and then when I heard the shots from inside? That was *it*. I wasn't going to be with a killer. Some things your partner will do that erases *all* of what may have went before that moment, and they can do so in a heartbeat. All the good times, the happiness and feeling that you could not love anyone more stronger.

Evaporated when your partner shows you who they *really* are and that they weren't the person that you'd thought them to be.

We left Ibiza that evening on a hastily booked flight for London. I tried to leave him, at the airport. His face, there in the departure lounge, while I had a meltdown - in front of hundreds of holiday makers waiting on their flights home - and screamed that I couldn't be married to a killer. He looked like he didn't know *what* to do and Peter Duncan *always* seemed to have himself a plan.

Quieting me down. He managed to change my mind by asking me to think back over everything that had happened since we'd had to leave Colombia and whether I thought it would be a good idea to try and go it alone, when god only knew what kind of people were looking for him and I. That we would be much safer together as a unit and besides, if I was to hang on a little further, he was going to come up with something that would solve *all* of our problems.

He denied killing the man that was in the room. Of course he did. I felt insulted that he would lie to me in this way, when *everything* pointed to the contrary.

Having talked me around, I went with him to London where - for my safety - he had me placed under a self imposed lockdown in our room at The Dorchester while he - ambiguously - went away for a couple of days on 'business.' Telling me that if I didn't hear or see him after a total of four days to then assume that his plan had failed.

Manny - Losing the disc - just as you had negotiated the fifty million dollar sale to the Mexicans - then to compound things, the sicarios sent from Bogota tracked you down. It all seems like the natural conclusion to someone who has lived hard in the narco industry, and was about to *die* hard. How did you escape what appeared to be your fate?

Peter - Well you have to give Stevie a little bit of credit. He willingly put his father into a pit filled with shit but at least had the decency to throw a rope in there for him to get himself back out of. In what would be the last time that we would speak to one another - until Amsterdam Two Thousand - in the shortest of calls he alerted me to the fact that Jorge and Gilberto were now in possession of my whereabouts and - logically - they were going to be visiting sooner than later.

It had been enough time to leave me, however, to put the necessary plans into place so that I would be ready for their arrival. Stevie, more or less saving my life - and Eva's - with that phone call.

The *one* thing that jars me to this day about it all, even though technically it doesn't matter anymore as I'm never going to see or speak to her again now.

Manny - What would that be, Peter?

Peter - That I never killed Gilberto 'La Cobra' Martinez in the cottage. But that Eva thinks that I *did*. Will *always* think that I did. No matter what I said or *how* I had put it across to her. She wouldn't believe me on that.

Manny - You left the room with Martinez still alive?

Peter - You know what? I stood over him and pointed that gun straight at him. I tried to consume myself with the thoughts of what *he'd* do, were the roles reversed. Remind myself that he was only lying on a tiled floor of an Ibiza stone built cottage with blood pouring out of him from bullet wounds *because* he had flown cross continent with the task of ending *me*.

I couldn't do it, though. I'm not a killer. Never claimed to be one and when it came down to it, *showed* that I wasn't one. I mean, it would've solved another problem to just take someone as dangerous as Gilberto Martinez out of the game, while there was the chance.

He was just like I'd been, though. When it came to working for Eddy and German. Nothing was personal, he just went where he was told to go. This thought was the swing vote in my head. Wheezing and pressing down into the leg wound that he had most of the blood coming from. He looked up at me and awaited the inevitable.

Out of frustration I unloaded what bullets were left in the gun into the wall.

I crouched down towards him so that I could whisper into his ear.

'Gilberto, I always liked you. Next to that dead piece off shit psychopath beside you, you were a stand up guy. I'm going to give you a second chance today. By the time that you get your way back to Bogota you're going to find that the wheels have already been set in motion that is going to see that your old employers are no longer in the business. You'll never see me again but - if you make it out of here before the men outside come back in to deal with the 'bodies' that's lying here - I hope that one day you remember who it was that gave you a second chance today. Adios hermano.'

Eva and I left straight away for the airport but from the tidy up call that I had made to Danny O'Halloran - one half of the notorious Scouse gangsters who'd supplied me with the bodyguards who had protected me from Jorge and Gilberto - I was not surprised - in the slightest - to find that when Danny's men had entered the house - following up my instructions to dispose of the dead bodies inside - they were to find only one Colombian lying there.

Trying to learn from my mistakes I thought that it would've been insane had I flown directly to Mexico City - on such a high stakes and potentially deadly trip - along with my wife in tow. Feeling that London was far away enough from Ibiza and - ideally - even further from Mexico, where I would head to try and arrange a deal that could either go very right for me or very, very wrong. I didn't want my wife *anywhere* near any of it.

I was hoping that Mexico City was as far as I would have to go and that all business would be conducted from there inside the capital. If I was to be asked to venture into Sinaloa - and all of the variables of what could go wrong in such a scenario - along with the disc, then the advantages, for the Sinaloans, would have only increased, greatly.

Before actually receiving payment for the disc. There were all manner of potential things that could go wrong. There is no disputing just how much Eddy and German needed the disc back. Who was to say that it hadn't *just* been El Jugador and La Cobra that they had dispatched off to Europe to find me? *Then* there were all the different varieties of how the Mexicans could have burned me, if they took such a decision to do so.

Knowing that I was now on my lonesome and with no cartel behind me as back up. They could easily have double crossed me. Simply 'taken' the disc and dropped me off at one of the many farmer's pig farms in the region. Easier still, have a bent copper arrest me on arrival in Culiacan on some fabricated charges and obtain the disc by those means? No matter how rich a cartel may be, if they can find a way to save fifty million American dollars, they're going to explore that avenue.

It was something that I had to keep in mind and be aware of the possibility. I left London for Mexico City later on in the same day that we had arrived from Ibiza. Telling Eva that she would know if I hadn't been in touch after a specific period of time that something would have happened to me.

After all that I had put her through. I couldn't have blamed her for not even *caring* if I came back from meeting the Sinaloans or not.

Manny - How did the Sinaloans receive you on getting to Mexico?

Peter - As far reaching and powerful as they were, they were in a bit of disarray at the time. It had been only the year before that their jefe, Chapo Guzman, had been given twenty years sentence and - as you'd expect in a situation like this - there were more than one person who felt that they should lead the cartel in Guzman's absence. This all at odds with the fact that while even behind bars 'El Chapo' had been able to manage cartel affairs without barely a hitch.

Guzman himself - Manuel Loerda advised me when we sat down at The Hilton by Mexico City International Airport - being instrumental in the initial contacting of Mikael and sounding him out over going behind the backs of Eddy and German. All the while sat in a jail cell at the 'maximum security' Puente Grande facility in Jalisco.

Manny - *laughs* I noticed the emphasis that you drew on how tight security is at Puente Grande.

Peter - *laughs* Well, yes. I understand that very recently señor Guzman managed to - with the help of guards - walk through an open jail cell door and helped into a laundry cart. *Then* taken down unguarded hallways, and through already opened electronic doors and into the car park where he simply jumped out of the laundry cart and into a waiting car. Yes, *very* Fort Knox-esque, Manfred.

Over lunch - and with the worst jet lag imaginable for someone who had flown from Ibiza to London and then straight to Mexico City - Manuel and I sat there and thrashed out a deal between the two of us. The fee itself had been agreed on back in Ibiza. It was now really a case of finding a way to come up with an exchange that I'd felt would have provided me with an element of security.

I just wanted to be back on that plane headed back to London along with the sum of fifty million sitting inside my Cayman Islands bank account and me *free* of the disc. As long as the Sinaloans were happy to keep up their part in things then there wouldn't have been any problems.

Manuel had been at pains to ensure me that his employers had no wish to burn me over it. We'd done business together - him and I - in the past and I'd always found him a smart, funny and amiable man. The cartels - with how abrasive their jefes could be - *needed* guys like Manuel and me. I think we saw a piece of us in the other and because of that there was an unspoken respect between the two of us.

He'd told me that - with the importance of the quote unquote Colombian Cartel diminishing, following Medellin and Cali falling, and the rules of how Cocaine being distributed across the world were starting to change. Sinaloa had sensed that this was now the chance to make a move on Bogota. The Culiacans - ever smart - cottoning onto something that Medellin and Cali had never quite managed to. That the weapons sales that Eddy and German generated was something that could not be ignored. Add that to the Cocaine that the Mexicans would be sending in place of from Bogota. Fifty million dollars, while a king's ransom to me, was 'affordable' to them.

Having had a chance to listen to *my* side of things. Where I'd explained that matters had turned serious, how I had to disappear, and that the disc was my chance to get out of the business once and for all. He explained how over the years that I had been dealing with them. The Sinaloans had began to look on me as a bit of a good egg and that they'd be happy to see me get my pay day and then never be seen or heard of again. Their view being that someone - who knew the kind of stuff that I did, like what was *on* the disc - who was comfortable and wealthy enough to live out the rest of his days in luxury was a *lot* less likely to be finding themselves in a position of wanting to give up information to save themselves.

They would get the disc and I would leave the narco business a very, very rich man. Everyone would be happy.

Manuel and I arranged for the trade to happen the next day, where we met in a city centre coffee shop. When I had received the confirmation - from the operator for Cayman National Bank - that the transfer of fifty million dollars - minus administration fee - had indeed been received into my account I handed the key with the number '**88**' stamped to a keyring for the locker matching that same number at the nearby 'Estacion Buenavista' train station.

'I assume that the disc *will* be inside the locker, Pedrito?' Manuel kind of half joked. I would not have been as stupid as to do anything other than that. I wasn't exactly brimming with pride over what I was doing to Eddy and German. By handing that key over to Manuel I was surely either signing their death or arrest warrants. This was a situation that I was having to 'react' to rather than instigate, however. I was trying to dig myself out of things. Manuel had no worries. The disc was there.

Manny - And once the Sinaloans got their hands on the disc?

Peter - Well, they systematically tore the Bogota Cartel apart through a campaign of damaging leaks regarding all of the police and politicians that the brothers had bribed, coupled with the more intimidatory tactics which saw them strong-arm their way into areas of the Ramirez brothers' businesses. In ways that saw little to zero resistance from Bogota.

Soon the Bogota Cartel - as we'd known it - had been decimated to the point of extinction.

Manny - There are various theories about what happened to Eddy and German Ramirez. Do you know, personally, what happened to them?

Peter - Well at this point, I think the only thing that *anyone* knows for sure is that they aren't sitting in an American jail, like some, I may add. Neither were their bodies found, either. From what I was told, from those back in Bogota who were apparently in the know and who had remained 'friendly faces to me.' The brothers - along with all family - disappeared into the night. One evening they were all on Eddy's ranch and by the next morning, they were gone. The place left looking like some narco Marie Celeste.

What I *do* know, however, is that if Eva and I had been able do a disappearing act with new identities and living in another continent, with our resources, then the hidden wealth that Eddy and German possessed would have been enough to see that they could've went anywhere or done *anything* they liked. They could all literally be on some private island bought through one of their shell companies, for all any of us truly knows.

Manny - Don't you think that they were simply murdered by the Sinaloans, to get them out of the way?

Peter - While obviously a possibility. Personally, I don't think so. Eddy and German Ramirez were two of the world's most famous narcotics and weapons exporters. Spent more time - on occasion - at the top of the Drug Enforcement Administration's most wanted chart than The Beatles did in the Top Forty. Could you *really* see Mexicans taking such a major scalp, and not boasting about it? You'd expect a Sinaloan operative to be stopping speeding traffic to tell the cars that they had assassinated the Ramirez brothers and sons.

My theory - and I know we all have our own right up to them being buried along with Jimmy Hoffa, Elvis and Shergar - is that they saw that the writing was on the wall, took the considerate wealth that they had stored away and decided to pull the eject cord.

It's a bit of a paradox but I'm happy if that's the case, even if it was a case of if I was still on the outside I'd have had to live life forever looking over my shoulder.

I never wanted the pair of them dead, or arrested. But then again, I wanted both of those things even *less* for myself.

It had been - without question - one of the most mentally draining fortnights of my life and let me assure you, the previous six years leading up to that period of time - and all it had been filled spent doing - had hardly been 'inactive.'

Sitting on that British Airways flight - somewhere over the Atlantic - heading back to London. I remember pouring a drink - out of the mini bottle of Malbec I'd ordered to go with dinner - and thinking to myself

'You did it, Duncan. I don't know *how* you pulled it off, but you did'

So proud of how I'd played things I even toasted myself.

There had been so many times - following fleeing Bogota - where I'd thought that it was the end of the line and that it was a case of me naturally reaching the conclusion of me running out of luck.

But no, there I was. Fifty million dollars richer, a free man and on my way to get the girl and - as cliched as it all sounds - ride off into the sunset.

Eva - One more day and I was going to have to start to assume that the worst had happened to him. Only for my husband to burst into the hotel room that evening, big smile on his face asking

'So are you ready to go to Bora Bora then or what?'

A paradise on earth that we - first of all - moved out to as holiday makers before purchasing a beautiful house that looked out onto the South Pacific. All the home comforts we needed, shipped from America and Europe. The plan being to live out the rest of our lives in some much needed peace and tranquility. A place where we would not have to lift a finger. Somewhere we would have *everything* we wanted and needed and wouldn't have to worry about a single thing. Well, until the next time.

With Peter Duncan, there was *always* a next time.

Chapter 34

Peter

I couldn't get the face - of Gilberto Martinez - out of my head. Lying there, gazing up at me with that look in his eyes, that knew he was about to die. I'd never seen *that* face before in my life and I hadn't ever again after that day. Talking to Manny about the events in Ibiza. It had left me thinking about Gilberto. How *his* story had gone. He was *undoubtedly* the ride or die type so if I'd been told that he'd died in the line of duty, while trying to defend Eddy and German from the Sinaloans? It would not have surprised, would've been even kind of fitting, almost. Even then - and assuming that he'd made it back to Colombia - Gilberto, the only surviving member out of him and El Jugador, would've be the one that had to return to the brothers and inform them that he didn't have the disc. Personally, I'd have rather stayed on the White Isle, given the circumstances.

The thing is, though. Someone - with La Cobra's reputation - like Gilberto. When *he* gets killed, you find out. When a narco figure like that leaves the world, people tend to notice. Folk singers construct narcocorridos in their honour, the stories of the man become committed to mythology - through the medium of song - as if in some kind of memoriam, with the person being spoken about in the past sense. There had been *none* of that in connection with La Cobra. If I'd had to take a guess - like his bosses - it would've been that he'd been still out there. Maybe he'd never left Ibiza, thinking he'd stick around there? That idea making me laugh, even if it was the least likely of possibilities.

'You've killed people before, Gal? *How* were you able to do it? Pull that trigger on them?' I asked Gary, following me telling him the story of being visited by the two sicarios in San Antonio that day, and how it all turned out.

'I'd have fucking blown the cunt's head off if he'd came looking to kill me on a contract. You're too soft, fella.'

Gary's take on the fact that I had one of the sicarios on the ground - a literal sitting target - and had taken the decision to spare his life instead of taking it from him, like he'd came to my house to do to me.

'Well, that's the thing, Pete. I saw it as my job and I'm guessing that lads like Jorge Lozano and Gilberto Martinez took that very same approach to *their* work. Take away the human side, make it purely transactional - and occupational - and it becomes much easier.'

The way Gary said it, literally brushing off the subject of killing someone as if it was just one of those everyday things like brushing one's teeth.

'No, but, when they're looking straight at you and you can see *that* fear in their eyes. What is - in all likeliness - going to be the last glimmer of life from them. How do you just go ahead and 'take' it?'

I - having found myself in that very same situation - could not wrap my head around how someone could press on and do it, though.

'What? The *puppy dogs*? Don't let those eyes fool you, mate. Given half the chance those same eyes would be fixed firmly on *you* with the gun pointing in *your* direction. You'd be amazed what someone will do - in their final moments - to avoid taking a bullet. Dignity and self respect, for some, goes right out the fucking window.'

I couldn't help but think that Gilberto - back in that stone cottage - had, at least, kept his dignity. Was he scared of the prospect of me unloading the clip from the Glock into him? Of course he was. I could see it in his eyes and you know what? Anyone who *doesn't* have that fear of life coming to an end really can't have much of a life to start off with. Yeah, 'La Cobra' was scared but if he was going to be departing this earth then he would do it on his own terms. Respect and dignity *completely* intact.

I'd actually admired Gilberto, in that moment. I mean, *he* didn't know that *I* hadn't the ability to pull the trigger on him - or anyone else for that matter - inside of me. He didn't plead, he didn't lie and he didn't start to offer me all kinds of riches in return for me sparing his life.

'You should've fucking slotted the cunt. All the pain and mystery that him and his dead mate had caused in the region. You'd have been doing a *lot* of Colombians a favour, fella.'

Gary continued. La Cobra and El Jugador two hitmen whose reputations went before them across Colombia and beyond. Assassins that my English intercom friend had most certainly heard of as part of his own travels across the continent on behalf of queen and country.

'And as for that fucking rat bastard Finn.' He's fucking lucky that he'd already had his throat slit because the moment I'd latched onto what he'd been up to behind my back I'd have fucking did it myself.'

My heart sank at the image - once again and not for the first time over the day - of Miki sitting there, tongue through his throat and a massive pool of blood sitting around him.

'In fact, the shit he pulled and what he dropped on you in his death. I'd be fucking *exhuming* his body *just* so I could fucking shoot the cunt out of my own need for self satisfaction.'

He was putting some fucked up mental images into my head. It had got me thinking, though. What would the Colombians have *done* with Mikael, once the boy had been discovered by the authorities. Would he have been buried? Cremated? Thrown to pigs? I was surprised to find that out of all of the thoughts I'd had on the Mikael subject I'd been so wrapped up in all of the other variables that I hadn't given any kind of thoughts with regards to Mikael and what happened *after* I'd left the country. Hey, maybe his parents claimed the body and he was lying in a Helsinki graveyard? What did it matter, anyway? Talk about making your own bed, wherever that ends up being.

For what he'd done to me he deserved to be lying in a sewer along with all of the other rats.

'A mate, Gal? If I hadn't been able to murder a hitman, whose specific remit had been to track me and my wife down and kill us. How the fuck was *ever* going to kill the person who I had looked upon as my best friend.'

I asked him. Not really looking for an answer, as such. I didn't believe that there was anything that he would've been able to tell me that would've showed me a path to having been able to do such a thing to Mikael.

'Mate? He wasn't your mate, Pete. He pretty much told you as much, with his actions. Had I been in *your* world, as opposed to mines, he'd have had to go. No debate.'

'You aint nothing but a cold blooded KILLA' I joked back with him. Trying to sound like some gangster rapper but *still* sounding like a man with an accent that didn't know what it wanted to be. Scottish, English or even a Latin *speaking* Scottish Englishman.

'So, Gal. Lets say you and me had known and worked with each other, on the outside, like, and then you found out that I had been skimming from the top of our money *or* had been planning some kind of side move exit strategy of sorts. You'd have - with no sentiment whatsoever - just dealt with me, like you would've with someone like Mikael?'

I decided to play devil's advocate.

'Mate, I'd have done it in a heartbeat and *without* sentiment. If you let sentiment in, that's when your decision making can become a little cloudy. *That's* why you blank that shit out. Have you any idea just how close I was to you on some of those trips? Could've popped you at *any* time. Of course, British intelligence agents can't just run around foreign countries clipping narcotics and weapons dealers, though. As much as Bond films would suggest otherwise. Lucky for you, eh, mate?'

You could tell that he wasn't joking around and that he was nothing other than deadly serious in what he was saying. It led me to think of the times that him and I had been in the same cities at the same time as each other. Leaving me unsettled that - had he been instructed to - he'd have just taken my life away from me, indiscriminately.

I know that the pair of us had habitually joked back and forward with each other over the fact that we'd been thrown together in the ADX - despite coming from either sides of the fence - and how ironic two people, one law enforcement the other the antithesis of that, would be given a chance to become friends and talk each night. We'd rib each other over this side of life. This felt, I don't know, more personal. It was possibly because - like the other phone calls with Manny Ruiz - I had other things, from my past, on my mind and had felt a little sensitive and raw. While we would bust each others balls. This felt, different. Gary telling me, without a hint of the jovial about it, how - no matter how good friends we were, the type that I had *actually* put us down as in the ADX - he wouldn't hesitate to take me out if the situation required it. It wasn't what I really needed to be hearing. I'd sat and talked through Mikael's killing and all that followed. It had been one of the worst periods of my life - having to flee from a life that I *loved* - and it had been inevitable that Manny and I would get around to talking about it. Now that we had, it had unlocked a lot of deep and repressed memories. Ones that I had been more than happy to keep hidden away under lock and key.

I could've probably done with a night of Gal being his usual daft self and giving me a laugh but well, conversations go in their own directions at times. I wanted to find the reverse gear to get us back out of it again and onto something I considered a little more *light* of a topic. Sometimes once you're into something, though, it's difficult to get yourself back out again.

'Jesus, Gal. Really?' All I could get out.

'And don't make yourself out to be Mr fucking Ethics, either, Pete. Yeah you don't have it in you to pull a trigger but *who* is it that puts the guns *into* people's hands? Yeah, you didn't have the bottle to pull a trigger yourself but you certainly had enough 'courage' to put the guns into the hands of others, and fill yer pockets in the process.'

I don't quite know where it happened - or came from - but things spiralled from there. Gary telling me that the sleazy suits that exist in the underworld - making a note to specifically add 'suits like you' - were the worst of all, worse than the killers. The merchants of doom *purposely* putting guns and drugs onto the streets while - in a premeditated sense - already *knowing* just how much death and destruction both would cause in all of the cities and suburbs that they popped up in. How someone like Gary had pretty much dedicated his life to Great Britain to *protect* it from people like, me. There was no joking around by then, from either of us.

'You *do* know that the queen or Thatcher's not going to shag you, mate?'

I asked, trying to bring us back to a better place while dealing, personally, with the unfortunate image of the absolute worst threesome possible. A question like that would *normally* have done the trick with the banter that we enjoyed with each other.

'What do you know about the fucking queen, Pete. You don't know *what* it's like to serve someone, put your own interests last and your country ahead of you, always. As long as *you're* all good then fuck everyone else.'

There really had been no need for things to get so personal. They had, regardless.

'Well you know what? Which one out of us travelled the world, living life at the very fucking top, and made millions in the process. And who's the one that gave up their own personal life in return for a shitty government pay to *watch* the other one live their best life? And *where* did they **both** end up, regardless. I'd feel a little bit of a mug if I were you, Gal. Never mind though, Rule Britannia, and that. '

If he wanted to go there then, you know? Fuck it. So would I, and did.

'Fuck you, you narco piece of shit.' He shouted through the intercom at me.

'Yeah and fuck you, too. Fucking serf. Remember to stand up for the national anthem before you go to bed now, mate.'

I started to imitate a trumpet playing 'God save the Queen' to accompany this.

'Tell you what, fella. Yeah, I might've killed more people than I can even remember but *know* one thing. I can *still* sleep more soundly each night than you - and the history that you have - will *ever* be able to.'

Not on that 'bed' made out of poured in concrete in your cell you won't, I thought to myself.

'I don't know, you'd be surprised, Gal. I sleep pretty soundly in the knowledge that I never physically forced a gun into anyone's hand or a line of Cocaine up their nose. Adults make adult decisions. My conscience is clear. If I hadn't, someone else would've. You don't want to admit it but the world *needs* people like me.'

My conscience was anything *but* clear but I wasn't going to admit that to Gal. The two alphas were coming up against each other in that moment and there could be no weakness, whatsoever, put on display.

'Yeah, you keep telling yourself that, pal. You *do* know that's what they all say to placate themselves? That if they didn't someone else would.' He laughed back in a mock show of humouring me.

Sensibly, I decided that the best policy - for the conversation and our friendship in general - would be to abort and get out of it. Gary had been the only thing that you could've come close to describing as a friend since my arrest in Amsterdam and I had very quickly grown to love the nightly back and forth that we had.

No one likes to hear someone - that they regard as a good and valued friend - say how they would kill you in a heartbeat, if required. It had been what had set everything off and I knew that - had we continued speaking - things were only going to go further - and faster - downhill from there on. I wanted to at least *try* and leave things on some sort of decent terms even if, in reality, we had already went past that point.

'Well, talking of sleeping soundly, I'm gonna take myself off to that king sized four poster of mines and get some beauty sleep.' I announced.

There was no reply and I didn't look any further for one.

He'd seemed a little *off* during the intercom call. You know? Other than the subject that we had found ourselves speaking of - off the back of mines and Manny's phone conversation during the day - he had seemed both a little subdued *and* irritable on the occasions when he *had* spoken.

ADX brings ADX emotions, I thought to myself as I lay down for the night on that hard and uncomfortable 'bed' to try and get myself some sleep before it was time for the neighborhood Jihadists to wake me with with their first prayer of the day.

Sleep didn't come easy to me that night, not through Gary and how our conversation had went but through my phone call with Manny from The Post.

It had involved talking over a time of my life that I rank up there as the most saddest that I'd had to live through, and I say that from the position of someone who had the 'luxury' of experiencing something like United States of America Department of Justice indictments and imprisonment inside the most secure and isolated prison inside the country's borders.

Ibiza - and why I was even there - marked the end of the greatest days of my life. The *one* thing that I'd actually ever been *good* at. That I'd enjoyed the exhilarating thrill and buzz of doing each day, even if during some particular moments I'd have told you the *exact* opposite.

It had *always* made me sad, to think of how it all ended and how it was something that was out-with my own control. No one will ever be able to persuade me otherwise that - through Mikael's actions - I too wouldn't have been murdered by Bogota. As much as I loved Eddy and German, and they loved me back. To have assumed otherwise - after the years I had worked for the cartel - would have been nothing other than naivety that would have left me - and without question, Eva - a dead man.

Like Gary said, all sentiment would've been put to the side. It's what the Colombians excelled at.

I'd had to react - the way that I did that summer - in that *exact* way to ensure my survival.

It had always cut me, how it all came to an end for me, though. They were without a shadow of a doubt the absolute *best* days of my life and that - moving on from the deal with Sinaloa for the disc - the one thing I would've been able to put up as a cast iron guarantee was that life would never be the same again for me.

I drifted off to sleep while a mini montage of moments from those crazy days played around and round in my mind.

Some of the cars, the suits, the glamorous - and sometimes not so - settings I'd find myself. The sights of briefcases full to the brim with American dollars and warehouses holding keys of Cocaine and wooden crates of automatic rifles, Hawaiian shirted sicarios with sub machine guns and Coked up models dancing to nightclub beats in Miami. The twin towers falling in Manhattan and Osama bin Laden sitting there in that camouflage jacket staring at me.

All of these related thoughts merging into each other and popping up individually as if a carousel had been going round in my mind. Eventually each individual thought would drop off the carousel and halt from popping into my mind until the carousel stopped completely, allowing me to drop off for the night.

Chapter 35

El Corazon Valiente - The Ballad of Peter Duncan cont

Manny - You had pulled off the deal of a lifetime. The kind that would allow, the opportunity to remove yourself from the narcotics and weapons lifestyle altogether, free from threats from the DEA, CIA and ATF, or rival cartels. Living out the rest of your days in the beautiful setting of Bora Bora, French Polynesia. Considering all of your previous and frequent movements across the world over the years leading up to that. This seemed like the very point in your life where you would be *least* likely to be arrested. Yet you were? How come?

Peter - My libido, Manfred. My libido.

I would say that it was the most expensive f**k of my life but that's the very best part. I didn't even *have* sex, even though it had been the promise of such activities that had taken me all the way from Bora Bora to Amsterdam on 'business.'

I'd found the shift from travelling around on behalf of Eddy and German to lazing around by our pool - or down by the beach - every day in Bora Bora, challenging.

Manny - A lot of ex criminals admit to missing the thrill and buzz of the job.

Peter - Oh yeah, we're a lot like professional sports people once they've retired, in that way. *laughs*

On the surface of things I was living out someone's dream. Not having to worry about money *ever* again. Having the freedom to get up each day without concern for where I'm going to bring funds in from, or the need to go out and work for anyone. A man, literally, of complete leisure.

The thing was, and I was never going to realise this until *after* the event but - while working for the brothers back in Colombia - I had been riding a wave of adrenaline for a number of years and once it had all came to an end. Normal life just wasn't *ever* going to be good enough. Normal life - I'd found - was, well, *normal*. Kind of empty, almost.

Despite having everything that - technically - I could have ever wanted. Money, beautiful wife, sun on my back every day, I was restless. Bored, even.

We'd made friends with other couples who also stayed there on the island. Went for dinner on occasions and had everyone over to ours. Shit? I'd even taken up golf, having had no real interest in the sport but figuring that it might've, if anything, helped things on a social level. It was no use, though. While I had the money to mix with these types who - just like me - had retired to a place in the sun. They weren't *my* types of people.

Hedge fund bankers, ex NBA and NFL players, retired Ivy League trained lawyers. I'd always hailed myself as being able to connect with people on *whatever* level it was that they required me to. That had never been an issue and *wasn't* there on the island of Bora Bora.

Having to toe the line and pretend that Eva and I were lottery winners from Britain who had been forced to leave the U.K due to the incessant requests for money we'd get morning noon and night from people - instead of being able to say who I *really* was - got old very quickly.

Who knows? Maybe I would've got myself past all of that and settled down there and began to actually *enjoy* this new chapter in life? I never gave myself the chance though and, instead - and not for the first time in my life - chose to press the self destruct button.

Manny - I find it surprising that - in such a beautiful setting and how life was for you and your wife - there was even such a thing as a self destruct button that could even *be* pressed.

Peter - Oh, if there's one, I'll find it, Manfred. And there's *always* one, if you look hard enough.

Well, first of all I need to clarify. I am not someone who habitually slept with escorts during my time with the cartel. Have you any *idea* just how much skirt being a cartel associate can bring you, Manfred? Don't answer that, I'm being rhetorical. All of the girls laid on for you at the parties and then those you would encounter at all of the hotels that you would stay in across the world. I could've had more sex than Ron Jeremy, if I'd wanted to.

Manny - Here comes the justification train. *laughs*

Peter - Oh you better believe it is, pal. Pulling into the station right now, please stand back, CHOO CHOOOOO. *laughs*

So, as you are now waiting on me saying, there was one night in Istanbul where I employed an escort. She was American, believe it or not, but - like me - travelled the world, conducting business.

It was just the one night with no repeat. The torture that I'd put myself through - by cheating on Eva - had been enough to ensure that I didn't go back again for any more with her, or any other escorts and call girls that it would only have taken you a micro second to find hanging around at ground level of a hotel.

I've said it before and, I guess, I'm saying it again. There was just *something* about the woman. Well *evidently* there had because she had been enough for me to risk *everything* that I had gone through - with the Colombians and then the Mexicans - and *all* that I now had for myself in life, just for a few more nights with her.

Figuring that if I was going to cross continents to have sex with someone else other than my wife I'd have been as well lying to her about events. Telling Eva that I was going to Chechnya - specifically choosing a 'hot' area of the world that she'd have had absolutely no interest in tagging along with me to - to help an oligarch on a consultancy basis that was going to bring us in a few extra million dollars.

Manny - And this, in a way, took you almost full circle. *Back* to Amsterdam, the city that things all began for you?

Peter - Almost poetic, isn't it? Anyway, it was the worst mistake of my life, heading to Amsterdam. While I may have given you a warts and all account of how life has been for me - all be it a condensed version because you and I had absolutely *no* chance of covering things over four phone calls, not even close - I feel that there are certain things that your readers don't actually *want* to know, or that you won't even go as far as to print.

Manny - Well, you know? You could let the readers and or my editor to decide that?

Peter - No, I'll pass on that, thanks. Let's just say that I had wasted my time flying the best part of twenty four hours, escort wise.

Manny - Didn't she appear?

Peter - Oh she appeared, alright, Manfred. *Appeared* not to be interested in meeting her client's 'needs.' Like I said, a complete bust. Obviously, I was in Amsterdam, though. What else was I going to do other than get out there and reacquaint myself with my old stomping ground again? Yeah, I'd been there over the years on Bogota business but that was Bogota business. This was *my* business.

Later on that evening I found myself sitting in a city centre bar and, I guess, *this* was where the gods had conspired to place me in. All the precarious places that I had been in my life, spent in the company of some of the truly *worst* people imaginable. And yet where does it all come crashing down for me? In the chilled, cosy and warm environment of an Amsterdam bar with soft lighting - and even softer mood music - while I'm sitting there having a glass of scotch and talking to an ex pat who - like I had years before - had found themselves working in the Dutch capital.

Manny - So what was it that led to your arrest?

Peter - Well *that* was put down to 'Dutch Intelligence' but I don't know? There were a *lot* of coincidences that night, leading up to my arrest. The kinds that - sitting here in the ADX at night - I find myself replaying over and over again.

Manny - Coincidences?

Peter - Well, look, I need to choose my words carefully here because I'm in danger of straying into the territory that I already said I'd keep away from.

Manny - The trouble that your son had found himself in?

Peter - Correct! Look, lets just leave it at the lad was in a lot of trouble and I helped him out. Now - without really giving you the ins and the outs - if were to extend that a little further I could say that by helping

Stevie, I possibly ended up taking advantage and profiting out of the situation myself, along with my Edinburgh based associate. And as *part* of helping out my son - and myself - at the start of the Nineties it so turned out that someone - who was also part of that particular story - ended up in prison for ten years.

Following me so far?

Manny - A-ha, please continue.

Peter - So all of this taking place towards the end of Nineteen Ninety. Fast forward to ten years later. Explain how I just so happen to wind up in an Amsterdam bar casually speaking to the very *same* individual who I had been instrumental in them going to prison, the same prison that they were now *in* Amsterdam and on the run from, having escaped? Farcically, neither of us knew who the other was because we didn't know what the other looked liked. We literally sat there laughing and joking with each other for a few hours inside there, sharing stories and getting on like the proverbial house that's caught fire, completely oblivious to the realities things.

Manny - And how was this matter of confusion overcome?

Peter - Well, with the dangerous character that he was, it would've been far better - for me, anyway - if the confusion over our identities had *never* been cleared up. As for who it *was* that brought some clarity to the room? Well that's where shit got *really* weird.

Do you know who Jeremy Beadle is, Manfred?

Manny - No

Peter - Ok, doesn't matter. My point is though, when my son Stevie and Simon - his friend who I'd met in Ibiza in Ninety Six - then walked into the same bar. The pair of them looking like they'd each done twelve rounds with Marvin Hagler. Cuts and bruises covering both their faces, jackets ripped and looking every inch like two men who had just returned back from war, it all began to feel like a set up. I'd never seen nor spoken to him following the summer of Ninety Six in Ibiza and he just happens to walk into the *same* bar that I'm in when visiting the city for a few days. A bar that I shouldn't have even *been* in, considering the plans that I'd previously made for the night.

Manny - I cannot even begin to imagine what the odds of that are.

Peter - I don't think that there's a scientist in the *world* who would be able to calculate the probability of all of that coming to pass. For all of those components to be thrown together, in such a way? The three of us - and the history that we all, collectively, shared - put in the one room was like some human game of stone paper scissors. All three of us with the ability to cancel out the other one's dislike for the other.

The man - on the run from prison - on seeing Stevie, and in turn realising *who* it was that he had just spent the past couple of hours drinking with, wasted no time in shaking me down. Threatening to put a smashed tumbler straight through my throat unless I provided him with *adequate reimbursement,* to make up for the years that he had been in prison for as a result of the move that I'd made on him at the start of the Nineties. What he was asking for was - in reality - a drop in the ocean to me. Old habits die hard, however. Instead of just sucking it up and paying him, I tried to haggle.

It was a delaying tactic that would turn out to cost me a *lot* more than a few paltry thousand dollars.

I've overplayed *that* so many times in my head. Timing is everything in life. Every thing. He was happy to let me go, following the transfer of the funds. Something that he was about to do - receiving his confirmation of the transfer - *exactly* when the team of Dutch police came into the bar and slapped the cuffs on me.

If I'd just paid the man, even as little as two minutes earlier than I had. I'd have been gone, disappearing into the Amsterdam night with no trace left behind. Soon to return back to Bora Bora free of the guilt of cheating on Eva and ready to have another crack at that whole living in paradise gig.

My *need* to negotiate, everything and anything. The way that I had become pre wired that way - due to my work for Eddy and German - and extremely good at it I was too, had come back to bite me on the behind, and in such a devastatingly cruel way.

Manny - Of all the bars in the world you walk into, as they say.

Stevie - Amsterdam, aye? That was wild, mate. Absolutely mental. That day, though. Full stop from start to finish, mind. Most of it not for your publication you understand but that day - by the end of it - you were left feeling like you had quite literally been on a tour of Iraq or Afghanistan. Long after my pops had been huckled by the Amsterdam police I was sitting in an Emergency Room at the hospital, waiting on someone sorting out my broken nose. It was a *very* long day. That stuff with my dad and Nora, though? I'm not even sure that a couple of years later I can quite fathom out how the universe managed to steer us all in the path of that Amsterdam boozer that night. I stayed in the city, which at least increased the chances by a few percent but considering Nora *should've* been tucked up inside a Glasgow jail cell and my dad was living wherever he had been?

Manny - Nora? Wasn't it another man that was in the bar that night, with your father?

Stevie - Oh aye, it was. Just a daft name. You know how some nicknames don't always make sense for some people? Like when you see someone called Barry the Hat but it's because he doesn't *wear* a hat, ken?

Best way I can describe things to you, Manny, is that Nora didn't much like me and he *definitely* didn't like my father. What with him seeing to it that he would spend the majority of the Nineties behind bars in a Scottish prison. That type of stuff must smart, like? All of this was all good though because well, Nora was in jail. *I* was living in Amsterdam and my father? Well who knew where but it wasn't a Scottish prison and probably not Amsterdam either. It was assumed that he was happy - wherever he was - and so was I. Nora, possibly not so much because he'd *escaped* from Barlinnie Prison, along with some narco lawyer from Peru.

Manny - Yes, Sebastian Montoya's 'daring escape' from a foreign prison is something already committed to narco folklore back in Lima.

Stevie - From what I saw on the news - about it - he walked out the front door dressed like a painter? Hardly death defying stuff, mate! Anyway, things were all good. Me or my dad were never going to see Nora again in our life, *or* each other, right? Only - and for whatever reason that I'll never be able to wrap my mind around - that night, and through our own independent choices and actions. We found ourselves all together in that same small bar, out of the hundreds that you could've picked from inside the city of Amsterdam.

I had a lot of choices to make for a 'first impression' when I walked into the bar along with my mate Si. I hadn't seen dad since he'd fled from Ibiza, having almost had my girlfriend killed. Nora in even longer, since the start of the Nineties, back in the days when he had waged a campaign of terror on me - myself, only sixteen at the time - as part of when I was in a gang of football hooligans. And for the avoidance of doubt, Manny. When I say 'football' I mean the sport where sportsmen run up and down a pitch kicking a ball with their feet, as opposed to the one where the players stand around half the time doing absolutely f**k all and the ball barely ever *sees* a player's foot.

Manny - I see what you did there.

Stevie - Ah, simply a wee reminder over just how mental you guys are when it comes to naming things at times. Any excuse I get I'll take, mate. *laughs* A sport that has a World Series that only includes teams from North America. Too mad, Manny.

My first impression, though, walking - well, limping, actually - into that Amsterdam boozer? What the F**K are those two doing drinking together? Did I miss a meeting somewhere along the lines? That was my first thought. The secondary, why Nora was not in jail following soon after.

Very quickly, however, it appeared to be the case that the pair of them had been sitting oblivious to who the other was. What were the chances? I honestly didn't think Nora knew *what* to do. He looked like he wanted to decapitate me there and then on sight but then - seeing Simon heading straight to talk to my father and in turn, showing that he wasn't just a random stranger - he had to do an about turn.

Now let's be clear. Nora is was and forever will be one of life's more sinister and dangerous individuals. I've never met anyone *more* intimidating in life who has had the ability to frighten me like he had, and I'd dealt with Colombian sicarios in Ibiza, to give you some kind of an indicator.

Instead of acting on his impulse to right the wrongs from Nineteen Ninety, and just end me there and then inside the bar. He chose to instruct me to keep my father talking and that he would be back in a few minutes.

He left the bar, for what reason I did not know. It could've been to get himself a more suitable weapon than a broken tumbler for all I could've guessed and would not have been surprised had that indeed been the case. This was not a predictable man that we were dealing with here, by any means. In fact, with the mood swings that I had witnessed as a fifteen and sixteen year old when around him, he was the complete polar opposite of *predictable*.

Si and myself sat and had a chat with my father, where me and him had an attempt at trying to talk over the past but it didn't exactly go well. Even then, it was only the briefest of chats before Nora, once again, returned back to the bar to join us.

We kept ourselves to the sidelines while my dad and Nora talked about money. Bread that Nora had felt my father was owed him. It wasn't anything to do with us so Si and myself stayed out of things, having a drink and nursing the wounds that we'd collected over the course of the night and I really mean 'over the course' as we'd been spat on, kicked, punched, showered with coins and tear gassed from our trip to see Dundee United - our team back in Scotland - play Ajax. I kept picking up certain parts of the conversation. Nora trying to equate for how much my father would compensate him. This based on potential losses that Nora had incurred by being in prison which would - naturally - prevent him from earning any money in the drugs game, where most of his money would invariably come from on the outside.

The early Nineties - from a drug dealers perspective - was the boom times in the U.K. An absolute explosion of kids and young adults who had never taken a drug before - and had barely even had a chance yet to experiment with *alcohol* - all taking Ecstasy and smoking weed. And Nora had missed it, stuck in his prison cell in Glasgow.

My dad trying to haggle with him. Laughed straight in his face at the amount that Nora was asking him for. They haggled some more, and then some more. Well, I say 'haggle' but from what had been picked up. Nora got *every single penny* that he had originally asked for. The look on his face when he had got his confirmation that the transfer had been successfully sent. The kind that should've been reserved for one of those c***s that you see holding up a novelty sized cheque when they win the lottery.

It wasn't even a full minute from my father making that funds transfer before the Dutch coppers started filing into the bar. I'll be honest, Simon and myself hadn't exactly been fine and upstanding citizens across Amsterdam that night and, for a brief moment, I'd thought that they were there for *us*. That was one of the funny parts to it all, though. All *four* of us inside the bar - stood together - had our own personal reasons for being nervous around a bar full of police officers. Us because we had been fighting and involved in multiple examples of public disorder over the night, and our looks provided smoking gun evidence of this. Nora was, well, he was on the run in another country, having escaped prison, so you could say that he would've had a pretty good excuse to have his arse going ten to the dozen at the sight of them and then, you had my dad.

The thought of why *he* would be nervous - around coppers - really should've spoken for itself. Not that he ever seemed to *get* nervous, though.

Peter - I was literally in the process of trying to get up from the bar to leave when I found the cuffs slapped on me with a - frankly - concerning amount of charges being thrown my way. I tried to play it off - there in the bar - but as that small rotund Amsterdam copper read out the list of charges that I was wanted in connection with. They *all* made sense. Each and every one of them.

Conspiracy to distribute and import a controlled substance.

Trafficking as part of a criminal organisation.

Suspicion of murder.

Funding a terrorist organisation.

Trading of illegal arms.

Money laundering.

Bribery.

The list went on, and on.

Stevie - And that was the last time that I saw my father. The fact that I hadn't seen him for four years since Ibiza, and *six* years previously from that, in Blackburn. It kind of softened the blow, a little. *laughs*

Look, no matter our history between each other. I didn't ever want to see the man either killed or jailed even though - with his choice of occupation - I don't think that he could've picked a job where he would be of *more* risk of either happening. It was a sad end for him because that's what it felt like when I saw him looking round to me and telling me not to worry (I didn't) about him. The end. He knew it. He *must've* known, hearing that list of charges read out by that wee copper.

While he had kept the majority of his work secret from me. The amount of *serious* charges that the Amsterdam inspector was accusing my dad of was the stuff that you would never see one single day as a free man again. Thinking that he was wrapped up in the drugs game, with a Colombian cartel was bad enough, Almost - in a perverse way - on the side of cool, to have a father involved in that industry. The *terrorism* stuff, though? I didn't want to believe any of that but the Dutch boy seemed to be quite sure of himself.

Outside of a website or news channel, I haven't seen him again since.

Manny - So what did the Dutch authorities do with you once you had been captured?

Peter - Well I'll tell you one thing that they *didn't* do. Tell the Yanquis to go f**k themselves when they - predictably - came calling about my extradition. Couldn't get rid of me quick enough, the clog wearing bastards. The lawyer that I'd ended up hiring had assured me that with all of the frivolous appeals and counter appeals that he was going to be submitting he would tie the legal system up in knots for years, and that I would be an old man before I even went to trial, if at all.

This, proving to be a complete steaming pile. Me arriving in New York - and to the Brooklyn detention centre where I would be staying leading up to my trial - less than six months after my arrest in Amsterdam.

In what was an 'ironic' twist of fate and what had been - as far as I'd ever known - a first. The DEA *and* CIA, in a cross agency collaboration, had shared all of the intelligence, that they individually had gathered on me, with the Department of Justice which had highlighted just how bang to rights they had me in a case that no one would have wanted to have seen to be on the side of the 'narco and arms trader.'

My stateside lawyer - while not exactly telling me what I had wanted to hear - had been brutally honest with me. Advising that with the sheer amount of evidence that the American authorities held on me it was a case of lots of shit and no paddles.

As he viewed things. There was going to be *no* getting out of any of it.

Admittedly, I *had* been a busy boy, working for Eddy and German over the years. I'd done so, however, with no concept of just *how much* it had all been documented by the Yanquis. I'd always assumed that a percentage of what they came out with was them on fishing trips or just bluffs. They, in fact, were not bluffing.

Even so, you had to keep your spirits up by believing that - somehow - you would beat the charges, despite everything pointing to the contrary. Hey, I played with fire for *many* years. I couldn't have exactly complained on feeling the most extreme heat I'd ever come by, like I was then experiencing. Still, the very worst of times, though, Manfred.

All the confusion over Eva - who I had not been able to speak to on account of her being arrested in Bora Bora soon after my Amsterdam detainment - never mind what was going to happen to myself.

Manny - Eva, your wife, was arrested?

Peter - I understand that to be the case, yes. Look, details are a little sketchy on that because I haven't technically *spoken* to her since I left Bora Bora for Amsterdam in Two Thousand. From what I understand, she was arrested, held for god knows how long only for all charges to be suddenly dropped. A paranoid man would have said that she had 'assisted' authorities but, thankfully, I'm not one of those. And besides, with all of the evidence the CIA and the Administration had on me, it's not like they *needed* anything to help nail my conviction down any further. I'd have said that they were doing ok in that arena, if I'm being honest.

When I'd been arrested in Amsterdam - and under the charges I was being held - I'd been treated as if I was one of the most dangerous men in the world. I'd thought back to what Branson had said about how they would - one day - possibly look on me *as* a terrorist. It sure felt like that in my detention centre - somewhere between Amsterdam and Utrecht - while I waited on my extradition being processed. No phone calls, visits, or communication with the outside world. It was as if you didn't even exist. I'm sure all kinds of human rights were being infringed upon but hey? Who would listen to the narcotics and weapons peddling, politician and police bribing guy with links to a South American cartel and Osama bin Laden on speed dial, right?

I didn't need a phone call with her to know that my marriage was over. She'd thought that I'd went to Grozny. You could only have imagined what she'd have said when she found out that I hadn't went to Chechnya and was, in actual fact, in Amsterdam enjoying a two day jolly? Like any wife would, to be fair, she'd have had an opinion on things, as well as a *lot* of questions.

Apart from that. She had already threatened to leave me a few times before. Notably at the end of the Ninety Six Ibiza trip. Saying that she couldn't live with a killer, which - once again, for the record - I wasn't. I'd managed to talk her around, reminding her just how much danger we were both in and how she would've been much safer sticking around with me. At that point I was in the process of trying to secure the money from the Sinaloans that would offer Eva and I as much protection as we needed. Her going it alone and taking herself back to Manchester? Yeah good luck with that, Eva.

Things - over the following years - had left us forever on the point of her leaving me. Knowing her as I did. Being arrested in connection to her life with someone known as a Bogota Cartel operative and slung in jail, and all of the attention this would've brought. *That* would've been the thing to tip her over the edge, if the news that I had lied and went to Amsterdam hadn't already, of course.

It was like a lot of things around that time, a sad ending. I loved her, always will, Manfred, and there are memories of the two of us that - despite how things all ended - I will hold up top and think of from time to time to get me through living in this hell hole. We were - most likely - not right for each other but due to the parts that made up her and I, we just about made things fit.

I hope she's able to make a go at life. She's still young and smart enough.

It was a ride of a lifetime and I for one am glad that she played a part in it.

Manny - From the four phone calls that we have had with each other over the recording of the article, I can only agree. It was some ride, amigo. They'll write books and make TV shows about you. I promise you that. You already have the narcocorrido written in your honour - which I will seek out to listen to - so you're already on your way!

I guess that brings us full circle? I cannot thank you enough for your cooperation on this project. You're an interesting guy, Peter, and I put that mildly. Is there anything else that you'd like to add before we wrap things up?

Peter - I'd like to thank you, too, for handing me the outlet to tell *my* story. From our correspondence away from these phone calls, you are aware of the deep distrust that I've been left with the Western media. History will prove which side of the fence you will fall on but, I don't know? You're ok, Manfred, I've got a pretty good feeling that you're going to be as good as your word and print the story, not the myth.

Especially when the story is even *better* than the myth?

Manny - *Exact-amundo*

Peter - Look, those times, back in Scotland, then Holland. Good times, my friend. To a much larger extent, however. Colombia, Eddy and German Ramirez? They truly were the *best* of times. I *know* that what I was up to was highly illegal but what can I say? They were the greatest, most fun, enjoyable and thrilling days of my life and for the majority of it, I don't regret a single thing.

A time where I was *something*. Someone who made a difference, for good *or* bad. Now while you never came close to hearing my *full* story. I've already told you. The stories collected over those years working for Bogota I could sit and tell you for years and years but, as things stand, given the time constrictions placed on us, I hope I've given you *enough* for the article. You know where to come if you ever want to do a follow up, if, of course, your boss doesn't fire you for running *this* one.

laughs Give me a call, I'm pretty much free for the rest of my life, last time I checked my diary.

They were great days indeed and while I *know* that I'm not meant to be proud of the things that I did, as I sit here in my near permanent isolation, but you know what? I *am*. I made a tonne of money, saw pretty much every part of the world that there is to see - and some areas that you absolutely positively would *not* wish to - and had a brilliant time along the way. I'll never deny that.

And one last thing. With my sense for survival and street smarts mixed with entrepreneurial spirit, I wasn't half bloody good at it, as well.

Manny - I just can't but help feel that if you'd channeled your mind in a different direction you'd probably be chief of General Motors right now instead of sitting in a Colorado supermax prison. *laughs*

Peter - *laughs* Yeah well, maybe that's waiting for me in the next life, eh?

Chapter 36

El Corazon Valiente - The Ballad of Peter Duncan cont

Manny - Eva, Peter left Bora Bora for a business trip to Chechnya and never came back?

Eva - Yeah, his 'popping out for a pack of smokes' moment. Peter *always* had to do the spectacular, though, didn't he? Can't just disappear quietly out of someone's life - like most men - by just upping and leaving one day and becoming a ghost to his former partner. No, his version of that is to leave you and then offer a follow up blow by having Interpol come and arrest you while you're ignorantly - but blissfully - lying on a French Polynesian beach without a care in the world.

I felt such a fool, over what Peter had done. The lying to me about where he had been going to when leaving Bora Bora. The possibility of a visit from some kind of law enforcement agency was something that had *always* hung over us. That this visit - abruptly pulling me out of the bliss that I (rather than *we*) had created for myself there on the island - had been through my dickhead of a husband flying to a completely different destination than he had told me he was off to? I'm telling you, Manny. The man was lucky that he was destined never to be in the same room with me again. Any husband who thinks that he can disappear off to a city like Amsterdam for a couple of days and then have it glossed over when they return is fooling themselves.

He'd been talking about some business that he had lined up near Russia which would bring in a couple of million. Money that he said it would've been mad to have turned down. I had tried to tell him to leave it. He hadn't done a single piece of business since we had left for Bora Bora and had kept his head down. We were still unsure of who or who may not have been out there in the world, looking for us. His enforced situation - in addition to the funds we had behind us - effectively putting him into retirement.

Peter having told me that as long as neither of us did anything to attract any attention, the issue with his old bosses would soon be fixed in some way or other but until then we should lay low in Bora Bora while everything played out. We had more than enough money to last us the rest of our life. We were set and didn't have a need or want for anything. It all came *to* us, there on the island. *That* was what was so unusual for him to come out with - one evening as we sat eating dinner - when he told me that an old contact from Grozny had reached out to him about some consultation that he wanted Peter to do for him. The businessman was "apparently" looking to enter into negotiations with an old associate of Peter's in Eastern Europe and was looking for Peter to smooth things along in that department.

I'd told my husband that he didn't have to do it and that he should just stay there on the island and not risk any unwanted attention when he was off the relative safety of the island. I didn't say it to him but had felt that with it being an old business contact - from his days working for Bogota - that there was the possibility that this could have been a trap to flush Peter out of the woodwork. Offer him an amount of money that he would find difficult to turn down. Providing him with just enough of an incentive to bring him out of hiding.

Initially, I'd thought that I would accompany him on the trip but when he'd told me *where* the meeting had been arranged for. Grozny, and I fully admit to having had to go away and have a quick google to find out some more about it. One web search later while Peter is telling me that he will be protected at all times, driven around in bullet proof cars and things like that. I decided that he could go there alone. I was staying put. You know? Had he been going to a Milan or a Paris, perhaps. Grozny, Chechnya? I was less enthusiastic over.

He flew off, telling me that - taking the full twenty four hours worth of travelling there and back into account - he'd be home again in approximately four days time again. It's hard to describe the mix of emotions I had on him leaving. I was worried and scared that he was going to wind up killed yet - and while never wishing any harm on my husband - I was glad to get some space. Despite the paradise that we were living in it could never, at any point have been classed as a *truly* happy time. The feelings of having wanted to leave him had never fully dissolved.

He'd Jedi mind tricked me into thinking that I'd have been in danger on my own - following leaving Bogota - and how, with his finances, we could just disappear from public life and how I'd be safe and looked after in every way. You can see how *that* would've been an attractive prospect to me? Doing it under the feeling of duress, though.

Going along with it, with a man that you'd already decided to leave back in Ibiza due to being a murderer? It was not the way for a relationship - a marriage, even - to go forward and despite the idyllic surroundings of where we relocated to. It was done so - I'd felt, anyway - in a way where I had been really just waiting on the upheaval coming again. The feeling of just getting acclimated to your new life before having the carpet pulled from underneath you, something I was starting to become conditioned to.

This finally arriving the day where - I'd expected Peter to be somewhere still in the air on his way back home - I had been down on Matira Beach having a swim in the ocean and was now lying back out on the beach to dry off. Lying there with my eyes closed behind my sunglasses, listening to the Macy Gray album that I'd recently had shipped, along with a selection of other recently released CD's in the U.K. Funnily enough, an island like Bora Bora not exactly being full of record shops to peruse through.

Enjoying the sun while tapping my sand covered feet slowly to the music. I was brought out of my blissful sun kissed state by the feeling of one of my headphones being pulled away from me ear with another hand forcibly grabbing at my arm.

While still on my back, I looked up and - despite the sunglasses - squinted through the sun to see who it was. My first thought had been that I had got my time differences wrong and that Peter had arrived home earlier than I'd expected. Once I'd been able to focus, I realised that it, in fact, wasn't. I'd made the assumption simply through what the man was wearing. A nicely fitted suit *exactly* like you would've seen my husband in.

Looking to the side I could see another man, similarly dressed. The pair of them both in sunglasses. Sitting up and pulling my headphones from off my head and around my neck - the sound of Macy Gray still audible from each earphone - I looked behind me to find two local police officers holding rifles in their hands.

The one - who had pulled on my headphones and grabbed my arm to bring me out of the blissful setting I'd found myself in - introduced himself as David Tigana, and his partner, Enzo Claasens. Both from

Interpol and that they were arresting me on suspicion of a whole raft of charges from conspiracy - involving Peter's work for the Colombians - possession of Cocaine, travelling under a false identity, owning a hairdressing salon in San Fernando, California (that, incidentally I didn't know I owned) which the IRS had retrospectively found breaching several money laundering red flags over a number of consecutive years, all the way to multiple charges of *murder?!* I went completely numb at that point. The man in the suit kept talking but I wasn't hearing any words that he was saying. It was like I had some white noise fill my head as I saw images of myself behind bars somewhere. Prisoner Cell Block H vibes.

Manny - *Multiple* murder charges?

Eva - I've never so much as killed a spider in my life and I was being accused of fleeing Colombia with my husband while leaving behind a dead business partner, along with a dead sicario in Ibiza. Someone who Peter had been assured - apparently - had been disposed off with no way of leading back to him.

The killing of Mikael? It wasn't the world I was from but I'd have thought that even an intermediate level of police officer would have known who had killed Peter's partner, and it wouldn't have been Peter, and *obviously* not me. That's the thing, though. If factions of the Bogota police are being *paid* what to think then that can kind of change things.

Manny - So how did you fight the charges?

Eva - With the help of a good lawyer. I knew such a day would come although I'd never thought that it could have ever been with such levels of seriousness, personally. Peter, evidently *had*. Knowing that when it arrived the authorities were going to immediately close off all access to our funds. He had been smart enough to leave a considerably large amount of money 'behind the bar' for me at one of Chicago's top law firms, Penneywell, Larsson, Mancino & Schwarz. While they may have sounded like the members of a European boy band they were in fact absolute superstars of a law firm and ran complete rings around the American Department of Justice.

Cutting right through some of the Interpol crap straight away. The 'murder' charges were laughed at once my lawyer, Lance Larsson, had been given a chance to go over things. No prints or, in fact even any evidence that I had *ever* visited Mikael's home on the Bogota side of things while in Ibiza the dug up decomposed corpse of the man who had been sent to kill us both - apparently only recognisable through his Colombian passport being found in his back pocket - had produced nothing more than some whispers to police that the same man had been seen around, town asking the whereabouts of Peter.

I suppose it possibly didn't look too good that each time Peter and I had fled the country, following a death, though? Regardless, those potential charges were completely shut down by Lance and soon dropped. Not that any of this took a few days and some phone calls to take care of, of course. I spent months being held in a Texas detention facility while - between my lawyers and the Department of Justice - it was decided just what the hell they were going to do with me.

I could not believe just how quickly it took to end life - on Bora Bora - that day although, given how it had all ended in Bogota, I should've. I woke in the morning thinking I would go to the beach and then go to the local market and pick up something for dinner and, instead, *by* dinner time I was sitting in a local jail cell while my flight out of there was being arranged by Interpol.

That beautiful beachfront house. All my clothes and possessions that were left - *once more* - inside it. All gone in an instant. If what had been left behind in Bogota had been more of an 'enforced' choice for us. This wasn't, it was a full scale take over of what you had thought of as 'yours.'

Well I say *all* my clothes and possessions. *laughs*

Manny - Why the laugh?

Eva - I'd decided to leave Peter, back in the summer of Ninety Six. He'd persuaded me otherwise, however. Rightly or wrongly, I went along with him but *did so* safe in the knowledge that a day like that - in Bora Bora - would eventually arrive. *No one* can swan around the globe, doing exactly as they pleased - like my husband - without having to pay the piper at some point. He was going to get burned, sooner or later, and when that happened, those close to him were going to feel the heat along with him. Either just by association or *because* he had turned the flame in their direction, to save himself.

Either that day was going to come, or I was going to end up leaving him. One or the other, with no exception to it and I guess him flying to Amsterdam - for whatever the reason, although I've made my own judgments there - merely expedited the process. He simply would not have been able to resist the chance to take a risk over something or other and completely f**k things up for him and I. Be it then or at some point in the future.

I'm hardly Mystic Meg but - back in Ninety Six - I had been able to see as far into the future *as* that day in Bora Bora, on the beach. Yeah, didn't know *where* in the world I would be when the authorities came and took away the life that I'd thought was mines. And even as far back as Ibiza Airport - in that departure lounge for London - having just had Peter talk me around from getting on a flight to a *different* part of England, I began to plan my escape route for another life, when that moment was to come around.

Manny - Stevie, your father arrested before your eyes with almost every charge apart from stealing Christmas and non payment of parking charges thrown at him. Worldwide news. How did it impact you, personally?

Stevie - Oh, mate? You've no clue, like. Bad times, squire. *Everyone* was speaking about it in the House Music industry, on the internet message boards, printed magazines, at afters, all of that stuff. Not that cool when everyone is all talking about you, you know? Obviously the kind of gig that I have. The mad thing is that you *want* everyone talking about you. For your skills behind the decks, though. Not because they've seen your dad - a narco and weapons dealer wanted by the CIA and DEA - getting himself huckled by the police.

Lee - my manager - tried to tell me that no publicity was bad publicity but I didn't agree with him. He knew better, though. Managers, eh? Had me getting my first feature in the big magazines like Mixmag and DJ but that was the thing, I was only in there *because* of my dad, not because I'd done a residency at Space on the terrace or was playing all the big festivals year in year out by then. No, because of Peter Duncan. It's died down a wee bit now as there's always something else that'll come along in House Music. Some DJ who'll have taken too much gear and made an arse of it behind the decks or spoken out on a subject that they know f**k all about and have landed themselves in trouble over. I just wanted to make sure that people would recognise me for myself, rather than my dad. Kind of like Jordi Cruyff or something like that, eh?

Aye, impact though, Manny? Brutal mate.

Manny - Compared to Eva - your step mom - who was arrested and, initially, charged with various offenses all the way up to murder. It appears that the closer a person were to Peter Duncan the more the impact was felt when it all fell down.

Stevie - *Murder?* Jesus, mate. I didn't know *that*! I kind of feel a bit of a dick now for moaning about people gossiping about me in kitchens at nine in the morning. First world problems, eh? You know, Manny? I've hardly really been told *most* of the details with how everything went and am actually looking forward to reading your article because I reckon you probably know a lot more about it than I do. I only met Eva the once over a short trip to San Antonio, mind. Great girl but married the wrong man, evidently. I don't think anyone will debate me on that, not even my dad. I didn't see her again - after Ibiza - and never spoke or messaged. Her and my father had dropped off the face of the earth for four years, after they'd left the White Isle.

A couple of days after my father had been lifted in the Amsterdam bar I'd seen a report on CNN saying that Eva had been arrested too, on a South Pacific island or something. Some time later, couldn't even tell you how long it was but definitely a good half a year, probably more. I saw something saying that the authorities in America were dropping all charges and that she was flying back to Manchester the next day. Was even on the British news. Murder though? That must've been just mind games that they were playing with her to try and get her to agree to something else. No way was she going to be murdering anyone. Her or my dad? Hardly Fred and Rose West, the pair of them.

I'd always hoped that she'd have seen sense and got out of dodge with my dad so when it came out that she'd been arrested - in connection to her life with him - I feared the worst for her. Was brilliant to see her get released and allowed to come home, though. Bet my dad was well jealous when he clocked that had happened, like. No point the two of them being banged up though, is there? And, let's be honest here. There's only *one* out of them who you could say *deserves to* be behind bars.

I hope that she's doing well, though. Managing to rebuild the life that Peter Duncan comes into - for certain people - and obliterates like a wrecking ball in one go, simply through the man's energy. I'm sure that if you were to set up some sort of Peter Duncan 'survivor support group' you wouldn't see yourself short of applicants who had felt the *touch* of the man in some way or other.

Manny - Guys? What was the reaction of the news that Peter Duncan - traveling under the name of 'Brad Coleman' - had been apprehended in Amsterdam, Netherlands?

Vinnie Valencia - Me and Tommy were on a stakeout sitting bored to tears while feeling our asses grow, eating Wendy's, when Tommy took the call. You could see the smile growing on his face.

'And that's a confirmation? On the I.D?'

'And you're one hundred on that?'

'Aha, and where is he being held?'

He looked at me - while still listening to the other end of the call - as if he was going to burst if he couldn't tell me what he had just learned.

Tommy Ambrosini - Steve Worchowski had seen the cable come in as he sat at his desk and called me straight away.

'Tommy, I figured you'd want to know this A-SAP. Peter Duncan has been arrested in Holland.'

'We gottim' I said, triumphantly to Vinnie, the second I flipped my phone closed.

Manny - *You* got him? I'd say the Dutch authorities who had paraded Duncan out on display to the world's media - as some kind of a trophy - may say differently. You had tried to get a conviction on the man for slightly over ten years before he was eventually captured, *outside* America. Had it not been for the Dutch it could be argued that Peter Duncan would have still been at large. Isn't it true that him and his wife had completely dropped off the map years before, with your trail going completely dead through him breaking ranks from the Bogota Cartel?

Vinnie - Listen, pal. When it comes to an individual like Peter Duncan, its a *team* effort. Whoever catches him, and where. It don't really matter. At the end of the day, we *all* win out of it. And anyways, here's a little piece of intel that the triumphant Dutch neglected to mention to the world's press. That they had *not* been on the tail of Duncan while he was inside the country and that it had actually been down to a tip off from a helpful member of the public who had alerted them to the fact that they had seen him in a city center bar. Claiming that they had seen a documentary on the Bogota cartel on the Discovery Channel and recognised the fugitive from that. Funny how the Dutch don't shout that part from the rooftops?

'Anti crime and corruption intelligence' was how they had put it, or something to that effect. Even that was as much as Duncan knew. In reality, it was bullcrap. Duncan had fallen into their laps and they know it. We read the debriefing from our connection at Interpol which explained things - regarding how he came to be arrested - but at the end of the day, who cares *who* got the collar, and how?

Tommy - Yeah, you really think Vinnie and I give a rats furry ass about the name of the person who arrested Duncan and whether their name was Frank or Franck? We got the guy, and in a country that - friendly to America - would have no objections in seeing to it that the man would be sent - Stateside - to face big delicious steaming hot bowls of justice, served up by Uncle Sam.

Vinnie - Together - and along with the CIA - we had supplied enough evidence to the Attorney General on Duncan that would see to it that he would never see the world as a free man ever again.

Tommy - While it had been unknown to us, initially. Once the CIA began sharing intelligence on him we found out about the Al Qaeda links. With connections to an organisation who had carried out an attack on American soil and with the evidence that the company's counterterrorist unit possessed, that Duncan had *collaborated* with them on more than one occasion in the supply of weapons, the DOJ were pushing for the death penalty which - following talks between the SDNY attorneys and Duncan's - was subsequently withdrawn.

Manny - It was highlighted in court - in his trial - that Duncan had not worked for the Bogota Cartel since Nineteen Ninety Six. How can you justify the millions of dollars of American public's tax payers money that was spent on the prosecution of someone who was no longer a threat to national security and had removed themselves from society to live on a secluded and remote island in retirement. The DOJ prosecutors, at times, making out to the court that Duncan was the devil incarnate.

Vinnie - Careful now, Patty Hearst. Your Stockholm syndrome is starting to show a little, buddy. Wasn't he, though? Isn't that the *exact* work of El Diablo, what Peter Duncan engaged in?

Tommy - *laughs* We actually had a theory, Vinnie and me, that Duncan *was* the devil. Having done our homework on the man. The more we found out about him, the more he suited the role. Someone who would come with warm smiles. The likable type that you didn't even see the harm that he was doing until it was too late. Coming with guns and drugs. Seducing people with the promise of the riches that they could make out of such illegal practices.

Vinnie - To answer your question, though. How could America justify *not* prosecuting Peter Duncan. After the threat - along with all the other narcos - that he had caused our country for the first half of the Nineties? What? We just say 'yeah you helped flood our country with narcotics and assisted Osama bin Laden and his disciples but well, you've retired now so we'll give you a pass?'

Tommy - *No* passes handed out on that shit, my friend. And anyway, that whole 'he hadn't been active with the Bogota cartel' bullcrap. He'd have *still* been working with them today had it not been for events that he had not been able to control, that led to things spiralling. Lets put an end to any talk that Peter Duncan saw the light and - morally - felt that he had to remove himself from such matters, ok?

Vinnie - Yeah, even in his final days - before dropping off any agency radar - we know that he had been in possession of evidence that, had he handed over to the authorities, would've helped take down the Bogota Cartel. Instead, he chose to *sell* it and in doing so causing hundreds of deaths in Colombia - and Miami - through the Sinaloans cleaning house. A man who had suddenly saw the light and wanted to repent, he wasn't, so lets cut the Robin Hood crap, Manny. Peter Duncan was not the guy.

Tommy - Like any of the other narcos, he had to be made an example of. Regardless if his need to cause death and destruction - indirectly or not - had dimmed considerably, due to the money he now had sitting in the bank.

Us guys have to think of the scenario of when a man like Peter Duncan - and the business brain that he has - starts to run out of money and *how* he'll be able to make himself some more again.

Vinnie - Well that's one thing he won't need to worry about from now on. His three meals a day are covered for the rest of his days. Unlimited credit. Same with his living conditions. Completely on the house. *laughs*

Tommy - Yeah, you may question the resources spent - over the course of a period of ten years - on catching the man. And then all of the millions - from the public's purse - required to take him to trial and prosecute him. But you know what? It was worth every *single* dime to prosecute Duncan, whether he was a 'retired narco' or not. There's always another hundred Peter Duncan's out there and they need to know that if you f**k with the DEA they *will* catch you and you *will* spend the rest of your days in prison. Examples need to be set for the next Peter Duncan to keep in mind.

Vinnie - I'm gonna have to correct you on something there, Tommy. There definitely is *not* another hundred Peter Duncan's out there or a 'next' one coming along. That dude was some kind of prototype that had ended up being shelved for mass production and sent out into the world in error. And thank god that was the case.

Tommy - *laughs* Yeah, point taken. If the job had been full of Peter Duncans I'd have quit after a week.

Manny - Given that El Corazon Valiente had been something of a nemesis to you and that the three of you never quite had that long conversation that you'd hoped you would, and also that he will be reading this article at some point in the future. Do you have any words that you'd like to say to him, via the medium of this newspaper piece?

Vinnie - Yeah YOU LOOOOOSE! YOU GET NOTHING, *laughs* How you like that Willie Wonka type shit, *El Corazon Valiente?*

Tommy - *laughs* You know? If you *are* reading this, in that seven by twelve foot cell. Sitting on your cold and uncomfortable stone bed. The same cell where you can safely drop the soap *all* day long -

unmolested - due to just how separately lonely and isolated things are. I just want you to know that it was nothing personal. We both kind of liked you, in fact. But here's the thing? You can't run around the United States of America, the *greatest* country in the damn world - and the *rest* of the globe - doing exactly as you please.

That's not how *real* life works. I know that you seemed to feel that you were some form of exception to that rule but well, look around you and you will see that you, my friend, are *not*. I hope you remember both our names as your years in the ADX go by at a snails pace. We won't forget *yours* in a hurry. *laughs*

Vinnie - We shall, no doubt, see you again when we all reach hell, motherf**ker. Until that day comes, enjoy your *other* hell.

*Attempts to reach out to the Central Intelligence Agency with regards to receiving comments from Agent, Walt Branson were declined by Langley, along with firm denials that 'The Company' had - presently *or* previously - *had* an agent going by that name on their staff.

Manny - So you had been planning an exit strategy, so to speak. For when it all crashed down around you. Something that you had already expected to happen. Only, you didn't expect the charges that the Americans would throw at you? How do you find yourself sitting in Manchester, England talking to me rather than in a women's correctional facility on *this* side of the pond?

Eva - It really was a case of my legal team fighting one battle at a time, and there were quite a few of them needing fought, with all of what the Americans were trying to make stick.

Thankfully, the murder charges - and by *far* the most worrying of everything - had been taken care of. That allowed my team to get to work on chipping away at the remaining ones. You know? It didn't help that I was actually *guilty* of some of what the authorities were accusing me of. The possession? Peter and I *both* would have the occasional sniff. Well, 'some' would have it on a *more* than occasional basis but whose bedside cabinet was the contents of the freshly arrived ounce - that Peter had arranged to be flown in from his usual connect - sitting in the morning that Interpol came and went through our house with a fine tooth comb? The drugs possession, along with the fake passport and birth certificate were charges that I could not argue a single thing over.

Not concerning themselves on the things that they could not change, or alter at *that* stage of my arrest, they, instead, focussed on chipping away at the other potential charges that the American authorities were trying to lay at my door.

The hairdressers? That ex husband of mines? I honestly can't, at times with him. The DOJ were accusing me of owning a hairdressing salon in California, and then willingly funneling Peter's Bogota income through it. The Americans all so very sure about themselves when they produced evidence that I had previously stayed in a San Fernando hotel. Documents proving that I had been in the region for the period of a week in Ninety Five. This technically true, Peter had taken us there for some rest and recovery at a beautiful spa in the Valley. I hadn't been anywhere *near* a hairdressers, however.

Then once my lawyers started to dig deeper into this they discovered that the salon had been 'purchased' by me back in Ninety Two. A year that I was working in a coffee shop in Manchester and - by that point - had not travelled outside of Europe in my entire life. And they were saying that someone like *me* was in the process of opening American based hairdressing salons? Handwriting experts were hired and brought in who were able to prove that the signature on the sale documents of the salon clearly did not match mines. The independent hand writing adjudicator, there on behalf of the DOJ also left with no choice but to agree with them.

No signature match and, obviously, no bank records to link me and the purchase with. Another charge bit the dust.

Eventually, my legal team had reduced things all the way down to the two charges that I *couldn't* give the Department of Justice a satisfactory explanation for. *Technically,* the Cocaine possession had been in *another* country but the two agents from the DEA who had come to visit me - Mr Valencia and Ambrosini, two complete muppets of men who had brought an air of rushing around after the stable door had been left open and a horse galloping down the road - had assured me that they would lean on the Bora Bora local police force to press charges in my absence and that America would *happily* take care of for them, under some treaty that had been agreed back in the Eighties when the island had found itself a haven for criminals on the run. It was something that my legal team argued over its legalities.

As for the traveling with fake documents? Well the reason for that was because my moron of a husband had put a price on our heads and he had been left with no choice other than to procure a new identity for me. I'd been left with no say in *that*. As Lance Larsson said to me when we went over things. With all the charges that your husband is facing, there won't be a single judge or jury in the land who would not sympathise with you. The falsification of documents, motivated through fear of life than for any *intentional* reason such as fraud. I hadn't used the fake documents to attain any form of financial recompense which allowed Larsson to play the frightened victim card.

Lance had assured me that things did not appear to be as bad as they may have first seemed, when I was being marched off that Bora Bora beach.

These two DEA agents wouldn't drop things, though. Larsson had said that he'd spent a career dealing with agents like that. Small dick syndrome guys. He'd said that because the pair of them had been chasing my husband for years - with no success - and that when finally Peter *was* arrested, it wasn't by them. Because of this, they were trying to get themselves a win from somewhere, anywhere. Something that they could - most likely - boast about to their buddies at the bar. Something for them to dine out on. If it meant twisting the knife into Peter *through* his wife, then these agents weren't above such antics.

'Can you give them anything?'

Lance asked me in a visit to the detention centre to update me on how matters were moving.

'I think these two Administration agents will cut you a deal and let you walk. But you're going to have to give them something in return.'

Considering how secretive Peter had been - telling me that it would have been safer for me if I *wasn't* to know certain things - giving them 'anything' of value wouldn't have been an easy thing to do. Or not as easy as my lawyer - or, indeed, the two DEA agents - would have possibly believed.

'Don't worry about going behind Peter's back to the DEA, if you *do* have anything. Pragmatically, he's going away on multiple life sentences *regardless* of if you open your mouth to Valencia and Ambrosini or not. If Peter loves you, like a husband is meant to. If you have anything, he would want you to use it to your advantage. Your loyalty towards him right now will only hurt you and I say that as I am to a client but it is advice that I would urge any human being to take, if left in your predicament.'

'Your statement will make *no* difference to the years that Peter receives. It may not even be *used* in his trial. This is more about these two Administration agents than it is convicting your husband. Give them something and we'll have you out of here in no time.'

The way that Lance had spelled it out. If Peter was left a little put out over my show of 'disloyalty,' on learning of it, then he clearly wasn't good at maths. Then again, I'm pretty sure *that* was why he had Mikael added as a partner in the first place. *laughs*

If he was going to be served with *multiple* life sentences - which to credit Lance and his predictions, Peter was - then me serving out some time on my side would not have got him out any quicker from his own sentence.

Larsson told me to take a few days to think over his proposition and he would be back in touch.

I'm not a religious person, by any stretch but I firmly believe that sometimes the lord will send out the occasional signal to someone in the hope that they will pick up what he has dropped down. Hours after Lance had left, some poor Eighteen year old girl was murdered in the rec room. Found with a pool cue shoved into each of her eye sockets. That, I guess, was my cue to leave.

Manny - Such a grisly pun.

Eva - You think I'd joke about something gruesome like that? Please. *That* was my signal to get myself out of there, America full stop. My experience of 'The American Dream' had been enough to stop me from ever visiting the country in my life again. It was time that I checked out. Actually, the maids were outside banging on the door wanting to clean the room ahead of the next visitors. *That's* how far past checking out time I was at.

I got the message to Larsson the next day that I would sit down and talk to the DEA agents. Lance informing me that he would have everything we needed in writing. Confirming that should I assist them with their enquiries, my narcotics possession and falsification of documents charges - in addition to immunity from any connection to Peter Duncan and his misdeeds - would be dropped.

They were so cocky, the pair of them. A real pair of a**holes. I found it amusing how much of a parody they actually were. Like, how it appeared that *they* were trying to behave like the two agents out of Miami Vice when in reality it was the actors in the TV show trying to portray DEA agents!

I must've relived my whole life with Peter, inside that interrogation room, with the diverse range of questions they had for me. I sat and cooperated in all ways that they wanted me to, only stopping to answer on the times when prompted by Lance to do so. On the whole, though, I was as close to cooperative as they could ever have met, considering their job occupation. I answered every question they had for me, completely openly and honestly.

I hadn't been getting any kind of reaction from them, however, that signalled that I had given them any kind of shock and awe level of 'information.' I'd hoped that by just playing along and answering every question put to me it would have been enough to secure my release. I'd willingly agreed to sit down with the agents and answer their questions. Something I did. They still weren't happy, though.

'Tell us something we don't know already?' The one called Vinnie Valencia - not too much the bad cop out of the pair, they were *both* bad, he was the less worse out of the two, though - said impatiently.

'Well maybe you can ask *better* questions then?' I reacted, tired of the unrelenting quizzing being fired at me from both of them. And *they* weren't happy with my answers?

'Hey, we can send you right back to the detention facility. Just you say the goddam word, Eva.' Tommy, the other one shouted back at me with Lance standing up and getting in between us.

'Ok, how about we step out for a cup of coffee and a cigarette and leave you and your attorney to talk things over. When we return, we hope you're gonna have something for us because, otherwise, your cute ass is going back behind bars again, darling.'

Tommy Ambrosini said with the underlying threat that you knew had actions waiting to be used behind it as him and Valencia left the room. Wisely, leaving us all to cool down a little.

'Ok, Eva. I'll level with you. I'm all outta ideas. I'd have thought, hoped even, that in the line of your questioning, they would have asked you something that would have led them somewhere, in whatever way they needed you to.'

'Like I said, Lance. Peter kept me out of a lot of things. I can't tell you what he didn't tell me, can I?' It was as simple as that and I spelled it out to him.

'And there's nothing that you possibly, perhaps, overheard him saying, or that you happened to stumble across found written down by him? Think hard, Eva. Your freedom depends on it. Any moments of weakness that he showed when drunk - or high - where he possibly told you something more than he'd intended to?'

Manny - And *had there* been?

Eva - Well ok, yeah, there was. There had *always* been one but I had hoped that it would not have had to reach the point where I would have to go so far as to have to *tell* the two DEA agents it. Then again, in an ideal world you *would* get to sit down and talk with a couple of Drug Enforcement Administration agents, come away securing your freedom while not having to mention the ten million dollar's worth of Microsoft shares that you know your husband had hidden away.

Now be honest, Manny. Wouldn't *you* hold back that kind of information from the Feds, until it was the absolute *worst case* nuclear option?

Manny - No comment. *laughs*

Eva - One night, I think it was still inside our first six months in Bora Bora. This having followed Ibiza and Peter securing *some* kind of bag for us that would provide for the rest of our lives. He was low on details but you could tell simply from the man's energy - returning back from Mexico City - that he had scored us something *big*. We were sitting outside our house, one evening, having a few glasses of wine watching the sun go down and we had got onto the subject of all the missing money, that Peter lost through his murdered lawyer in Barcelona. Millions. Not an insignificant amount of money and the majority of it being what Peter had worked and risked his life for.

Peter had waved that amount away as if it had been a sack of small potatoes but my point was still valid. What had happened before could happen again and I had asked him if he had safeguarded our money from any potential 'issues' in the future. He said that he had it covered but I had kept nipping and pulling at him enough to make him share with me that he had bought ten million dollar's worth of Microsoft shares. Telling me that computers were about to explode and that our ten million could end up becoming *TEN* times that amount, over the years. I remember laughing at the irony of him sinking as much money into a product that he knew the square route of nothing about, yet was telling me that it was the future.

As all wives would've done in a situation - where your secretive husband has let you in on the fact that there is ten million dollars of your money sitting somewhere - I asked to be given joint access to the shares. I actually found it quite fun. Bora Bora was so laid back with all chill and not much in the way of *excitement*. *D*oing something like checking the stock price of Microsoft was something that actually got the blood going any day that you would check it. Would it be *up* and your original outlay showing as something higher - or - would the share price have fallen and you now showing as in the red and worried about the prospect of falling even further. Leaving you ready to give your husband earache for wasting our money on magic beans.

I could not have told you *where* the rest of our money was, or how much we had of it. But the Microsoft shares? I knew, at times on an hourly basis *exactly* where they were, and how much they were worth, down to the nearest dollar. It's like I had treated is *as* my money because for once, it was money on a screen that I was able to actually *see*. Like, *this* was real in the way that it was visible, as opposed to the 'fairy money' that just seemed to always come from somewhere, as and when we needed it.

In what had appeared to be him humouring me and leaving me to it while he looked after the *real* money. I watched the share price grow as the years went in. Typical lucky Peter but his prediction was coming true. Our ten million - while being an initial place to store our money safe from any Federal intervention - had soon churned out our first million in profit, then another. Agonisingly, by the time I was handing over the details of the shares to Valencia and Ambrosini. The money had grown to an impressive *twenty seven, point four,* million.

You can understand how I didn't want to hand over 'my baby.' When learning of Peter's arrest and then witnessing the subsequent seizure of our property, possession and bank accounts. *All* assets. Well, not all. By law, Lance had been required to inform me of any of the assets that had been seized by Interpol, and the Microsoft shares were not on the long and detailed list that he'd presented me with.

With the shares missing, I thought it prudent not to bring them up.

Faced with an extended stay in an American penitentiary, though. I coughed them up. Lance assuring me that with shares worth *that* amount of dollars, it would hand the two agents the piece of 'gold' that they had come for.

I could have cried that afternoon when handing over the username and password that would gain them access to our shares.

Manny - Well, you *had* just handed over an extremely large amount of money. That would've affected most people.

Eva - Undeniably, it was. There's been some - back here in Manchester - who have told me that I should've just done my bird, (jail) kept my head down and the shares would've been worth even *more* by the time I got out.

Which is also true.

I couldn't face years on the inside, in America. I chose to buy my way out of it. Figuring what good would those millions be to me if I was a broken, mentally scarred basket case of a woman by the time I got back out again. And besides, I had a Plan B. Peter had steered me wrong in so many ways over the years but he had always been good for something - like the advance payment to lawyers which possibly had not helped get him out of jail but certainly did for me - even if it was just a little piece of sage advice every now and then.

'We're travelling at forty thousand feet in this lifestyle, Eva. *Always* have a parachute ready for if and when the engines fail.'

It had obviously meant more to him - knowing more about the business that he was working in - but I had taken the message that he was trying to put across to me, even if my actions would not have been what he'd have intended, when advising me of that. Then again, it was Peter. He'd possibly have been *proud* of the parachute that I'd made for myself. I mentioned to you earlier on during our chat about how one moment I was planning what to have for dinner that evening and the next again all of my possessions had been seized.

Well, not quite *all* possessions.

You know one thing that all my friends and family always said about me, when I was back home in Manchester? That I was the type of person who would've given you my pot to piss in, if you didn't have one yourself. Generous, sometimes to a fault.

So, you know? From Ninety Six - and me deciding that I was already on some kind of countdown of doom that was ticking towards the day where I either left Peter, he was killed in revenge for what he did to the Colombians or the authorities and or karma caught up with him - I decided to take my husband's advice, and start making a little 'parachute' for myself.

I'd 'gift' my mam a Cartier watch here. My friend Jenni a pair or two of red bottoms, there. What with Peter's spiralling sniff addiction from Ninety Five onwards, he didn't know half the time what he had gifted me from one time to another or not. I took some real risks like sending thousands of pounds in hard currency, by simple air mail, to avoid the paper trail. Literally *anything* that left the island destined for Manchester could've and should've had Securicor looking after it.

Over the course of four years - and leading up to Peter's Amsterdam arrest - I had syphoned off enough money, jewelry, clothes and watches that - once everything had all died down - I'd been left with enough money to put together to buy - outright - a city centre flat. *Easily* a better position than I'd been in when I had left Manchester for Bogota, years before.

Thankfully, I can sit here and tell you all of this *free* from prosecution due to a tiny piece of paper that the Department of Justice gave me on my release and when I was in the process of getting myself out of the country.

What is it that boxing guy with the mad frizzy grey hair always says?

'Only in America.'

It was a wild, outlandish experience - meeting and sharing a life with Peter Duncan - but you know? As sad is it may be when things come to an end. No one likes an ending, or saying goodbye, do they?

They should try and spend a few years as the other half of the man who was my husband and *then* they can come back and give me their opinion on how they feel about endings.

It was a dream, turned nightmare. Eventually, though. I woke up from it.

Manny - Stevie, you and your father's relationship, and the contact that you kept up with each other, could hardly be described as prolific or joined at the hip. I understand that you haven't reached out to him since being detained by the authorities. Is there anything that you'd like to say to him? Given that he will have the luxury of reading this article in the coming weeks. Call this a fast tracked way of getting a message to him, considering the length it takes for a message to be either sent to or from out of the ADX in Florence.

Stevie - Oh, man. Well putting me on the spot with that stuff, Manny, like. Kind of seems weird to say - what I want to say to my dad - but to you. Someone who's *then* going to take my words and put them in print for the rest of the world to read. Ken what, though? Despite him being my dad, I have a feeling that I'm about to find out as much about him as *most* of your readership with this article so f**k it, full disclosure, mate.

Dad, I'm assuming you're reading this because you'd have to be off your head otherwise to let a national newspaper write something about you, and you not have a wee look at it for *quality checking* purposes. No offence, Manny but there's too many journalists that are slippery c**t's out there that give the sound ones - like you - a bad name, eh? Anyway, you're a smart guy, dad. I've probably never told you this, probably never told you a lot of *other* stuff though, to be fair. That's not what you and me were about though, eh? Well like I was saying, probably never told you before but you're the smartest man I've ever met - with what you did with your life and what you made of it - but by going and getting yourself huckled in Amsterdam you're also the *dumbest* f**king person as well. I'm sorry but its true, pops.

Nora told me - later on - *why* you were in Amsterdam, with you mouthing off to him in that bar - before Si and me came back from the match - about all your woes to him that evening, before you had clocked *who* he was. Imagine giving up *everything* that you had in life, for a ride. And you didn't even *get* one?

I'm sorry - when you were on the outside - that me and you didn't make a go of the whole father and son gig. Some would say that we were too alike but that, I'm afraid, would be a lot of pish. There's only one out of the two of us that would let someone - like a young girl - be murdered by sicarios, while they had the chance to save her. Sorry for the dig there but aye, I've not forgotten about it, and probably never will.

It's over with now, though, and while I don't think that you'd do anything different, if left in the same position again. The fact is, you'll not *get* to be in the same position again so I'm willing to put it in the past and move on. You were only looking after yourself after all. Which was kind of your default position at the end of the day but you know what, pops? I kind of get it, I think. And I'm hoping that this article will cement all of that. I've tried to tell myself that you were the way that you were - and I'm sorry if I speak about you in the past tense but you're in a f**king supermax prison in Colorado so, you know? You kind of *are* in the past - because you *had to* be because to put anyone other than yourself first - in the world that you existed in - would've meant weakness, death, capture. Stuff like that?

Maybe you - or quite possibly, even the written work of this fine and upstanding journalist I've been talking to - will be able tell me just how wide or close to the mark I am with that line of thinking?

Who knows? With me flying over the world and being in - or passing through - America, on occasion. I can maybe schedule a visit to come and see you? If you don't mind, though. I think I'll hold off on scheduling any visits until *after* the article comes out. You've always had the ability to surprise and shock and I'm assuming that this interview is going to be no different? If it's alright with you - given your track record - I'll wait to see what you've got in store *this* time around before I go making any travel plans!

Until we're next in contact. You look after yourself. Get fresh air, read books and don't let those bastards get you down.

It's not words we've exchanged too much in life but I love you, pops. Even if - at times - it has more resembled me loving *hating* you.

laughs Remember that, though. Take care of yourself, Pedro, and keep your head up and hopefully I'll get to see you soon.

Manny - Thank you, Stevie. Having spoken with Peter over the course of this article I can assure you that your words will mean the world to him.

Stevie - Well, if it keeps the big man's spirits up inside there then they were words well spoken.

Manny - Thank you for your cooperation with the article, also. The contributions from all those who were close to him - in one way or another - have offered a well rounded view on your father. I hope you enjoy reading it as much as I did speaking with everyone.

Stevie - Pleasure, Manny. Pleasure, my man. Before I hang up can I please take the opportunity to remind your readers of my upcoming six date mini South American tour? Coming up at the start of Two Thousand and Three.

Beginning in Medellin before moving onto Bogota, Lima, Sao Paulo, Rio De Janeiro, finishing in Bueno Aires.

Manny - You just did, although, I will reiterate that once you have read the article on your father you may think of reconsidering *some* of those tour dates. *laughs*

Stevie - Please, mate. I used to run into mobs of ASC and CCS when I was a daft sixteen year old at the football with the casuals. South America will be tranquilo, hermano. Cucumbers, mate.

Manny - Thank you, once more.

Stevie - You're good, Manny. Keep in touch, my man, you hear?

Eva - Any last words for Peter Duncan? Shit. Well, that's the thing. It really *will* be last words, as far as towards my soon to be *ex* husband.

I guess if you *are* reading this, Peter. There's a *lot* of things that I could sit here and verbally attack you with. We had quite the journey, you and I but that's the thing with journeys, they have to come to an end, even if that comes through just *one* of the passengers wanting to get off. I will *never* forget the trip - while I was on it - though. Living a life of absolutes with you - like we did - was both thrilling and frightening. Only *you* could place us on such a paradise on earth like Bora Bora and it end with me being marched off a beach by Interpol.

It was never dull. I will never, ever take that away from you but - at times - you, and your profession, was tiring and I'd had enough years of it before it all came crashing down but I loved you - and still do - and wanted to try and be there for you for when you *did* settle down.

The shit that you put me - us - through at times, though?

But I'm not going to dwell on any of that. I want to focus on the things that I want to *thank you* for.

I thank you for always trying to make me feel like I was the most beautiful and special person in the world, in your own way, even if sometimes you fell short. I could never compete with the devotion and attention that you had for Peter Duncan and I never took it personally whenever I came second to him.

I thank you for the love that you showed me. I was just a young girl when we met so hadn't had much experience to *see* what men were like, in general. You would not have seen me move across to Colombia had you not showed me that side of how you felt about me.

I thank you for all of the security that you provided me as your partner - and then wife - with not a *single thing* that I ever had to go without, no matter *where* in the world we were.

I thank you for your generosity and - due to that - the fun times we had when we were globetrotting. The shopping trips. The clothes, shoes, jewelry. You *know* that I'm not a materialistic girl. A girl in her early twenties working in a Manchester coffee shop, how *could* I have been? To be treated by you. Wearing the type of clothes and labels that I could not have dreamed about owning otherwise? It made a girl feel special, for a while, in a way that I'd never really had the luxury of feeling before in my life.

Above *all* else, though. From the bottom of my heart Thank *you, thank you, **thank you*** for listening to me back in Ninety Seven - god knows how many times you *didn't* - you know? When I told you that we should double up on those ten million dollars worth of Microsoft shares, in a separate account, once I had noticed that the initial outlay was beginning to make us a serious return. And for agreeing to allow me to purchase *another* ten million dollar's worth of shares for us, in a separate portfolio.

Our airplane didn't experience the *engine problems* that you predicted that it might, years before. It was *you* who threw me from it - when you got yourself arrested in Holland - and from a great height.

Thank you for providing me with the safest of *parachutes* to break my fall, though, darling.

Manny - A *separate* account. With Microsof *..

Eva - *laughs before the line goes dead*

Writing about the topic of narcotics and arms dealer Peter Liam Duncan, the man known inside Colombia - and further afield - as 'El Corazon Valiente,' was never going to be anything *other* than subjective. The article that you have read, I fully appreciate, will have both carried the ability to help see things *from* Duncan's side or assist in cementing *everything* that you already thought that you knew about him from the cable news reports to the extensive coverage of his trial that was across the networks and newspaper corporations.

For some, we have a fascination to talk and read about the 'bad guys.' Doing so, and seeing how they live life, reminds us just how good people *we* are, or at least *tell* ourselves that we are.

The outcry over Peter Duncan - by Americans - inside a country that makes so much money a year through guns and rifles and has the largest amount of Cocaine users in the world, a clear example of the stench of hypocrisy that runs within our borders.

I am certainly not sitting here claiming that Peter Duncan *isn't* a bad guy. His own words - inside this article - will be his own judge, jury and executioner. I simply wanted to show the world that sometimes, and only sometimes, the 'bad guy' doing the heinous things in life isn't *always* the monster that we all look at, think of and judge them as.

I will leave it down to you, the reader, to decide if Peter Duncan is - or is not - one of life's monsters or devils.

Manny Ruiz

Words by Manny Ruiz with special thanks to Peter Duncan, Stevie 'DJ Selecao' Duncan, Eva Duncan, Tommy Ambrosini, Vinnie Valencia and Governor Bill Blazjowski of the Florence ADX for his co-operation.

*I received no further clarification with regards to Eva Duncan's final comment. Peter Duncan's ex wife choosing to end the call with the slightest and mischievous of giggles before hanging up on me. Despite extensive phone calls between her, her estranged husband and others who knew El Corazon Valiente, this journalist - at the time of going to print - is still unsure whether Mrs Duncan had been simply joking around - a theory being, to play with the minds of both Vinnie Valencia and Tommy Ambrosini who, it would be fair to assume, will also see this article and two men who had left her with a bad taste in her mouth from her experience - or, in fact, was deadly serious with her claims to be in possession of further Microsoft shares, paid for by her husband's narcotics and arms trade gains. Something that, legally and through her immunity deal, she now could take out a full page ad here at The Washington Post telling the whole world about - if she so desired - and not lose a single share as a result.

Chapter 37

Peter

Ah, that enormous indignant feeling of having to strip bollock naked and forced to bend over and part your ass cheeks *just* so you can sample a piece of fresh air. Oh how I'd missed it for the previous few days that I had "enjoyed" on my self imposed seclusion from the world. I was worried, however, that I was starting to go all a little Howard Hughes so had forced myself to get out for some recreation. Took every single piece of will power *in* me to get up and *go* out, though. A real battle of wills. Lethargy had began to set in and it was something that had to be met head on before it started to run riot with my mind body and soul.

It didn't help being the middle of November and us - inside the ADX - all now firmly into winter. Not that it impacted on the inmates, apart from the effort made to give us a meal to reflect what time of year it was. We were approaching Thanksgiving. Apart from not having been given a trip to Death Row when our sentences were being handed down, what really did any of us in Colorado *have* to give thanks for?

Shit, was it *cold* down at the foot of those mountains at that time of the year, though. While it might have been so suffocatingly humid in the summer - as is frequently the case with America - it was the opposite in the winter. A country of absolute extremes, in so many ways. The irony of me *wishing* to go out - on a freezing day like that - hadn't been lost on me. A day for curling up on the sofa with a hot cocoa and a good book. I had my own points to prove to myself that day, though.

For the previous forty eight hours I'd been feeling *more* like a prisoner, an inmate, convict. I mean, the prime reason for the ADX was to *make* you feel like that but I'd managed to stay on top of things, for the most part. Gal and me hadn't spoke for a few nights and I think that the lack of *escape* - that our conversations brought - had been magnified during its absence. Without it, there was nothing other than the TV, books or the 'entertainment' which was the constant noise that the wing was filled with.

Gary had been a bit 'funny' of late - over the past week - and I had recognised that he was maybe having a bit of a bad time but that, through my help, he would get past it again. The United States Government had literally got all of the best minds together to *plan* a place like the ADX. It wasn't just some jail thrown up at the foot of the Rockies to follow the formula of any other American detention centre. No, these nasty bastards all got around the table to brainstorm just *how* they could make it such a hell for anyone who was unlucky enough to wind up there.

For it to *not* affect Gary would have been *more* noticeable. Doesn't matter all of his experience that he'd accumulated working as an agent for MI5. All of that counts for nothing, when that cell door closes and you're left alone inside such a small space. It's the thing that levels out the playing field for us all. No matter if you're an Islamic terrorist, narco Mr Fixit or a spy working for the queen. We were all in the *same* boat, in there. No matter *what* our background or beliefs were.

He'd been really quiet. Had lost that zip and zest to his personality that had stuck out so much before. Had become a bit withdrawn but hadn't been really open to talking about things so - you know how it is - I didn't press him on matters further. Just gave him some advice from someone who had already done that initial early period inside the ADX and was passing on tips that I, myself, would have killed for back in those early days of my imprisonment in Florence.

We'd not spoken for a few nights. Any attempts from my side - via the intercom, and our special combination of numbers to connect each other - had been met with silence. We all have moments that we need to take a little time out. Maybe we don't want to speak to *anyone*? Even Axl Rose sung about it in 'November Rain.' That I got, so it wasn't as if I had been spending my night constantly pressing the intercom to get his attention. Just a few tries at the beginning of the night with a final message of reminder to him that I was on the other end if he wanted to talk before getting on with my night. Telling myself that should we reach a week - without contact - then there would have been cause for concern. *That* alone could have meant something more serious such as the guards discovering that he'd been left with the ability to make contact with the outside world - with me - or the even graver possibility that he'd went and done something stupid although it has to be noted that the guards at the ADX - who appeared to be in *complete* control at all times - left the options of being able to *do* anything stupid severely limited to you short of banging your head off a wall repeatedly until you were left with brain damage.

I'd also been under *no* illusions that Gal and me were going to be *lifelong* friends, there in the ADX. Prisoners being moved cells was an unfortunate reality of the place and that - sooner or later - one, or both, of us was going to find ourselves being moved and, as a result, having our mode of contact completely pulled. Leaving us knowing that the other existed in there but that we would never see or talk to the other again in our life.

'Ok, buddy, you're good to go.'

Chuck - according to the name tag on his prison guard uniform shirt - who had come to collect me that day, said. Happy that I wasn't carrying anything that I shouldn't have been and motioning for me to put my clothes back on and get out into the Rec area. He'd walked me down the seemingly never ending main hallway outside of my cell and down towards what we called 'The Kennel' where recreation and exercise took place for prisoners. Walking in those shackles up to the kennel always seeing to it that a seemingly never ending walk down the main hall was made to feel even more gruelling.

The Kennel resembled - pretty much - an empty swimming pool for the inmates to run or walk around in or - if they chose - simply sit and look up at the sky, the only part of the ADX where they were ever given that option of one of life's simples pleasures.

'Tell you what, pal? This Colorado climate isn't good for the old shrinkage, eh?' I tried to make a joke with him over the reduced size of my penis - something that he hadn't exactly been shy about when looking at me - while I quickly scrambled to get my underwear and orange prison two piece on.

Jokes were wasted on the guards in there. I think that they came pre wired and without the capacity to show *anything* that even resembled a human or empathetic side. Don't get me wrong, they're dealing with a hell of a different amount of prisoners but I don't know? If I was a guard and a prisoner appeared to be normal and civil? Take that shit when it's going - I'd say - because you never know if the next prisoner is going to be quite as nice. Maybe they're not *allowed* to be more personal, in case it leads to them letting their guards down and some sociopath slash psychopath ends up preying on the weakness shown?

With my uniform back on - and free of the shackles - Chuck advised that I had 'ninety minutes' worth of recreation, should I want it. Letting me through the gate and into The Kennel before closing it again and allowing me the run - or more walk, in my case - of the place to myself.

I sucked in a huge breath of fresh air and puffed it back out with the impressive smoke blowing skills of a dragon. Despite the clear chill in the air I *did* love the crispness and how fresh the air was on days like that. Where if you were half asleep before taking a deep breath you wouldn't be by the time you've finished it.

There was not a chance that I was - like some others in The Kennel - going to go for a run around the pool. Choosing to just clear my mind by walking in a clockwise circle. Occasionally looking up through the grated opening towards the sky anytime I heard a passenger liner flying. Regardless of where the plane was going to, me stood looking up at it and wishing I was sat up there at forty thousand feet, with a drink in my hand reading GQ. Hell, I'd have even sat in economy, if it came to it.

Walking around and round. I tried to imagine what I would be doing with myself on such a crisp and fresh day with not a cloud in it. I laughed at me looking for some examples like going for a five mile hike with my dog or something to that effect, when I wasn't even that type of person. I'd have spent such a beautiful day doing something a *lot* less strenuous than rambling and I knew it. The ADX had a habit of doing that to you, though. Making you reevaluate things and yearn for doing activities that you never did in the first fucking place. That Colorado supermax being the ultimate place for reminding you that your life as you once knew it is now over and that pretty much everything that you put off on the outside you have now lost your choice, as well as chance, to do *forever.*

It was almost tantric but walking around that empty swimming pool I had managed to take myself away - from out of the fact that I was pacing in a circle inside a maximum security prison - from my surroundings. From somewhere I had plucked out a memory of taking a young Stevie - could've only been two and getting on his feet - to the local park. Swings, roundabout, cheese cutter and see saws, that kind of set up. I could literally hear his giggles as he was being gently pushed forward in the swing and then his feeling of propelling back down to me again.

It had been a memory that even I hadn't been aware that I'd been left with. So much of life had happened in the more recent of years that had made the past look extremely like it had literally been another life altogether.

Remembering that day - at the park - however. It was as if it had just taken place the week before. The smell of the freshly cut grass, the clear sign of the council vans parked up nearby showing that it had *just* been cut, fresh that day. The graffiti scribbled all over the seats of the swings in black marker pen. Someone loves someone else. Another - with a different handwriting - wanting the world, or that area of Fife at least, to know that they had 'been there.' Stevie's giggles, though. The memory of that little kid in the swing, sitting there with no knowledge of all of the madness waiting to come into his life. The smile that I had on my face - as lost to my own stream of consciousness as I was - so fixed that I could feel the cheeks on my face beginning to strain through being left sitting out of position for so long. I'd almost forgotten *how* to smile.

'Watcha, Pete.'

It was weird. So sucked into my memory of taking my infant son to the park and so removed from the ADX. When the guard spoke to me - I'd assumed that he was telling me that it was time to leave, even if it *had* felt like a rather quick hour and a half of walking around - he had sounded more of a Cockney than a Coloradan, though. I wheeled around, - looking towards the nine of clock stage of my three hundred and sixty degrees marching area - it *wasn't* Chuck, the guard.

Stood there - staring back at me - was someone *also* in the same orange two piece as me. Unkempt beard and even more unattended greasy hair that looked like it was stuck to his head rather than free flowing, with how much of it there was, it should've been. The gate from The Kennel lying open behind him.

Due to how deep I'd been in thought. I'd never heard anyone come in and even when they'd spoken, I'd only partially heard them and - having not anticipated anyone speaking - hadn't been prepared to listen out for it.

The man looked like he had tears in his eyes as he looked back at me but while doing all he could to avoid looking me *directly* in the eyes. He looked a mess, in general. Almost as if he was going through the stages of cold turkey but Florence had no time for such stuff. You needed to be *on* drugs in there - first of all - for a chance to then experience the withdrawal symptoms that they may bring.

We just stood, with around six to eight foot separating each other, looking back at the other. I was confused for the first few moments. I - technically - shouldn't have been in the same space as him. Glancing towards the gate, I couldn't make out any guards on the other side or nearby.

'You been good, fella?'

He broke his silence and confirmed that I hadn't been hearing things with the Londoner voice from a few moments before. Fuck! It *was* Gary. How, though? There were too many questions I had for that moment that could have even been answered by him.

There was no light or smiles to him though, as you would have imagined for such an unlikely of moments for the two of us to end up in the same recreation yard. No sparkle in his eyes on meeting the 'other side' of the nightly intercom chats.

I should have seen it for what it was straight away. Don't even know how a man like me - who had lived life on his toes - *hadn't* realised. It was in his eyes from the moment I'd looked into them. The ADX weakens the mind, though, they say?

'Gal? What the fucking fuck are you?'

I attempted to ask but then trailed off. Noticing - for the first time - that one of his arms that were hanging down. There was a shank in his hand. Arm hanging loosely but hand gripping firmly to the blade.

'Oh.'

I said, looking at the weapon and then back up to him again. Heart beginning to thump inside me. Obviously, his 'stringent' strip search had not managed to produce the knife that he was carrying. I had nothing to fight back with. Even if it had been hand to hand, I'd have still been up shit creek, minus the required paddle. I wasn't wired for 'prison yard scraps,' scuffles, handbags, barneys or anything else that you wanted to call them.

The tears in his eyes had began to build up to the point that actual tear drops had now started to slowly run down his cheeks.

'I'm sorry, mate. I am so *so* fucking sorry. It's, it's my kids, Pete. They're gonna kill em, if I don't pass on this message to you.'

It was only *then* that I fully realised what was happening. There was too much things to think about, take on board and make sense of in that moment and not even close enough time for to do so.

'*Who* has your kids, Gal?' Clearly someone was threatening those closest to Gary's life - if he didn't take mines - but who? With the work that I had done in the previous decade. To find that there was possibly someone out there with an axe to grind with me. You'd needed to have narrowed down things, considerably. I'd have said that - in that lifestyle - I had *felt* that I had been liked. You can always tell from talking to people if they like you or not. Still, it would have been practically impossible to have lived life - in that arena - and *not* picked up a few enemies along the way.

He appeared to be too preoccupied with what he was about to do to engage with me. Almost as if had I *been* able to get him to speak to me it might have been enough to change his mind. I tried to exploit this. Reminding him about some of the laughs that we'd had back and forward and how when the pair of us got out he was going to take me to watch his team. It was a waste of time. Offers to help get his kids back through some connections that he could have done with their help. All received by him without even any hint of importance on his face.

'CHUCK CHUCCCKKKKKK I'M DONE WITH REC FOR THE DAY.'

This - I'd felt - was going to be the only thing that was now going to come along and save me. I'd been mildly disturbed by the fact that he'd left his gaze on my penis and scrotum for much longer than socially acceptable, if that's even a thing? Shit, if he'd suddenly reappeared and saved me from the 'man with the knife' he'd have been welcome to stare at it all day long, if he'd wanted.

'CHUCKKKKK, YOU THERE, PAL?'

Nothing.

'Chuck's not coming, Pete, mate.'

Gal said, almost looking like he'd felt a little pity that I was at the point of naively shouting for a guard who may well have been the one who had *let* him into The Kennel in the first place.

Reluctantly and hesitantly, he moved towards me.

'I'm so fucking sorry, Pete. I'm gonna have to live with this the rest of my fucking life but, Eddy and German Ramirez say hello.'

Faced with someone who was the antithesis of the Peter Duncan that existed in the outside world. Someone who would do *whatever* it took, to save not themselves, but someone else.

I think I *understood* what was happening.

Pragmatically speaking. I *got it.*

Thinking quickly of some of the 'unflattering' decisions and choices I'd made in my life.

This wasn't just a message being sent to me by Eddy and German Ramirez. It was a message from the universe. That it was time for me to settle up my account.

Chapter 38

Peter Duncan
Inmate - 387765
5880 CO-67
Florence
Colorado
81226
United States

10/27/2002

Stevie Duncan
C/O Ragamuffin Talent
27a Brick Lane
Spitalfields
London
E1 6PU

Well, SURPRISE!!!

I guess I always was good at those out of the blue visits (if you can call this a visit? Put it this way, it's as close to one you'll be fucking getting from your pops) although I BET you never thought you'd get one from a supermax prison in America, eh? Yeah, me too, unfortunately.

I was thinking about you tonight, son. Quite a lot, so thought I would act on it and grab that weird excuse for a pen (they give us these things that you can't stab yourself or anyone else with, or write) and jot down some words to you. Didn't have your Amsterdam address or know if you're even still in that part of the world anymore but <u>did</u> remember the name of your manager's agency so managed to piece things together from there to get this to you.

Well, I 'hope' it gets to you, anyway.

I hope that life is going good for you, Stevie? The fact that your old man saw you at The Grammies is a pretty good indicator that things seem to be moving in the right direction or, knowing you, you're probably worried about appearing too mainstream now?! The daily struggles of life, eh? As long as you're happy and safe that's all that really matters and I say that with the benefit of experience behind me. Talking about The Grammies. Now that you know that I saw you there on the TV I just want you to know that I understand, the way that you reacted. That interviewer was a complete bitch to throw that question at you, on a big night like that, for your own career.

You know me, though? At the time? I was calling you for everything while I bounced up and down on my bed. Well, if you can ever really bounce up and down on a bed that has been designed by pouring concrete into the rough 'shape' of a bed?

If there's one thing that this place provides you with, though. It's time to think. Too much bloody time actually but there's occasions where - sat there with your thoughts - you can actually begin to make some sense of your car crash of a life that has landed you IN a building like the ADX.

When it comes to you, I've been able to really go deep and think about how bad a father I've been. I mean, some might say that I haven't been one AT ALL.

I've brought you more trouble in life than the other way around? What kind of father is that? I've seen you three times in just over ten years and what were those three occasions like? You were out of your mind so didn't know but I was there in Blackburn in my capacity as an Ecstasy dealer. That particular story you can wait for The Washington Post article to come out. Secondly I brought you cold blooded Colombian killers to Ibiza, almost tanking your career and leaving your girlfriend murdered, and thirdly - and most recently - you were treated to the spectacle of your father being arrested under suspicion of just about any serious crime that you could think of.

Father? Yeah, I fell short. Way, way short. To be a good father you need to be prepared to put yourself last. I couldn't do it and I'm sorry for that, Stevie. You deserved better than what you got and while it's a little late for this I just want you to know that I recognise it now. I may never have done so on the outside world with how life always seemed to be for me but I sure as hell see it all for what it is when I'm inside this cell for twenty two to twenty four hours a day. I just hope that - through time - you might be able to find it within yourself to forgive me?

When we were reunited, back in Nineteen Ninety, *that* should have been my cue to make up for lost time. Carpe Diem, you know. Take the chance that was there to take note of the brilliant son I'd had (and lost) and appreciate him. Grow a relationship. It wasn't easy, though. For that to have happened, I'd have had to give up my work for the Colombians and - you might already appreciate this - you don't just walk away from people like that and stop working for them.

You and me were victims of the circumstances that had been put into place the year before we met in Blackburn. By then, I was in too deep with the Colombians. It made me nervous to co exist having a son while working in such a dangerous environment. And well, it led to what it led to. Apathy and loathing between us where it was never anything other than my work that was the wedge between us.

Having the superhero like ability of hindsight. I can see all of the perspectives from your side of things and can now understand where I went wrong. I expressed my disgust to you - in Ibiza - over my seeing you as having taken someone else's side over me, family. I see that day differently now, Stevie. I look back on what you did in an entirely different light and am PROUD of you for the decision that you took to save that young girl's life.

It showed that YOU had more heart, courage and empathy than your old man, who was double your age.

When I think back to those times I actually look UP to you.

I just want to say I'm sorry for it all. Despite everything, you know? I don't think I ever DID say sorry. I am deeply and I would like you to tell that to Flo once you've read this letter. I was selfish, thought only of me and Flo could've been Queen Elizabeth for all I'd have cared. She'd have still had the plastic bag over her head if it would've been enough to save me from a couple of bullets in the head. Queen or not.

If there really is a god then I guess - one day - I'll have to square up the bill with him over some of those moments that have not left me exactly cast me in the best of lights?

Until then, I just want you to know that 'I' know. Maybe it's too late for me to have this epiphany but I got there as quickly as I could, son. I just needed the rest of life to slow down for me, is all.

I've put the address for me here at the top of this letter. If you want to write back you can reach me via there. I'd like it if you did, more than you could ever possibly imagine.

For now though, son. I'll sign off.

Keep yourself safe, Stevie. And remember and make sure that nut of yours stays screwed on, I know what you can be like!

Love you and know that I'm <u>always</u> proud of you.

Dad x

Also by Johnny Proctor

The Zico trilogy

Ninety

A great portrait of a seminal time for youth culture in the U.K. A nostalgic must read for those who experienced it and an exciting and intriguing read for those that didn't' Dean Cavanagh - Award winning screenwriter.

Meet Zico. 16 years old in 1990 Scotland. Still at school and preparing himself for entering the big bad world while already finding himself on the wrong side of the tracks. A teenager who, despite his young years, is already no stranger to the bad in life. A member of the notorious Dundee Utility Crew who wreak havoc across the country every Saturday on match day.

Then along comes a girl, Acid House and Ecstasy gatecrashing into his life showing him that there other paths that can be chosen. When you're on a pre set course of self destruction however. Sometimes changing direction isn't so easy. Ninety is a tale of what can happen when a teenager grows up faster than they should ever have to while finding themselves pulled into a dangerous turn of events that threatens their very own existence.

Set against the backdrop of a pivotal and defining period of time for the British working class youth when terrace culture and Acid House collided. Infectiously changing lives and attitudes along the way.

Ninety Six

Ninety Six - The second installment of the Zico trilogy.

Six years on and following events from 'Ninety' ... When Stevie "Zico" Duncan bags a residency at one of Ibiza's most legendary clubs, marking the rising star that he is becoming in the House Music scene. Life could not appear more perfect. Zico and perfect, however, have rarely ever went together.

Set during the summer of Euro 96. Three months on an island of sun, sea and sand as well as the Ibiza nightlife and everything that comes with it. What could possibly go wrong? It's coming home but will Zico?

Noughty

Bringing a close to the most crucial and important decade of all.

Noughty - The third book from Johnny Proctor. Following the events of the infamous summer of Ninety Six in Ibiza. Three years on the effects are still being felt inside the world of Stevie 'Zico' Duncan and those closest to him. Now having relocated to Amsterdam it's all change for the soccer casual turned house deejay however, as Zico soon begins to find. The more that things change the more they seem to stay the same. Noughty signals the end of the 90's trilogy of books which celebrated the decade that changed the face, and attitudes, of UK youth culture and beyond.

Muirhouse

Living in the 'Naughty North' of Edinburgh, for some, can be difficult. For the Carson family, however? Life's never dull. You'll give them that.

'Muirhouse' by Johnny Proctor is a story of the fortunes of Joe 'Strings' Carson.

Midfield general for infamous amateur football team 'Muirhouse Violet' on a Sunday and petty criminal every other day of the week. Above all, though. Strings is a family man and, like any self respecting husband and father, will do whatever it takes to protect his household.

A commitment and loyalty that he's about to find being put to the ultimate test.

Available through DM to help support the independents.

Twitter @johnnyroc73

Instagram @johnnyproctor90

www.paninaropublishing.co.uk

Also available through Apple Books, Kindle, Amazon, Waterstones and other book shops.